S0-AWI-606

"Catch him!" came the cry. . . .

Ramagar bolted into the dumbstruck crowds gathered at the gate's edge. A band of mounted troops came charging from the street, whips flaying, sending the frightened citizens into a panic. Mariana, in the meantime, had lifted herself from the ground and made her way back inside. Everywhere she looked there was frenzy.

"He's dressed as a Karshi," Mariana heard a captain shout. "He won't be hard to find!"

Amid the chaos a group of soldiers had cornered someone, and Mariana strained to see. Was it Ramagar? Her heart sank as never before. The Karshi robe was unmistakable. The soldiers closed ranks and raised their weapons.

"Kill him!" the commander barked. And Mariana screamed. . . .

UNABLE TO FIND FAWCETT PAPERBACKS AT
YOUR LOCAL BOOKSTORE OR NEWSSTAND?

If you are unable to locate a book published by Fawcett, or, if you wish to see a
list of all available Fawcett Crest, Gold Medal and Popular Library titles, write
for our FREE Order Form. Just send us your name and address and 35¢ to help
defray postage and handling costs. Mail to:

FAWCETT BOOKS GROUP
P.O. Box C730
524 Myrtle Ave.
Pratt Station, Brooklyn, N.Y. 11205

(Orders for less than 5 books must include 75¢ for the first book and 25¢ for
each additional book to cover postage and handling.)

The Thief of Kalimar

Graham Diamond

FAWCETT GOLD MEDAL • NEW YORK

Map by Edward Meehan

THE THIEF OF KALIMAR

© 1979 Graham Diamond
All rights reserved

Published by Fawcett Gold Medal Books, a unit of CBS Publications, the Consumer Publishing Division of CBS Inc.

All the characters in this book are fictitious, and any resemblance to actual persons living or dead is purely coincidental.

ISBN 0-449-14214-0

Printed in the United States of America

10   9   8   7   6   5   4   3   2   1

*For Daniel Zitin, and all those others who know
anything is possible . . . if you believe*

SPECA

ARAN

BRITTAN

THE ETERNAL DARK

Valan

Great
Western
Sea

Palav

Tents of
Haj Burly

Kalima

KILOMETERS
0   100

ICE ~ CONTINENT

FAR NORTH
Cenulam   Nebumai

Seafaring   Lands

Malik

Tarta

Lemba   Bants

Culsi   Eastern Sea

Olsia

EASTERN
KINGDOMS

Land of the
Baboons

South Lands

I

Thief of Thieves

1

Ramagar stood silently, his back against the cold stones, his long fingers nervously grappling at the roughness of the wall. His keen black eyes stared intently into the shadowy street as he struggled not to blink against the cold biting wind. For even in an instant he might miss some far-off movement, some half-hidden sign that a mark was close. No, Ramagar knew he must not stir, only keep watching and waiting until tonight's long vigil was done.

And then it came. A dim darkness against the black at first. Then a blurred silhouette outlined briefly when the crescent moon peeked from behind the heavy clouds. Ramagar squinted. He had to be careful. It could be anyone at this hour. After all, in the Jandari, the night was still young.

The shuffling sound of boots over cobblestones brought the faintest of smiles to Ramagar's lips. The silhouette began to loom larger and the thief stealthily crossed the alley.

The mark was well-dressed: well-heeled also, if Ramagar was any judge. A portly man, his finely woven cloak haphazardly flung over his shoulders. The tip of his boot made a scraping sound as he stumbled across a loose stone. He almost fell; only the reflex action of his hands finding the nearest wall saved him from losing balance completely and tumbling flat on his face. Clearly his bellyful of wine was more than he could handle.

Ramagar sneered. It would be an easy mark after all. But still he must be quick. Who could tell what others—servants or companions—might be close behind?

With the swiftness of a leopard the thief leaped into the open street. The drunken prey gasped, realizing what was about, and foolishly made to run off. Ramagar lost no time; the fist came up and the drunk doubled over, wheezing and coughing, vainly trying to scream for help. Before he had even fallen to the ground the deed was done. Quick fingers expertly yanked the purse from the belt, lifted off the emerald ring, tore the small gold pendant from his throat.

Fleshy buttocks hit the street with a thud. The prey stared bewildered as the lightning-like thief paused to bow before him and whisper a hasty "Thank you, sir" before dashing back off into the alley and becoming lost among the shadows.

The prey sat with his jaw agape; it was a long time before he was able to manage to raise a shout.

Over the low wall jumped Ramagar, thief of thieves; then he darted down an alleyway, up along the twisting back street where only the dim candles in the windows of the prostitutes could be seen, and dashed high and low among the shadows of the plaza until he reached the far corner where he ducked into a doorway. A beggar lay at his feet in a drunken stupor. Ramagar observed him disdainfully for a moment, then no longer paid any heed.

Panting, he poured the contents of the purse into his calloused palm and counted with halting breath. He closed his eyes and whistled softly. Eight pieces of silver and one of gold. His eyes opened to count again. Glittering in his hand they remained. Eight of silver, one of gold.

That fate was on his side tonight, there was no question. His mark must have been a man much wealthier than he had dared hope. In a single stroke he had earned more money than he usually could in a month. And the emerald ring and the gold pendant—tiny though it was—these would bring a pretty penny at Oro's stall.

Tonight's good fortune changed matters considerably. Further work was suddenly not only unnecessary, but also risky now that the soldiers would surely be seeking the robber of such a wealthy man.

Serves the fool right, though, Ramagar thought as he put the coins in his pocket. Teach him not to come to the Jandari bearing so much wealth. And in many ways the poor fool was lucky. Yes, lucky. To be robbed by Ramagar meant not to be hurt in any way. The thief of thieves abhorred violence when not needed. But there were many others in the Jandari who looked upon the matter quite differently. A swift blade could silence a tongue forever—as many visitors to the quarter had found out to their sorrow.

Stepping over the twitching body of the beggar, Ramagar tossed the empty purse to the shadows and briskly began to walk in the direction of the Jandari's main avenues.

The Street of Thieves was filled with life. The air reeked of pungent meats and cheap perfumes. Women of the night, even in winter clad only in the barest of flimsy garments, flashed their eyes at him and smiled while they jostled through the crowds, seeking an easy pocket to pick while

12

searching for the next customer. If Ramagar had worn a hat, which he never did, he would have tipped it to them. He knew them all by face, if not by name, and counted many among his friends. After all, the Jandari was their home as well as his, and he was at ease with everyone: the con men, pickpockets, thieves, whores, drug dealers, and even murderers. Rogues of every conceivable description: his own kind.

Beyond the last of the shouting merchants hawking their stolen wares in hand-pulled carts stood the Demon's Horn. As Ramagar came to the arched street a smile formed on his lips. He walked more slowly as the dim glow of candlelight from the shuttered tavern window enticed him, the faint smell of heady wine already filling his nostrils.

He pushed open the heavy door and was greeted by a flood of light. Worn boots kicked up a small cloud of sawdust at his feet and made him sneeze. The landlord looked up at the sound.

"Ah, Ramagar," he laughed, standing beside the closer tables and tapping his stubby fingers along the multiple folds of his belly. "What brings you here so early? Was the night's chill not to your liking?"

A few small cackles came from the scattered handful of patrons at the more distant tables where the shadows hid their faces from unwanted stares. A thin haze of smoke billowed and swirled at the ceiling, as Ramagar, paying no attention to the landlord's remark, strode to the open hearth and rubbed his cold hands over the glowing embers.

It was a dirty, ill-kept tavern, this Demon's Horn, offering little in the way of comfort or good food. Yet to Ramagar, and those of his ilk, it was at least a safe haven, a place where even the boldest of the Khalir's soldiers dared not enter, and boasting no less than three hidden exits to flee just in case one night they did.

"Will tonight be credit or cash?" the landlord asked, belching loudly. "You've run up a tidy bill in weeks past, my friend—"

The thief of thieves ignored the remark. Reaching into his pocket he drew out a silver coin and tossed it in the innkeeper's direction. A quick hand shot out and caught it, the red face glowing with the realization of its value.

"Tonight I'm thirsty," said Ramagar. "Make sure you bring the best you have."

The landlord bowed respectfully. He knew the silver coin

would erase the previous bill, provide tonight's wine, and leave him a fine profit besides.

He tucked the coin safely away beneath his apron. "For you, Ramagar, only the best." And shouting to the servant girl, he demanded that a fresh bottle be brought. One from his private cellar.

The thief straightened his shoulders and took a small table near the back. There he placed his hands openly on the table, in time-honored tradition to show that he bore no secret weapon, and sat in silence as he waited.

A whore wearing an outlandish green wig slid from a nearby table to his. The fake gold necklace she wore glittered in his face as she smiled, bending low beside him so that her ample breasts just brushed against his cloak.

Ramagar shook his head. The whore lingered a moment, false eyelashes fluttering, then frowned and returned to her seat. It was no secret in the Demon's Horn that she favored him. Always had, ever since her coming to the Jandari three years before. But not once had the thief taken up on her offers, even when she had made it plain that for him her pleasures would come without charge.

Moments later the servant girl was back. The landlord took the bottle from her and brought it himself. A dirty goblet was placed on the table and the landlord poured. He stood beaming while the thief tasted the wine and nodded in approval.

The landlord leaned in closer, glancing about to see if anyone was watching. Then, assured that everyone minded his own business, he said, "Someone has been looking for you."

Ramagar raised his brow. "Who?"

"Vlashi, the pickpocket. He was in earlier, asking for you. He gave me a message to say that he has matters to discuss. Important matters, he says."

The thief ran a hand along the edge of his trimmed black beard. For one reason or other, the wispy pickpocket was always seeking him out, always offering him new schemes to make them both rich. Yet it was always Ramagar's wine that was drunk, and his own purse that was forced to pay for it.

"If he returns tell him to go away," the thief replied. "Tonight I have other things on my mind."

The landlord clasped his hands and frowned. "Would that I could, my friend. But, alas, it may be too late."

Ramagar looked to the door and there he stood. The pickpocket's beady eyes were already busily scanning the inn, seeking him out. Vlashi saw him and grinned, displaying a mouthful of decayed teeth. And without being asked, he strode to the thief's table and plopped himself easily into the chair opposite. His nervous eyes gazed at the bottle of fine wine. A tongue darted from between fat lips and ran from one corner of his mouth to the other.

"Bring another glass," Ramagar sighed.

While the thief poured, his companion warmed his hands by rubbing them over the wax lamp. A glint of mischief flickered in his eyes.

Vlashi took the drink greedily and downed it with a single swallow, not caring that excess wine dripped from his mouth over his beard and onto his seedy, torn cloak.

He winked at the thief. "You must have had a fine mark tonight to afford such a quality brew," he observed.

Ramagar eyed him slowly. "I hear you've been looking for me," he said, purposely ignoring the question. Vlashi, not the brightest of men, was unaware of the slight.

Leaning his body over the table and bringing his dirtied face so close that Ramagar could smell his foul breath, he smiled. "I, too, have been fortunate tonight," he whispered. "Yes, most fortunate."

"Then the gods must have favored us both. Perhaps you can pay back the three coppers you owe me."

Vlashi looked at him sourly. "Coppers? Ah, a mere trifle, my friend. A matter of no consequence. Not with what I have to show you."

"And what might that be?"

The pickpocket poured himself another drink and finished it off in the same manner as the first. Ramagar sat back and waited while the cutpurse looked carefully around the room. At the closest table the patron was half-strewn across the table, snoring loudly. At the next, the green-haired whore was sitting with her eyes on the door, too interested in the possible next customer to be paying any attention. Two other patrons were dealing in whispers of their own, while the servant girl doted on a group of newcomers to the Jandari who obviously had no idea where they were.

"It's safe," said Ramagar, beginning to stir with impatience. "You can speak."

The decayed teeth flashed with the smile. Vlashi nodded in agreement and slowly put his hand inside his faded tunic.

A long curved object glittered as it first caught the light. Ramagar stared as the pickpocket placed the object in his hand. It was a tiny, jeweled scimitar, not much longer than a

15

man's hand, but intricately woven with fine design along both sides of the scabbard, which, as the thief had no trouble realizing, was made of pure gold.

Before Ramagar could inspect it more closely, Vlashi pulled it back and began to fondle it affectionately.

"Now *this* is a prize, eh, my friend?"

The thief was too stunned to answer. He narrowed his eyes and gazed at the jewels, tiny baubles that reflected dancing light onto the wall. The whore turned to look, and Vlashi quickly put the blade back in his tunic.

"Look this way again and I'll slice your tongue!" he hissed at her.

Undaunted, the girl was about to reply when the thief's angry eyes caught her own, sending her back into silence.

"She'll cause no trouble," assured the thief. "Now tell me more about this, er, prize. Where did you get it?"

Vlashi chuckled. So the thief was interested after all. Perhaps more interested than he was willing to admit.

Ramagar read the thought. At once his face returned to impassivity, his voice no longer betrayed emotion.

"How I came upon this prize is in itself a tale to tell," Vlashi said quickly. "Ah, Ramagar, it is not to be believed! Never in a thousand, thousand years could it happen again. I swear that if I—"

"Yes, yes," growled Ramagar. "I am sure you could take all night to explain to me in detail. But get to the point. I have very little time to waste . . ."

Vlashi's face twisted slightly into a grimace. "I lifted it from a beggar."

The thief roared. "Very well, Vlashi. Perhaps I had no business in asking. It bears no merit—"

"But I swear to you!" cried the pickpocket. "I was not trying to keep anything from you, Ramagar. This very prize that I now hold was truly lifted from the pocket of a beggar!"

The thief scrutinized him carefully. Such a thing was impossible, he knew. Where would a beggar come to possess such a prize? And if he did, surely he would no longer have to beg for a living. The scimitar was a gift of princes, or even kings.

"Tell me more," said the thief, and his companion was all too eager to comply.

"It was a man in rags. A peculiar fellow—yellow-haired. A foreigner. I first saw him wandering aimlessly along the streets and into the plaza." Vlashi's eyes brightened and he

16

paused to pour himself yet another glass of wine. "Normally I would not have given such a man a second look, much less a piece of my valuable time. But . . ." He seemed to grope for the right words. "But there was something else about him, something I cannot explain, that left me intrigued. His dress and open palms said beggar, yet he carried himself like no other I have ever seen . . ."

"And then?"

The pickpocket hunched his shoulders and leaned closer. "And then I began to follow him. Why, I cannot say. But whatever the reason that drove me on, I felt somehow compelled to find out what the lout was up to. I assumed the bulge behind his rags to be no more than a cheap dagger of sorts, causing me to think that perhaps my prey was in truth a murderer only disguised as a beggar or brought to this low state by circumstances I could not guess." He shrugged and grinned wanly. "But, as times are hard, and business was poor, I felt that if I could lift even a copper dagger it might bring me a few coins to pay for a good meal and bottle of wine.

"So I spent the day in waiting. His eyes were as cunning as mine, I tell you. I saw the way he looked at passersby, saw the way he was able to define their stations even as you or I have been taught to do. The sun was all but gone when I made my move. The beggar had paused to drink at the fountain. And like the wind I struck. I jostled him and turned him, leaving him gaping. My cold hands had never been faster. Within the blink of an eye I lifted my prize. The beggar gave chase—can you imagine? I, Vlashi, the fleetest foot next to your own in all the Jandari, being chased and cursed by a beggar? Well, no matter. I easily lost him, although I have to admit I was forced to hide for hours until I dared come out into the streets again. You can imagine my surprise—and delight—when I discovered what I had found. The beggar had made me a rich man. Yes, a very rich man."

Ramagar nodded his head slowly. "There is no doubt as to the beauty of your prize," he said. "Or even its value." As he spoke he poured Vlashi another glass. "But tell me, have you found a buyer for it yet?"

The pickpocket's eyes twinkled like a child's. "Finding a buyer is easy," he said with a giggle. "A hundred merchants in the Jandari would beg me for the chance to own such a gift. But finding one who will meet the right price, ah,

17

Ramagar, that is a different matter. A very different matter. I must not be hasty. No, not hasty."

Ramagar hid his amusement. "I agree. So have you come to ask my help?"

"I have. Unless of course," he said slyly, "you might wish to purchase the prize yourself."

The rogue among rogues, thief among thieves, smiled and leaned back in his chair. All the while that Vlashi looked him in the eye Ramagar's mind was clicking. He studied his companion, wondered if a bit more wine might not lower his asking price, and just how much he would really have to pay for it.

"How much do you want?" he asked directly.

Vlashi frowned and gazed at his glass. "For a quick sale, and for a friend, I can let you have it for a nominal sum. Yes, a very nominal sum."

Ramagar became stern. "How much"

"A hundred pieces of silver," to which he hastily added, "and ten of gold."

The thief grimaced. "Your price is preposterous," he said with irritation. "No man would pay so much."

"You take me for a fool, my friend. It's worth that and more. And you know it!"

Ramagar was at a loss to disagree. The prince who had the prize forged might have paid as much as a hundred pieces in gold. "Take it somewhere else, Vlashi. I cannot meet your price." And the thief rose to leave.

"My friend," replied the pickpocket, "resume your place, please. The night is young, and we have yet to begin our discussion in earnest."

Ramagar sat down, pretending to be vexed. His first ruse had worked, for he had no intention of giving up easily.

"Let me see it again," he said gruffly.

Reluctantly, as if parting with a part of his very being, the pickpocket once more handed over his prize. Ramagar, sheltering it from the prying eyes of others, held it up to the light and slowly turned it round and round. He slid the blade out from the scabbard and held his breath in wonder. The steel glowed ice-blue. Ramagar knew this blade had been forged with the care that a craftsman gives only to a king. The edge was so sharp that the slightest touch of his finger against it brought forth blood.

Ramagar slid the blade back, handed it over. "Fifty in silver. Not a copper more."

18

Hurt showed on Vlashi's pockmarked face. "You play games with me, thief. Twice the price is a bargain."

"Then sell it—if you can," Ramagar replied. "A prize such as this will be missed by its true owner. The soldiers will be seeking it. And the man found with it in his possession risks losing his head. No, my pickpocket friend, the price you ask is far too high. Slit your own throat if you like, but do not ask me to slit mine."

Vlashi began to sweat. He had not thought of the consequences Ramagar had described. And it was most certainly true; carrying the prize around made him a marked man. Every soldier, every mercenary, every brigand, and every thief would desire it. Men who would stop at nothing to get it. Vlashi realized that he would be better off without it. Let the next owner live with such fear. He would sell it now and be done. Yet, his Jandari instinct was still not about to let him part with it without receiving at least a measure of its true value.

"Eighty, no less. Cash, paid tonight. Have we a bargain?"

The thief shook his head. "Sixty and no more . . ."

"Do you jest? Even Oro would offer more. A dirty swine like that would make me a better offer. Ah, Ramagar, you do me an injustice. My feelings are hurt. We are friends. Seventy-five . . ."

Ramagar laughed and called to the landlord. "Bring us some playing cards," he demanded. The landlord snapped his fingers and the servant girl came running with a fresh deck which she spread in front of them and placed on the table before she withdrew.

Ramagar took the cards in his hand and began to shuffle. His black eyes gazed into Vlashi's. "I make you a proposition, my friend. One that can leave neither of us with hurt feelings." He spread the cards evenly across the table, face down. "A single game of jackals and hounds. If you win, I pay seventy-five . . ."

Vlashi grinned like a cat. Jackals and hounds was his game. No man, not even Ramagar, could beat him at it.

The thief stopped him as he tried to draw a card. "But if *I* win," Ramagar continued, "you sell the prize for forty."

"Forty!"

Vlashi's outraged scream caught the attention of others.

"Hush, my impatient friend."

The pickpocket stuttered, trying to get the words out as fast as he could. "But moments ago you offered me sixty!"

"Now it is you that hurt me, Vlashi. We are both men of the world, are we not? Men of the Jandari. Willing to risk our lives every day in the gamble of life. Play me this single game. Seventy-five is yours tonight if you win. Seventy-five! And even if you lose, you still walk away a man of wealth. Forty pieces of silver . . . Enough to keep your belly full for months. Women to share your bed, a new cloak, the finest wine available . . ."

Vlashi smacked his lips and swallowed. He glanced at the green-haired whore, her full breasts taunting and tantalizing him. The roundness of her hips, her sensuous mouth perhaps upon his own later this night.

"Make your offer fifty, Ramagar, and the bargain will be sealed."

Ramagar nodded. Fifty it would be.

A new bottle of wine was called for and brought; each man poured a glass filled to the brim. Vlashi downed his nervously while Ramagar sipped. Then they each, in turn, drew three face-down cards, held them close, and eyed them carefully.

"You first," said the pickpocket.

The thief was in no hurry. He studied his cards and after a long moment's time, while Vlashi sweated, placed the first card face up on the table. It was a serpent. A red-eyed cobra.

Vlashi chortled and put down his own. A bear.

"My bear takes your serpent," he wheezed triumphantly. And he scooped up both cards and placed them beside him. It was his turn to throw first.

The card was a strong one. A hound.

Ramagar kept his stare to Vlashi's face and put his own second card beside it. The pickpocket winced. It was a fox. Both cards were of the same value and no one could claim them. The entire game would now rest on the final throw, the winner claiming all four, and taking the match.

Tiny beads of sweat broke out across Vlashi's forehead. He put down his third card, palm still covering it. Ramagar did the same. At last Vlashi ventured forth and showed his strength.

"A jackal!" he cooed. "Only one card in the deck is stronger. The game is mine!"

Vlashi's face glowed when he saw the thief frown. He was certain he had won. Ramagar had only one chance in a hundred to beat him. And the thought of seventy-five pieces of silver in his pockets made Vlashi shake with laughter.

"The game is not done yet, pickpocket," growled Ramagar. And when Ramagar's hand was removed, Vlashi's jaw hung open wider than a street urchin's.

The card was a dragon—a wild card, and all-powerful. Even the mighty jackal fell to its presence.

Vlashi slammed his fist onto the table, causing the bottles and glasses to quiver. Ramagar laughed loudly and held out his hand for the prize.

Vlashi pouted but there was nothing he could do. Ramagar had won fairly; at least Vlashi knew that he could never prove that he hadn't.

"Not so fast," said the pickpocket, offended at the waiting hand. "The agreed price was fifty. Where's my money?"

Ramagar quickly begun to empty his pockets, pieces of silver jingling on the table. Vlashi began to count. There were seven pieces of silver, one of gold, a handful of coppers that Ramagar had been saving.

"Where's the rest?"

The thief took out the emerald ring. "This is worth twenty," he said, handing it over. Vlashi took it and examined. He nodded. Ramagar showed him the gold pendant. "This is worth ten more." The pickpocket grabbed it. "What else?"

Ramagar slid the wine bottles to his side of the table. "You paid for these as well. That should make us more than even."

Vlashi drew a long breath and sighed, sure that somehow he was getting the poorer end of the bargain. But to refuse now, and try and keep the prize, could easily so arouse the thief that he might end up minus the scimitar and the money as well. Not to mention a few broken ribs.

"Don't act so dejected, my friend," said Ramagar, smiling broadly. "You have both the wine and her," he glanced at the waiting whore, "to console you. And I'm sure you'll find them equally pleasing."

Vlashi reached inside the tunic again, and for the last time fondled his prize. Ramagar snatched it and quickly stood up from the table. "Take care, Vlashi," he called, flinging his cloak. And turning on his heels he strode from the tavern.

"Ah, well," mumbled the pickpocket. He downed another gulp of wine and looked up at the whore. When she smiled he beckoned her with his finger, soon to forget this day and the strange turn of events it had brought.

The hour was late. The busy Street of Thieves and all the others in the Jandari had become quiet in the hours before dawn. Ramagar felt the night chill, the cruel winter wind blowing harsher as it always did before the sun came up.

He had not a penny to his name; not a halfpenny to buy a few slices of bread. Everything he possessed had been given to Vlashi, but he was certain that come the morrow he would be a wealthy man for it. There was still time left for him to seek another benefactor, as he fondly called his victims. Somewhere he might yet find some poor soul too drunk to stand with a purse containing a few pieces of copper. But Ramagar's thoughts strayed from such notions; he could think only of the prize he clutched in his pocket, and of bringing it to Mariana to see.

Far from the Street of Thieves, past the Avenue of Pigs he walked. The byways narrowed, taking on an eerie silence. Occasionally Ramagar glanced this way or that at a sudden noise, only to realize that it was the banging of shutters that caused his unease. The bitter wind was his only companion.

The life of a thief is a lonely one. For Ramagar, it was at this time of night that he was forced to face this obvious truth. As a boy, alone and awake in the night, prowling the alleys like a cat, he would fight back tears in a losing battle, only to stop when there were no more tears to cry. Ramagar had no home. Not then, not now. No mother, no father. Only the streets. Only the dark shadows in which he prowled incessantly, stealing a piece of bread, a slice of fruit. By day he would climb to the roofs of the hovels and there, bathing in the warm, gentle sun that blessed these lands nearly every day of the year, he would curl himself up against the wall and sleep. And when he woke, the sun would be all but gone. The shadows would begin to descend before his eyes and he would greet them like old friends. And under their cloak he would descend to the streets, seeking another piece of bread, another piece of fruit, anything that might sustain him till the day when the cycle would begin anew.

When he was eleven he met one-eyed Jackal. The old man was renowned throughout the Jandari and young Ramagar had stood in awe. Who in the entire city had not at one time or another heard fearful tales of the best thief the Jandari had ever known? Once, it was said, a cohort of soldiers had combed the alleys and catacombs for an entire month to find the wily rogue. But the Jackal was too smart for mere men; with fire in his eye and laughter on his lips he eluded them. Eluded them one and all—and made a laughingstock of the entire Regent's Garrison.

But that had been when the Jackal was young. Before his capture and torture. His right eye gouged from its socket, his face bloodied and broken, the Jackal somehow managed to escape. But he was never the same. The loss of his eye had taken much of his skill, and, Ramagar knew, much of his spirit. But not his wits. No, never that.

For reasons the young Ramagar never learned, one-eyed Jackal had taken a liking to him. Perhaps he saw the lad as the son he never had, or perhaps he saw in him some of the qualities that he himself had possessed as a youth. For whatever reason, the Jackal had taken Ramagar under his wing. And he vowed a vow; that he would take this urchin, this stealer of bread and fruit, and make him not merely a thief, but a thief of thieves. Through Ramagar, the Jackal would live again.

Day after day the Jackal would walk with him through the bazaars, teach him how to spot men of substance, show him how to recognize true nobility from that of con men and hucksters. He showed the lad just where a merchant's purse might be found, where a dowager might carry her gold. He refined his speech, taught the letters of the alphabet so that the lad might read the wall posters and notices and learn better the doings of the city. Picking pockets was easy for the boy. It was a natural talent. But any fool can learn that lowly trade. Indeed thieves, true thieves that is, held only contempt for such men. A real thief has finesse; a nobility of his own, if you will. An understanding of who will make the better mark. And a thief of thieves, well, he must know all these things better than any other.

So it was, after a reasonable time of training, that the Jackal, one-eyed and hobbled, took the lad every night into the alleys and made him learn to walk them with eyes shut. Then it was the streets themselves, and not just of the Jandari, but in finer quarters where those such as Ramagar had never been before. He would gape at the fine, stately homes, stare in disbelief that anything so luxurious could exist. Real grass in front of the houses—and walls of brick that did not crumble. The Jackal would laugh at the boy's gasps. "These are your marks," he would say. "Learn everything you can. A man from this house carries no coppers nor silver. Only gold, Ramagar, only gold."

And the lad would listen and nod. One-eyed Jackal gave him the finest education anyone could receive. Those lessons were never forgotten, even now, years after the Jackal had

23

died a miserable death in an alley and Ramagar became alone again.

Yet Ramagar knew that his friend would be proud; his legacy would never die, not as long as the thief of thieves still lived. Not as long as Ramagar held breath in his body.

Saddened by these fond memories, Ramagar made his way to the tiny arched street at the very edge of the district. Mariana's street.

Now, as everyone knows, a thief can never have a real home, nor a wife to share his bed and give him children. Yet a man must have somewhere he can turn. Someplace where he knows he is welcome and will be received, where he can rest in the knowledge that he is as safe as a thief can possibly hope to be. Equally important, he needs someone to love and to love him in return. And Ramagar loved the dancing girl. Perhaps his shyness would not let him say so in words. But his kisses would not lie. Women he had known for all his life; from prostitutes to servant girls, once even a priestess from the temple. Never, though, had there been the attraction that he felt the first time he had seen her. So struck was he by her loveliness that he was unable to work the entire night. Instead, he spent his money and his time finding out just who she was. And when he learned her name he whispered it upon his lips a thousand times over. Mariana, Mariana. The sweetest sound he had ever known.

As he came close to the two-story house he glanced up at the corner window. It was dark and he frowned. Either Mariana had not come home yet or, angered at his being so late, she had put out the lamp and gone to sleep.

Probably the latter, he thought with a sigh. Lately she had been trying harder than ever to domesticate him, to make him a husband in deed if not in name. Oh, he might bark and carry on at her nagging, but in truth he was pleased. It showed how important to her he was. For the first time since the Jackal's death he was wanted again. It was a feeling he hoped never to lose.

Still, if Mariana was as angry as he feared there would be hell to pay. It could take days to placate her. But then he thought of the scimitar, the fabulous prize in his pocket. He smiled. He could picture the glow in her eyes when she saw it.

A chilly gust of wind blew leaves at his feet as he came to the door. His sharp senses picked up the faintest of sounds from behind.

Ramagar whirled; his fist lashed out at the darting silhou-

24

ette. There was a groan and a gasp when the fist connected, and the attacking figure rolled in pain to the cobblestones. The thief was about to deliver a swift kick to the face when he was stopped by a pair of haunting eyes; sad, pitiful eyes. He peered more closely at the shadowy face. It was a boy's. Not even a boy's, it was a child's.

"Please, please, sir! Don't strike!"

Hands on hips, Ramagar said, "Get out of here! Fast! Be glad I let you off so easily. And the next time you seek a mark be certain he's someone you can handle!"

The boy staggered to his feet, and Ramagar got his first good look at his face. It was drawn and haggard, the eyes puffed, the lips blue from the cold. The boy wore no covering on his feet. No boots, no sandals, not even rags.

"Thank you for letting me go," the boy rasped sincerely. "Forgive me . . . I had no idea it was you . . ."

The thief cast a wary glance. "You know who I am?"

"Oh, yes! You're Ramagar. The finest thief in all of the Jandari. The master of thieves . . ."

Ramagar stifled a chuckle and looked at the boy sternly. "When was the last time you ate?"

The lad shrugged. "Yesterday, I think."

The thief's heart ached for the lad, although he would not let himself show it. And he took pity on him, perhaps in the same way one-eyed Jackal had done, so long ago. But Ramagar had no money, no spare coppers to put into the boy's palm.

"See that window?" he asked, pointing above.

The street urchin nodded.

"Wait for the light to go on. Then stand directly below. Take what I throw you and be off."

The youth's jaw dropped, his eyes grew wide with excitement. What would he tell his friends? Who would believe that Ramagar had offered him not only his life back, but was going to feed him as well!

"I will wait, Ramagar. As long as you say. I am indebted to you forever—"

Ramagar grimaced. "Be indebted to no man, boy," he said. "That is the best advice I can give. Hold your own counsel and trust no one and nothing. Do you understand?"

The boy shivered as he nodded. His tattered cloak looked as though it was about to tear into shreds.

Ramagar turned abruptly, flaring his cloak behind, and entered the house and climbed the stairs. The hallway was black. Only his night sight allowed him to find the right door. The muffled cry of an infant came from somewhere below. Ramagar ignored it and knocked.

"Who's there?" came a sleepy voice.

"Me. Open up."

The door cracked open, and he could see the pupil of one eye. "Oh. It *is* you, isn't it. What do you want?"

"Very funny. Let me in."

The voice was a sneer. "Go sleep in a gutter."

Ramagar gritted his teeth. "Don't make bad jokes, Mariana. Look, it's cold out there. Freezing."

"Too bad. Come see me tomorrow."

He groaned out loud. "Open the door or I'll break it down."

"Try it and I'll make you a eunuch."

The woman was incorrigible! But what was he to do? "Please listen, Mariana," he said wearily, holding his hand firmly against the wood so she could not shut the door in his face, "I meant to come hours ago, like I promised. But I was detained."

"By that whore from the Demon's Horn?"

He threw up his hands in exasperation. "With Vlashi."

"That's worse."

"Please, Mariana, let me in just for a few minutes. We have to talk. It's important." Here his eyes narrowed into slits and he looked at her seriously. His voice became a whisper. "Perhaps the most important thing that's ever happened to either one of us."

She eyed him skeptically, then reluctantly opened the door wide. "All right," she agreed, putting her hand to her mouth to stifle a yawn. "But not for the night, mind you. Just to talk."

Ramagar nodded appreciatively and closed the door behind. The girl struck a match and lit the single wax lamp on the table. The light flickered, then burst into yellow and blue flame, brightening the tiny room and sending long shadows bouncing off the walls.

Ramagar smiled as he faced her. Mariana, aware of his amorous tricks, stepped back a pace, hands tightened into tiny fists at her side. Long black hair flowed over her shoulders, down the pink nightgown, the edges curling just below her round, firm breasts. Brooding eyes peered at him from below thin dark brows.

"Now what's so important?" she asked.

26

"Just a moment," replied the thief. She gaped while he went to her purse and drew a few coppers. From the small wardrobe he pulled one of his old cloaks.

"What are you doing?"

"Keeping a promise." His eyes scanned the room quickly, focusing on the fruit bowl set aside on the ledge. He took a few apples and pears, then wrapped them, along with the coppers, into the old cloak.

The girl looked on while he opened the window, straining to make it budge.

"Are you insane?"

"*Shh!*" Then he poked his head out, calling in a whisper, "Hey, boy! Catch!"

The bundle fell to the earth, and Mariana heard the shuffle of feet running down the cobblestones. Ramagar smiled and shut the window. She came to his side. She had not seen the urchin, but she knew her lover well enough, knew his soft heart's charity.

Ramagar turned to the dancing girl and kissed her on the cheek. She turned her head away. "Pig," she mumbled.

"Don't be angry. Not tonight . . ."

Black eyes flashed as she snarled, "And why shouldn't I be angry? Where in hell have you been? I haven't seen you for days."

He patted her on the behind, then slumped wearily onto the worn divan, which, except for the bed curtained off in the corner, was the only major piece of furniture in the flat.

"By all means, make yourself at home," she told him sarcastically.

The rogue grinned and closed his eyes. "You look beautiful, Mariana. Why don't you come over here?"

She rudely intimated that his parents were unwed and gazed at him with her hands on her hips. "I suppose you're hungry?"

"Ravished. It's been a very long night and I haven't a copper."

"Serves you right. Just remember that you owe me those coppers you just took."

Propping himself up on his elbow, his head resting gently on the laced pillow, he said, "But the night wasn't a complete waste. I do have something to show you. Something you might want to examine for me."

"I'm not interested. Take it to Oro."

He unsnapped his cloak, placed it beside him on the floor.

Then he reached into his pocket and took out the scimitar, which he dangled loosely between two fingers.

Now, Mariana was a shrewd girl; perhaps the shrewdest he had ever known. She possessed a vast knowledge of many matters. Not only could she read and write properly—which in itself was a rarity for a dancing girl—but she knew more about the city and the world than Ramagar would ever know. Whenever a matter puzzled him, he could be sure that Mariana would be able to find the answer. And tonight he was more puzzled than anytime he could remember.

"What *is* that?" she asked, the dazzle of the scabbard holding her attention.

He handed it to her without a word.

Her eyes lit up like stars and she stood breathless. Never in all her twenty years had she seen anything like it. "It . . . It's magnificent," she whispered. "God above, you must have lifted it from a king."

The thief laughed. "I didn't lift it at all. Vlashi did—and he claims his mark was a beggar."

"Don't joke with me, thief," she snapped.

He held out open palms. "I'm not! It's the truth. I paid Vlashi everything I had to get it. And even then I had to cheat him at jackals and hounds to make the price."

While he was speaking Mariana examined the scabbard, her heart thumping louder with every new jewel she recognized. Slumping down next to him, she spoke with amazement, mumbling softly.

"A ransom . . . It must be worth a king's ransom."

Ramagar took her hand and scowled. "I know that much myself. But look it over carefully." He pointed to the strange markings near the hilt. So tiny, so intricately woven into the design that they could easily be overlooked.

Mariana was quick to comply. Straining her eyes, she held it close to the lamp, searching for the engraver's mark, the telltale sign of who made it and where.

"The craftsmanship is superb," she told him, observing everything, missing not even the slightest nick or scratch, of which there were many. "But it's old. Very old. Ancient, perhaps. I've never seen a prize so fine."

"Was it made in the city?"

The girl pursed her lips and shook her head. "Definitely not. Look." She ran her finger along the edge. "I can't understand the inscription. The writing is foreign, like nothing ever done in Kalimar."

The thief whistled. Kalimar was a vast land, extending between two great seas. It included many cities, including his own. But if the scimitar was indeed from somewhere foreign, then it must have traveled thousands of miles to reach its destination in the Jandari. And Ramagar could only wonder what strange adventures it must have known during its long journey.

"I wonder who its original owner could have been."

The girl hardly heard. She was too busy studying the peculiar mark close to the hilt. It was a tiny circle, no larger than one of the lesser jewels, and within the circle was an X-like rune with an arrow-like letter running through the middle.

"How much do you think we can sell it for?" he asked.

She took a long time in answering, and when she did, she said, "I think we should try to find out more about it before we sell it. It could be rarer than either of us realizes."

"Not sell it?" He looked at her incredulously. "But we have to sell it! What use is there in keeping it? Imagine all the things we could do with the money."

"You're impatient, Ramagar. Don't let it slip out of your hands so easily. Not until we know all there is to know."

Her reasoning did make sense, he had to admit, even if he didn't particularly like the idea of hanging onto it. After all, what he had told Vlashi was in part true; its owners would surely be seeking it back. And the man caught with it . . .

He scratched at his beard. "How can we find out more about it?"

The girl shrugged and sighed. "I suppose we'll have to take it to Oro after all . . ."

"That dog? I wouldn't trust him with a copper!"

She ruefully agreed. But the hunchbacked merchant was a cagey old devil. And a foreigner. For twenty years he had dealt in stolen and smuggled merchandise, and in that time learned more about such matters than any man in the Jandari.

"I don't trust him either," she said. "But at least he'll be able to tell us more than we can find out ourselves. If only we can learn where it comes from, we might get a true idea of its value. Why, if it was taken from a prince, then the reward for returning it should make us rich."

"Return it?"

"Why not? Its owner would certainly be most grateful—"

"Ah, Mariana, you're dreaming again. But never mind. Tomorrow we'll see what to do." He blew out the candle and

29

tucked the scimitar under the pillow. Then he pulled the dancing girl close and pressed his lips to hers. Mariana squealed with pleasure in his embrace, offered no resistance when his hand loosened the string of her nightgown and slid it to the floor. She closed her eyes and forgot about the harsh world outside. She was his; he was hers. For tonight that was more than enough. And then she smiled, knowing that the golden scimitar would change their lives forever—and make all of her foolish girl's dreams come true.

2

The starry black sky changed slowly to indigo as dawn crept its way across the horizon, then the winter sun itself flamed into sight, to warm Kalimar from the inland sea in the east all the way to the nameless ocean that swept endlessly in the west.

As always, it was the tall golden spires of the city that first caught the light, slanting morning shadows across the domes and temples, along the high walls, and to the citadel of the palace itself. Hooded priests with faces aglow in crimson took their places in the minarets and cried from tower to tower, in prayer, the coming of the new day. And life in the city began to stir. Golden rays poured across the brightly colored roofs of slate, filtering down unevenly into nooks and crannies and all the darkest places, nudging beneath tightly locked shutters and doors, creeping into ten thousand bedrooms like a herald to announce the day's arrival.

The faint haze that had come with dawn quickly disappeared and in its place the soft heat shimmered and danced against cobble and flagstone, touching softly in the alleys and byways, bursting in splendor along the old, weaving roads that led to each of the Nine Gates of Kalimar.

The city was awake, from the plazas and the bazaars to the busy port where a dozen ships stood ready to berth and unload their wares. Only in the quarter called the Jandari did the streets remain silent. Only there did the stalls and shops remain tightly locked. Beggars, who had lined the pavements only hours before, now hid from the light in doorways and alleys, replaced in the gutters by stray cats and prowling dogs

30

seeking their meals among the heaps of rotting garbage discarded the night before.

But not everyone slept; there were some who stayed awake plotting and scheming their plans for the coming night, while others dared not sleep. Each sound from below sent them scurrying to the windows with hearts beating like drums and wary eyes in search of marching soldiers come to drag them from their beds.

There were many reasons not to sleep, but on this morning none had better than the thief and the dancing girl. Their business could not wait until dark. Under prying unseen eyes they stealthily made their way along the Avenue of Pigs and paused only when they reached the iron-braced door of Oro's shop.

While Ramagar looked up and down the avenue, Mariana knocked. A tiny slit was quickly pulled aside, and two beady eyes peered out. It took only a moment until recognition flickered and Mariana could hear the unbolting of locks. The door creaked as it opened to reveal a small man with hunched shoulders and a slight hump. His face was lined and creased, though not so much with age as with memories of a lifetime of bitterness. Deformed at birth, he grew up hating the laughter of other children. In later years the envy of other, stronger, men twisted his mind until he knew only rage for the world around him. But Oro was a cunning man, and in the dirty streets of the Jandari, where cunning was king, he had become a feared and respected figure. And no one dared to laugh.

Oro shaded his eyes from the light and looked greedily at the shapely girl before shifting his glance to the thief. He hid a frown from Ramagar, and without speaking beckoned them inside. The very fact that they had come to him in daylight assured him that they considered their business important. Above all else, Oro was a businessman.

The door shut, leaving only darkness. Black curtains covered the tiny window at the back, and the room was coated with dust and the dried dung which filtered inside from the courtyard beyond the hidden back door.

As their eyes adjusted to the dark, Oro led them to his counter. There a burning candle cast an eerie yellow pall in which a moth danced.

Mariana shuddered involuntarily and slipped closer to her lover. Oro caught her uneasiness and smiled inwardly.

"So," he rasped in his thick, accented voice as he took his

31

place behind the counter. "What brings you here so early in the day?"

The thief met his steely gaze. "We brought something for you to examine."

"Oh?" His dark brows rose malevolently. He had as much love for Ramagar as the thief had for him. "And what might that be, eh?"

Ramagar hesitated before reaching inside his pocket and bringing out the scimitar. The dagger glittered in the candle's light and the dealer in stolen goods stared. The thief closed his hand around his prize and held it tightly.

"I cannot examine your merchandise unless you give it to me," Oro growled impatiently.

Ramagar shot a quick glance to Mariana and she nodded, although with much of the same apprehension that he was feeling. Then with a sigh and a look that promised violence if Oro tried any clever manipulation or sleight of hand, he handed it over.

The merchant put an eyeglass to his eye and inspected it closely. His head bobbed up and down, and he muttered, "Yes, yes," over and over. At last he took the glass from his eye and turned to his visitors. "Have you brought this to sell?" he asked.

"That depends," replied the thief. "First we want to know what you can tell us about it."

Oro shrugged. "It is a very fine piece of work. Indeed it is. But you know that as well as I, Ramagar . . ." In a gesture of good will he placed it down in front of the thief. "I am prepared to offer you a handsome price. In cash, of course."

"How handsome?"

Oro grinned toothlessly. Mariana stepped back a pace at the smell of his hot, foul breath. The merchant rolled his eyes as if in some mental calculation, saying at last, "Fifty pieces of silver."

Ramagar laughed. The very offer he had given Vlashi! He shook his head and sneered. Oro looked at him suspiciously. His face remained blank, but inwardly he was annoyed that the thief obviously knew more of its value than he had let on.

"Such a fine jewel as this will be difficult to be rid of," he said, looking first to Mariana, then to the thief.

"Perhaps so. But I'm not interested." Ramagar put his hand to the scimitar and pulled it out of Oro's reach. The rubies and emeralds scattered colored light in all their faces.

32

Oro hunched in closer. He wiped his mouth with the back of his hand.

"How much do you ask, then?"

The girl flashed her eyes, replying before Ramagar could answer: "Have you seen the engraver's mark?"

"I have," came a slow, measured reply.

"Then you know how rare it is. A true value would be more like a thousand pieces—in gold."

The beady eyes screwed in anger. Then Oro laughed, looking hard at the full-bosomed dancing girl with pangs of growing desire. For more than a year he had watched her from afar, watched her dance at the taverns. The single time he had approached her she had spit in his eye, caring nothing for the silver he offered in return for meeting his lewd cravings. And her arrogance had angered him as much as her spurning. But he blamed not the girl, no indeed, but rather he blamed the thief. It was her lover alone who was responsible, and secretly he despised Ramagar for it.

"Your price is outrageous, dancing girl. Fit for princes with overflowing coffers. I cannot meet it. Nor can any merchant in the Jandari."

Mariana scooped it up. "Then we keep it."

Oro's face twisted with annoyance. Dealing with the girl was going to be harder than dealing with the thief. *Damnable girl!*

"Why be so hasty?" he said with a smile. He drew a bottle of wine from the drawer beneath the counter and filled a glass for Ramagar. "Perhaps," he said, running a stubby finger alongside his nose, "I can make my offer a hundred and twenty-five. In silver . . ."

Ramagar downed the wine and grinned. This was more like it. "Actually, I had more like two hundred in mind . . ."

Oro shared his mirth. "Ah, Ramagar," he sighed, "you are too clever for me. What am I to do? Two hundred, you say? Can we agree on one seventy-five?"

Ramagar paused, but was about to agree.

"Done?" asked Oro, holding out his hand.

"Not done!"

The dancing girl pounded her fist on the counter, disturbing a thin layer of dust. "It is no longer for sale!" And she clasped the scimitar firmly against her breast.

Oro reddened. "What? What are you saying?"

Even Ramagar seemed perturbed. "Listen to me, Mariana," he soothed, thinking her unreasonable.

"Are you mad?" she flared. Her eyes glowered at the merchant. "Ramagar is not as aware of your tricks as I am," she hissed. Oro was so taken aback that he very nearly cringed at the sight of the enraged girl.

"What is she talking about?" he stammered to Ramagar.

"The rune, you dog!" she bristled. "You saw it as well as I, didn't you? Tell us, Oro, where was this dagger forged? In what land, at what time?"

Oro drew to his full height, right shoulder arched forward and higher than the left. "What matter to you, girl?" he countered. "Its origin would only have value to a collector. To you it means nothing." He turned back to Ramagar, hands slightly shaking. "Do we have a bargain or no? Two hundred pieces, thief. I'll meet the full price. What do you say?"

Although he tried not to show it, Ramagar was truly astounded at the merchant's eagerness to buy the prize. Never before had he seen Oro take such an interest. Always his best offer was given with a take-it-or-leave-it attitude. And Ramagar felt puzzled by this sudden change.

Mariana, still clutching the dagger, looked at her lover with pleading eyes. Eyes that cried out: "Don't be a fool!"

The thief pondered, taking delight in seeing Oro fidgit and squirm. "Where *was* the dagger forged?" he asked at last.

Oro sighed. "I am not sure," he sighed. "But not in Kalimar, that much is certain. Perhaps it came from one of the northern kingdoms, Sakhra or Lanohor . . ."

"Or Speca?"

At that, Oro's eyes widened and his jaw dropped. He looked at the girl carefully, wondering how she could possibly know. Or even suspect.

"What do you know of Speca?"

"Only that their craftsmanship was the finest in the world. The finest the world has ever known, or ever will know." She gazed up at Ramagar, adding, "I suspected it last night, but I was reluctant to tell you because I knew I might be wrong."

Ramagar could feel his blood race with his pulse. Specian art was indeed the rarest known—as well as the most valuable. "But what makes you sure now?" he asked.

She glared at Oro. "*He* does. His greed to own the dagger, his willingness to pay anything to get it. Anything."

"Is that true?" asked the thief.

Oro swallowed. He had made his best effort—and lost.

"Bah," he growled. "Only an expert can decipher Specian runes. Their language and culture have been dead a thousand years. At best I can only guess or speculate, as Mariana is doing now."

The girl shivered when she saw the indecisive look on her lover's face. "Don't listen to him, Ramagar. Please—"

"Two hundred fifty pieces, thief. In cash. My final offer. What do you say to that? It will make you a rich man."

"No!" cried Mariana.

Ramagar wanted to sell, wanted to badly. Yet Mariana had never led him astray before. Her counsel had always proved the best he had known. He knew he should listen to her now, as well.

"Let me think about it, Oro. I'll be back tomorrow."

"Thief of thieves, indeed," rasped the merchant in scorn. "Does a woman make your decisions for you, Ramagar? A dancing girl, little better than a common slut bought for a few coppers?"

In rage the thief grabbed him by his tunic and half lifted him off the floor. "If I ever hear you say that again," he whispered, "I'll slice that hump off your back!" And he pushed him against the wall, slamming him so hard that a multitude of objects fell off the grim shelves and clattered loudly onto the floor.

"Get out! Get out!" squawked Oro in a high-pitched squeal. "Don't ever dare come back here again!"

Ramagar put his hands on his hips and laughed defiantly.

"Don't think I'll forget this day, thief!" Oro was openly trembling, trying to pick himself up. "And your prize will be sought, you can be sure—"

"Are you threatening me?" His fist was clenched and ready to strike.

Oro drew back, content to pay for his bravery with the muscles of others. "A warning, Ramagar. Just a warning."

Hands open on the counter, the thief leaned forward and locked Oro's eyes. "If you speak one word of this to anyone, I'll come back and make you suffer." Then he spun on his heels, and, taking Mariana by the hand, whisked her into the sunlight.

Ramagar walked briskly, unspeaking, and Mariana had to almost run to keep up with him. "Are you angry?" she asked, panting to catch her breath.

He shook his head.

"But you're sorry? About not taking the two hundred fifty?"

The thief stopped in his tracks, looked down at her haunt-

35

ing childlike face, and smiled. "No, you were right. A Specian artifact is too valuable to sell without careful thought. But we'll have to find another dealer. I wouldn't let Oro have it no matter what he offered. Not after what he said."

Mariana blushed and smiled, knowing that Ramagar had been willing to fight for her honor and reputation. She stood up on her toes and kissed him lightly, thinking him more a prince than a thief.

"But you'll have to be careful, Ramagar," she warned. "The old goat wants it badly. Badly enough to stop at nothing to get it, I'm afraid."

Putting his arm around her, the thief laughed. "Don't worry. He'll not dare to even look at you again."

Her eyes were wide and pensive as she said, "Not me, Ramagar. You. It's you I'm frightened for."

He frowned. "Me? What can a gutter rat do to me? Listen, this sun is killing my eyes. Why don't we forget all this nonsense, go home, eat some breakfast, and go back to sleep like normal people?"

Mariana nodded and smiled. Then she took his hand and led him home, glad the morning's task was done, and not even suspecting the series of events that would begin that evening.

3

Ramagar awoke with a start. He put his hands to his ears, trying to cut off the screams and cries of his nightmare. But as wakefulness took over he realized that the screams were no dream—they were real. Glancing to the sleeping girl, he threw off his covers and soundlessly hurried to the window. The screaming was growing louder; among the grind and shuffle of running boots he was certain he could hear the distant clomp of horses' hooves drawing steadily nearer.

He unbolted the shutters, opened them wide, and put his hand before his eyes to blot out the rush of late afternoon sun. Below, the tiny street was in confusion. Street people were pushing and shoving, scrambling helter-skelter to reach the safety of doorways and alleys, diving this way and that with total disregard for those poor souls too slow to avoid being trampled underfoot.

Ramagar poked his head out and searched below. "You there!" he called, recognizing a face. "What's going on?"

The urchin paused in his run. Had it been any other than Ramagar who had called he would have paid no attention whatsoever. But the warm new cloak he wore and the jingling coppers in his pocket were too great a debt to ignore.

Face sweaty and paled, anxiety plain in his eyes, he shouted, "The soldiers are coming! Searching every street!"

"But why? What's happened?"

The reply was fast and breathless. "A noble has been murdered in the Jandari! Hundreds have been taken to the dungeons for questioning." And with that, the urchin fled as fast as his feet could carry him. Ramagar, above all, could not blame him. Few who had known the regent's cells below the sewers came out the same as they went in. The Jackal had taught him that as his first lesson.

Ramagar quickly closed the shutters, leaving a single slat open so he could observe at least partially what was going on. Meanwhile, his mind raced as he put together an escape route across the roofs if it came to that.

A wanted man takes no chances.

Down the arched street came riding six black-caped guards. Stern, grim men, sworn to uphold Kalimar's ancient laws and earn favor in the minister's eyes. Purple plumes fluttered from their gray helmets, long, glittering swords dangled from their sides. Red stallion-shaped crests were sewn into their tunics above the heart, telling all who saw that they belonged to the crack regiment known as Inquisitors, the most fearful of the regent's troops.

Women screamed and bundled their infants as the soldiers recklessly tore across the ancient flagstones. Iron hooves struck like flints, sending sparks flying in the late afternoon calm. Old men and cripples hobbled out of harm's way, beggars and pickpockets slipped like lizards into every available nook. Still, within moments a large crowd of citizens had been gathered and pushed with their backs against the walls.

The captain of the soldiers dismounted with an unmasked look of disdain on his face. A dour man in the best of times, he was in no mood for wasting time. The death had caused a minor uproar within the palace walls, even though the victim had been considered an ill-mannered fop, and the captain's orders were plain: if the culprit was not soon found, his own head would be placed on the block in his stead.

Losing not a moment, he drew his sword and brandished it

at the faces of his captives. The frightened group huddled and shivered. He eyed each and every one carefully, rapidly weeding out the riffraff from those of more serious intent.

"Who has information for me?" he questioned with contempt. No one answered; they dipped their heads and shied their eyes from his malevolent gaze. "Speak up now," the soldier warned. "It will save you all a great deal of trouble later."

His companions snickered at the obvious reference to the waiting dungeons.

The captain pursed his lips and sighed. Dealing with them like honest, decent folk would be useless, he could see. They had to be treated as the gutter trash they were. And if he were minister and had his way, this entire district would have been burned to the ground years ago, its filthy inhabitants trapped like rats in the flames. Good riddance to them all. Most were better off dead anyway.

He paced before them and then, on a whim, grabbed hold of an old beggar and hurled him into the gutter, where he splashed clumsily into a reeking cesspool.

"W-What have I done?" cried the beggar.

"That remains to be seen, my friend," said the captain as he ran a finger lightly along the side of his drooping moustache. "Now, can you account for your whereabouts today?"

The beggar was shaking, too frightened to reply. All he could manage to do was whimper his innocence of the crime and beg not to be hurt.

That this man was obviously too dim-witted to be capable of murder the captain knew as well as everyone else. Yet he would provide a good example to the rest: that no life was safe until the murderer was apprehended and Kalimar's justice served.

Ramagar watched from above in anger. He gritted his teeth and cursed softly under his breath as the little scene unfolded.

The wily captain drew back a pace from his newly found suspect, glancing at the others, pretending to be finished with the man. Then he whirled, foot flying upward, his heavy boot smashing against the beggar's sagging jaw. The beggar reeled and howled like a stuck pig.

"Perhaps that will change your mind, eh?" cackled the sadistic soldier. He kneeled down, yanked the man by the hair with one hand and drew the tip of his short sword up against

38

the beggar's jugular with the other. The beggar's eyes widened in terror. The slighest movement of his head would cut the vein.

"Well?"

"I—I am innocent," he rasped. "Please—"

"Then who is guilty?"

"I have been . . . sleeping . . . all day . . . I saw nothing . . ."

The captain grimaced, pushed the man's face into the cesspool, and let him go. Cleaning his hands with a handkerchief, he looked again to the others. A slight weasel of a man met his eyes briefly, then quickly hid them from the steely glare.

The captain flashed a cruel smile. "You, there," he barked. "Yes, you. Come forward." He beckoned him with his finger. "Don't I know you?"

Vlashi shook so hard that even Ramagar in his lofty height could see his knees quiver.

The soldier snickered. He had seen this man before, he was sure, but what matter? There were so many like him in the Jandari, hundreds, thousands even. It was impossible to keep track of them all.

"No, sir," whispered Vlashi, "we have never seen one another before . . ."

"Is that so, my shivering friend?" He brought his face so close that Vlashi could feel the heat of his breath. "What information have you for me, eh? What have your eyes seen this day?"

Vlashi looked away, and his gaze fell on the miserable beggar who was trying to scrape himself up from the gutter.

"Well?"

"I know nothing, sir. Nothing."

"He claims ignorance," marveled the captain with folded arms as he addressed his watching men. "Perhaps we'll have to find a way to loosen his memory." Slitting his eyes and scratching at his chin, he pondered several time-tested ways for dealing with the situation. At length he looked back at the shivering pickpocket and said, "Hold out your hand, my friend."

"Sir?"

The captain set his jaw and raised his powerful frame so that he stood towering over the slight pickpocket. His clenched fist was as large as Vlashi's face.

Vlashi, awareness dawning on what was in store, shakily

did as told. The captain snapped a finger, and one of his men rushed to his side with his weapon drawn.

"Remove the hand," said the first to the second. The soldier grinned. His blade flashed in the crimson sun as he raised the weapon high above his head.

Vlashi took a quick look at his tormentor. Eyes rolling and veins popping, he fainted, collapsing in a heap at the captain's feet. The other soldiers broke into raucous laughter. The captain slapped Vlashi back into wakefulness and smiled. "How many pockets shall you be able to pick with but one hand, eh? Or will you be forced to become a beggar?" He paused to let the meaning of his words sink in and take hold.

Vlashi was white as sheets. "N-Not that," he stammered. "I-I beg you, not that!"

"Then tell me everything you know—right now! What have you seen today? Who has committed the crime?"

The pickpocket's mind was racing frantically. An answer was needed fast; any answer at all, no matter how absurd. As long as it was convincing to his captor.

"It—It was a beggar that killed your noble," he blurted with a sigh and a prayer. "A foreigner, new to the Jandari, new to Kalimar—"

A calloused hand surrounded the pickpocket's frail throat. A freckled tongue protruded from between lips which turned blue, as Vlashi gasped for breath. Soon his entire complexion was dark purple.

"What sort of imbecile do you take me for?" seethed the soldier. "Do I appear to be such a dolt that a fable like that should be believed?"

Vlashi twitched and moaned as the fingers tightened their grip.

"T-T-Truth . . ." he wheezed. "T-Truth . . ."

With scorn the captain let go. Vlashi doubled over and heaved to fill his lungs. The captain marked time while the pickpocket vomited.

"Now then," he said when Vlashi was done, "do you still claim the crime to have been committed by a wandering vagabond?" He drummed his fingers impatiently on the hilt of his sword.

"I have not lied," replied the pickpocket swiftly. "There is such a stranger in the Jandari. I have seen him myself only yesterday. He is like no other beggar, I assure you. To look into his eyes is to look into death itself—"

The captain listened skeptically; the tale was growing more

outrageous with every word. "And where," he queried with ridicule, "might this stranger be found?"

"Yesterday I saw him in the plaza—"

"A thousand beggars line the Jandari's plazas, each one the twin of the next. No, my weasely friend, I fear you send me on a fool's errand."

"But you are wrong!" Vlashi protested. "This one sets himself apart from other men. Indeed, he will betray himself to you the moment you see him."

The soldier cocked a curious brow. "How so, gutter rat?"

Vlashi rubbed his hands and chortled. "By his hair, good captain. Tell me, how many in Kalimar have hair of yellow?"

The captain was suddenly forced to give at least an inkling of credence to the ridiculous tale. Yellow hair was indeed a rarity of rarities in Kalimar, the mark of a foreigner from a distant land. Such a man should not prove difficult to find.

He looked sternly at the pickpocket. Jandari street people were notorious liars, willing to say and do anything if it might save their wretched necks. "And you," he said, "will be willing to swear to this man's guilt?"

Vlashi nodded and made the sacred sign. "I will do whatever needs be done."

Although the pickpocket did not know it, he had saved the wary captain from many hours of grief. A suspect was demanded by the regent at any cost; now, Vlashi had not only provided one but was willing to attest to his guilt as well. Clean and simple. By tomorrow another head would have rolled, another example set to the Jandari. The regent would be pleased, the captain would gain favor in his eyes. Everyone would be satisfied. Except, of course, for the poor wretch they caught. But someone had to pay the price for the vile deed, guilty or not.

All that remained was to find the yellow-haired beggar.

"Ride to the barracks and bring a cohort of men," the captain barked to his aide. "If need be, we'll comb every inch of this accursed place from the plazas to the sewers. This yellow-haired murderer must not be allowed to escape. Kalimar's justice must be served!"

With a bow and a sweep of his cape the aide mounted his fine steed and galloped swiftly down the street.

"What about *them*?" another soldier asked contemptuously of the frightened crowd. "Shall we bind them and haul them in?"

The captain smiled slyly. "Let the wretches go," he commanded with a flippant gesture. This new development was reason enough to let him act so magnanimously.

No sooner had he spoken than the crowd scattered into a dozen different directions, vanishing from sight before the soldier could have a change of heart. Even Vlashi was allowed to flee; the captain had marked him well and would know where to find him.

Then the soldiers mounted their horses and thundered away as quickly as they had come.

Ramagar stood watching these events until they were done and sadly shook his head. There was no doubt as to who Vlashi had accused; it could only be the same man from whom he stole the prize. And the thief, to his own surprise, found himself feeling pity for the unsuspecting beggar. He knew what would happen when the man was found; actual guilt or innocence meant little in the streets of Kalimar.

4

It was a sultry wind that descended on Kalimar that evening as the sun went down. It swept in low and fast from the mountains, across the plains, bringing with it thick clouds of dust that permeated the air and blew into every crevice and cranny from the palace to the Jandari.

It was an ill omen, this hot wind, and the street people responded with shudders as they huddled behind their closely locked and guarded doors. In the streets the cohort of Inquisitors pressed on with their duty. Faces masked from the swirling dust, they marched from alley to alley, avenue to avenue, byway to byway, intent on capturing the man they sought. Long into the night their business continued, each grim step becoming more difficult. Faces harrowed, lungs aching, eyes grown red and blurry they searched. No force in Kalimar, not even the violent storm, could for a single moment deter them. One way or another they were determined to take their prisoner before the coming of the new dawn.

In the shadows he hid, a tall figure, blending in with the undefined shapes of darkness until he appeared as no more than a shadow himself. Only a pair of small, beady eyes, cat's eyes, were visible. Cunning, shrewd, frightened. Hour after hour they followed the obscured movements of the Inquisitors as they passed from alley to alley in their search. He heard them cough, heard them shout commands at one another, and heard them pass, unaware that he had been within their very grasp.

Slinking his way from his hiding place, hunched low in the stance of a humble beggar, he dared at last to cross from the alley. A long hood covered his features, a rag of a kerchief served to filter the dust from his nostrils. He had lost many hours in evading the soldiers. Valuable time he was not sure he could make up. But his mission left no time for such thoughts; he must accomplish his goal, now, tonight, before it was too late. Find the pickpocket among a thousand others, single him out and regain what was his. For without it, his cherished dreams would become empty hopes—and a lifetime of planning would have been snatched away forever on the dusty, dirty streets of this wretched city that desert men called Kalimar.

Vlashi raised himself slowly from his comfortable chair and moved to the door of the Demon's Horn. His twenty-four-hour binge was beginning to show. Staggering, he poured the last contents of his bottle into his mouth and stepped out into the night. The wind was still howling, the dust still flying in his eyes. But the storm had eased somewhat, and he knew that calm would soon return.

Leaning with his back to the wall he pushed down the sudden urge to vomit. He thought of the long hours spent this night in the tiny room and the pleasures they had brought. Bought was a better word; the girl had managed to wrest from him quite a few of his coins. In fact, when that expenditure was put together with the cost of his wine (the finest of the finest, naturally), Vlashi realized that the entertainment had cost almost half of his fortune. He put his hand into his pocket and frowned at the feel of the few paltry coppers. But he still had the emerald ring Ramagar had traded him, and also the gold locket. Tomorrow he would go to Oro and sell them both. Tonight, though, it was time he cleared his head enough to return to work.

The soldiers would not bother him, he knew. So it was only a matter of finding a mark who was drunker than he was. Some poor merchant seeking the company of a woman would not be sober enough to notice when the pickpocket's not-so-nimble fingers lifted his purse.

Vlashi bundled up against the wind and stumbled away from the dim tavern light into the blackness of the street. The combination of foul weather and searching soldiers left the avenues nearly deserted. Normally the Street of Thieves and the Avenue of Pigs would be swarming. Tonight, all he saw was a scattering of locals. A few beggars, an occasional urchin, a group of dim-witted vagabonds fighting over a found dreg-filled bottle of cheap swill.

The pickpocket ignored them all; preferring if not better company than none at all. For some time he walked, mostly among the arched streets which wound high and low against the hills. Once in a while he paused, as much to rest as to scrutinize some possible mark. But it seemed that luck was against him. There was not a soul worth the effort.

Yawning, too sleepy to continue in the fruitless effort, his thoughts returned to the green-haired whore, who likely as not would still be available. Perhaps even anticipating his return. Ah, well, he ruminated, what is money if not to be spent and enjoyed? With a shrug and a sigh he turned around, content to let this night pass into oblivion. Tomorrow would be another day and—who knows?—maybe another prize to catch. This time, though, he warned himself, the master thief would not buy his wares so cheaply. Ramagar would have to pay full value—through the nose.

Vlashi chuckled. How very much he would like to outwit Ramagar. Just once.

Lost in his musings he was hardly aware of the beggar who set cross-legged before him at the edge of an alley.

An open hand groped out, catching him unaware.

"A coin, good sir. A single coin, if you please . . ."

Vlashi looked down, startled. "You frightened me," he growled. "Get out of here! Go sit under some light!"

"Please, sir . . . A coin . . ."

Vlashi narrowed his eyes and slid his hand under his tunic to where he kept a hidden dagger. "I told you to be gone. Now go!"

The beggar nervously got to his feet and shuffled backward out of sight. For all he knew the pickpocket was a cutthroat and he was not about to take any chances.

Vlashi snickered in self-importance as the man disappeared. Then, with a happy whistle upon his lips, he continued his journey back to the Demon's Horn.

It was a few moments later that he heard footsteps from
44

behind. Turning, he stopped and stared at the shadowy man in rags. "You again," he barked. "Are you following me?"

The man stopped in his place and did not move. It took Vlashi a long time to realize that this beggar was not the same man he had encountered only minutes earlier. Vlashi squirmed. There was something about this beggar that made him uneasy. Without knowing quite why, he drew a copper from his tunic and threw it to the waiting man. "Here," he sneered, "take it. Now go away."

The coin jingled loudly as it bounced on the flagstones. The beggar's eyes followed the coin until it had stopped, but he neither made to pick it up nor to leave. Vlashi was now more afraid than before.

"W-What do you want?" he whispered. His hand once more moved toward the unseen dagger. In all his years Vlashi had never had to use it. But something told him tonight could be different.

The beggar came a step closer. He was a muscular man, and his bold, defiant stance was out of character for the role he played. Meeting the pickpocket's widening gaze, he whispered, "Where is it?"

Vlashi froze. Recognition was at last beginning to creep into his wine-dazed brain. And with recognition came terror.

"W-W-Where is what?" he stammered. "I-I don't know what you're talking about."

The man in rags parted his lips in a hint of a smile. His hand reached out and grabbed Vlashi by the collar of his worn tunic. The pickpocket broke out in a cold sweat.

"The scimitar," hissed the man in rags. He threw his hood from his face, exposing a headful of curled blond hair that twisted over his ears and at the nape of his neck.

Vlashi nearly passed out. "I don't have any scimitar," he squealed.

But the beggar was in no mood for the pickpocket's games. His fist came up into Vlashi's stomach. Vlashi wheezed and staggered and fell to the ground.

"Now where is it?"

"The soldiers will catch you!" Vlashi whined. "Catch you and kill you! You're a murderer!"

The beggar's eyes blazed in anger. He knew well that he was being sought—sought for a crime of which he had not the slightest knowledge. He also knew who was responsible for his plight. But all that meant little to him. The scimitar was all that mattered. For that, he would face any danger, any host, any foreign army. Without it, his life had no meaning and he would just as soon succumb to Kalimar's "justice."

Kneeling beside Vlashi, he pressed his thumb against the pickpocket's right eye. Vlashi winced with pain.

"I'll blind you, pickpocket, if you don't give it back to me—"

Vlashi tried to squirm away but the beggar pushed him down hard against the ground, his free arm powerfully pinning the pickpocket and making it impossible to wriggle free. Meanwhile the thumb was applying more pressure; Vlashi could feel his eyeball squash under the weight.

"I'll tell you!" he moaned, tears streaming from his good eye.

The beggar released his thumb and waited.

Vlashi put his hand to his face and opened the eye. Its vision was blurred and dark. "I don't have the blade any longer," he cried. "I—I sold it—"

The thumb resumed its work, only this time digging in an upward motion from under the eyelid, as if to gouge out the eye. Vlashi wailed. "I swear to you! I sold it! I sold your scimitar yesterday!"

Stunned, his adversary released him. Vlashi quickly began to empty his pockets, letting the coppers roll across the ground, placing the ring and the locket at his side. "Here," he wallowed, "this was my payment. Take it. Take it all. It's yours, I give it to you."

The beggar was incredulous. Breathless and dazed, he said, "You're telling me the truth? You actually sold it? For *money?*"

Vlashi panted and nodded. A thin line of blood began to spill over his eyelids and onto his face.

"You fool! You *fool!*"

The man was in a rage. His lips and hands began to tremble with fury and Vlashi covered his head with his arms, burying himself into a ball and whimpering.

The beggar wrenched him by the arm and sent him sprawling. Vlashi's head hit against the stones; he tried to scramble to his feet. As he made it to his knees the beggar grabbed his neck from behind, yanked up under the pickpocket's jaw, and slammed him against the wall.

"Who?" he seethed, desperately trying to control his fury. "Who did you sell it to?"

Now more than ever Vlashi felt his panic rise. If he told,

Ramagar would kill him for it tomorrow. But if he didn't tell, this deranged beggar would surely kill him for it today. He mumbled incoherently under his breath, wishing he could think a bit faster and concoct a story as he had for the soldiers.

But the man in rags was too clever for any such ruse; twisting the pickpocket's arm behind his back until it nearly snapped, he repeated his demand.

"Tell me the name! Tell me the name!"

"I sold it in a tavern," cried Vlashi in pain. "To a thief—"

"His name!"

Vlashi saw stars as his head banged roughly against the stones.

"Ramagar! I sold it to the thief called Ramagar!"

The beggar's breath was on his face. "And where can he be found? Where does this thief live?"

"He has no home," Vlashi swore truthfully. "He is of the Jandari, the alleys are his only home."

The beggar threw the pickpocket to the floor and stood over him with glaring eyes. "If you've lied to me, my gutter rat friend . . ."

Vlashi shuddered. "Ramagar is . . . well-known. Ask, you will have no trouble in finding him." And so, betraying his only friend, Vlashi slumped into a heap and wept, unaware that his assailant had gone back into the shadows and could no longer hear what he said.

The door shook furiously. Mariana sat up straight at the side of the bed and put her hands to her ears. The flickering candle was nearing its end, the first light of a new dawn was little by little inching its way through the clefts and cracks of the shutters. The banging grew louder as she shook the sleep from her mind. Harsh, gravelly voices rang in her ears. "Open up! Open up at once!"

Mariana threw her gown over her shoulders and ran to the door.

"Who is it? Who's there?"

A deep resonant voice boomed in response: "King's soldiers. Open the door or we'll break it down!"

Frightened, her hands trembling, she unbolted the latch. The door flew open, pushing her back and causing her to lose balance. Three husky men barged inside, each brandishing a short curved sword. Hand to her mouth, Mariana fell back against the wall. Two of the intruders paid her not the slightest bit of attention; they rummaged through the room, turning over everything in their way, pushing aside curtains, searching every inch of the floor and walls for hidden hatches and doors.

As Mariana watched breathlessly the third of the soldiers wielded the tip of his blade before her eyes. Without hearing his voice she knew who he was. And the captain of the Inquisitors smiled grimly. "Where is he?" he demanded.

"Where is who?"

The wily soldier broadened his grin and Mariana shuddered as she felt his eyes poring over her. He pressed the tip of his sword lightly against the supple flesh of her breast. "Your lover. Where is Ramagar?"

There was no way she could hide the fear in her eyes. "He's . . . not here," she replied truthfully, biting her lip to subdue her rising terror. Then she drew all her courage and lied. "I—I haven't seen him for days."

The soldier applied just enough pressure on the blade so that a needle prick of blood was drawn.

She stiffened and he snickered. His left hand reached out and gently caressed the side of her face. Her skin was a marvelous gold, softly blended against full lips and dark eyes whose quick intelligence showed even through fear. The soldier leered appreciatively. He knew her loveliness was due to natural beauty and not to the cosmetics so freely used by the more aristocratic women of Kalimar. And he recalled seeing Mariana in her dance, her lithe form twirling across sawdust floors, causing heartbeats to quicken and desire to rise while patrons sipped their honeyed wine. It was indeed a pity, he mused, that such a girl was wasted on a common thief. But then, after this day, perhaps that situation would be remedied.

Mariana felt sickened and disgusted as his hardened fingers slipped gingerly across her mouth and played with the twisting curls at the edge of her hair. She wanted to squirm from his grasp but the feel of the blade prevented her from moving a muscle. Holding her slim, soft hands at her side, she forced herself to meet his glowering stare, and whispered, "I told you he's not here. What do you want?"

The soldier did not answer; he looked to his companions, who by now were busy tearing and breaking everything in sight. One of them took hold of the laced pillow at the edge of the divan and scrutinized it. Mariana held her breath. The scimitar had been carefully hidden within the feathers, the

48

seams resewn. If he looked carefully enough he was sure to find it. Then the pillow was tossed haphazardly across the floor, and she secretly breathed a sigh of relief.

"Nothing here of any worth," one soldier told the captain. "Just a lot of useless junk." He was tinkering with her costume jewelry and frowning. The captain sheathed his sword and sighed. "All right. That's enough." While his men disappointedly marched from the room he returned his attention to the girl. "Best for you that the thief wasn't with you tonight," he snarled. "Consorting with a known criminal is a serious offense." Here he smiled. "A very serious offense. I'd have been forced to take action."

Mariana stood defiant. "Not in the Jandari—"

"Oh, no?" His face returned to its dour mask. "This time your lover has outsmarted himself. And we're going to catch him one way or another. This time Ramagar is going to pay with his head."

The panic was rising again, she knew. There was more afoot than she understood. Why indeed were the Inquisitors so intent on finding a mere thief? And what crime might he have committed that required his life in payment? Or could it be that they somehow knew about the scimitar?

Wide-eyed, holding her breath, Mariana said, "What is he accused of? What has he done?"

The captain laughed bitingly. "Murder. He's killed a noble."

"But that's impossible!" she cried. The girl was beside herself, unable to grasp what she had been told. "You're lying! Ramagar never killed anyone!"

It was a wicked, sly smile that crossed his lips. He knew that after tonight the dancing girl could be his for the taking. To enslave, to throw in the dungeons, or even to disfigure her brooding face so that no man would ever want to watch her dance again.

His tone was cold and impassive. "We have a witness. The noble was murdered for his gold—and the killer was your lover."

Her head was spinning. "But they say a stranger murdered this noble. A foreigner. You yourself—"

"We were deceived," countered the captain. "Taken for fools. The beggar we sought does not exist. And the pickpocket who devised this deception will pay as dearly as your lover. We now have positive proof that Ramagar is the one

49

who committed the crime. We have a witness whose word cannot be refuted—even in the Jandari."

"It's not true!" Mariana flared. "This witness is a liar and I can prove it! Ramagar was with me yesterday. All day and all night. I'll swear to it with my last breath."

He smiled thinly and cruelly, yet also with a tinge of admiration. The loyalty of the girl to her lover was without question and he would wager every copper he owned that rather than see him punished she would admit to the crime herself. But the word of a dancing girl, even if it were true, would carry little weight in the courts of Kalimar. No, the thief of thieves would have to pay, guilty or not. His cunning and wits would avail him no longer.

Mariana burst into tears as the soldier turned to go. "Tell your lover we'll be back," he warned. "And we'll tear apart the Jandari brick by brick if we have to. This time he'll not get away."

And then he was gone. Mariana scampered to the door and bolted it, as if in this way she could pretend to herself that the world outside was safely locked out.

But she knew too well it wasn't. Without a second thought, she scooped up the pillow and slit the new seam. The scimitar glistened in the morning light. She knew she must find Ramagar. Find him quickly and warn him before it was too late. He must escape the city, escape the Jandari and Kalimar completely. It was his only chance.

But where was she to look? There were ten thousand alleys and ten thousand roofs. Shadows to cloak each and every one. In which of a hundred hiding places might he be found? Or was it too late already? Perhaps by now the unsuspecting thief was bound and gagged, lying helpless somewhere in the labyrinth of dungeons within the palace walls.

It was with desperation that she fled her room and hurried into the bright daylight of the street. Giving neither thought nor care to her own safety she raced in the direction of the Demon's Horn. Only there might someone be able to say where her lover had gone after he left her in the middle of night. Only there might there be someone she could trust.

Oro the hunchback ducked swiftly into the doorway when he saw her leave. His twisted features hidden by his hood, he leaned back and chuckled, rubbing his hands in a slow, deliberate motion.

Ah, yes. Today would be a day never to forget. The Inquis-

50

itors would pay him handsomely for his lies. And now, with the thief as good as dead, both the mysterious scimitar and the dancing girl would soon be his. All that he had ever desired was about to be gained in a single stroke. The thief of thieves would be a thorn in his side no more.

5

It was the longest day of her life. Hour after hour she had searched, high and low, in and out of every alley and every byway both familiar and unfamiliar. But all her efforts had been futile. Bravely she had climbed to the roofs, investigated the winding, endless narrow alleys that weaved in and out among streets ancient and crumbling where only urchins and packs of wild dogs could be found. Panting from fatigue and hunger, her body glistening in perspiration, she went relentlessly on, vowing never to give up until he was found and warned of the dangers that lurked from every direction.

Now, though, as the shadows of day deepened, Mariana began to despair. Up to the present, her search had been relatively easy, seeking her lover in places he was known to frequent. The night could only serve to complicate matters, adding personal risk and peril to her search. Not only must she avoid the patrols, who seemingly had preceded her every step of the way, but now also the robbers and cutthroats, men who would not hesitate to deal with a woman as harshly and callously as with any other mark caught in the web of their private territory.

But this danger made no difference. Upheld by sincere love, she would never regret her actions, rash and dangerous as they were.

Nightfall spread across Kalimar, bringing calm and quiet. Mariana listened as the last of the priests sang evening prayer from the distant minarets and considered which avenue she should try next. Candlelight from the windows above illuminated the streets, which slowly began to swell with life as the Jandari prepared for another evening. The odor of sweetmeats and sour sauces permeated the air. The glow of cooking fires from stalls and hearths brightened the byways and sent shadows dancing above her head. Mariana put a hand to her brow and tried to compile a list of all the places she had

51

searched, and those she had yet to seek. But there were so very many, and her task seemed to become more and more impossible. Yet there was a measure of comfort with her despair. For if Ramagar could keep so well hidden from her, then he may have managed to elude the cohort of soldiers who shared her eagerness to find him.

At last she made up her mind and changing directions decided to follow the old gutted street that ran parallel to the Avenue of Pigs. The crumbling hovels, mere shells of what they had been during the Jandari's moments of glory, towered above her at either side. Once upon a time they had housed the finest families in all of Kalimar, centuries ago, before the desert winds had swept across the land and turned her fertile plains into dry and barren wastes. Every kingdom and every empire has its day, and Kalimar was no exception. But now its glories were past, faded into recorded memory. A thousand years of splendor were lost upon the rotting brick and dusty streets of a once proud city. Its founders and heroes were dust scattered to the winds; the vultures remained to feed off what was left. And the street people of the Jandari were only mirror images of the ugly world around them.

But gentle Mariana was unaware of all these things as she passed the ancient relics. She could think only of her lover, and her urgent need to save him.

A strange silence followed her as she made her way among the piles of stone and garbage. Alone and frightened, she ran as quickly as she could, anxious to reach the wharves and her lover's secret hiding places among the abandoned warehouses.

As she crossed the narrowing road, avoiding the path of a pack of lean scavenger rats that poked their heads up among the refuse, she stopped short with a gasp. Lying in the middle of the road was a man—a sad, pathetic figure, writhing and moaning upon the ground. At first she wondered if this was a ruse and the man was actually a cutthroat of some sort, playing this role while waiting for his mark.

Backstepping slowly, her hand reached to the pocket of her cloak and she clutched tightly at the scimitar. The razor-sharp blade felt as cold as ice. She was ready to use it if the need arose, and not in the least bit reluctant.

The writhing man caught sight of her and stuck out his arm, fingers groping in the air as if to grab her. Mariana sidestepped him and drew the blade, ready to plunge. Then, as her arm rose and the blade glittered in the starlight, she froze.

A pair of small tortured eyes peered sharply at her; tormented, sad eyes, bloodied and bruised.

"*Az'il*" she cursed, the whispered word rolling off her tongue.

The man on the ground cleared his throat and tried to speak. A rasping, labored and pained. "Mariana . . ."

"Vlashi! Sweet paradise! Is that you? What's happened? Who did this?"

The pickpocket tried to lift himself and Mariana kneeled down beside him, using her handkerchief to wipe away some of the drying smears of blood.

Vlashi struggled to his knees, holding onto the girl's arm for balance. "Ramagar," he rasped, "where's . . . Ramagar?"

Mariana's eyes began to flood and she felt the terror rising inside her again as it had all day.

"I—don't know," she replied. "I can't find him anywhere."

"Must find him," Vlashi grunted. "Must find him and warn him. Danger, terrible danger . . ."

Feeling pity for the injured man, she tried to soothe and assure him. "Shh, Vlashi. Leave it to me. You must rest, find some shelter, and tend your injuries."

His hand grasped her shoulder and she winced, feeling his fingernails dig through the cloth into her flesh. "You don't understand, Mariana. There is . . . no time. Ramagar must be found and warned—before it's too late."

The girl drew back, her eyes now narrowing and searching his. Vlashi, unable to meet her gaze, hung his head on his chest and put his hands to his eyes. And to the dancing girl's surprise, he began to sob.

Mariana took hold of his shoulders and forced him to look at her. "Tell me what's happened, Vlashi," she said calmly. "I can't help any of us if I don't understand what you're trying to tell me."

Tears rolled down the pickpocket's cheeks, mixing with the grime and dirt. His normally tanned face was white and his eyes hollow and vacant. He took a deep breath and drew his courage. "Forgive me, Mariana," he implored. "I didn't mean to do it. But I had no choice, no choice at all. I would have been killed if I didn't tell everything . . ."

Mariana shuddered, fearful of what he was going to say. "Who, Vlashi? Who forced you? The soldiers?"

Vlashi clutched at his aching ribs and moaned while the girl waited in exasperation. Then he shook his head, forcing the words to come, aware that now he must admit the

53

truth—no matter what the cost. And he told her how the beggar found him and beat him, forcing him to tell that Ramagar was now the owner of the precious scimitar. Mariana listened in shock.

It was hard for her to accept what she had heard, hard for her to accept the pickpocket's treachery. The laws that governed the Jandari were simple; when a man betrayed a friend, when a thief betrayed another thief, he himself would be forever marked, disgraced, and scorned, with no hope of ever redeeming himself in the eyes of his peers. Vlashi knew this as well as the dancing girl. He knew Ramagar had the right to kill him for his deed, and half expected the girl to commit the act in his place.

Mariana stood over him, trembling. She wanted to hate the little weasel of a man for what he had done, but all she could feel was pity.

Vlashi reached out and tugged at her sleeve, his eyes red and watery. "This beggar will stop at nothing to regain his prize," he sniveled. "He will kill Ramagar to get it back. Kill him without a second thought. Find him first, Mariana, I beg you. And tell . . . tell Ramagar that I'm sorry . . ."

Her eyes flashed with burning rage. Right there and then she would have struck him, plunged the bejeweled blade into his heart. But her own heart was too gentle, and she saw in Vlashi now only the pathetic man that he was. His blood on her hands would prove nothing, settle nothing. Leaving him to live with his conscience was a far greater punishment.

Her mind was swimming deliriously. Matters had become even worse than she had realized. For now there was a double threat against the thief; not only were the inquisitors searching for him for a crime he did not commit, but this strange and mysterious beggar as well. A man cunning enough to walk brazenly among the shadows and not be seen, crazed in his desire to reclaim his blade, and willing to pay any price to ensure he got it back. And Ramagar was aware of none of it.

Leaving the pickpocket to bemoan his fate, she spun and raced for the closest byway. The night wind rushed by her, cold against her sweat-drenched clothes. Mariana ran as fast as she could, panting, taking breath only in short, quick spurts, and far too fearful to pause for even a second lest in that brief moment her lover might be found.

The lanterns of the wharves shone dim and yellow in the evening pall. The moon, crescent and low, had turned hazy behind a thin film of fog that rolled slowly across the water.

She could dimly hear laughter from the distant Street of Thieves, where the night crowd of visitors and merrymakers would be at its height.

A ship's horn sounded lonely and forlorn in the night. The sound echoed in her ears, mingled with the subdued shouts of the captain cajoling his crew as they slipped closer into berth. From across the estuary a thousand lights glittered from the palace. It rose high at the top of the largest hill, overlooking the sprawl of Kalimar, and she could make out the tiny forms of sentries patrolling the long walls. Curved swords dangled from their sides and the colorful plumes in their helmets rustled in the breeze.

She skirted the rows of warehouses still in use, avoiding the watchful eyes of guards marching back and forth along the piers and docks. Across the footbridge she dashed, coming at last to the old port. Filled with decayed and weatherbeaten wooden structures, it had been unused since the time of the last fires which had almost destroyed half of the city.

Pulling her cloak more tightly about her, she wandered down the broadest of the deserted streets and kept a careful lookout for signs of being followed. Often Ramagar had spoken of his hiding places in these warehouses. Places shown to him by his tutor and friend, the Jackal. A wanted man's dream; a virtual labyrinth of dark cellars and lofts so multiple and so complex that a man using all his wiles might be able to hide for a lifetime without ever being found out. And it was here, Mariana knew, that Ramagar would have come if he had fled the Jandari. At least that was her prayer, for after here there would be no other place for her to turn.

Crisscrossing back and forth to avoid unwanted eyes, she at last reached the long stone wall that surrounded the massive array of storehouses known as the old compound. The familiar black doorway loomed ahead and she nervously bit her lip as she entered.

The passageway was totally black; not the slimmest beam of starlight passed between the cracks in the rotting beams. Her shoes disturbed a thin layer of dust as she walked cautiously in the center, careful to keep away from the walls, where water rats and mice nestled in clusters among the holes in the corners. Somewhere beyond this passage Ramagar might be found. Somewhere high in the highest loft, above the alley and courtyard.

Silently she ventured, her hand held out before her, feeling her way in the dank, dismal gloom. The only sound was that

55

of her own breath. And then, suddenly, she could see glimpses of sky ahead. She walked faster now, until at last she was out in the open and at the edge of the alley. A chilly wind was blowing down from the river; she could almost taste the salt in the air carried west from the inland sea.

Stepping over the stones, she inched her way close to the low fence where it wound in a semicircle toward the enclosed courtyard. A large gray cat hissed from its perch on an empty windowsill. Mariana tensed, caught sight of the cat, and smiled with relief. The cat straddled the sill, tail lifted, and followed her until she turned the corner.

Then, as the hiding place came into view, she turned around one more time, her sweeping glance taking in the fence and the black wall of the compound as well as the alley and the courtyard and the gaping black exit of the passageway. And she knew she was alone. Completely alone, with no chance she had been followed. For that much, at least, she was more than thankful.

Cupping her hand to her mouth, she tilted her head up toward the looming lofts that obliterated half her view of the sky. The signal was brief; a low cuya bird whistle, no more than a soft drone that blended perfectly with the sounds of night.

But, save for the wind that rustled between the aged wooden beams, there was nothing to hear at all.

She wet her lips and tried again, praying that he was close and that this long search would at last end for her. She strained her ears to listen for his answer, but still none came.

Mariana sank her head and tried to stop the tears from flowing. Once more she would have to begin anew. She would have to return to the Jandari and comb the maze of alleys yet again. Only this time it might truly be too late, what with the news Vlashi had given. Suddenly she turned to go, her hopes crushed. For some reason she had been so sure that she would find him here. So positive of it. It was hard to admit she had been wrong.

There was a soft shuffle from somewhere atop the corrugated roof. And then a voice, low, but strong. "Mariana! Mariana! Up here!"

She whirled, dress flaring, her heart thumping in her chest. Squinting, she peered up to the top, standing on her toes to see. And there he was, Ramagar, her lover, the thief of thieves, nestling perfectly among the lumbering shadows.

Her face lit up with happiness. Straightening her shoulders, throwing back her head so that her hair swirled behind, she sighed. "Ramagar, thank the heavens I've found you at last."

He hushed her and bounded down to a lower roof, his weight making only the softest of noises. Then down a pipe he slid, landing on the ground with the agility of a cat, grinning at her like a misbehaved child and taking her in his arms.

"How did you ever find me?" he asked.

She smiled sheepishly. "It wasn't easy. I've been searching all day."

He frowned briefly, then the grin returned. Taking her by the hand, he led her inside the warehouse and down a small flight of wooden steps to the cellar. There, she looked on in wonder. A small oil lamp lit a tiny room, complete with straw for a bed, blankets, a shelf well stocked with jars of preserves, salted meats, and a bottle of sweet wine.

Ramagar laughed. "Let's say this is my home away from home," he teased. "At least it's warm, and safe."

She looked at him sharply. "Then you know?"

"A thief makes it his business to know everything. The moment I entered the street last night I realized that something was the matter. So I hid, and then, when I saw the soldiers come to your room, I put two and two together."

"You saw them?" she gasped. "You were there, hiding?"

He nodded. "On your roof."

Her temper began to rise. "Then why didn't you let me know? I've been driving myself crazy trying to find you and warn you. And now you tell me you've known all along!" He bent to kiss her and she pulled away.

"Ah, Mariana, I couldn't tell you. Not then. Don't you see? The soldiers would have been watching everywhere, and had they seen me slip into your room . . ." He let his words trail off slowly. "No, all I could do was plan my escape from the Jandari as best I could, and keep you far from any harm. Besides," here he smiled again with a twinkle in his eye, "I knew you'd find me sooner or later."

Mariana realized that this was reasonable enough. Better a cautious lover than a dead one.

Ramagar sat back against the straw and put a bent piece of twig between his teeth. At his side rested a half-full cup of wine and he stared disconsolately into the still, dark brew. "Why are they after me, girl?" he asked. "What have I been accused of that Inquisitors would break down your door?"

"Then you really don't know?"

The smile turned wan. "I didn't stick around to ask."

Mariana flew to his side, kneeling beside him and holding his hand between both of her own. There were tears falling down her soft, unblemished cheeks. "They say a noble was murdered in the Jandari yesterday," she said slowly, her voice little more than a whisper. She closed her eyes and felt her lashes press against the wetness. "And the soldiers say that you . . . you . . ."

Ramagar stared at her in dawning understanding. "They accuse me of the crime?"

She nodded slowly, painfully, putting her head to his chest, burying her face so that he couldn't see her while she cried. The thief ran his hand through her long black hair and whispered her name softly. "Do you . . . believe them?" he asked.

She lifted her head and gazed at him sharply. "Of course I don't! It's all a lie—a cruel and terrible lie. And I told them as much!"

"Ah, Mariana," he sighed, "if only the soldiers of Kalimar had your trust, your love . . ."

She sniffed and blew her nose into the worn handkerchief he gave her. At that moment she seemed little more than a frightened child, lost and forlorn, caught in a web of events she did not understand and could not alter.

"What are we to do?" she asked haltingly. "The Inquisitors are combing every inch of the Jandari. They'll never give up. Never."

He spit the piece of wood from his mouth and scowled. "I never killed any man," he said, "although I can think of some I should have." There was venom in his voice, deep-seated anger and hatred she had never known him to express before. And it frightened her even more.

"What are you saying?" she asked breathlessly.

His eyes darkened. "Someone was paid to tell this lie," he growled. "And he was paid by someone who might benefit with me dead."

She gasped. "Oro!"

"Yes, Oro. That little weasel would stop at nothing if he felt he had something to gain."

In her despair she covered her face with her hand, sobbing so hard that her shoulders shook. "It's my fault," she cried, "because of me it's come to this. Because of the dagger—"

He grabbed her wrist tightly. "The soldiers didn't find it, did they?"

She shook her head and he drew a long breath of relief.

58

Possession of the glittering blade had become a more dangerous risk than he had ever dreamed. But as long as he still had it he controlled his fate. Too many men would be willing to make any bargain to claim it as their own.

"It's clear that the soldiers will never believe I'm innocent," he said at last. "And if they finally do manage to catch me—"

"You'll never see the light of day again," Mariana finished the thought with a voice that cracked. "Oh, Ramagar! What can we do?"

He downed his wine with a single swallow and tossed the cup across the floor. A small water mouse scurried out of harm's way, then dashed back into the hole in the wall.

"You've got to flee the city," pleaded Mariana. "Right away, as fast as you can."

The thief nodded sullenly. The Jandari was not a place many men could love; indeed most dreamed of one day being able to make their way far from it. Yet to Ramagar the Jandari was home, the only one he had ever known.

He stood and walked to the tiny slit in the wall that served as a window and stared out across the dark shadowy wharves. Dim lights were flickering from across the estuary, beyond them dimmer lights. Jandari lights. He thought of its streets, its maze of alleys, its rooftops and gutted sewers. All suddenly seemed like a distant memory, lost but faintly recaptured in the furthest recesses of his mind. Had not the dancing girl been at his side he knew he would have cried.

"You know," he said, turning to her and looking sadly into her wide, pensive eyes, "once I leave, I can't come back. Not now, not ever."

The girl suppressed a tiny squeal of pain. "Forget your life here, forget everything about this wretched city. Forget Kalimar and never think of it again."

Resting his back against the wall, he said, "And will I be able to forget you as well?"

Her mouth opened, speechless. She pursed her trembling lips and gazed at him with distraught eyes.

Then casting her own feelings aside, shying away from his gaze, she said, "Where will you go?"

The thief shrugged, a bitter smile upon his lips. "What matter? I'll be a man without a home, a land. Perhaps in the south—"

"Across the desert?"

"If I must. There are trade routes to be followed, caravans that cross beyond the borders. I've heard tales of the southern

59

lands. They are said to be places where a soldier of fortune can be in great demand."

"Ramagar, no! To fight among some unknown army, to die in battle against some barbarian host, is that what you want?"

"What choice do I have?" he countered. "Few cities will welcome a thief—especially one whose head has a price on it." He looked back to his window, rested his arm on the sill, and frowned. He could almost make out the range of flat-topped craggy mountains hazy and distant along the horizon. "Perhaps I could go north," he said. "Maybe reach the sea. I suppose I might find some captain in need of a pair of strong hands, and who won't ask any names . . ."

Mariana could no longer hide her feelings. She hung her head and took a few steps toward him. "I don't care which way you decide," she whispered through salted tears. "All I ask is that you take me with you, wherever it may be."

Ramagar stared, wide-eyed. "You want to come with me?"

"Anywhere. Any place on earth. It doesn't matter, as long as I'm with you, beside you."

"But how can I take you? You know the risks as well as I. The roads from the city will be watched constantly, they'll be expecting me to make a break for it. It's going to take all my skill, all my luck, just to get past the city walls. If they catch me, it'll mean my head. And if you're with me, it will be your own as well."

"I don't care!" cried the dancing girl. "I'll not stay in Kalimar without you—not for a single day. I'll follow you on my own if I have to, every step of the way!"

Ramagar took her hand and brought her to him. Tilting her chin with his fingers, he kissed her gently. "I love you, Mariana. I want you to know and believe that. I always will. But no, I can't take you with me. The dangers are just too great. I'll not endanger your life because of me."

She pulled away from his grasp and bristled, eyes wetly flashing. "You men!" she seethed. "What do you know of dangers? A woman in the Jandari faces them every day of her life, time and time again." The thief looked on in sheer amazement as Mariana's face grew hard and her eyes so cold that he could feel the chill.

"And what do you suppose will happen to me once you're gone?" she snapped. "Be taken and forced into a brothel? Or shall I walk the streets at night like the other whores, selling myself for a few coppers to fat, pompous fools with purses that bulge like their bellies?"

60

"Mariana! What are you saying?"

She sneered at him. "Or shall I become the mistress of some soldier, only to be tossed aside like a rag when he's done and given to any man in the barracks? Perhaps I can become someone's wife—someone who wants me, like Oro——"

Ramagar slammed a clenched fist against the wall. "Enough! I don't want you to talk like that ever again!"

Mariana smiled thinly, standing defiantly with her hands on her hips. "Well? Then what do you think will happen to me once you're gone?".

Her point was well made, he knew. Time and again he had pitied the fate of other attractive women unfortunate enough to have been born in a place as cruel and heartless as the Jandari. The very thought that Mariana—*his* Mariana— might someday have to share their fate left him anguished and sickened.

"All right," he said after a few moments' thought. "Maybe I can figure out some way for us to escape together." He looked at her seriously. "As long as you know the risks—and the penalty if we're caught."

She bit her lip. "You mean that? Then I can come?"

The thief of thieves nodded glumly, then was surprised as the girl threw her arms around his neck, stood on her toes, and smothered him with wet, joyful kisses. "You won't regret this," she vowed. "You'll see. We'll find a place for ourselves, a place together where no man, no soldiers, can ever frighten us again."

He laughed and slapped her on the behind. "We'll discuss it later. Right now, though, we've got to find some way to get beyond the walls." He turned from her and paced the floor, all the while nervously biting his lip and rubbing his hands together. Then he said, "Maybe if we can get word to Vlashi he can give us some help . . ."

At the mention of the pickpocket's name Mariana's heart skipped a beat. "Vlashi!" she gasped, recalling the earlier event she had almost forgotten.

Ramagar stopped in his tracks and glanced at her troubled face. His own features grew impassive as he said, "What is it, girl? What's happened to Vlashi?"

"He—he begged me to warn you—"

"Warn me? About what? The soldiers?"

She shook her head ruefully, cursing at herself for not tell- ing him sooner about this new peril the thief faced. With the color draining from her cheeks, she said, "The beggar who

61

owned the scimitar found Vlashi and hurt him. He threatened to kill him if Vlashi didn't give it back."

Ramagar sighed, rubbed gently at the side of his face with an open palm. He shuddered to hear what was coming next, although he knew it to be as predictable as the sun after a summer thunderstorm.

"Poor Vlashi was frightened out of his wits when I saw him," continued the girl. "And I'm sure he didn't understand what he was doing." She glanced up to her lover's face, seeking a reaction. Then abruptly she said, "Vlashi broke the code, Ramagar. He told, told the beggar everything there was to know. How he sold the scimitar to you—and just who you were."

This time when the thief slammed his fist the weak beams shook, dislodging a thin layer of dust that quickly descended over the floor. Ramagar clenched his teeth and did everything he could to control his temper. He should have known the pickpocket was untrustworthy, should have known that buying that cursed dagger was going to bring him ill fortune.

He folded his arms and drew a deep breath of the stagnant air. "Did Vlashi give you a description of this beggar?" he asked.

Mariana stared blankly. "No, he only said that the beggar was determined to find you at any cost—and that you had to be warned. He's cunning, this beggar, Ramagar. He's also eluded the Inquisitors. By now he might be anywhere in Kalimar, searching for you this very moment."

The thief grimaced and began to pace again. "I should have known," he rasped. "What a fool I am! I should have known!"

Mariana raised her brows inquisitively. "Known what?"

Deep in thought, Ramagar leaned on the far wall and clenched his hands together, rubbing them in a slow, deliberate motion. "All day," he said, "ever since I fled from your roof, I've had this uneasy feeling, like I was being watched or followed. And more than once, even after I fled from the Jandari and made my way to the wharves, I kept seeing this same beggar; keeping his distance from me to be sure, but it was the same man everywhere I went. At first I thought it only a bad case of nerves. After all, there must be ten thousand beggars in Kalimar. But now, now I'm beginning to wonder . . ."

Mariana put a hand to her mouth. *"Az'i!* What if I've helped lead him to you?" She looked around with a feeling of

62

helplessness. "He could be here on the docks, in this very warehouse, waiting for us to show, biding his time."

Ramagar put a finger to her pale lips and smiled. "Shh. We're safe enough. What harm can a single beggar do me, the thief of thieves?" He laughed caustically. "Today I've managed to fend off a full cohort of regent's soldiers—what do I have to fear from a single beggar?"

The girl was not put off by his taking the matter so lightly. She knew very well it was only his way of trying to put her own thoughts at ease, no easy task under the circumstances.

"What shall we do?"

He scratched at his beard. "We'll have to think of a way to get out of Kalimar before worrying about other matters. Have you got any money?"

The girl turned sideways, put a hand inside her blouse, and unpinned the tiny purse. "It's everything I have," she said, offering it to him. "Just a handful of coppers and a silver piece."

"More than enough," replied the thief. "You hold onto it. And where's the scimitar?"

Mariana smiled. "Well tucked away under my skirt—where even you won't get at it."

"As good a place as any, I should think," he answered dryly. "Now what about us trying to get out of here? With any luck, we can be far away by daybreak."

Mariana began to pick at the loose straw clinging to her cloak and smoothed down her skirt with an open hand. Ramagar drew beside her, grinning, and put his arm around her shoulder. At that moment she felt all her fears begin to vanish. Of all the men she had ever met, in the Jandari and indeed in all of Kalimar, it was only this handsome rogue who could make her forget so many tears with but a single smile. What sorcery or magic he had she didn't know, nor did she care. Being with Ramagar was all that mattered now, all that had ever mattered in her young life. She was more than willing to share any fate with him.

"The first thing we have to do is get us some horses," said the thief as he led her to the door.

"Where? It's the middle of the night. Besides, my few coins won't nearly be enough to buy one, let alone two."

Ramagar grinned like a cat. "Then we'll steal them—that is, if you don't have any objections."

Mariana shrugged. "How you earn your living is no business of mine," she observed merrily. But then she hesitated and cast her gaze to the ground. "There's one thing, though, that I think I'd better tell you."

He cocked one eye. "Oh? What?"

"I don't know how to ride."

The thief of Kalimar groaned.

6

Hand in hand they ran from the warehouse and the courtyard, dancing among the shadows, following the path beside the endless rows of decrepit quays and abandoned storage sheds until at last they came to the ancient footbridge that spanned the estuary at its narrowest point. Aging wood creaked and moaned beneath their feet. Around them they could hear the gentle slapping of waves against the docks and the occasional faraway blast of a ship's horn piercing the fog-shrouded night.

In such tense moments the wily thief was at his best—every muscle taunt and strained, every sense fully alert, poised and prepared for unseen peril. With the night vision of a panther Ramagar led the dancing girl across the bridge. Where Mariana could see only shadows, he saw shapes and forms with animal clarity. But sometimes even a thief of thieves can err; and it would take only a single mistake to shatter all their hopes and dreams.

Beneath the bridge itself he followed. Wading slowly through the muddy, shallow water, hunching low under the planks, he listened to every footstep above. The water was foul; filled with moss and clinging slime, crabs and jellyfish that swam between his legs and crawled in the mud each step of the way. But the cunning beggar gave no thought to these things, not even when his tender flesh felt the sting of claws tightening around his ankles. As the thief and the girl moved he matched them with every pace. When they paused, he paused, when they hurried, he hurried. In the silence of night they almost breathed together, each hunted, each hunting. The beggar's eyes watched, his ears listened. And the smallest hint of a smile parted his lips. At last, he thought, at last his search was nearing its end. Soon the precious scimitar would be in his possession again—where it rightfully belonged—and he could continue his long journey anew.

"This way," whispered the thief, taking the girl by the arm and hurrying her onto land again. A berthed ship loomed high to their left, and Mariana glanced briefly at the tall, bared masts, the lonely silhouette of a sailor standing grimly at his post upon the quarterdeck.

Ramagar adroitly slipped them back into the safety of the lumbering shadows. The fog was rolling in more quickly now, tumbling down across the water and dimming the scattered lanterns and torches set along the wharves. Ramagar smiled; the mist was an ally, and never could one have come at a better time.

Shadows merged and merged again; Mariana held her breath trying not to listen to the grisly sounds of the wind. Kalimarians were a superstitious people, and their lore was filled with tales and legends of strange happenings that befell the city on nights such as this. As the fog became denser she fancied that above the wild throbs of her heart she could hear these legends come to life; fiendish voices calling to her, laughing, taunting; the flutter of huge unseen wings that at any moment would swoop down from the starless sky and whisk both her and her lover away to some bottomless pit where the fires of hell raged and crackled with laughter at the chance of capturing yet another hapless soul.

Such were her fears when Ramagar yanked her strongly and pulled her off her feet into a dark, deserted doorway.

He put a finger to his lips to keep her from venting her fright, then pointed his hand to the unseen street. A few seconds later she heard the sound, dim at first but steadily growing louder. The harsh scraping of hooves slowing moving toward them. *Soldiers!* And she bit her lip so as not to cry out.

Then there were voices, casual banter between the riders as they cautiously negotiated the tricky path. She strained to hear what they were saying.

". . . or cut off his balls," one shouted, to the hilarity of his companions. Then something else was muttered among them, something she couldn't hear, and their laughter became louder.

Mariana was shaking. If only they would pass! If only time were speeded so she and Ramagar could run again, back to the shadows without being seen.

It seemed like forever, but at last they were gone. The last of the hoofbeats faded into the night and her prayer had been answered. Her sweat-drenched hand closed on Ramagar's own and they stole from their hiding place. Racing along the broken cobblestone, they dodged helter-skelter among the warehouses, once nearly tripping over a drunken sailor lying in the middle of the road, another time zigging and zagging at sharp angles to avoid the roving eyes of a well-armed night watchman.

Away from the quays and storehouses at last, the lovers ran through a street of deserted, crumbling markets. Once this place had been the pride of all Kalimar, a central bazaar where goods from a dozen lands were hawked to milling throngs of shoppers from every district of the city. Now, as with so much else, it had fallen into disarray. Where stalls and gaily lit shops had stood there was nothing but the corrosion of time: crumbling brick, splintered wood. A virtual jungle of vegetation and sand had overrun the ruins.

At the end of the grim road they paused to catch their breath.

"What next?" Mariana asked, panting.

Ramagar furrowed his brow. "We still need those horses," he said. "If we follow the road to the palace we're bound to come to a stable."

"You'd steal our horses from right under the regent's nose?" she said, bewildered.

Ramagar chuckled. "Sort of poetic justice, isn't it?"

Soon the road had broadened and they found themselves reaching even higher ground, a place where the fog was merely the thinnest of hazes and they could look back almost without obstruction at the harbor below. There, the fog was still spreading out like a blanket, settling slowly over the estuary, obliterating all of the eastern half of the city including the Jandari.

Mariana took a deep breath of the clean, fresh air and sighed thankfully. She could see the moon, hazy and high above the distant palace walls, and the dim glitter of stars flickering against the velvet black sky.

A low stone wall, partially covered by twirling boughs of ivy, twisted up and down the road's shoulder. Behind the wall stood rows and rows of leafy palms, willows, figs, and a plethora of other colorful fruit trees. They paused to rest and take a drink from a brook. Ramagar bounded the wall and came back in a moment grinning, his hands filled with apples.

Mariana sat on the wall, her bare feet dangling over the side and her toes barely nudging the cold water. Her scuffed, worn boots at her side, she eagerly took one of the apples and savored her first bite. On either side of the wide road stood an array of homes, the likes of which she had never seen before. They were made of brick, with real glass set into the windows and spryly colored roofs of tile. She stared at them in amazement. Tall iron gates stood before every one; there were gardens and flowers and ponds overflowing with color. So far removed was she from the squalor of the Jandari that for a while she wondered if this entire setting was not just part of a dream.

Ramagar chomped loudly into his apple and threw away the core. "We'd best be on our way," he said. "We can't afford time to dawdle."

Mariana sighed and began to put her boots back on. Then Ramagar suddenly stood up and pushed her harshly off the wall and into the grass. Before she could lift her head he was beside her again, telling her not to make a sound.

Ahead down the road, making their way through the peaceful streets, rode three soldiers, their blue tunics shining in the moonlight. Mariana and Ramagar at once knew them to be palace guards—probably on their nightly patrol of the western edges of the city. Stern-faced and handsome, they spoke little among themselves, content to keep their eyes straight ahead and their hands on the hilts of their curved swords.

"Do you think they've seen us?" she whispered.

Ramagar bit at his lower lip. "I don't know. I hope not."

"But they're not Inquisitors," protested the girl. "They won't be looking for us . . ."

He looked at her with steely, cold eyes. "We can't take any chances." Then, to Mariana's shock, he drew a dagger of his own from inside his shirt.

"Ramagar, no! There are three of them!"

The voice was rough and deep. "Come out of there!" it barked.

Mariana froze. Peeking above the wall, she saw that one of the soldiers had ridden ahead of the others and had now stopped some twenty paces before the wall.

Ramagar was about to leap, dagger at the ready, when the girl quickly pushed him down from sight. She stood up slowly, smoothing the wrinkles out of her skirt as best she could, all the while widening her shy gaze at the demanding soldier. Ramagar crouched low beside the wall and watched the girl in puzzlement.

The keen-eyed soldier gaped at the sight of the girl, certainly surprised at his catch, and secretly somewhat delighted. One hand held firm on the reins and the other loosened the hold on his weapon. His eyes wandered over her from head to foot, noticing the opened buttons, the firm, supple breasts half exposed in the soft silver moonlight. He looked deeply into her eyes, black as coals, luminous and entreating, stirred at the sight of her slightly parted lips, nothing less than seductive.

"Who are you, girl?" he barked down at her, controlling his restless stallion. "What are you doing here?"

Mariana sat down on the edge of the wall, her arms stretched behind and her chin held high. She made sure that her dress was raised slightly higher than normal modesty would permit. Then, secure in the knowledge that the soldier's attentions were undivided, she coolly put the apple to her mouth and took another bite.

"Well?" said the soldier, sounding vexed. "I asked you a question."

"I came to visit a friend," she replied with a smile.

A shadow crossed the soldier's brow. "Oh? You have friends here, in this part of the city?"

"Very important friends, Captain. Influential, as well. They pay me quite handsomely to visit them."

The soldier eyed her shrewdly. "Where do you come from?"

Mariana tossed back her head and laughed. "From the Jandari, of course."

On the surface her story was preposterous; after all, what gutter slut from across the river could possibly claim to have friends within sight of the palace walls? Yet the girl was indeed a beauty; who could say for certain that some high-ranking court minister had not sent for her to share an idle evening's pleasures? This possibility struck a note of caution in the soldier. A single angry note written by such a minister could dispatch him to a life of cleaning out the regent's stables.

"What's your name?" he asked.

"Mariana, Captain. Perhaps you may have seen me dance—"

The soldier scratched his chin and nodded. She did seem vaguely familiar. He beckoned her to come closer.

68

Mariana lowered herself from the wall and, hips swaying, stood before him. Their eyes locked and hers danced with merriment. Although she would never admit it to Ramagar, she was beginning to enjoy this little ruse.

He leaned over and touched the edges of her flowing hair. "Do you often come to this side of the river, my dancing princess?" he asked.

Mariana shrugged and pursed her lips. "Men pay better here—or didn't you know that?"

The soldier laughed heartily, beginning now to like this little vixen from the Jandari. Her obvious charms were difficult not to appreciate. He began to wonder now if this chance encounter could not somehow be turned to his personal advantage.

Reading his every thought, she looked up at him and grinned. "Would you like for me to come with you now?"

The soldier fidgeted and looked back over his shoulder. His two mounted companions were hanging back in the distance, feigning lack of interest.

"I—I'm still on duty," he said, clearing his throat nervously. "But I'll be off at dawn. That's not too long to wait for me, is it?"

He's hooked! she thought.

"Then why not come to my room, Captain? Perhaps you'd like to spend the day with me? I'm sure it would be an enjoyable experience for you . . ."

The soldier swallowed hard and nodded. "What street?"

Without thinking, she gave him Oro's address, trying not to smirk at the thought of the handsome soldier knocking at the door and the ugly little hunchback coming to answer it.

The soldier committed the address to memory and stirred when Mariana added, "Don't forget. I'll be waiting."

The captain threw her a quick kiss and turned his stallion sharply. Then he rode off down the road to rejoin his waiting companions. No sooner had he disappeared from sight than Ramagar bounded from the wall with all the haste he could muster.

"Why in the name of heaven did you do that?" he bullied, so livid that tiny veins were bulging from his throat.

"Would you rather have fought all three all by yourself?"

"Of course not!" he ranted. "But don't you think your own measures were a little extreme?"

Mariana felt her face flush, and she stood on her toes and

kissed her lover fleetingly. "Why, Ramagar," she chided, "I didn't know you were so jealous."

The thief grunted and wisely let the matter drop.

Holding hands, the two continued their journey toward the tall spires of the palace, unaware that the little incident, from inception to conclusion, had been carefully observed. From behind the massive trunks of the willows the blond-haired stranger in rags stood and bemusedly shook his head. Clearly this rogue and his beautiful girl were not going to be as easy to fool as he had thought.

It was easy for the thief to pick the lock of the black iron gate, far easier than he ever imagined it would be. What a shame, he mused, that he would not have the opportunity to tell his peers back at the Demon's Horn of this daring exploit. Here he was, in the small hours before dawn with little but the most rudimentary of tools, casually picking the locks of the regent's finest stables. True, and most unfortunate, that these were not their liege's private stables; still they were royal property—and it amused Ramagar no end that he and Mariana would make their escape upon steeds whose backs had previously known only royal behinds.

The lock snapped with a quick *click*. Mariana swung the gate open carefully, her eyes darting in every direction, while Ramagar bolted through the opening and raced for the stable. The lone senty posted at the gate rolled over and moaned, a hand resting on the swelling bruise the thief had expertly delivered to his jaw only minutes before.

Ramagar dashed across the bridle path, avoiding the shadows cast by the barrack-like servants' quarters, and panting, slipped like a lizard inside the slightly ajar stable door. He stifled a sneeze as his nostrils were greeted by the musty sawdust air. Then he gazed around in wonder. There were easily two dozen horses in the stable, each with its own stall, and piles of hay in the back were stacked right to the ceiling.

He walked slowly to the first stall and peered over the gate. A fine black stallion shook its mane and whinnied. "Hush, hush," Ramagar whispered, and he reached over and stroked the nervous animal's nose. The horse calmed and Ramagar opened the gate and led him out gently, so as not to frighten the other watching horses. He looked the stallion over and admired the regent's taste. He was a beautiful specimen. Tall, sturdy, defiant. The sort of horse every man in Kalimar must dream of one day owning.

He kept the stallion occupied with a clump of hay and went on to inspect the next stall. A short, stocky mare stared back at him with dumb, pensive eyes. Ramagar nodded to himself, turned, and cast his gaze along the wall. Bridles and harnesses were all firmly in place. The first bridle he slipped over the gray mare, the second onto the waiting black stallion. Then he darted to the door and called softly to the girl. Mariana came running as fast as she could.

"We'd better hurry," she said anxiously, looking first to her lover and then to the horses. "That guard you hit is going to wake up any minute."

The thief smiled grimly. "Everything's all set. The mare is yours." And he handed her the reins.

Mariana took one look and gulped. "But what about a saddle?" she moaned.

Ramagar frowned. "There aren't any. Maybe we can buy one somewhere tomorrow. For now it will have to be bareback."

The dancing girl closed her eyes and sighed. Already she could feel the stinging bruises on her behind. She said nothing as he helped her mount and watched him while he took the stallion firmly in hand.

"I'm scared," she said, as they prepared to ride.

"Not as scared as you're going to be if we don't manage to get out of the city. Anyway, you'll get used to it. Just show her that you're the one in control. Keep your body loose, try to sway with her as she runs."

Mariana nodded.

"Ready?" he asked.

"Whenever you say—"

All of a sudden, they both looked up, startled. The stable doors had been flung open wide, and a sleepy-eyed servant stood staring at them, a small lantern dangling from his hands. And beside the servant stood two of the most vicious dogs that either of them had ever seen.

"Who are you?" demanded the servant in a shaky voice.

Ramagar whooped and slapped the mare and his stallion. Both horses bolted ahead. The servant wisely jumped to the side and rolled onto the grass as the horses thundered past. The hounds gave chase, yelping and snarling, barking at the top of their lungs, yapping at the horses' heels. Lamps began to be lit in a dozen windows, and a great commotion started as others servants and soldiers came running, pants unbuttoned into the chilly night air.

"Stop them!" someone cried. "Don't let them escape!" called another. "Bring them back!" chimed a third.

But it was too late; the unseen riders had long broken for the road, darting among the trees and well away from the palace and its environs. Soon even the dogs were left panting behind, exhausted and whimpering, uselessly continuing to bark sporadically after their prey. By the time the first group of soldiers rode from the gate, they could only scratch their heads in confusion, trying to figure out which of many ways the thieves might have gone. It made no difference though. The riders were too well along their way to be caught.

7

The sky was changing color from black to azure, violet, and plum, then suddenly blood-red pouring up from the corners of the horizon. Along the sandy road came the caravan, a kilometer-long procession of camels and packmules and donkeys, all worn and weary, all shuffling slowly under the weight of their burdens. Snorting and wheezing, they moved to the crack and the sting of the taskmaster's whip and the shouts and whistles of the muleskinners until the time when the gates of Kalimar came into sight and the long journey was at an end.

The tradesmen lifted themselves from their wagons and beasts, and shook the dust from their flaming-colored robes, watching with sly eyes while the host of laborers unpacked their wares. It was then that the soldiers and inspectors came onto the scene. They assessed the wares and tallied the levies to be imposed, blindly misreading the scales at the feel of silver passing clandestinely into their palms.

While all this transpired the city began to awaken from the long night. As always, it was the sound of morning prayers cried from the minarets that brought most from their slumber. Soon the streets and bazaars would be crowded with the throngs crossing from one side of the river to the other. Most citizens would be completely oblivious to the numerous patrols of soldiers marching through the streets and guarding each of the Nine Gates. Most, that is, except for those who had something to fear, those whose escape meant the difference between life and death.

Mariana walked slowly and casually along the perimeter of the caravan. Unsought by the Inquisitors, she had passed through the gate with hardly a glance, although she was still careful to keep her gaze low and her veil high. Three times they had been thwarted in their plan. *Three times!* Alert guards posted at the road beside the Old Wall had signaled the alarm before their horses could even attempt to make the dangerous ride through. They had been forced to turn back, seek another route. But Ramagar's next choice proved equally disastrous; dodging whistling arrows, they had barely made it away in time. Fortune in the shape of night had been with them, though, and they had managed to elude all chasing sentries. But now it was day, and there was little refuge they might seek if this fourth attempt for freedom failed.

Mariana's eyes scanned the road and the attentive soldiers on either side. She felt uncomfortable in the new clothes Ramagar had stolen for her. Her moccasins, a size too loose and poorly laced, slipped with every step. The tunic blouse with its high gathered neck irritated her throat, and the sleeves, far too long for a girl her height, kept falling below her knuckles, trapping her hands. Her hair was pinned up now, tightly bunched under a white headcloth. With her veil firmly in place, she knew she looked the part her lover had intended her to play: that of an anxious merchant's wife come to the caravan to find her long-missed husband.

She strolled among the crowd, here and there pretending to catch sight of some traveler or other she recognized. Then, hiding her distraught eyes, she sluggishly drew away from the caravan and passed back beneath the arched wall into the city.

Well away, in a side street that led to the central markets, Ramagar stood waiting. The horses were watering in a slime-filled trough, and the thief, dressed in the outrageous brown robes of a Karshi religious fanatic, paced up and down the flagstones with his hood covering his head and shading his face.

The sight of the girl and her downcast eyes told him the result of her foray.

"It's no use," she said. "Soldiers are everywhere. *Az'i!* I've never seen so many in one place at a single time. They're sending a whole army to catch you."

The thief wiped his brow and cursed the heat of the day. How these damnable fanatics wore their robes even at high noon left him bewildered. Here it was, less than an hour after dawn, and already his body was drenched in sweat. He gazed

73

up at the rising run. Time was running out, he knew. Hour by hour the noose was tightening. He must make his move soon, while he could, while there was still a move to make.

Mariana watched as he took the horses by the bridles and walked them back to the edge of the street. "What are you going to do?" she asked.

"They're expecting us to come riding through the gate like demons from hell," he replied sullenly. "Charging down the road like crazed, trapped animals. Well, we're going to fool them."

Mariana held her breath. "How?"

"We're going to walk. Slowly, leisurely. One at a time. You'll have no trouble, you've already proved as much—"

Her pulse was throbbing. "And what about you?"

He smiled thinly. "I'll be close behind. A Karshi fanatic, on his way to self-flagellation in the desert. They do it all the time, you know. I shouldn't cause any attention."

The dancing girl grasped her hand around his sleeve. "But what if you're asked to lower your hood? They'll want to see your face before you pass, Ramagar. They'd be fools not to."

"Then," he drawled, sucking in the hot air through his mouth, "you keep on going. Don't stop, don't pause, don't even turn around."

Her eyes met his. "I—I don't think I can," she whispered.

The thief took her hand and smiled; a kind smile behind red and weary eyes. "You have to, Mariana. That's the way I want it. The way it has to be. Look, you asked me to take you with me, and I agreed. Well, we've done our best. But I'll not allow you to be dragged off to the dungeons with me."

"I'll not leave you," she said firmly.

"Yes, you will." His voice was cold and devoid of emotion. "You'll do exactly as I tell you or I'll leave you here right now. I mean it, Mariana. Now will you do as I ask?"

Mariana nodded her head slowly, knowing that this time there would be no changing his mind.

He put his hand to the side of her face and gently ran his fingers over her lips. "It's best this way, girl," he consoled her. "No matter what happens at least you'll be safe—and free. Sell the scimitar as quickly as you can. You'll be a lady, Mariana. A lady of quality."

"Not without you. I'm nothing without you." A single tear rolled down her cheek and the thief wiped it away. Then Ramagar turned swiftly.

"We'd better get going," he said.

Silently, Mariana took the reins of her mare and began to walk along the avenue back to the gate. The clomping of the stallion's hooves behind was the only assurance she had that her lover was still close. She was determined to do everything he asked, and not even to look at him again if turning around was against his wishes. But her tears were another matter. They flowed freely from her eyes and she was not ashamed of them. If this was to be the end, then let it come quickly. Let Ramagar die right away. He must not be forced to suffer the indignities and tortures the Inquisitors had promised. And rather than stand by and allow such a thing to happen, Mariana knew she would take the thief's life herself; slay her lover if need be with the bejeweled dagger she carried, the one men so highly prized, and then toss it to the wind when the deed was done. It was an evil thing, she decided. It had brought Ramagar—and herself—nothing but grief. She wondered what devils had bewitched it so, what curse had been laid upon its gold so that all who claimed possession would know only misery.

Yes, she would be rid of it if ill befell Ramagar. Be rid of it once and for all. And woe be unto the poor soul who claimed its ownership next.

Mariana passed beneath the shadows and the arched wall with little but these thoughts in mind. Eyes straight ahead, never wavering, although she ached to look behind, she led her mare away toward the edge of the road, carefully following the thief's instructions, and praying that his escape would come as easily as her own. Seconds drifted like hours; she felt her body grow stiffer, her muscles tense, her brow wet with perspiration, and her mouth become dry. Merchants, finished with their barter with the inspectors, were beginning to pass by now, a few of them stopping to bow their heads politely. Mariana was unaware of their attention. Reaching the clumps of grass alongside the resting camels, she paused. Her heart pounded like a kettledrum; she dried her wet palms on her tunic. So far so good, she assured herself. By now surely Ramagar would have passed beyond the gate as well. Soon they would both be safe; she would greet him, fly into his arms. Once on the open road they could never be stopped.

She shut her eyes briefly and prayed: Please! Let it be so!

The various soldiers scattered nearby all seemed preoccupied with assorted duties. Not a one among them seemed the least bit suspicious either of her or the Karshi religious fanatic who was close behind her. And Mariana drew encouragement. It's going to work! It's really going to work! Just a little bit longer; a few more minutes at most . . .

Suddenly she stopped cold in her tracks. Off to the side, close to the hastily set merchants' tents, a small group of men had gathered and were going through the motions of haggling with each other over their merchandise. Something, though, seemed most peculiar. Beneath the colorful robes the men wore swords—most strange attire for a caravan journey. Then her heart skipped a beat and she stifled a gasp. There was no mistaking it. Oro, the hunchbacked trader, was among them. His ugly little face was busily scrutinizing her as he drew himself from the crowd.

Mariana spun around as quick as she could, crying, "Flee! It's a trap! Run back to the city!"

The grim-faced Inquisitors shed their robes in a frenzy and, weapons drawn, came racing to the gate. Honest merchants and brokers standing in the way began to run and hide. Women began to scream. In a split second all was pandemonium.

Ramagar whipped out his dagger and barely blocked the thrust of the first sword in time. Bending, he scooped up sand and threw it into the attacker's eyes. From the side two more soldiers rushed at him. He dived to the ground, caught one off balance and slammed his fist into his gut. The soldier doubled over, wheezing. Then the thief was back on his feet, grappling with the next soldier, fists flying, sending him sprawling to the dirt.

From the wall, arrows came whizzing, kicking up sand, landing inches from his feet. Mariana watched in despair. Other running soldiers knocked her down, shouting commands, rushing the gate, and calling for it to be shut.

Before the cunning thief could mount his steed, hands were all over him and pulling him down. Then the black stallion lurched in pain. Arrows slammed into its flanks, its neck, its back. The animal whinnied, standing high on its hind legs and kicking. A soldier screamed in terror as the animal lost its balance and fell onto him with a powerful thud.

Ramagar ran for the gate. Two sentries were in his way. One's jawbone he cracked with the force of his fist; the second he picked up by the collar and sent flying into the arms of his rushing comrades.

"Catch him!" came the cry.

The wily rogue bolted into the dumbstruck crowds gathered at the gate's edge. A band of mounted troops came charging from the street, whips flaying, sending the frightened citizens into a panic. Mariana, in the meantime, had lifted herself from the ground and made her way back inside. Everywhere she looked there was a frenzy, a terrible melee of a hundred soldiers giving chase, kicking and knocking to the earth anyone and everyone who got in their way.

"He's dressed as a Karshi," she heard the captain shout. "He won't be hard to find!"

Amid the chaos, a group of soldiers had cornered someone, and Mariana strained to see. Her heart sank as never before. The Karshi robe was unmistakable; the man was completely surrounded. The soldiers closed ranks and raised their weapons, steadily moving in on the hooded fanatic. "Watch out!" someone warned. "He's as slippery as an eel!"

The fanatic stood his ground for a moment, then suddenly tried to bolt to the side. More soldiers closed in. The robed man no longer tried to run. He lifted his arms into the air and sagged his shoulders.

Mariana watched the scene with growing horror. It was plain that Ramagar was giving himself up—but it was equally clear that the soldiers now had no intention of taking him alive.

"Kill him!" the commander barked. And Mariana screamed. Blade after blade plunged into the body. While it still lay writhing upon the earth, the soldiers pressed in closer and, as a man, began to kick and spit at the dying form.

Sobbing, wailing, beating her fists at the laughing soldiers, Mariana worked herself inside the ring of death and knelt beside the corpse. Her tunic stained with blood as she took his hand and pressed it against her cheek. "You bastards," she cried. "He was innocent! *Innocent!*"

The captain of the troops paid no heed; tugging at his brush moustache, he barked to the man beside him, "Uncover his face. I want to take a final look at the master thief."

"Kalimar won't miss him," the second man growled. Then he knelt down and pushed back the hood. The soldiers stood speechless; Mariana swallowed hard and drew the courage to take one last glance at her lover's bloody face. She too was stunned speechless at the sight of the pockmarked and clean-shaven face.

"Gods of mercy," whispered one of the soldiers. "That's not Ramagar! It's the wrong man! We've slain the wrong man!"

Then from the roofs behind came a billowing laugh, a laugh Mariana would recognize anywhere.

"After him, you fools!" urged the captain. "That's Ramagar up there!"

And Mariana laughed through her tears as the soldiers gathered their horses and drew their weapons once more.

It was quiet. Evening prayer was done, the streets returned to their dusty desolation. Mariana sat alone watching the sun-baked domes glint in the failing light. She could think now only of the coming shadows; the welcome cloak that would hide her lover at least through the night. But where he was, she had no idea. He certainly could not risk going back to his hiding place at the wharves, nor could he chance returning to the Jandari. He would have to hide as best he could. A few moments here, an hour there. Spies would be everywhere, she knew, more than eager to help the soldiers in their search and claim the newly posted reward of twenty gold pieces.

This time she was certain she would never see him again. He would never dare come to her, not even for a fleeting moment. And how could she blame him? Her room would be constantly watched, even perhaps her every movement. She glanced up at the squalid buildings beyond the plaza and wondered if they were watching her at this very second. What broke her heart was the knowledge that even had she known his whereabouts she could not go. It would only hasten his doom.

No, they could never meet again. The time they shared, the love, and the dreams they planned were all behind. Sooner or later the thief would be caught, more than likely betrayed by a friend. And she, well, she would have to face her future without him. All that was left were her memories, memories she would cling to until the last breath had left her body.

With such sorrow in her heart, Mariana slowly lifted herself from the stone bench and began the long walk back to the Jandari. She would never dance or love again. Her life would know only long and empty years. Barren, joyless years.

"Pssst!"

She glanced sideways to the shadows in the dark doorway. A bony finger nervously beckoned. *"Pssst!* Over here!"

She screwed her eyes and stared. It was a boy who was calling her. Ragged, thin, and yellowed. Normally she would not have paid him the slightest bit of attention, but the cloak he wore, ill-fitting and far too long for him, seemed strangely familiar.

Mariana took a wary step closer.

"Follow me, Mariana," rasped the boy, turning his back to her and climbing up a winding flight of crumbling stairs.

Mariana crossed the threshold of the doorway and stopped. "Who are you?" she questioned. "And how do you know my name?"

The boy stopped his climb and looked back at her with a grin. "Ramagar helped me once," he said, fingering the cloak. And the girl nodded. She recalled the evening when he had first brought the scimitar to her, and how he had thrown a few old clothes and some coppers to a hungry street urchin waiting below.

"I remember," she said. "What do you want?"

"To help you, Mariana."

"Help me how?"

The boy shook his head impatiently. "Trust me, Mariana. Say nothing and follow me."

Her hand gripped the banister for support. She took a single step and then stopped. "Why should I trust you?" she said abruptly, her dark eyes flashing. "Why should I do as you ask?"

"Because," replied the boy with a sigh of exasperation, "I think I can help Ramagar to flee Kalimar."

At this she let her mouth open soundlessly. Her eyes widened in disbelief. "*You* can help Ramagar escape?"

He nodded. "I know someone who knows a way out of the city. A way that not even a thief like your lover is aware of."

Her first inclination was to laugh. Who was this urchin to claim more knowledge of Kalimar's secrets than the city's most masterful rogue? His very words rankled her. And then she thought: perhaps his words were a ruse—a clever ploy to enlist her aid in finding Ramagar so the urchin could turn him in and collect the reward.

She raised her chin and glared squarely at him. "I don't believe what you're telling me," she said flatly. "And I'm not going to follow you a single step farther."

"Then perhaps you'll believe *me*."

Her eyes darted up to the top of the stairs. Whoever it was who had spoken sounded unfamiliar, and she strained her eyes to catch a glimpse of the shadowed figure.

"And who are you?"

The man didn't answer. He opened the small door that led to the roof; all Mariana could see besides his silhouette was the darkening sky and the few early evening stars twinkling above.

The stranger held out an open hand, gesturing for her to come up. "Please," he said softly. "Do as we ask. We are not your enemies. And we do mean to help you if we can."

Something in his tone was reassuring to her, and although still hesitant, she decided to do as asked. The steps crumbled as she climbed; the urchin offered his hand to help but Mariana refused. Once at the top, she bent her head and slipped out onto the roof. The boy stood fixed at her side, his eyes moving back and forth from his shadowy companion to her.

Though the stranger remained concealed in the shadows, Mariana made a quick assessment of what there was to see. A hood covered his head and his cloak was tightly wrapped. It was clear that he was young; his stance told her that he was proud; and his manner was proof enough of his good breeding.

There was a small wooden box placed close to the doorway and the stranger gestured for her to sit. Mariana did as asked, and said, "What is this all about? How can you help me, and why do you want to?"

Her companions could not doubt her mistrust.

"Your lover cannot hope to hide for much longer," said the stranger. "Another day, two at the most. Then they'll catch him and behead him."

Mariana squirmed. She found his frankness a bit too much to take. "First they have to find him," she snapped.

The stranger folded his arms and stared out into the night. Across the city the lamps were being lit in ten thousand windows. "Be assured they will find him. No stone will remain unturned in the effort."

Mariana was growing more uncomfortable each moment. This man sounded more like an enemy with every word that passed his lips. She began to rise.

"I can help him," the stranger promised.

"We both can help him," added the urchin, seemingly eager for her to believe him.

She looked at them both blankly. "Why?"

"Because Ramagar showed kindness to me," replied the urchin quickly. He met her gaze, then lowered his own. "And he was the only man in my entire life who ever did."

80

Mariana accepted that without a second thought. Who knew better than she the harsh pitiless life Jandarians were forced to live? If her lover had shown this lad a small kindness then the boy was now more than willing to repay it a hundredfold. For that she was more than grateful. She smiled at the youth and turned back to the stranger. "And what's your reason?" she asked.

The hooded man smiled a sly smile. "Ramagar has something that belongs to me. Something very important."

At this the girl shuddered. Comprehension was beginning to dawn and she felt her calm unhinge. The stranger pushed off his hood and she stared at the flowing golden hair, the penetrating ice-blue eyes. The beggar! She gasped. The mysterious man in rags!

"I'll never help you!" she flared uncontrollably. "You want me to help you find Ramagar so you can kill him yourself!" And she jumped up from her place and stepped backward until she was against the wall, trembling, trying to plan her escape to the street.

The stranger stayed unperturbed. "I'm not seeking to kill your lover, Mariana," he drawled slowly. "Only to regain what is rightfully mine—"

"Ha! Don't make me laugh! And where did you steal it from, I wonder? What pocket did you pick to dare claim it as your own?"

Anger fired briefly in his eyes, but by the time he replied it was gone. "I did not steal it," he answered. "It belonged only to me."

She gazed up and down his ragged dress. "You? A beggar? You expect me to believe such nonsense?"

"Believe what you like," he replied. Then he narrowed his eyes and locked them with hers. "But I *will* have the scimitar back, I promise you that much. It matters not to me if I take it from a dead thief or a living one."

"Worm! Then find him by yourself!"

Skirt flaring she turned to go, but the urchin's hand on her sleeve stopped her. "We do want to help him," the boy insisted, his own eyes large and honest. "Please, hear us out—"

"What have you to lose, Mariana?" added the stranger. "Ramagar is doomed in any case. So why not listen to what I have to say?"

She eyed him suspiciously, filled with loathing and contempt. If he dared make the slightest threatening move toward her, she would take out the dagger he so badly

81

desired, and indeed give it back—straight through his black heart. But it did amuse her to think that while he so fretfully sought the blade, in truth it was only paces away.

"Well?" said the stranger.

"Talk, then. I'll hear you out."

Nodding, he said, "There's an old route out from the city that few living men even dream exists. A way out where not a single soldier will be looking."

"An unused road?"

"No, not a road. Not a land route at all."

"Then what?" she sneered. "Will we all fly over the walls like birds?"

Ignoring her sarcasm, he replied, "Through the sewers, the ancient pipe system built thirty meters below the earth, long unused and longer forgotten."

"It's true, Mariana," chimed in the urchin. "I've seen these sewers myself. It would be a perfect escape for him and for you. For all of us, if it came to that."

"But only I know the exact route," warned the stranger. "Deviate from it ten paces and a man would find himself lost in a hopeless labyrinth without a chance of ever getting out."

Mariana could feel her heartbeat quickening again. She was by no means convinced of what he was saying, but if it were *true* . . .

"How do you know all this?" she asked. "You're a stranger to Kalimar, a foreigner. What proof do you have that you actually know a way out beyond the walls?"

"Ah, but do you forget that I was also sought by your soldiers? Unlike Ramagar I chose to hide not above the ground but below it. For days now I have studied this system of underground pipes. I cannot be wrong. The sewers will lead us to the river, more than a kilometer from the walls. Under the cover of darkness your escape will be easy. I will be your guide, fighting to protect your lives if I must. Then, when we are safely away, you can go your way and I shall go mine . . ."

"And the price we must pay for your assistance is the scimitar."

He smiled caustically. "You understand me perfectly, Mariana. But for you it's a bargain at any price. Ramagar will live, and you will be at his side. Think it over."

The street urchin pressed her further. "Listen to him, Mariana. You'll come to trust him as I have. He means us no ill. None of us. And this dagger he seeks *is* rightfully his. You

82

know as much yourself. Give it back, Mariana, please. Implore Ramagar to listen."

The girl sighed and tried to clear her confused thoughts. Events were happening now so fast. Friends had become enemies, enemies were offering to become friends. In a quandary, she leaned against the opened doorway, sagging her shoulders as she sighed. Would Ramagar trust this soft-spoken stranger, she wondered. Would these soothing words have convinced him half as much as she had been? Yet what other choices were there? Trusting this man was certainly a risk, but without his help what else might come? Only more despair, and death.

"I cannot speak for Ramagar," she said at last, turning herself and fully facing the stranger, "but I agree to your terms. Take us as far away from Kalimar as you can and the scimitar will be yours again."

The blond-haired stranger smiled. "Trust that you've made a wise decision."

Mariana looked at him sharply. "Have I?" she asked. "Let's hope Ramagar feels the same—that is if we can ever find him."

The street urchin's face lit up in a broad grin. "And that is where both of you need *me*," he said. "In all of Kalimar I'm the only one with any idea where he is."

8

Ramagar sat with his arms folded around his knees and his body arched forward, away from the damp planks dug into the earth. Above his head splintery beams dripped a steady flow of dirtied water. The ground at his feet was cold and coarse and he shivered every time the gusty wind forced itself between the boards.

Opposite him crouched the street urchin. Drooping his head, staring at the scattered pebbles in the dirt, he waited for the thief to give his answer. Since the very first day he heard of Ramagar the boy had held the master rogue in awe and admiration. Now, though, it was a sad, hollow man who sat before him, and the boy's features showed only sorrow and deep emotion. For here, close to the great ancient locks of Kalimar's canal, beneath a decrepit, rattling walkway overlooking foul cesspools, the greatest thief in the Jandari was forced to hide like a frightened animal, as broken as his dreams.

Ramagar sighed, lost in thought, pinching the bridge of his nose with thumb and forefinger. When his eyes finally opened the boy saw that they were sunken and tired, attesting grimly to his plight.

"And you swear that Mariana trusts him?" queried the thief.

The urchin nodded with conviction. "I give my word, Ramagar. There is no treachery to fear. Only an honest trade—your freedom for the dagger."

Ramagar listened attentively, then cast his forlorn gaze heavenward. How much he wanted to see Mariana again, even if only for a few precious moments. To hold her close to him, kiss her, feel the softness of her skin against his own.

"You must believe what I've said," pressed the boy. His darting eyes made plain that he was nervously aware of the passing patrols diligently searching every nook and cranny from one side of the river to the other. "Won't you come with me now, Ramagar? Mariana is waiting for us, for you . . ."

The thief shivered at the mention of her name. And he asked himself if it had really been trust that led her into this strange alliance with the beggar. Or, as he secretly feared, was it nothing more than blind love and sheer desperation forcing her to close her eyes to the possibility of a carefully laid trap?

The wind grew stronger and the boy listened for the sound of hoofbeats it carried. The soldiers were closing in. "We've so little time," said the urchin to the rogue. "These patrols have been crisscrossing the city since dusk. If you agree to the offer, you'll have to come with me now." And as if to add emphasis to his words he placed his ragamuffin hand tightly around Ramagar's sleeve.

"Tell me, lad," said the thief, looking deeply into the boy's eyes, "do *you* put your trust in this man?"

"I trust him with my life." It was said swiftly, without hesitation. Ramagar knew the lad spoke with sincerity, although why he loved the beggar so was a complete mystery.

Once again Ramagar sighed, this time leaning back and weighing the scales before giving his answer. It was a risky business to say the least, walking these sewers. A very risky business. He knew little of them; only that the superstitious folk of Kalimar held them in terror, daring to speak of them only in soft whispers—and even then never after the sun had set. These tunnels, by all accounts, were a honeycomb of rodent- and leech-infested arteries as black as midnight devils, colder than a graveyard. For more than a century they had been unused, with nary a man bold enough to venture so deep into the bowels of the earth. For it was said that once a man lost his way, he would never find it again. Insanity and death were surely all that awaited him.

Ramagar knew what foolishness this darkened journey might prove to be. Yet, his state of affairs was such that even a plan like this offered a brighter future than the one surely faced if he turned the offer down. If his life had any value remaining, he had no choice but to put it into the hands of the strange beggar who called the prize of a prince his own, and claimed to know the long-forgotten exit which led beyond the walls. Ramagar did not mind putting his own life in jeopardy; indeed, the risk meant little. But the thought of Mariana sharing the burden—albeit willingly—sank his heart and left him in despair. This decision was the most difficult he had ever faced.

At length he lifted his head and looked to the boy. "Very well; I accept the offer. The scimitar in exchange for freedom. In any case, I'd rather die in the sewers than let Oro and his goons gloat with satisfaction at the removal of my head in a public square."

The urchin twisted his way from under the footbridge and out into the open. He breathed a thankful sigh, then squinted his eyes and looked far into the night. He could see nothing, but as before the wind carried the distant sound of hooves.

"Which way?" said the thief, coming to his side.

The urchin smiled. How proud he was at that moment; the thief of thieves at his side, and together they would elude the pressing legions of the Inquisitors. "This way, Ramagar," he said, pointing to the wet dung-smeared horse trail above the bank of the estuary. And side by side they disappeared among the shadows.

Mariana held her breath at the sight of the two figures hugging the alley wall as they made their way toward her. Then she flew into Ramagar's arms, weeping with happiness. They kissed briefly; the thief held her face in his hands and looked at her longingly. Mariana untied her headcloth and let

85

it fall to the ground. Unpinning her hair, she shook it loose until it tumbled windblown and free over her shoulders.

"I never thought I'd see you again," she confessed.

"Nor I you," admitted the thief.

They could have stayed that way for an hour, unspeaking, content to gaze into each other's star-filled eyes. But there were other matters at hand; matters that could not wait. Ramagar held her close and looked to the beggar. Aloof, unconcerned with these matters of the heart, the yellow-haired stranger lifted his gaze from the crater-like hole at the far end of the alley and stared at the thief. For a while the eyes of these two strong-willed men locked; partly in anger, partly in respect. Mariana looked on with trepidation while they took long measure of each other, and she feared that this encounter might yet turn to confrontation.

The fear, though, was short-lived. The stranger's mouth cracked at the corners and a small smile appeared. "So," he said in his accented voice, "you are Ramagar. We meet at last."

The thief nodded. "And I have kept my part of the bargain."

"You carry my blade?"

"It is in my possession, yes. Once we are taken to safety it shall be returned."

"I would see it now," said the stranger. "Not that I don't trust you, master thief. Merely as a precaution that you still have it."

"A fair enough request," replied Ramagar. Then he turned to Mariana and said, "Let him see it."

The stranger's eyes widened in wonder as the dancing girl modestly turned from view and reached inside her tunic. Even in the darkness of night the golden blade glimmered as she held it.

The stranger was agog; all this time of searching and plotting had been futilely spent. It had been within his very grasp—and he never once suspected. But the humor of this episode had not escaped him; he mulled his foolishness over and laughed. "You tricked me well, Mariana," he said. "Have you had it all along?"

She smiled mischievously. "From the very beginning."

The stranger scratched his head and sighed. "What more needs to be said? You've both kept your agreements; come, I shall keep mine."

With that, he beckoned them to follow. The entrance to

the sewers seemed little more than a gaping hole on first inspection. Concave, crack-ridden, and seeping raw sewage, it was literally a black pit. A pile of rubble had recently been removed to expose a badly decomposed set of steps leading about ten meters down and ending at the base of a large, shadow-concealed metal doorway.

Mariana tightened her hold on Ramagar's arm and looked down with disgust. Small maggots and lice by the hundreds were crawling under and over the steps, swimming in the black, liquid pools that formed below the several exposed corroded pipes.

Ramagar breathed through his mouth to blot out the stench. "Are the tunnels beyond that door?" he asked.

The stranger shook his head. "Only the entrance to them. We'll have to go deeper than that, I'm afraid. Much deeper."

Mariana bravely began to descend, the thief at her side, the stranger and the urchin taking the lead. The stranger was the first to reach the landing, whereupon he began to scrutinize the entrance while his hands deftly felt for the springed catch to unlock it.

"What will we use for light?" asked the thief uneasily.

The urchin provided the answer. He had wrapped a handful of oil-soaked rags around a fat stick of wood. Ramagar's flints struck and caught; immediately the rags became a smoking blaze of fire.

The catch-spring *twanged* and the stranger smiled. He pushed the door with all his weight and it slowly opened with a groan. Blackness fell back to the torchlight and Mariana gasped as a dozen sewer mice dashed helter-skelter for the distant darkness. The tunnel was not steep, although its incline semed constant. And it was only then that the thief and his girl grasped the true nature of the journey they faced. Green slime and moss covered the walls of rock; the entrance reeked of stale air and foul droppings.

"I never said it would be easy," said the stranger. "And it only gets worse the deeper we go. The tunnels we must use won't even be reached for hours—and one wrong turn might mean we'll never find them at all . . ."

"There's no turning back now," said Mariana, fighting with all her strength to overcome her abject terror. "Lead on. The quicker we make this vile passage the sooner we'll be out."

"And you feel the same?" he asked of the thief. "You want to go on?"

Ramagar nodded grimly. He drew his dagger and clutched

it firmly in his sweaty hand. "I didn't come all this way just to turn back now."

The stranger smiled. "Very well." And he shut the metal door behind. The lock sprang back into position and they knew they could no longer get out even if they wanted to. The only other exit was somewhere out there in the black; all they could do was go forward and find it.

Holding the torch high, the urchin took the lead. Down, down, ever down they went, feeling the damp and the chill cut to their bones. There was little talk among them, and then only in quick whispers. The sounds of their marching feet echoed grimly in places they had passed: the slow, steady steps of the boy; the assured, confident, harsh steps of the stranger; Ramagar's long, firm strides; Mariana's moccasined light step hurrying to keep pace with the others.

The initial leg of the journey had not in truth taken very long, but to Mariana it seemed like hours. At a place where the tunnel broadened dramatically before separating into three small tunnels, the stranger stopped. From somewhere unseen but close they could all hear a steady *drip drip drip* of trickling water. Mariana looked back at the ascending shaft and shuddered. In the black she could see a pair of staring eyes. Rat's eyes. Cunning, frightened, hungry. The rodents, unseen, had been following every step of the way. Watching, waiting. Perhaps biding their time.

"Which way now?" said Ramagar, blowing hot air into his cold hands.

"The tunnel on the left," replied the yellow-haired stranger. "It's the only one that leads beneath the river."

"The river?" gasped the girl. "You mean we'll be traveling below the water? These tunnels were built a thousand years ago. What if one gives way? We'll all drown!"

"It's the only way," said the stranger impatiently. "We'll move fast. We'll be safe. I've never seen the water rise higher than a man's waist."

Ramagar looked at him with questioning eyes. "Then the tunnels do flood?" And he frowned when the stranger replied, "All the time." Still, there was no choice but to move ahead.

The urchin remained in the lead, taking them into a narrow, uneven tunnel where the ceiling was so low that all but the boy had to lower their heads. And the longer they walked it, the narrower it became; so narrow that Mariana had only to stretch her arms halfway out to feel the rough, mica-encrusted wall at either side. Water was seeping everywhere, through cracks in the ceiling and in the walls; she could feel the ground soften and her moccasins squish through mud. What sickened her most, though, was the sight of the roaches, disgusting brown and yellow things that wormed and scurried between the crevices as the offensive torchlight disturbed their search for food. But there was plenty of that, Mariana saw. Worms and spiders, weed and moss, not to mention the maggot-ridden flesh of dead rodents.

"We'll soon be out of here," said the stranger to his companions. "This tunnel ends abruptly, if I recall, and we'll come to a wide cavern where the sewers used to meet."

"Brrr," shivered Mariana. "I can hardly wait."

As far as she could judge, by now the sun would have long risen. She thought wistfully of the blazing ball of fire in the sky, its warmth and comfort. And in a way she felt pity for these repulsive sewer-dwelling creatures who had never known daylight or warmth, and never would.

The tunnel turned suddenly, sharply, becoming wider. They were still on something of a descent, but now it was leveling off. Occasionally they passed smaller tunnels leading off at angles at the side; deep, silent arches as grim as tombs. Mariana could only wonder where they led, but she was definitely not curious enough to explore.

As the stranger had predicted, this tunnel came to an end without warning. The small band found themselves standing on the threshold of an enormous cavern, its ceiling up to fifty meters high in places. And the ceiling was studded with incredible formations: icicle-shaped stalactites sculptured from the limestone and dolomite that glittered in hues of gold and scarlet and flaming yellows above the pale light of the torch.

Mariana and Ramagar stared in awe at the breathtaking beauty of the forebidding grotto. Their yellow-haired companion glanced at them and grinned. "Impressive, isn't it? All the more so, when you bear in mind that this is part of a sewer."

"It's stunning," stammered Mariana, her gaze held high. "It sweeps you away, like nothing I've ever seen before."

"A shame that no one else will ever see it," added the thief. "It should be a shrine."

The stranger lifted his head and stared for a long while at the dripping, motionless cones of sparkling rock. "I don't think I will ever come to understand this land of Kalimar," he said with a sigh. "There is so much beauty to be found here, so much potential for your people. Yet you knowingly have let it all fall to such waste. A terrible pity. A crime.

Beneath the earth there is so much wealth to be mined, above it, so much land that could be reclaimed from your deserts. Yet you allow it to remain barren, empty. No," he shook his head, "I shall never understand."

Mariana and Ramagar exchanged quick, puzzled glances. This blond-haired beggar was certainly the oddest man they had ever known. Yesterday his mind and heart were filled with hatred and murder, today he spoke softly of beauty and nature.

"Who are you, stranger?" said the thief suddenly. "Who are you really?"

The stranger shook off his musings and smiled. "I am many men," he answered mysteriously. "A wayfarer, a vagabond, yes, even a beggar."

His hard features had somehow softened, Mariana saw. And she was certain that behind his stony, rugged facade he was in truth a kind and gentle man, even as Ramagar was.

"You have been many things, stranger," she said. "How came you to Kalimar?"

In no hurry to reply, he walked to the center of the cavern and stared harrowingly into a deep pool of dark water. He stared at his reflection for a while, then said, "The road I have traveled has been a very long and difficult one, Mariana. I have seen many places, many cities. Kalimar was meant to be only the briefest of stops, I assure you." He glanced to Ramagar and smiled. "Let's just say that my journey has been unavoidably delayed. But once I have my blade I can begin anew."

"From what land do you come?" asked the thief.

"And where will this journey end?" chimed in the girl.

A hint of mystery returned to the stranger's eyes and he shook his head sadly. "I have been asked that question countless times. I will give you an answer, but one that you may not readily understand." He paused here, seeing the urchin listen as curiously as the others. Then he said, "I seek whence I have come, and I have come whence I seek."

"You pose us a riddle, stranger," said Ramagar. "Can't you be plain?"

Mariana, though, seemed less puzzled than the others. Pushing hair away from her eyes, she said, "I think perhaps I can solve this riddle."

"You understand it?" said the thief.

She nodded and locked her gaze with the stranger's.

"Many have guessed it," he told her, "but few have under-stood—"

"The answer is simple. You seek whence you have come, you have come whence you seek. Home. You are going home."

Clearly taken aback, the handsome beggar raised himself to his full height, eyes grown wide with surprise, and looked to Ramagar, who seemed just as astounded as he was.

"She is a very wise young woman, master thief," he said admiringly, "and you are a most fortunate man. Be sure to take good care of her. She is far too great a prize ever to lose."

"I know it well," replied the thief, watching Mariana blush as he put his arm around her shoulder and cradled her close to him. "I almost did lose her once—but never again. She means more to me than anything, including your bejeweled dagger."

The stranger nodded sagely. "Then, my friends, you are both very wise . . ."

"Best we be on our way," interrupted the urchin, breaking the spirit of the moment. The stranger sighed and nodded.

There were so many things that Mariana and Ramagar wanted to ask their new companion; so many puzzles that de-manded solutions. But now, they knew, was not the time. Too many more urgent matters pressed. With resignation, they prepared to move on.

The stranger took the torch from the boy and pointed it in the direction of a grim shaft set at the farthest corner of the magnificent cavern.

"From here on I will lead the way," he told them. "Stay as close behind me as you can—and cry out swiftly if you sense any danger."

Mariana gulped; she wasn't sure just what he was referring to, but didn't feel brave enough to ask. Ramagar again took hold of his dagger and gripped the girl's arm with his free hand. The street urchin brought up the rear, and the little band moved on deeper into the threatening channel.

One by one they crossed the cave until the gaping hole loomed menacingly before them. "This tunnel will take us under the river," said the stranger as he poked the torch in-side. Eerie shadows cascaded over green corroded iron pipes. The fiery light awoke a slumbering nest of tiny bats who screeched at the flame and darted on frenzied wings deeper into the gloom.

"They'll not harm us," assured the beggar, and he boldly strode inside. The others followed in his footsteps.

"*Az'il*" moaned Mariana, placing her foot down lightly in the dark, smelly tunnel. The rusting pipe and gravel floor was covered with a thick coating of wet, green-tinted slime that had settled into stagnant pools at their feet. The slime was barely ankle-deep at first, but the farther they crossed into the tunnel the deeper it became.

Cautiously the band walked through the muck, often slipping, sometimes sliding, cursing beneath their breaths, and straining their eyes for some clearer path where they might find relief from this misery. But the dark ooze only deepened, encumbering them until they were virtually wading through it.

"Has this quagmire no end?" groaned Ramagar.

"At this rate it will take us a day to get out of here," grumbled the urchin.

"And where did all this stuff come from?" wondered the girl.

The stranger counseled their patience and then said no more.

As they sloshed their way in silence, torchlight pushed away some shadows, and Mariana recoiled in horror at the sight of a procession of rats sitting on the edges of the pipes above and along the ledges of the wall of rock. The rodents hardly stirred; their beady red eyes followed the intruders' every movement.

It was then that the stranger trampled something underfoot, something that crunched beneath the weight of his boot. He stopped, handed the torch to Mariana, and lowered his hands deep into the slime. He lifted out a large, round object, encased in jelly-like muck.

"What is it?" panted the girl.

The stranger began to wipe away the jelly, bit by bit until there was no longer any doubt. It was a skull—a human skull.

Mariana gasped. The gaping black sockets where eyes had once lodged stared at her, and the death mask seemed to be grinning.

"I wonder who he might have been," said Ramagar, huddling close to Mariana and inspecting the skull.

"Probably someone who got lost and couldn't find his way out," replied the stranger. "He must have starved to death—then the rats took over."

"Poor fellow," lamented the thief. "I wonder how many others might have shared his fate?" Then with a sigh he dropped the skull back into the slime. It plopped, splashing dully, and sank limply back to the bottom.

Mariana shivered. She gave the torch back, saying, "Let's get away from here as quick as we can."

And more grim than ever, the tiny band continued on.

Soon the awful slime became more shallow, and some of the nauseating stench disappeared. They were still wading, but now in water. Overhead pipes dripped a steady trickle of raw sewage; it poured down the walls where tiny wingless insects fed hungrily on the filth. The shaft widened, descended sharply. Mariana felt her ears begin to plug, then crackle.

"It's only the pressure," assured the stranger. "We're directly under the river. Five minutes more and we'll be on the other side."

It was cold under the river; colder than Mariana could ever recall being. Her teeth were chattering, her lips turning blue. Sensation in her fingertips had dulled, and her legs had become numb so long ago she no longer even bothered to think about them.

Suddenly the water was draining; running off into downward catchbasins at the side of the wall. It gurgled and gushed in whirlpools, receding blissfully until the pebbly earth could be seen again, sparkling wet rocks shimmering in the light.

The stranger wiped his cold nose and mouth with his hand, turned back to his companions, and grinned. "We did it. We're across."

"Thank the heavens for that," mumbled Ramagar, flexing his fingers and bringing them back to life. "Then the worst is over."

"Not quite, master thief. True, we're on the other side, but it's still a long way to go until we see the sky again. But come, beyond the next tunnel there's another cavern, a small one, but with a stream of fresh water."

Mariana's face brightened noticeably. "Water? Pure water? To drink and to wash in?" She glanced down at her tunic; it was smeared with a filmy residue of green slime. Her only consolation was that her companions' clothes had not fared any better.

The urchin picked up one foot and groaned. "There's something bothering me," he said. "Something digging at me . . ."

The stranger's eyes fired darkly. "Quick! Take off that boot!"

The boy seemed startled. "But why? What's—"

"Just do as I say! Now!"

The urchin sat precariously against the rocks and winced as Ramagar and the stranger cut the leather and slid the boot off. Blood was trickling along the instep, up near the ankle. The entire foot was discolored and swollen—filled with oblong black blotches that were moving; slowly pulsating and digging into tender skin. The boy stared at them and screamed, "They're alive!"

"Leeches!" cried Mariana. "He's stepped into a nest of them!"

"Quick," shouted the thief, bolting to the stricken lad's side, "bring over the torch!"

The urchin gritted his teeth and moaned as the hot flame singed both a leech and his flesh. The stranger grasped the wriggling worm and tore it off, hurling it back toward the river tunnel. Then Ramagar put the flame close again and the boy writhed with pain. A second bloodsucker was pulled off, then a third, and a forth, all thrown back into the dark.

"Now the other boot," said Ramagar, tensely wiping sweat from his brow. Mariana took his dagger and cut the seam with a single stroke. The soggy, worn boot dangled, then fell. Mariana looked and reeled back in revulsion. The foot was covered with them, creeping, crawling, sinking their teeth into soft flesh all the way up to his calf.

"Filthy parasites," rasped Ramagar.

The urchin whimpered with the next sting of heat, and then in panic at the sight of the leeches running farther up his body, tried to get up and run. The stranger restrained him, but only briefly. In his wild desperation the boy shook him loose and pushed him to the ground. Screaming, he flayed his arms and tried to run back to the tunnel. Ramagar quickly dropped the torch, drew back a powerful fist, and let it crack against the urchin's jaw. The boy reeled and slammed back against the stone wall, banging his head, then slowly sliding to the floor in a crumpled heap.

"We've got to get them off fast," cried the stranger, picking himself up. "Otherwise they'll work their poison throughout his body."

Mariana cradled the urchin's head while the others went to work. She put her hand to his forehead and gasped. He was

94

burning up, wracked with fever, his eyes half-opened and rolling deliriously.

"Can we still save him?" she asked, frightened.

The stranger moved his head from side to side, biting his lip. "We might—if we're in time. I know something of the healing arts, just enough to save him, I think. But then he'll need herbs, medicinal brews to nourish him . . ."

"We'll worry about that later," said Ramagar, holding up a squirming leech between his thumb and forefinger and examining it before tossing it away.

One by one they pulled the leeches from his leg. They tore open his shirt, found another already beginning to feed on his soft belly; found yet another inching its way from his back toward his neck. The boy's tormented body was riddled with wounds, some of them oozing pus as well as blood.

Ramagar unsnapped his cloak and wrapped it around the boy like a blanket. "We need to clean those wounds," he said, lifting the urchin up and carrying him with both arms. "How far to that fresh water you spoke about?"

"Only a few minutes, if we run."

The thief of Kalimar shifted his burden and nodded. Mariana held up the torch. "Then we run," he said. "And pray we can save his life."

Swiftly they passed through a high, weed-infested channel. But the ground was dry and level and before they knew it they had come to the cavern. Ramagar spread his cloak beside the clean water and rested the urchin upon it. With nothing but rags, the three travelers cleaned the wounds thoroughly and tended to his needs before taking a well-deserved rest for themselves.

Mariana and Ramagar quenched their thirst greedily, savoring the clear, cold water, then falling exhausted when they had done. The stranger, though, had yet to drink a sip. He placed himself next to the boy and sat motionless, his head hung low against his breast and his arms hanging loosely at his sides.

Ramagar closed his eyes and fell into a light peaceful sleep. Mariana sat up, leaning against a wall, and watched the stranger as he held the boy's hand and soothed his brow. She was deeply touched by his devotion.

"The boy means a great deal to you, doesn't he?" she said quietly.

The stranger raised his head and looked at her with saddened, tired eyes. Eyes that told her they had seen much in the world, and now were truly wearied.

"Yes, the lad does mean a great deal to me," he said. "In all my long and lonely days in Kalimar only this boy, this hapless urchin, cared enough for a stranger to help him in his plight. He showed me where to hide, shared his blanket when we slept. Once, he even gave to me a crust of bread."

"A crust of bread isn't very much . . ."

"No, perhaps not. But it was everything he owned."

Mariana turned away her gaze and felt a lump rise in her throat.

"It's odd, though," he continued. "We shared so much together these last days. I don't even know his name."

"He has no name," said the girl. "No street urchin does. They have no mothers, they have no fathers. No homes, no friends—"

"But surely even a penniless boy has a name?"

Mariana smiled bitterly. "You *are* foreign to this city, aren't you? There are thousands like him. They live, they hide among shadows, they beg and they steal. And they die. No one knows who they are. No one cares very much. They are faceless children, unwanted and unloved. Vagabonds, wastrels, urchins—all without names." Mariana sniffed as she finished and the stranger noticed the welling tears in the corners of her eyes. He smiled warmly.

"Then we shall have to remedy this unjust situation by ourselves," he said, offering a bit of cheer into their shared gloom. "We'll give the lad a name of our own choosing. But it will have to be something the boy will like . . ."

Mariana dried her eyes and, looking at the boy, forced a tiny smile of her own. "You are kind, stranger. He will like that. And he will be proud."

"And so shall his name be proud! But what shall we call him? Let me think . . ."

He slitted his ice-blue eyes and ran a hand along his stubbled chin, lost in deep thought. Then he looked at Mariana and grinned. "I have it!" he cried, snapping his fingers. "A good name. A fine name. Noble and exalted. One worthy of his character. We shall call him: Homer. In my own land it means 'the Wanderer' . . ."

Mariana rolled the word over her tongue. Homer. *Homer.* Yes, it was a very fine name. Her eyes sparkled with approval. "I like it. It fits him well. You have chosen wisely."

The stranger beamed, his features growing boyish. Just

hen, the boy began to stir and they both flew to his side. Mariana put her lips to his forehead and laughed. "The fever is breaking," she said gleefully. "See for yourself!"

And the boy opened his eyes, staring up at the pensive faces. Recognition flickered in his eyes. "What happened?" he whispered. "I can't remember a thing . . ." He put his hand to his bruised jaw and winced with the sting.

"You've been ill," said the stranger, tightening Ramagar's cloak around him. "But soon you'll be well. How do you feel?"

"Thirsty . . ."

Mariana laughed and drew some water. The stranger sighed a deep sigh of relief. The poisons had not entered his bloodstream after all. The boy would live. Homer would live.

"Sleep for a while," he said to the boy. "We're all exhausted and need some rest. And don't fret; the worst of our journey is done. Now we begin the ascent to the surface. In a half day's time we'll see the sun."

Mariana glowed with the thought. The sun! Warm, gentle. Trees, grass, and birds. Flowing streams where she could bathe. A real bath. Perhaps she could find some soap, and she could scrub herself until her skin glowed and tingled. Wash her clothes spanking clean and forget the horrors of this dreaded sewer forever. It was a wonderful thought. She sighed with pleasure and closed her eyes. And when she fell asleep she dreamed only of the new life she and Ramagar would soon be able to lead.

The harsh wind howled and whipped its way down to the bottom of the shaft. The torch had long extinguished and the travelers were forced to climb the tunnel in darkness, stumbling step by step, stretching their hands to the walls for orientation. Soon, though, the fissures above began to show needle-thin beams of light. Not very much, but enough to guide the way and lift their spirits by assuring them their ordeal was near an end. The wind was cold; its fury fueled their desire to move faster even as it bit through their flimsy cloaks and nibbled away at their tender flesh.

Hungry and aching, they pressed on, following the increasingly narrow pipes, breath labored as the incline steepened and steepened again. Then they took a turn from the frigid tunnel, thankful to be well away from the wind, but only to find themselves in a new black passage every bit as dismal and despairing as any they had seen before.

97

"What happened to the light?" gulped Homer, shivering and gazing about into the void.

"Are we lost?" asked Mariana.

The stranger put his hand to the wall and felt the smooth, almost uncorroded iron. "Have no fear, my friends," he said. "We are walking within a pipe; the last channel of our journey." He rapped a knuckle loudly against the metal and it clanged dully. "Beyond this channel lies the doorway to freedom."

"But how will we find the way?" wondered Ramagar, his booming voice dimly echoing all the way back to the bitter shaft.

"We'll feel our way," replied the stranger. "Just follow me. Each one will hold onto the cloak of his companion in front. This way we'll be sure that we are together at all times."

Everybody did as asked and took hold. The stranger led the way, Ramagar grasping his cloak tightly and feeling Mariana clutch even more tightly to him, and Homer bringing up the rear, one hand placed firmly on the dancing girl's loose tunic.

Upward, ever upward, the huge pipe took them. And then a fringe of pale light glimmered fleetingly far ahead. They hurried on to reach it, knowing it to be the door, the massive stone exit that would bring them to the surface at last.

Both the stranger and Ramagar set their shoulders against the awesome slab, and with a mighty heave they pushed it ajar. Bright morning sunlight blinded them all. Like children they groped their way through the narrow opening and fell in heaps upon a field of tall grass. They basked under the sky shuddering at the memory of hours past, and shared in joyous mirth the sight of Kalimar's high walls shimmering in the distance beneath fast-rolling clouds.

Mariana closed her eyes and said a silent prayer. Ramagar stood up, hands on hips, his face encrusted with grime. His eyes stared harrowingly past the field and to the open parched lands that stretched as far as the faded mountains rippling up and down the edge of the horizon. And he smiled.

"Your word was well kept, stranger," he said, offering his hand.

The youthful beggar rose and took it. His gaze fixed on the thief, he grinned. "My part of the bargain is complete."

"And so it is." Ramagar looked to Mariana, and the girl took out the golden scimitar from beneath her tunic. Th stranger's eyes stared at the glistening blade, its jewel-studded scabbard. He took it greedily, thankfully, and pressed it firmly against his breast.

"At last," he sighed, tears coming to his eyes. "I've regained you at last. Now we may begin anew." He fondled his prize like a lover and placed it carefully beneath his soiled, bedraggled shirt. "You have both been good companions and friends," he said at length to the thief and the dancing girl. "Now, though, I fear it is time for me to depart. I have wasted far too much time in Kalimar, I can waste no more." He walked to Mariana, lifted the startled girl's hand, and kissed it. "Walk in heaven's light, my lady," he said. "Your loveliness will be a fond memory to me forever."

Mariana was left breathless. A lady. He had called her a lady. It was the first time in her life anyone had ever spoken to her in such a fashion and she did not know how to respond.

"Must you leave so soon?" said an equally perplexed Ramagar.

"Alas, yes, master thief. My road is longer than your own. Each day only adds to the burden."

"You've never told us the purpose of your quest," said Mariana, glad that the journey was done, but saddened that they would be parting so soon after completing it.

The stranger tilted his head and searched the skies. He caught sight of a great bird rising higher and higher against the sun, then abruptly turning and gliding beak first back toward the earth. "My quest will take me farther than the swiftest bird can ever hope to fly," he told her wistfully, sounding as mysterious as ever. "A task awaits me that can no longer be shunned. A people cry out in their desperation for help where there is none. Only Darkness. Eternal Darkness. On my shoulders must this burden be carried. The weight is heavy, but I must bear it no matter what . . ."

Homer slipped beside his friend and looked at him with reverent eyes. "And I shall follow the stranger," he said, pride unmistakable in his voice. "We agreed upon it since even before we joined forces to flee Kalimar. Whatever the road he must walk, whatever peril he must overcome, whatever pain he must endure, I shall willingly share it."

The stranger's eyes brightened and he clasped the boy around the shoulder. Mariana exchanged a quick glance with Ramagar. The thief frowned briefly and sighed. "Mariana and I have no set destination," he said truthfully. "And like

99

yourself, we seek to cross Kalimar's borders as quickly as possible. You have answered our questions only with riddles, but I for one would be pleased if we could share company, at least until our paths are forced to part. What say you, stranger? Would you be pleased to let us share your journey for a time?"

"It is good to have companions you can trust," reminded the girl. "We know nothing of the dangers you say you must face, but I do know that you saved Ramagar's life, and brought happiness back into my own. Now, perhaps we can help you . . ."

The stranger's face glowed. "It is good to have companions, as you said. But it is even better to have friends. Thank you both. I will be grateful to have you with me for a time. I have traveled alone for so long that sometimes I've forgotten the pleasure of another voice."

Ramagar laughed loudly. "Not to mention another pair of strong hands. I'll wager we'll have need of both."

This time when they shook hands it was firmer than before. "Agreed," said the stranger. "We have struck another bargain. We'll travel together and share all we have."

"Good," said the thief. "Now which way do we go?"

The yellow-haired beggar pushed back his hair and straightened. His eyes fixed on something far in the distance. "First we go north, then to the river. And then to the sea."

Mariana tingled with excitement. The sea! What girl of the Jandari had ever dared dream that someday she would see the sea?

"But there's a long way to go before even the river comes back into sight," said the thief. "And we'll only grow hungrier and more weary if we stay here and chat. Lead on, my beggar friend. Our journey begins again."

And laughing, filled with gladdened hearts, the small band set off toward the mountains, thinking only of a new and brighter future. It had been a strange set of circumstances that had brought these four together and made them companions—and even stranger circumstances that had brought them to share their lives. A thief, a dancing girl, a child of the streets, and a most unusual beggar. If they had thought that their adventure was past, they were badly misled. If anything, their odyssey had just begun.

II

The Beggar Prince

9

The tents of haj Burlu the swineherd were set at the base of the scrub hills, beyond the dunes, some twenty leagues from the great walls of Kalimar. And there, on this windswept night, when the sand swirled over the plain and across the parched ridges, he sat by himself merrily waiting for the pot of stew to boil.

An ox of a man, thick-necked and broad-shouldered, with a short fiery red beard now flecked with gray, he lazed back against the worn and patched cushions and sniffed with satisfaction at the spicy aroma swelling his nostrils.

It was good to be inside on such a night, he told himself. Let others chase sheep and cajole cows from their grazing. He would spend his time more productively; practicing his culinary skills and reaping the rewards when the meal was done. Burlu was proud of his cooking ability, even if other hajeen on occasion teased him for it. Cooking was woman's work, and even more so for a haj. Burlu, of course, scoffed at this foolish banter. Besides, his only serving girl was hardly worthy of handling his kitchen; he was not about to ruin his stomach any further.

He dunked the ladle into the pot and tasted. A wide grin broke over his cracked lips; it was a meal worthy of any haj. Indeed of a king, he chuckled silently. A shame that on this night there was no one to share it with.

He filled the wooden bowl to the brim, placed it carefully down on the mat beside the pitcher of honeyed wine, and cross-legged, began to eat. Empty cushions stared back across the tent. He glanced at the gold-threaded rug, the one his wife had painstakenly woven over so many years, and heaved a long sigh. He missed the woman, missed her more with every passing year. It was cruel for her to have been taken from him long years before her time. They should have aged together, slowly and gracefully, the way they had intended. Her death after only seven years of marriage had been a terrible blow. Yet Burlu was a religious man, as were all the people of these lands, and never once did he question the will of heaven.

Five children had come from this union. Five beautiful

103

children. Three sons, two daughters. For a long time haj Burlu's tents were blessed with their laughter and happiness. But even that had changed. One son, headstrong like his mother, had long ago left his home. To sail the seas, he said. To discover strange lands of mystery and wealth and one day return a hero. Burlu had ranted and raved but to no avail. His son was gone. The second son was a more practical man. He left home for the city, to seek a young man's fortune and fame. The third son, ah, he had been the favorite. Burlu's heart had never sunk to lower depths than when the local hajeen, their faces long and low, came to tell him that his son had been killed during the hunt. The old haj had wept and wailed; but as always, he never questioned. Three sons. And now there were none.

As for his daughters, well, that was a different matter. They had taken fine husbands and left his tents forever. It was only on the days he saw his grandchildren that his old heart again knew joy. Still, though, Burlu the haj, the beloved swineherd of the hills, lived alone. Yet as long as he had sheep and swine to be tended, fresh game to hunt on the scrub plains, he would consider himself a lucky man.

He ate slowly, savoring the lamb and the hot vegetables, washing the food down with wine. So lost was he with his meal that he almost did not hear the yapping of his dogs. He put down his spoon and listened, hushing the serving girl, who came running into the tent, panting that something was amiss.

The haj rose, his fine long robe flowing. Screwing his dark eyes, he pushed back the flap of the tent and stepped out into the night. Dust and sand swirled before him and obliterated his vision. The dogs were carrying on in a frenzy, running in broad circles all the way down to the edge of the horse path.

There must be a wild animal about, he reasoned. Some hungry beast on the prowl, possibly come down from the hills. A bear, perhaps. And his sheep and swine, not to mention his goats or chickens, would make fine prey. With his hand at the hilt of his hunting knife, he cautiously crossed the hard ground toward the road. The wind was against him and he had to struggle forward, using the broad side of his arm to cover his eyes.

The dogs were all around him, jumping, snapping, howling at the top of their lungs. Burlu strained to see. There were dark figures on the path, and again he pressed forward for a better look. It was with surprise that he realized they were men, and not lurking beasts as he had suspected. Still, what were they doing on the road? A night such as this was certainly not meant for traveling. And if they *were* travelers, where were their horses? Few travelers ever came along this out-of-the-way path, he knew, but those that did were always mounted. To travel any other way, especially at night, was foolhardy to say the least.

Puzzled, the lumbering haj, old in years but as keen and as powerful as ever, approached. He pushed away the shock of silver-red hair blowing in front of his eyes and called out, "Who goes by my tents?" He drew his knife from the scabbard and clutched it tightly. The haj was anything but a violent man, but these were mistrustful times in the world and no man could be too careful.

"Please, farmer," came a harried voice, broken by the wind. "Call off your dogs. We mean no harm—"

The haj squinted, his hand to his eyes. The images were at last coming into a sharper focus and he could make out their garb. These people, whoever they were, certainly were not farmers. Nor were they neighbors.

"What do you want here?"

One of the travelers, using his cloak to shield his face, approached the haj with his head lowered respectfully. He folded his hands before him, to show he was unarmed. Two great black dogs were yapping at his feet.

"We are travelers from Kalimar, good haj," said Ramagar, "and have been caught in the storm. We would ask your hospitality, if you will, just until the morrow . . ."

"From Kalimar, is it?" said Burlu, rubbing his beard and thinking of his second son somewhere in the capital city. "Where are your horses?"

"We have none, haj. Nor mules, nor camels. We have walked—"

"Walked?" Burlu was incredulous. He looked at the stranger's boots, badly worn and riddled with pebble-pierced holes.

Ramagar nodded, his eyes now shut and tearing from the sand. "Three days we've been on our journey, but until today we had little difficulty. We are weary and hungry, haj. But we do not beg. True, we have no money, but we will be more than willing to work for whatever you would give. Your stable will be more than adequate for us to sleep . . ."

Burlu was so astounded at what he had heard that he almost forgot his good manners. "Please," he said, gesturing toward the tents, "come inside. You are more than welcome to share what I have."

"There are four of us, haj. We mean no imposition . . ."

"Whatever the number, you are welcome. Now hurry. The wind will only rise and grow colder. Call your companions and tell them to follow. Supper is ready, and after it we can talk."

The haj's tents were more than inviting. One by one the bone-weary farers lowered their heads at the entrance and came inside. They looked on in wonder at the heavily piled rugs scattered over the floor, the thick, soft cushions placed in a semicircle around the stone cooking fire. Drapes and tapestries hung from the tent's walls, soft fabric, translucent and dyed in bright colors. Mariana looked about, dazzled.

Burlu seated himself upon his carmine cushion and bid his guests to take places of their own. He sat back smiling as the serving girl brought bowls and chalices, placing them beside each of the fatigued travelers.

Ramagar dipped a piece of fresh bread into his bowl and took a bite. "Your food is delicious," he said to the pleased haj. "Your serving girl is a marvelous cook."

"Quite so, quite so," added the yellow-haired beggar. He swallowed a mouthful and washed it down with wine. "I have been many places, eaten the most exotic cuisines, but your own surpasses them all."

The haj thanked them politely, making no reference to who the cook really was. Naturally he had many questions to ask of these visitors from Kalimar, but doing so now would be most rude, most unworthy of a good host. He knew he would have to still his curiosity a little while longer. Not that he minded, though. The night was young.

Mariana was the first to finish. Declining a second helping, she let her gaze absorb the tent with a single sweep. The corner of the tent was filled with artifacts: small vases of blasted stone and polished marble; tiny hand-carved figurines of rare woods; hanging desert tapestries depicting windblown panoramas and blazing mountain suns. She was not sure that their host was a man of wealth, but he was certainly a man of good taste.

Burlu, noting the young girl's interest, said, "I am but a small collector of these things. But tell me, are you a lover of such art?"

Mariana smiled meekly. "Merely an admirer, haj," she told

106

him, lowering her eyes respectfully. "I have always enjoyed objects of beauty."

Burlu toyed with his emerald ring and nodded with understanding. And it was then that he began to take closer note of her. Strange, he mused, but in many ways—ways he could not name—she reminded him strongly of his beloved wife. And he became curious as to why this beautiful girl traveled the long journey from Kalimar.

The lamb stew finished at last, the serving girl withdrew the bowls and quickly replaced them with plates filled with varieties of fruit and dried nuts. Another pitcher of honeyed wine was soon to follow and the serving girl took great pains to fill every chalice to the brim.

Ramagar sat back contentedly, rubbing his full belly and feeling his head lightly swimming from the strong, sweet brew. "How can we ever repay you for this kindness, haj?" he said. "These past days my companions and I have eaten little but wild berries and plants, save, of course, for the occasional hare we managed to trap. By no means were we prepared for such a magnificent feast as you have laid before us."

Burlu bowed his head with respectful acknowledgment to his well-spoken guest. "My fare is simple, my friends, but I am always glad to share it with visitors. But perhaps you are yet hungry? Shall I have my serving girl prepare—"

"No, no," laughed Ramagar. "We have had more than enough. And your kindness shall not be forgotten."

"Then you must all be my guests for supper tomorrow. I promise you the best my hospitality can offer."

"You are most gracious, haj," said the stranger in response. "But alas, for myself at least, I cannot accept." Burlu furrowed his brows with obvious disappointment; it was good sharing his meals with pleasant company, and indeed he had been looking forward to having his guests stay at least for another day.

"But why, my friends?" he asked. "Surely after such a long journey you need rest . . ."

The stranger's resolve was firm. "Forgive me, haj, but I must be on my way no later than sunrise. Your tents are as warm a home as I have ever known, and had circumstances been different I would have liked to stay for as long as you will." Here his face grew dark and sad, and he sighed. "But my business is too important, too urgent, to delay."

"Ah, then I am sorry. But you will spend the night?"

107

"Thank you, yes."

By this time the haj's curiosity was more than fired. Most travelers on the road from the city would have been more than eager to while away a few comfortable days before continuing on. Especially at this time of year when the weather posed a greater hazard than any band of roving bandits ever could. His guests tonight, though, at least the yellow-haired foreigner, seemed not to be bothered by any of these dangers. And Burlu began to wonder just what their mission of such importance really was.

Now, being a hill man, and a haj to boot, Burlu knew it would be considered too rude to ask outright. A man's affairs, the hill folk believed, were strictly his own. Host or no, even a haj would be displaying the poorest of manners if he were to ask.

Burlu considered this as he sipped at his chalice and tugged gently at his earlobe. "And this journey of yours," he said very casually, feeling that a little prodding might answer all his questions without his having to ask them, "has it already taken you far?"

Outside, the wind was rising, blowing harder than before. The serving girl hastily ran to secure the flapping curtains at the entrance. The stranger held his cup and gazed into the dark honeyed wine. "My companions have only joined me since Kalimar," he said. "But as for myself, I have been seeking my destination for half a lifetime."

"Half a lifetime?" mimicked the haj with astonishment. In his own surprise he didn't notice that his other guests were equally astounded. "It must be a very long journey, friend, to have lasted so many years . . ."

"Longer than you can imagine, haj. Longer than any of you can imagine. Almost from one end of the world to the other. But now," here he sighed, "the glimpse of the end is all but in sight. And I am most eager for its conclusion, come what may."

Something in his last words caused Mariana to shiver. Suddenly she felt very cold; almost as cold as when they crossed the sewers, even though the haj's fire was still burning brightly. "What lies at the end of your road, stranger?" she asked with trepidation.

Looking into each of their faces in turn, he said, "Perhaps glory, perhaps death. Either way, I must do what I must do."

Burlu gulped down his wine and refilled the chalice. He had met enough travelers and wanderers in his years to know the makings of a good tale when he saw it. He clapped his hands and called for another pitcher. The night was barely begun, and he knew there was nothing in the world better than sweet honeyed wine to loosen even the most reluctant tongue.

Ramagar stirred, saying, "You once told us your intent to cross the sea. Is that where your quest will finish?"

"There, and beyond."

Beyond? Beyond the great sea? thought haj Burlu. He nervously twirled his emerald finger ring and listened with growing interest. The evening was becoming more entertaining by the moment.

"And what, if I might inquire, do you know of what is beyond?" he asked, twisting his body so as to fully face his yellow-haired guest. "You are a man of the north, are you not? Your golden hair and fair complexion tell me as much. And by your dress, and you admit you are not a mariner."

"I know more than you give me credit for," came the reply.

"Ah," said the haj thoughtfully, "then are you a scholar? Our ships have sailed all the seas for countless centuries. And our sailors have been to every shore from one end of the world to the other. They speak only of desolate lands to be found, many ice bound, others swamp and jungle, inhabited mainly by fearsome beasts and often terrible savages. Tell me, is this not so?"

The stranger took a small swallow from his chalice and said, "These sailors are wrong."

Burlu smiled thinly, one eyebrow raised slightly higher than the other. "So, you claim to speak with more knowledge than they?"

All became very quiet as the stranger pondered his answer. Apart from the wind, shrieking like a chorus, there was not a sound to be heard. "Have you never heard the legends of the Lost Empire? Or the Golden Isles?"

"All these and more," said the haj with a frown. "They are fanciful tales, to be sure. And had I a sheep or a goat or even a swine for every such tale I have heard I would be a very rich man. Men have quested for these places since the dawn of time. But to me they are wishful dreams and nothing more."

The stranger sat straighter and looked his host squarely in the eye. "There are tales, and then there are tales, good haj. Some, such as those I have mentioned, are spun merely for

109

children and the gullible, while others that have been passed from generation to generation reflect only truth." His eyes narrowed piercingly and the haj blinked. "Some may call them fanciful, while others know better . . ."

Burlu ran his tongue over lips that were becoming dry despite the wine. "And do . . . you . . . spin such tales?" he asked.

The cooking fire had dimmed, a few last embers crackling softly, glowing in tones of amber and orange. Dull shadows cascaded across the walls and ceiling of the tent. The stranger's face was covered by these shadows, and he looked to his companions one by one. "There is only one tale that I tell, good friends," he said in a voice so low that all had to strain their ears to hear. "It is not a myth or a legend, but the story of a people whose civilization even to this very day has never been rivaled. A people whose beautiful land was the fairest and most bountiful that the world has known . . ."

Ramagar leaned forward uneasily, holding his empty cup with both hands. "What land is this that you speak of?" he said.

Mariana felt her heart thump madly; she could think only of the golden scimitar and the strange runes inscribed on the scabbard. Runes that bore the markings of a land long lost.

"Have any of you," said the stranger, "ever heard of the Specian Kingdoms?"

A strong gust of wind forced itself past the flaps and whipped across the tent, startling them all except the stranger.

"I have heard something of the legend," said the haj slowly. "It was said to be a mighty land; powerful, yet peace-loving. Wise men say it vanished from the face of the world centuries ago."

"Not vanished, good friends. But enshrouded in Darkness. Eternal Darkness, so that other men can never find it and set it free."

Mariana shuddered. "Are you saying that Speca yet flourishes?"

The stranger's eyes burned with dark, smoldering fires. "Not flourishes, but yet exists. Crying out in whispers to be freed. Their voices carry across the sea, across the deserts. My dreams are filled with these cries, terrible nightmares that haunt me and will not let me rest until my quest is done."

The haj looked quickly to Ramagar, then to the girl. He wondered if his third guest had drunk too much honeyed wine or was demented.

"These things you say," said the haj, "make little sense. Would you have us believe that your journey is to reach this fabled land?"

"Yes—and to regain it."

"Regain it?" The haj was stunned beyond words. Ramagar listened incredulously, unsure if the wine had not altered his own senses as well. Only Mariana listened with calm and understanding, while even faithful Homer looked at his friend with uncertain disbelief.

The mysterious stranger smiled briefly and then sighed. "I know you think me mad," he told them wearily. "And I suppose I can't blame you for it. Whenever I have told my story my listeners have considered me to be a raving lunatic. Once I was nearly dragged to an asylum for speaking these matters. They tried to bind me in chains and lock me away forever." He began to rise. "Perhaps it would be best if I left you all now." He looked at his host, head lowered in respect. "I thank you, haj, for all you have done. All I ask is that you do not allow your views of me to reflect upon my companions. They are honest folk, kind and gentle. They know nothing of me or my task."

Burlu raised his hands, palms up. "Please, do not leave. Stay with us as you intended. And tell us your tale from the beginning. Then maybe we can all understand."

Mariana reached out and took the stranger's hand, gently pulling him back toward his place. "The haj is right," she said. "Tell the full story. We will not laugh, nor call you insane."

The stranger glanced at his companions with surprise. "You will listen?" he asked. "Hear all I have to say?"

"Every word," said Burlu, gesturing for him to sit. He called for another pitcher of wine, and everyone sat quietly while the serving girl refilled the goblets.

And then the stranger began. "The kingdom of which I speak was like no other. Lofty and amazing were its cities; fashioned of stone and polished marbles and fine woods. Its temples and palaces were splendorous, its kings and princes benevolent. The people tilled their soil and knew no hunger. Its craftsmen and merchants traded the finest handicrafts and art, while its engineers constructed a network of roads and dams that have never been surpassed. Specian mariners sailed the oceans upon vessels swift and sturdy, too numerous to count. Their goods were eagerly received at ports of every continent, including your own. Science, above all, flourished

111

as nowhere else. There was hardly a sickness in the world that its physicians did not have herbs to remedy. Proud and noble, Specian men were handsome and the women beautiful. For twenty centuries and more they knew only peace . . ."

"It must have been a wondrous land," sighed Mariana.

"And it was—until the Dark came and overshadowed all, turning a dignified people into cowering wretches forever watching the black sky and waiting for the sun to return."

The haj felt the palms of his hands dampen. "What disaster befell them so?" he asked. "Was it a plague of locusts? Perhaps terrible drought?"

"Alas, it was none of these things—nor any other that your mind would conceive. Sadly, their fate was far, far the worse; for at least drought and plague know an end, the plight of Speca does not."

He paused here to let his words be grasped, and then with a sigh he drew the scimitar from his cloak and turned his gaze to it. The jewels seemed to brighten and glow as his eyes became murky and dark. And he stared, stared deeply into the tiny baubles as his tale began to unfold.

"It was on a grim and starless night that the ship came upon Speca's golden shores. A strange ship, flying a black velvet flag with no marker or seal. Its great crimson sail swelled as if with wind, although that night was calm and there was none. Carved into the sprithead was the image of a dragon's head, terrible and fearsome. Jewels had been set for eyes; dark rubies that glowed malevolently. And upon its head were horns, great, twisting hulks of bone or ivory carved with ominous runes. The mouth of the beast spit fire. Yes, true fire; although what powers or trickery were used to summon it I cannot say. The sailors were broad, grim men. Hairy and savage. And as they slipped into our harbor they sang a low, rumbling chant in a tongue no man or woman in Speca had ever heard even though many of her citizens had traveled far and wide across the world.

"Needless to say there was great unease in Speca. The barbarians stepped upon our land and in a mighty procession marched toward the gates of the palace itself. In the lead, wearing a black cape and a crown of skull, came a shaman. A sorcerer, a wizard. Few could bring themselves to gaze upon his cruel face, and those who did watched speechlessly and breathless. Soldiers, even captains well renowned for their courage, trembled at the sight of him. And the shaman

112

laughed, mocking and scorning them, and demanding to see the famed Specian king.

"The message he brought was a fearful one: war and destruction would ravish their fair land, he said, if his own king's terms for immediate surrender were not met at once. The Specian king and his advisers were knowledgeable men, not easily given to fear of things they did not fully understand. In Speca, as in many other lands, magicians abounded. Their tricks, though, were harmless; mainly employed for carnivals and feasts or the amusement of children. The king believed that this man, as fearsome as he seemed, was no more powerful than these others. Average citizens might perhaps be awed by his presence, but he was not.

"So the king laughed in the shaman's face. 'Do you take us for idiots that we would hand over our kingdom because of your threats?' he scorned. 'Do what wizardry you will. Speca stands firm. Now begone while your head still sits upon your shoulders.'

"The wizard held his ground, spitting foul oaths and daring the Specian king with his contempt. 'Laugh not,' he warned, lest your land and your people suffer for it.' The king was inflamed. He rose to his full height and ridiculed the man, calling him a clown. To this the shaman made no reply; he turned with his companions, his black robes flowing, and strode quickly from the room. 'You have been warned,' he shouted. And then he was gone, leading his procession back to the ship. Word of the king's bravery spread through the city. Where before there had been fear now there was none. The citizens harangued the shaman, taunting him amid great hilarity. Speca was resolute. The people would neither cower nor bow either to him or to any other would-be conqueror. And rightly so; for Speca was indeed the mightiest nation on the earth. A hundred warships would be built if need be. A thousand. With her science and her great knowledge she would repulse any who dared threaten her shores. Yes, even the mightiest of wizards could not make her falter.

"So it was that the ship set sail and left. And for fully a month thereafter life in the Golden Kingdom and all its domains carried on as peacefully and serenely as ever before. The incident was fully forgotten. But then, one dismal rainy morn at the outset of winter came the storm. And what a terrible storm it was! The sea itself seemed to rise up against us as never before, swelling and rolling with such force that the seawalls, holding fast and sturdy for ten centuries, now began

113

to crumble. And then they broke, the sea lashing out in fury and washing over the land. Rivers flooded high beyond their banks, dams burst, whole villages and valleys washed away before all eyes. It was horrendous; all of Speca's princes, all of her generals, all of her engineers and scientists looked on in frightful wonder. For seventy-seven full days and seventy-seven full nights the land suffered beneath a constant barrage until only despair and gloom filled every heart. Even her sages and her finest scientists were unable to find a solution to remedy the havoc that raged like a demon from one end of the land to the other.

"On the seventy-eighth day the waters began to recede. Losing no time, the king ordered his ministers and his soldiers to set to the awesome task of reclaiming the land. But so much had been lost, it seemed a hopeless task. Yet Speca remained determined. It was that very morning, while the people came out of their homes and gasped at the destruction, that the king himself was urgently summoned by his aides to come to the highest tower of the palace. From that lofty height they frantically bade him to look again upon the sea. It was as still as glass; not a ripple of a wave could be seen. But on the horizon, distant and dark, came a host of ships. Crimson-sailed ships of war, all flying the dreaded black flags of the wizard and his king, all groaning under the weight of catapults and other machines of war, all filled with hundreds of the swarthy, chanting barbarians.

"Above the Specian palace the sky was blue and clear, the sun brightly shining. Yet above the distant ships, moving with similar speed and with the same purpose, came an all-encompassing shroud of black clouds. Dense and low, they swirled in the conjured wind and slowly fanned out to cover the length and breadth of Speca. What magic had brought this, the king did not know; only that without question it was a result of the foulest sorcery he had ever seen. Ominously the clouds moved in, blotting out all sunlight, bringing with them a damp and cold that chilled the very bones.

"Still, the king rallied his loyal troops and managed to instill courage. Speca's brave sailors hastily mustered the pitiful remnants of her once proud fleets and prepared to meet the invading host head-on in battle. And soon the battle was joined. Each and every Specian fought with skill and valor, and although they were outnumbered in ships at least three to one they carried the fight so bravely that at every turn a new shattering blow was dealt to the enemy. Again, though, the
114

enemy called upon their black arts to aid them. And the sea itself became a terrible maelstrom, a frightening whirlpool that dragged each and every defending ship down into the black while the ships of the invaders remained unscathed.

"The Specian king watched these events aghast. Shouting for his ministers, he bade them draw all citizens into the city and to prepare for siege. Submission, even in this bleakest hour, was still unthinkable, the word 'defeat' never once even contemplated. All Specians agreed; they would rather fight to the last man than surrender and become slaves under the domination of this beastly host.

"When the enemy ships reached shore the barbarians lost no time in rampaging through the countryside, looting, stealing, and wantonly ravishing the precious little that was left. Fires raged freely, destroying what had been beautiful forests and fields, harvests and gardens. While above, the black clouds descended, settling slowly like a fog until at midday the sky was as black as on the darkest night. And the people knew that this Darkness would remain—remain until the vile host was wiped from the land.

"With no sources of food and the enemy in complete control of all the kingdom save for the walled city, the king and his followers waited helplessly. Starvation was quick to come—and with it the scourge of disease, new and strange ailments that left the physicians baffled and discouraged. Men, women, and children were dying each day by the score, then the hundreds. And so, after nearly a half year of valiantly resisting, the Specian king admitted to himself that his kingdom was lost. He wept bitterly; not for himself or his titles, but for his people, a people who had put all their trust and faith in his ability. Now, he had let them down. Speca had new masters. Vile, evil men, ruled for millennia by a line of deranged dwarf-kings and wizard advisers. For a century and more these men from a distant island had coveted the kingdom, plotting and scheming and practicing their nefarious magic until the skills were perfected. Now, Speca was theirs; her women defiled, turned into slaves and whores, her men shackled and put under the yoke as if they were beasts of burden and nothing more.

"The brave and righteous king of Speca was imprisoned in a high tower and there forced to watch while members of his own family were humiliated and tortured before his eyes. One night, unable to live with his agony, he flung himself to his death—to the amusement of his Dwarf-king advisory,

115

who ordered his corpse left near the desert lands where the carrion could feast on his flesh. And then, one by one, the many members of Speca's large royal family were themselves put to death."

The stranger paused, tears welling at the corner of his eyes, and with a hand that was shaking with emotion put his chalice to his lips.

Mariana lifted herself from her shocked silence. The story had affected her deeply, as it had the others. Face paled, voice a whisper, she said, "And did not a single member of the family somehow manage to escape such a dastardly fate?"

It was a cold thin smile that passed the stranger's lips. "Yes, incredibly so, two did escape. A young prince and princess, second cousins to each other. It was under the cloak of the everlasting accursed Darkness that somehow they were able to slip past their guards and flee the palace and the city. They hid within the fields for weeks, daring not even to breathe while the search for them covered the land. But Fate and Fortune accompanied them, it seems, and one day while the Dwarf-king held a religious celebration they caught horses and fled far inland to the borders of another land. And what a sight it was for them. How can I possibly explain? Where they stood, before a shallow river, the sky was black, the air cold and damp; while on the other side of the water, perhaps a hundred meters away, they saw sunlight, could feel the warmth of summer radiating, see birds fly and hear them sing. It was a stirring moment, I promise you. They waded across as fast as they could, and at last they were free. Only once did they look back, and when they did they shuddered. All to be seen was the night; and the gloom of their experiences tore at their hearts. They could never come back, they knew. Never again gaze upon peaceful Speca. With longing sighs and tears, they made their way to a new life. Crossing mountains they made friends with the hill tribes, who, although they feared the dreaded sorcery one day being brought down upon their own lands, agreed to help the two Specians find a new home.

"At a small fishing port they came upon a passing ship, a merchant vessel whose captain was a kind and good man. He took them aboard and the young couple sailed away across half the world before their journey at last came to an end."

"And . . . what became of them?" asked Ramagar sadly.

"They wed, found new lives for themselves, raised a family. The new land they had adopted was fair and peace-

116

ful, yet the refugees knew they could never know peace of their own. Not while Speca lay languid and spoiled under its cruel domination. The lovers, then, never forgot their home; nor did their children, nor even their children's children. Each succeeding generation was well schooled in the Specian fashion, and each felt the pangs of heartbreak with every passing day. For you see, these grandchildren were now the only true heirs to the Specian throne. And one day, no matter how long it would have to take, one of them would begin the quest to reclaim it."

The haj rocked back and forth quietly as he listened to and digested all that his guest had spoken. At length he drew a deep breath and let it out with a long sigh of sorrow. He looked deeply at the yellow-haired foreigner, and saw etched out before him strong and proud features shaded in the vague shadows of the tent, features that assured him that this man was neither vagabond nor beggar, no matter what the paltry cloth he wore might indicate. Burlu was clearly bewildered; he looked again at the man, considered the tale, and wondered just how his guest had gathered so many facts of lost Speca's fate.

"Your story has been most fascinating, my friend," he said at last. "Vivid and detailed, lacking in nothing. It is worthy of the finest storytellers I have ever heard on such an ill night as this. Truly it is a sad account of a terrible injustice to a people who deserved no such destiny. But tell me, can you— or any man—say with certainty that all of these events did indeed happen as you say? Or is it that the legend has been distorted by the long finger of time, as legends so often are?"

"An understandable question," replied the stranger thoughtfully. "Any intelligent man would be quick, as you were, to ask it. But, good haj, let me assure you all, all my friends here with me tonight, that each and every event of which I told is the absolute truth. There is no question as to the authenticity of my tale, and I am one to know. Yet let me whet your appetites a bit further; I say that not only is my tale true, but that even to this very day the Specian Kingdoms yet exist. They are not a dead ruin of what once was, but a thriving land waiting for a redeemer. And although it still lies dormant and miserable beneath the Eternal Darkness and the shackles of its conquerors, one day soon all will change. And Speca will again see the sun."

Burlu's wizened eyes opened saucer-wide and he lost no time in downing the dregs of wine.

"How do you know all these things you spoke of?" asked Mariana.

The answer was brief, but told of much—much yet to come. "I know these things," he told her, "because of who I am."

Mariana felt her sudden chills returning again. Sitting tensely, she rubbed at her bare arms. The next question was eagerly anticipated by her companions. "And who is that?"

The stranger raised his hands and opened them to reveal the precious scimitar. "Have you forgotten this?" he asked rhetorically.

The haj froze and marveled at the glimmering dagger. The scabbard caught a glimpse of light from the all but extinguished flames and reflected them dramatically. The tiny jewels dazzled and sparkled their eyes and the haj and his serving girl silently gasped in unabashed awe.

"What is that prize that you hold?" Burlu stammered. "Gold? A blade of solid gold?"

His guest smiled broadly. "Yes, haj, but it is also more. Far more. In my land it is well-known. You see, it was stolen from the kingdom for a special purpose. Some call it the Blade of the Throne," he looked at Mariana, "but others know it by the inscription it bears: Blue Fire. Forged countless centuries ago, and handed down from king to king, it is a marvel like no other, nor can there ever be another like it. Its elements are unknown in any of the world's kingdoms; I would venture to guess that some men would quest a lifetime to have it." And he politely held out the blade for his host to inspect. Burlu took it hungrily.

"Magnificent," he gasped in awe. "Blue Fire, you say? What is its meaning?"

The beggar smiled. "Perhaps one day you will hear of it, good haj. For now, though, I cannot say. Forgive me."

"I understand, my friend. I shall not pry into its secrets." He fondled the blade gently, admiring the craftsmanship, the sparkling jewels inlaid in the scabbard. "Ah, I envy you," he said truthfully. "I see that your prize is more than just a scepter of kings; my own words cannot do it justice. But tell me, how came this into your keeping?"

The beggar's eyes glowed as strongly as the jewels. "The dagger is mine and mine by right," he said. "Handed to me by my father and before that to him by his father. Only our family know and understand its use and meanings. Since my

118

father has died I alone claim its ownership . . . though others, I fear, would deny me my heritage."

Mariana listened, reflecting on the riddle he had posed for her to solve and recalling its enigmatic solution. And then she suddenly knew and understood. It was fantastic; incredible. She dared not believe—yet she dared not doubt. "Then you must be," she whispered, "the true descendant of the royal lovers . . . the cousins who survived when Speca was conquered."

"Aye," chimed in Ramagar, now grasping the matter for himself. "You are yourself a prince—and the heir to Speca's lost throne!"

The stranger bowed his head graciously, placing his hands in a pyramid and touching his fingertips to his forehead.

"I am my father's son, master thief. First in line to our throne and the reclaiming of my kingdom and all its usurped lands. Now you all understand the urgency of my task; why I cannot delay even a single day while bondage and suffering bleed my people as well as my heart. And by the will of the Fates I shall succeed in this long, difficult quest. Succeed in all this, and more."

"No wonder you were willing to die to regain the dagger," said Ramagar with perception. "Without it you would have no proof of your heritage."

"Rightly so. Without the scimitar I am like a sailor bereft of a ship. A herder without a staff. Or," he grinned, "a thief without cunning. But with the blade I can do many things; in my grasp will be the power to lead my people from their oppression."

"Well put, gentle Prince," said the haj. Then he looked at his guest with a perplexed stare and sincere worry in his eyes. "Your cause is as noble as any I have ever heard. And only a man pure of heart and soul would even contemplate taking on the task. But I fear that living up to these ambitions will be far harder than speaking of them tonight. Are you not one man alone? And do you not face, by your own admission, a force of men who will be more than eager to get their hands on Speca's last true surviving prince? What of these black arts your adversaries so skillfully practice? Recall—this magic brought your whole empire to its knees, slaughtered your people, made wreckage of your fleets and your royal family. Is this not so?"

"I have never claimed that my task would be an easy one," the beggar prince replied gloomily. "The barbarians have

119

turned my land into one so forebidding that men who hear my tale sometimes recoil in terror at the spoken word. To this day mariners who pass Speca's shores are said to quiver and pray until the dark coast is a hundred leagues from sight—and even then they speak of it only in whispers."

"Yet still you are not deterred?" said the haj with some amazement.

"Nothing can deter me. Tell me, are you not willing to fight for your own homes, if you must? Good haj, if bandits swooped down from the mountains and claimed all your land, your swine, your sheep, your tents, would you not face them boldly and fight?"

Burlu nodded firmly. "What man would not? But your own plight is very different, I fear." He uncrossed his legs and leaned in closer to his guest. His lips were pursed and he rubbed his palms in a slow, circular motion. "Ah, good friend. We know each other not. But now I speak to you as though I were your father and you my favorite son. Give up these dreams to regain the throne. There is only a cold and lonely grave that can wait at the end of your journey. Death and death alone."

"Too many voices from the past cry out to me, haj," sighed the beggar Prince. "I cannot turn from them. They count on me to free my people, and what is a king but the servant of his flock? A humble servant."

Mariana put her hand to the Prince's shoulder in a sisterly fashion, her eyes pleading and distraught. "We are your friends," she told him with a ring of sincerity in her voice. "And the haj is right, you know. When your journey is finally complete and you have reached the land where the sun never shines, what will you do? How will you overcome the fearful odds against you? Banish these black powers from your kingdom? You must be a very brave and noble man to do what you say you must. But I am frightened for you. You are a man alone, with no one to share your burden."

All were silent for a time. The haj leaned forward and handed back the scimitar to the Prince in rags. The Prince took it without a word and stared sullenly at his fabulous prize.

"Speca had many allies once upon a time," he said at length. "I will seek out the boldest of them and try to bring them under my banner. Once they believe who I am, understand the worthiness of my cause, perhaps together we shall find a way . . ."

120

"And do these allies from days past know of your kingdom's fate?" asked Ramagar.

The Prince sighed. "They know it well. They have seen the dark enemy and given them a name: Druids. Men of Shadows. The land of my allies lies perilously close to Speca's own shores. It would be best for them to aid me in ridding the world of this scourge."

"Are they themselves knowledgeable in such black sorcery as the Druids possess?" asked the haj. The Prince shook his head ruefully, and the haj added, "Then have they armies so vast and strong that they can overcome Druid magic?"

Again the woeful Prince was forced to admit they did not.

"Then why should they fight for you? Surely they must know their own land will suffer for such folly. They will likely as not be forced to share Speca's fate."

The Prince sat thoughtfully, then said, "Perhaps not. The bonds between our peoples once ran strong; but I will offer far more than the memory of our ancient friendship. I intend to offer them wealth in return for their assistance—wealth beyond belief. Enough gold and jewels to fill every purse and every coffer. The riches of Kalimar and all the Eastern Kingdoms combined would look pale when compared to what I am offering."

Ramagar's brow knitted with surprise. "And you actually have all this wealth to offer?"

The Prince met the thief's steady gaze. "I do, my friend. All that and even more, I promise. Each and every man who will join my cause shall return home in the style and luxury of an Eastern king. He will want for nothing until his dying day."

The haj whistled. "Soldiers of fortune are easy enough to find," he observed. "Indeed, Kalimar's cities are filled with them. For what you will pay I daresay you could raise an entire army overnight. And a loyal one to boot, though all the black power be arrayed against you. Greed is blind to danger."

The thief of Kalimar stirred restlessly upon his cushion, and Mariana was well aware of the thoughts running wildly through his mind. "If you have all you claim," she said bluntly to the Prince, "then why are you not followed by a legion? Why do you travel alone and in the guise of a beggar? A man of such riches should be leading a worldwide crusade, his cause renowned in every land."

The yellow-haired pretender folded his arms and sighed. "I

121

think, my friends, that you misunderstand me. I travel alone because I must—"

"Then you have no money?"

He shook his head. "Not a penny. But wait—the riches I spoke of are real enough. Remember that Speca in her glory was the envy of every nation. In the palace storerooms alone are so much gold, so much silver, so many priceless artifacts that a hundred scribes could spend their lives in making the tally. You have all seen the scimitar I carry. The fortune I offer could buy a thousand of them. Ten thousand. We need only win back this wealth from the Druids and set Speca free. My people would call it a fair bargain indeed. A slave dreams not of gold or jewels—only his freedom."

The haj frowned. "Soldiers of fortune fight only for cash. The jingle of coins in their pockets."

"So I have learned," ruminated the Prince. "I have been laughed at, called a madman, a fool, been cursed with the foulest oaths men can utter." His shoulders sank and a weary look came to his eyes. "Not a man in all my travels has considered my cause worthy enough to risk his life for. Nor even for the promise of a fortune. As you said, dear Mariana, I am a man alone . . ."

"No!" came the cry, and Homer bounded to his feet, tears flowing down his face. "You are not alone! No longer! I will accompany you, I shall be at your side always!"

The Prince looked up at his faithful young friend and smiled warmly. "Thank you, Homer. Your offer means more to me than I can tell, because you give it out of love. But alas, I cannot ask it. What the haj and Mariana have said are simple truths. My road is far too perilous to allow you to travel it at my side."

"You won't stop me," cried the boy. "We made a bargain, you and I; that where you went, I would follow."

"True enough," replied the Prince in rags. "But only until our paths are forced to part. When we reach the sea—"

"I will be at your side," the boy interrupted firmly. "I want to fight for your cause. I want to assist you in setting your land free."

"He is but a child," Mariana said sadly.

"I was man enough to risk my head to set Ramagar free!" Homer rejoined angrily. "I am a child of the Jandari. My will is my own, my life to decide for myself."

"He is right, you know," said Ramagar, looking first to Mariana and then to the Prince. "Take him. A boy such as
122

he has no future in Kalimar or any of her nearby kingdoms. But with you he will learn and become a man to be proud of. Who knows, perhaps the two of you may even succeed in your quest . . ."

The Prince nodded with understanding. A street urchin in Kalimar was no more than so much rubbish. If nothing else, the quest to regain Speca would give the boy a sense of purpose, a pride in himself that he had never had before. Even a reason for living. And it was better to die fighting for a cause, if it came to that, than to rot in some hopeless dungeon.

"All right, then," said the Prince. He looked at Homer and grinned. "I shall take you with me when we sail. And this much I vow: that when my kingdom is redeemed I will not forget your help. From urchin to prince shall be your destiny. Homer: foreign-born prince of Speca."

The boy sat, silently weeping with happiness.

"I am glad at least that much is settled," said the haj with relief. "And what of the two of you?" he asked Mariana and Ramagar. "Where do your own travels lead? Will you also journey to distant lands, or perhaps one day return to Kalimar?"

Ramagar hung his head. "I will be honest with you, haj," he said. "I can never return to Kalimar. I am a wanted man, although falsely accused. Proving my innocence is impossible." He glanced up at the girl and smiled. "Neither Mariana nor myself can ever go home again."

"We seek a new life, haj," added the girl. "Just a simple life. One where we can live freely and spend our years together."

Burlu was touched by her sincerity. The fact that her lover was an accused criminal did not disturb him in the least. As a hill man it was none of his concern; he would never speak of it. But more than that, he knew of the city and its evil doings; knew that even a good, pure man could find himself forced to crime. The haj would cast no blame.

"So where will you go, then?"

Mariana shrugged. "We have no firm course to follow. Thus far we have traveled with the Prince, and shall probably continue to do so at least until we reach the sea."

The haj hid a small frown. "And then?"

"Wherever the Fates may will," answered the thief. "I had thought about sailing for southern lands, but those places are not for bringing a wife. Maybe we shall go north. I have heard tell of sheep country beyond the Great Divide. A land of peace and serenity."

Burlu listened patiently, all the while nervously tugging at his finger ring. "I wonder if I might be bold," he said at length. "I know we are still mostly strangers to each other, but I feel I know you both like my own children. There is plenty of land in these hills. Land I own and that I have no need for. True, much is barren, but a hard-working man can make a go of it, if he tries. Maybe," he smiled, "even become a haj. What say you? Would you accept such an offer?"

"A most gracious offer!" cried Mariana, flushing with emotion. "We are deeply, deeply honored. But . . ." She looked away so she couldn't see his eyes. "But we cannot accept. These lands are still within the dominion of Kalimar. Soldiers will come looking for us sooner or later. And then it will be you they'll come after. The penalty for harboring a fugitive from justice is death."

"Bah," scowled the haj. "Kalimar's soldiers do not frighten me. The men of the hills consider themselves free and independent of all. We laugh at city men and their ways."

"That may well be so," said Ramagar, sorrowful to have to decline the kind offer put before him. "But will you also laugh when they draw their swords and threaten your lives? Or when they put your tents and your fields to the torch?" He shook his head from side to side. "No, good haj, it must not be. Mariana and I cannot bring our own misfortunes atop your own head. As much as we have come to know you and respect you, we must turn down your generosity. At daybreak we will leave with our companions and search for our own destiny."

Burlu sighed deeply. "I am sorry," he said, "but I understand. Yet it truly grieves me to think that we shall never share each other's good company again." He clasped his hands together as if in prayer and said quietly, looking from one guest to the other, "May the Fates bless all of you always. It would make an old man's wish come true."

Tears came to Mariana's eyes as he spoke, and she thought of him now as the father both she and Ramagar had never had.

The Prince turned to the thief, saying, "You know that it will be hard on both of you no matter where you go. Like me, you will find yourselves strangers in a foreign land. Few men will prove as hospitable as our kind host has been. And what of these lands to the north you mentioned? It is true

124

that they are peaceful; but tell me, is the life of a sheepherder the one either of you would choose? Living lonely and desolate in a place as far away from civilization as a man can hope to get?"

"At least we'll be safe," Ramagar replied with a touch of bitterness. "Besides, what alternatives are open to us?"

"Come instead with me."

Mariana's eyes opened fully wide and she stared at the Prince. "You're asking Ramagar to join you on the quest?"

"I am asking you both," he replied soberly. "Listen to me, please. Hear me out and consider what I say before you refuse."

Ramagar put his arm around Mariana's shoulder and nodded.

"There are so many things to be done," said the Prince excitedly. "Far too many for just Homer and myself. I have great need of a man like you, master thief. Your talents and abilities are too valuable to be wasted on tending sheep. Think, just days ago we were all hunted by Kalimar's dreaded Inquisitors. On his own, each was lost. Yet when we banded together we made stuttering clowns of Kalimar's entire army. Stand with me, Ramagar. Be my right arm. In victory I will reward you beyond your wildest dreams. Name your price: land, title, gold. I will agree. You shall have it all."

"Dead men have little need of title and gold," remarked the dancing girl dryly. "You are asking him to throw away his life."

"You are wrong, Mariana," insisted the Prince. "The Druids can be beaten. I *know* they can. We must only find the key that unlocks the door to their secrets. With both of you at my side and my allies to give us support, we can break the hideous chains that bind my land. And my people will rise up beside us, themselves dealing our enemies the final blows. I need you, Mariana, even as I need your lover. Your cunning and intelligence shall be a heavy counterweight to Druid black art. What do you say?"

She sat there with her breath swept away. Yes, there was adventure and fortune to be found if she went with him, an opportunity as exciting as it was fearful. To cross half a world, see things few women or men ever imagined existed. Yet, this had to be balanced against the very real and dangerous peril that awaited should they fail. Who could say what terrible death they would meet at Druid hands? The thought of some ingenious torture made her shudder.

The Prince sat tensely waiting, and even the haj, normally the epitome of repose, could feel his hands moisten and his breath quicken.

Unspeaking, Mariana and Ramagar looked deeply into each other's eyes. They each knew and understood the risks, they each realized the slim chance of succeeding. But in one aspect the Prince had been right: as fugitives they would likely be hounded for the rest of their lives, at best forced to live in lonely isolation. Crossing the sea, no matter what the perils, would set them free from the fear of one day being found out for who they were. Even the rewards this prince offered for their help were small when compared to the freedom they sought.

Mariana's eyes darted to the scimitar, glimmering gaily as it rested in their companion's open hand. It was a strange, wondrous object, she knew. Men would fight for it, men would die for it. What tales it could tell if only it could speak. What mysteries it must know the answer to. It was the dagger itself that had brought them all together on this night to sit in the tents of the haj, the dagger that had caused all their lives to be turned upside down in less than a week.

Was it an instrument of good? Or of evil? Would it lead them to adventure and victory? Or only to doom? Mariana had no answers to these questions. But somehow she knew that her association with the blade had not yet ended. Forces beyond her and Ramagar's understanding seemed to control their destinies.

Ramagar finished the last of his wine and cast a weary eye to the entrance of the tent. The wind had all but calmed, and to his surprise he saw that the first hints of red sun were cracking spider-like across the far horizon. So intrigued had they been by the Prince and the tale he told that dawn had come swiftly upon them before they had a chance to sleep.

He drew Mariana closer, crushing her with his strong arm, and looked to the Prince. "I suppose I wouldn't have been much of a farmer anyway," he grumbled. "Besides, I hate sheep . . ."

The Prince straightened attentively. Eyes glued to the thief, he said, "Then you both accept my offer? You'll come?"

Ramagar glanced down at the sleepy-eyed dancing girl. Mariana drew a breath, sighed, and nodded. "We accept,"

126

she said softly. "For good or ill, our destinies will be irrevocably bound to your own."

A broad, cheerful grin crossed the stranger's face, and his eyes, wide awake and sparkling bluer than ever, danced merrily. "Then it's settled," he chortled, clapping his hands in delight. "And neither of you will ever regret your decision, I promise. Everything you ask shall be yours." He reached for the wine vessel and filled each cup to the brim, making sure to include an extra chalice for the silent serving girl sitting wearily in the corner.

"A toast to our fortunes," he said, raising his chalice high. "To our success, and the regained freedom of my kingdom."

They all lifted their cups and drank. The Prince downed his wine greedily and beamed. "At least my army has begun," he told them in a serious tone. "And never has there been a finer beginning."

"A ragtag army at best," observed Mariana. "We have neither weapons nor horses, nor even food to sustain us on our journey."

The haj lifted his head and searched the faces of his guests. They were honest faces, he knew. Kind and gentle for all their trials. It hurt him to think of the fate that awaited them. In so many ways they were merely children. Children on a noble quest with no one to guide or fend for them.

The sun appeared fully now, washing the tent in brilliant yellows and browns while thin streams of gold poured through the thick curtains. The red clay earth of the scrub hills sparkled in the light and even the yellowed, parched grass took on a deep intensity. Burlu's swine had begun to stir; so had his sheep and his cows. He could hear the soft patter of shuffled feet and low murmurings as his herders arose from their own tents and set out to start the day's chores, a routine that both they and the haj had followed nearly every day of their lives.

"I suppose you will be leaving soon," the haj said sullenly.

Mariana nodded, the smallest hint of a tear welling in her eyes. "We must," she said. "But we'll never forget you or your hospitality. And I'll recall you in my prayers."

The haj smiled. He had come to like them all, he knew. But of all his guests the dancing girl was his favorite. What was it about her, he wondered, that brought his beloved wife's image to mind every time he looked at her? Burlu shrugged and smiled to himself. He must truly be getting old,

127

he mused. Why else would he see the faces of the dead within those of the living?

Trembling slightly from these thoughts, he turned to the Prince. "What route to the sea have you chosen, if I might ask?"

"They say the northern road will lead to a great river," replied the Prince. "From there we will follow it west to the sea."

Ramagar concurred. "It's the caravan route to Palava. It's long, I know, but there isn't any other way."

"Ah, but there is, my friend," said the haj with a sly smile. "A way that could cut a month's travel, and also keep you far from the possibility of any chance encounter with Kalimar's soldiers seeking you on the road."

Ramagar furrowed his thick brows in contemplation. Certainly it would be well advised for them to avoid the main trade route. But Ramagar was a city man. What did he know of the broad sweep of rugged lands that formed Kalimar's northern frontiers? The main road, such as it was, was the only one he knew anything of.

"Which road do you speak about?" he asked, perplexed.

The wizened haj smiled slyly. "Not a road at all, my friend. But there is a way to the port—a short way, if you're willing to cross the desert."

"Walk across a sea of sand?" gasped Mariana. "We'd never make it. How could we possibly find our way over this ocean of dunes?"

The haj leaned forward, his smile vanishing. "There is a way to take you across in a single week's time. It will be difficult, I realize, even dangerous. Yet certainly no less perilous than what awaits in Speca . . ."

Ramagar looked to the Prince and the man in rags shrugged. "How do we find this path?" he queried.

"It will not be hard. You will begin by going north, but when the dry riverbed is reached you shall follow it west, to the rock country and the Land of the Baboons."

"Land of the Baboons?" repeated the thief, scratching his head. "What's that? I've lived in Kalimar all my life and I've never even heard of it."

"Of course not," replied the haj with a hint of a sneer at his city-bred guest. "But we of the hills know it well. All too well, perhaps. It is a vast region of mulga scrub. Many creatures dwell within its confines, particularly lizards and snakes.

128

The baboons, though, are master. It is their land, their king-dom."

"What do you mean by 'kingdom,'" asked the Prince. "Is this a jest? Do these . . . baboons . . . actually rule over a patch of desert?"

Burlu nodded darkly, saying, "I never take such matters lightly, my friend. The Land of the Baboons is as real a king-dom as any in the world of men. They are trained like war-riors, their armies led by skilled and cunning savage generals—"

"An army of monkeys?" gasped the thief.

The haj's eyes flashed impatiently. "You will not scoff if chance brings you face to face with them. The baboon king guards his fiefdom well—as the bleached bones of hapless men who wandered upon their lands will grimly attest. It will take a brave heart and total resolve to trespass their domain and cross safely."

"Still," protested Ramagar, "they're only monkeys. If we had good weapons there would be little to fear."

Burlu smiled thinly. "The proof will be if you make it out of there alive." He set his jaw and said no more.

"Brrr," rattled Mariana. "It sounds to me like we should forget this shortcut entirely and take our chances on the trade route. I'd rather risk running into some soldiers from Kalimar than what the haj has told us about."

The Prince pondered for a moment, then said to Burlu, "How long would it take us to cross through, er, monkeyland, and reach the port?"

"Seven days. No more." He smiled again. "Of course, you would have to know the exact course to follow. Otherwise you would never find your way out."

Ramagar frowned. "Well, that should disqualify us," he said. "We know absolutely nothing about any of these lands. We'd probably wind up as supper for a baboon feast. No, as much as the idea interests me, we can't take the chance. We'd be as lost as children, roaming endlessly in circles."

Disappointed, the Prince concurred. "It's useless to even debate the matter. We would never survive."

Here the haj's eyes widened and his teeth glittered like ivory with his mirth. "Yes, you could survive. It has been done. Trust that there is a way to cross in safety. Only you would have need of a guide . . ."

"And where will we find such a guide?" said Ramagar. "Who in his right mind would be willing to lead us on an expedition through monkeyland, risking his neck when there won't even be a penny in payment for his troubles?"

"I think," said the haj slowly, "that I can find someone for you."

"Who," questioned Mariana. "The man would have to be demented!"

Burlu pulled a face. "I am not demented," he said. "And I offer myself as your guide to the sea. Even beyond—if you will have me."

"You?" cried the girl, astounded beyond belief. "But you're a haj! A man of wealth, of land. You have many duties and responsibilities entrusted to you. Why would you possibly want to risk all that to make a dangerous journey on behalf of a handful of ragged strangers?"

The haj sighed deeply and looked at them all with sad eyes. "I have seen much in my lifetime," he said. "I have lived many, many years. The land has been good to me, I am considered in these parts to be a man of substance. Yet, I am alone and lonely. The only wife I chose to take has been dead for more years than I care to remember. My sons are gone their own ways, my daughters married with large families of their own. Do not think that I am ungrateful; I am not. Life has been kind, as unworthy as I may be. But I seek not further riches, nor the pleasures of the flesh. And I do not wish to spend my last years as you see me: sitting in comfort and growing fat while the world spins around me. My eyes are still sharp, my arms are as powerful as any man's. If I can be of service to you in your quest then perhaps I can find meaning to my life. I am not a man to mince words. In my own way, I have as much need of all of you as you yourselves have of me."

"But what will happen to your flocks," said Ramagar. "And your fields, and your swine? Who will tend them in your absence? Who will care for the families of herders who serve you and depend on you?"

Burlu put forward his palms. "All this will be taken care of," he assured. "My daughters' husbands are strong, stout fellows who will be more than willing to share in the task. I can have these matters properly attended to in a matter of hours." Then he folded his hands in his lap and smiled thinly. "And remember, my good friends, to you I can be of invaluable assistance. You need me, if only to lead you through the Land of the Baboons. I can provide mules for our journey and the weapons we will need for our protection, perhaps
130

even a bit of gold to help assure our passage across the sea. All this I willingly offer; you have but to say yes . . ."

No one said a word, so stunned were they all by their host's unexpected offer. At length the yellow-haired Prince turned his face to the haj and stared at him evenly. "Knowingly you will give up all you have," he gestured grandly, "and come with us to a foreign shore? A shore filled with such dangers?"

The haj nodded. "I will pay my part of the bargain, you have my oath. And let me assure you, good friend, that I myself am no stranger to adventure or risk."

The Prince turned to Mariana and the thief, and they both nodded. "Then welcome to our number," he said, extending his hand. "Come, then. Make all your preparations. At noon our journey will begin in earnest. We have no time to spare. Speca must be reached before the summer gales make crossing the sea impossible."

Hand over hand they each clasped the others' hands, proudly making their vows of allegiance in the light of the sun. Mariana gazed wistfully up at the sky, wondering how many more times they would see it rise before they reached the land where the sun never shone.

But there was a long way to go before they would come even that far. For now it was the Land of the Baboons that loomed heavily on their minds, the first terrible trial they would have to face.

III

Into Monkeyland . . .
And on to Palava

10

The red desert sand seemed eternal as they made their way from the tents. On either side, stretching as far as the eye could see, it formed long, ever shifting dunes, in some places capped by a surprising sparse cover of wilting grass, in other places stark and so bright it almost hurt to look.

Haj Burlu, the swineherd, took the lead, riding his sturdiest and favorite mule. He was a wondrous sight to watch, dressed as he was in his flowing robes. He wore a tasseled cloth headdress with an intricately knotted cord of crimson that both held it in place and served to show his title. The cord bobbed and bounced as he rode, and the poor mule wheezed and gasped under his weight, the haj whipping and cajoling her onward.

Paces behind came Ramagar and Mariana, riding side by side. The thief shifted uncomfortably in his heavy, loose-fitting robe. It had once belonged to the haj's eldest son, and Ramagar had taken it gratefully, even though it reminded him of the Karshi fanatic's robe he had stolen while still in Kalimar. He only hoped this one would bring him better luck.

Mariana's hair was tightly braided, streaking down both sides of her veiled face. The head cloth she wore was of a light, soft material, pure white in color, and well designed for reflecting the harsh desert sun. Her body moved lithely within the confines of a clean white tunic the serving girl had hastily provided. With the sleeves falling purposely over her hands, and her desert boots up over her calves, there was little to be seen, except around her eyes, of her well-tanned, supple skin.

The Prince came next, also in newly acquired garb, and faithful Homer brought up the rear, leading two packmules heavily laden with goatskins filled with water and other foodstuffs and supplies.

It was hot. Dreadfully hot. The sun passed its zenith and slowly began to slide along the arch of the sky. Burlu first led them north, skirting at times the well-trodden caravan road, then quite abruptly veered his party in the direction of the dipping sun. They came to a deep wadi that widened as it twisted through mounds of rock and scrub.

By dusk they had traveled quite a distance. A remarkable distance, in fact, the haj observed, taking into consideration his companions' unfamiliarity with the desert and its ways.

At length the band came to a halt at a grubby rise of red clay and rock. The haj turned and smiled at the dusty faces of his companions. He raised his arm and pointed to a tiny clump of dark trees clustered almost at the edge of the horizon.

"Alasi oasis," he said spryly. "We can reach it in another hour and spend the night. There is fresh water and fruit. From there we can plan our strategy. So make the most of the oasis while you can."

Mariana looked at him puzzled. Certainly the oasis was a welcome sight indeed, and the thought of being able to wash out the dust and grime was most enticing. It was the other reference that disturbed her.

"What sort of strategy?" she asked uneasily.

Haj Burlu drew out his long, curved dagger and glumly ran his thumb along the edge of the blade. "By tomorrow night we'll reach the Land of the Baboons," he said. "We'll have to travel fast and carefully, with our weapons at our sides. With Fortune beside us, we'll not be seen—"

"And if we are?" said Ramagar.

The haj narrowed his eyes cruelly. "We fight for our lives."

Against the starry velvet night they urged their mules forward, wearily straining themselves to the limit. The mules, though, needed little prodding; they, too, had spied the leafy palms, scented the grass and the water on the wind, and were as eager as any to take their well-deserved rest.

The haj was the first to arrive. While the others drank and rested he took his bow and a single arrow and set out to forage for dinner. His hunt was quickly over. Grinning like a schoolboy, he came back carrying the largest hare any of them had ever seen. Rabbit stew would be a hardy meal to conclude the first day's journey.

The evening was spent pleasantly; after supper everyone sat beside the tiny fire and spoke easily, relating cheerful and good-humored memories of happier times in their lives. The banter did not last long, though; not after the hard, grueling day they had been through. One by one they rolled themselves in their blankets, not bothered by the night chill, and quickly fell asleep.

Mariana smiled at the sight of them and, too pensive to sleep yet herself, restlessly went to sit beside the bank of the deep pool. The night was silent, save for the haj's heavy snoring, and she rested back on her elbows and gazed peacefully up at the multitude of stars lighting the desert sky. With a soft song on her lips, she casually found herself tossing pebbles into the water and listening as they plopped and sank to the gravelly floor. Then she glanced about at the cool, shadowed green of the oasis and sighed. It was good to be free, she mused. Good to feel the soil beneath her feet and the wind as it rushed through her hair.

Time drifted past; the shadows danced from the trees, from the boughs above her head. She was drifting off into a restful half-sleep when a sudden short, muffled noise interrupted her quietude. Eyes widening in apprehension, Mariana sat up straight, listening and watching while her hand slid down to the sheath of the dagger strapped onto her thigh.

Quiet resumed. She strained her eyes in every direction, noting the sandy mounds and dunes sweeping away from the oasis on all sides. Here and there she could see the tall stalks of desert plants and wildflowers, still and motionless within the shadows. Above her head the palm leaves rustled gently with the faintest hint of a night breeze.

I must be getting jumpy, she told herself. We're still leagues away from monkeyland. She tightened her blanket around her shoulders and continued her vigil. It must have been a small animal she had heard. A hare, perhaps. Or a lizard. Nothing to be concerned with.

The silence deepened; even the haj had stopped snoring. Mariana shifted into a more comfortable position, but for safety's sake kept her hand close to her weapon. Then she saw it: a fast-moving hump of a shadow darting away from the oasis and behind a wide rising dune.

This time she took no chances; leaping to her feet, she hurried to the sleeping haj and awakened him. Burlu poked his craggy face from under his blanket and stared at her blankly.

"There's something—or someone—afoot," whispered the girl.

Like lightning the burly haj bolted to his feet, his own weapon shimmering dully in the starlight. "This way," said Mariana, pointing to where she had been sitting.

Burlu took long, loping strides as noiseless as a mountain cat. His sleepy red eyes scanned the sands and the fauna from distance to distance. Then, cautioning the girl to remain where she was, he moved from the grass and slowly wound his way down onto the open sand. For a long moment he

137

stood perfectly still, listening and holding his breath. He saw that the mules had been awakened by the noise. Tethered near the trees, they were all restlessly bobbing their shaggy manes and digging hooves into the dirt.

Burlu began to move, sliding ahead toward the dunes in a low crouching position. Then he stopped, kneeled, began to sift his fingers through the sand. As Mariana watched, he regained his posture and without a sound loped back to the oasis and the girl.

"Did you see anything?" she whispered.

The towering haj scratched at his white-flecked red beard and looked down at her with obvious bewilderment. "I saw tracks, yes," he sighed.

Mariana shuddered. "Are the baboons watching us?"

"It was not a baboon track, child. It was a man's."

"A man? But that's impossible!" she cried. "What would a man be doing out here, so close to the dreaded monkey kingdom?"

"I am as mystified as you, dear girl. Very few men come this way—unless they have the strongest of reasons."

Mariana bit at her lips, stared down at the silent dunes. "Perhaps," she said, biting her nails, "it was a bandit. There are plenty of rogues in your hills, you told us as much yourself. The cutthroat may have seen our fire and thought to rob us while we slept."

The haj rocked his body slightly and nodded. "Anything is possible, child. But even brigands know better than to prowl too close to monkeyland." He screwed his sleepy eyes and spat between his legs. "No, I fear there is something more here than we understand. I think we are being followed . . ."

Mariana's eyes flashed with uncertainty. "But why would anyone want to follow us?" she protested. "It doesn't make any sense. No one even knows where we are."

Burlu drew a deep breath and flexed his cramped muscles. "That may well be," he replied. "But those tracks are a fact. Someone is close, hiding among the rocks, perhaps even watching us now."

"Then what do we do?"

The haj glanced at Ramagar, the Prince, and Homer. All three were still lost in a deep restful sleep. "I think for now we do nothing," he said at last. "For now this peculiar matter is better left unmentioned. There is no need to create undue worry, at least not with the baboons to contend with. Besides, perhaps our visitor will turn back. Only a fool would enter

138

the Land of the Baboons on his own. But even if he did, he would be the least of our problems."

Mariana nodded with understanding.

"Go back to sleep, child," said the haj. "Leave this problem to me." He went for his blanket and pulled it over his shoulders. "I'll stand watch tonight. And don't worry, if our friend reappears, bandit or no, I'll be ready."

By early morning the sun was as fierce and unrelenting as any of them had ever known. The travelers had risen long before the crack of dawn, eaten a quick breakfast of dried biscuits and dates, and lost no time in resuming their journey. With the tensions of the day yet ahead, both Mariana and Burlu all but forgot the strange incident of the night before. They now found themselves well away from the dunes and Alasi oasis, on the verge of entering a broad canyon of crumbled rock surrounded on either side by grim craggy peaks of glittering stone. It was filled with ridges and oddly shaped formations of granite that caught the sunlight and reflected it with mirror-like intensity. Where up till now the ground had been soft and sandy, now it was coarse and hard. A few weeds and plants poked themselves into view along the ruts in the rock walls; other than that, the land was as barren and foreboding as any in all the Eastern Kingdoms.

The band halted at the canyon's entrance and Ramagar rode up beside the haj, calming his nervous mule. He lifted his head, threw off his hood, and glanced warily up from side to side. The farther down the canyon he looked, the higher the cliffs seemed to rise, endlessly until they blended with the deep blue of the cloudless sky.

"We are at the border of the baboon kingdom," the haj told them all grimly. "From this place to where the hills become green is all their domain. And men are most unwelcome. Look." He pointed to a dusty pile of bones set in the middle of the wide path some fifty meters from where they stood.

Ramagar tugged at the reins and guided his mule in the direction indicated. The others followed slowly. Dismounting, the thief kicked at the bones, scattering dust that quickly settled and blended into the color of the stony landscape.

"Was it an animal?" asked the Prince, peering down.

Ramagar shook his head. "It was a man."

"And the skeleton was set here as a warning," added Burlu. "The baboons have put it here on the very border of their kingdom purposely. They are telling all would-be travelers to turn back now—while they still can. They want no humans treading on their soil."

Homer glanced about uneasily and shivered. "Maybe we should heed their warning," he said, trying to be practical.

Noonday shadows were climbing up the faces of the cliffs, and from somewhere unseen beyond the heights a solitary hyena gave its piercing gruesome laugh; a laugh that left them all holding their breath. And the mules stood trembling and terrified, swinging their ears and rolling their eyes.

"We had best decide right away," cautioned the haj. "The longer we stay debating, the better the chance for some baboon patrol to come along and spot us." He glanced about at his companions. "Are any of you of a mind to turn back as well?"

Ramagar got back up on his mule and clenched his teeth. "We've come this far, good haj, we'll not run away now. Lead on. Guide us through this miserable place."

And off they rode, deeper into hostile territory, determined to muster all their courage and be gone from the baboon kingdom as fast as possible.

It was well into the afternoon; Burlu led them across the canyon and then followed an ancient hunting trail that took them through a long and ever-deepening defile that twisted its way west and through the very heart of the kingdom. On and on they rode, aching and fatigued, winding among rough skirts and rougher scrub, up high tricky slopes, and then back down again where the going was every bit as treacherous. More than once the mules bolted at the sight of vicious sidewinding snakes that coiled over deadened boughs and lashed venomous tongues as they passed. Thornbush and sharp rock brushed and stung against hooves and fetlocks. The wind began to blow, gently at first so that the riders welcomed the breeze, but then more brutally until at last it whipped around their heads in a furious frenzy.

The haj grimaced and covered his face, his companions hastily doing the same. Sand swirled, it became almost impossible to see. At the end of a deep gorge they found a cave. Really little more than a windblown recess in the exposed surface of the mountain, it would at least provide adequate protection until dawn, when they could resume the journey again.

Speaking little among themselves, everyone set to work: Homer watering and tending the complaining mules, Ramagar and the Prince picking their way over the ledges for firewood, Mariana busily spreading the blankets and setting up camp, while the haj prepared to practice his culinary skills.

Evening had come and the windstorm eased when the thief, his arms well stocked with dry sticks and branches, suddenly froze in his tracks. Far above the ledge at the very precipice of the overhanging cliffs he caught sight of the marching scouting party. Sand was still swirling when Ramagar deftly dropped his bundle and dodged into a narrow cranny between two huge boulders. His heart was pounding; he slowly raised his head and peered toward the top of the cliffs.

The baboons were moving single file, occasionally grunting commands among themselves. There were about six of them, Ramagar saw, although it was hard to get an accurate count because of the whirling dust.

The leader of the baboons began to climb down the slope, hand over hand, grasping expertly onto minute steps embedded into the rock. One by one his companions followed. Ramagar drew back and took out his knife. The crags were growing dark as the sun faded and the thief of thieves swore softly under his breath. The patrol, either by coincidence or design, was heading perilously close to the undefended cave.

Several meters ahead was a slight elevation leading to a low mound of broken rock. Wanting to get a better view of the enemy, Ramagar crawled from his place and slithered silently up to the natural rampart. He saw, boldly outlined in the light of the moon, the features of the Prince. The young man whirled, dagger in hand, at the movement from behind. Then, upon realizing that it was only Ramagar and not a baboon soldier, he heaved a sigh of relief and slipped back to his concealed position.

Ramagar wriggled his way to the Prince's side. "So you've seen them, too," he whispered.

The Prince nodded. "Before you did, I'm sure. I was climbing to the top to reach an old stump when I heard their grim chatter carried on the wind. Smelled them, too. By the Seven Hells, these monkeys stink."

Ramagar frowned. "I wager they'd say the same about us . . ."

From their lower position on the hill the two men watched the hairy menace jump from ledge to ledge and finally land upright on the flat crest opposite. They were ugly creatures, these fighting baboons. Their heads were large, grotesquely swollen in size compared to their bodies. They had long, sharp teeth that glittered in the waning light. Their muzzles protruded hideously, mouths twisted like rabid dogs. Long arms dangled to their knees. Each had a cap of thick gray hair on its head and over its shoulders. In all other places their fur was either orange or rust brown, nearly blending with the color of the rocks and dunes.

For some time the baboons held their places while they carried on what seemed to be a heated discussion. At times one of the monkeys seemed to be insistent that they follow the path toward the cave. The baboon gestured in that direction with his arms, jumped up and down, stamped his feet. His leader, though, clearly had opinions of his own. Grunting and carrying on savagely, he bullied his adversary into submission, and the patrol docilely followed his lead as he moved away in the direction of distant slopes. Soon they were out of sight.

The Prince stood and mopped his brow. "That was close," he said nervously. "For a while I was positive they'd seen us."

"Me, too," Ramagar agreed. "But we'd better not press our luck. These monkeys may be back with more friends."

Sliding, stumbling, sometimes even limping in pain when thorns or thistles dug at their legs, they made their hurried way back to camp. When the haj heard the tale he sighed and shook his head. "One of their patrols must have found mule tracks in the canyon," he told them all. "Which means they know for certain that a band of men is somewhere about. If I know anything about baboons, they will spare no effort in catching us and hauling us before their king."

Ramagar beat a fist into his palm. "Then we're trapped," he seethed. "Like flies caught in a web—only this time it's an army of monkeys doing the spinning."

"Maybe not," counseled the haj. "Baboons aren't particularly adept at fighting at night. From now on we'll travel only while the sun is down. We'll use daylight for sleep, making certain to have someone constantly standing watch."

"It's sure we can't stay here, now," added Mariana thoughtfully. "Sooner or later those apes will double back this way. My vote is to get moving right away."

There was no argument; the ragtag army lost no time in packing up, loading the grumbling mules, and clearing out as quickly as possible. The going at night would be considerably

142

slower, they knew, perhaps causing them to spend an extra day in the baboons' kingdom. But it also had its advantages. They could more easily elude any approaching patrols, make full use of the stars to guide them as mariners do, and they would be out of the blazing sun.

The desert at night was amazingly beautiful. Placid and still, the sands sparkled in moonlight, and the surrounding hills took on a glow and radiance they concealed during the day. But night was also a more deadly time. It was then that the lizards dug out from beneath their rocks and crooks, then that sleeping snakes and spiders slithered and crawled from dark holes to prowl for supper under the soft glow of starlight.

It was less than an hour until dawn when Burlu deemed them a safe enough distance away from the cave to slow down. Mariana gritted her teeth and tried not to think about the sting of her leather saddle burning against her thighs. As the mare winded down to an easy pace she lifted herself in the stirrups and gazed at the open stretch of sand beyond. Off to the side stood another grim range of hills, easily as high and as treacherous as those she had seen in the canyon.

She shifted her weight, at last settling back in the saddle, and looked back over her shoulder. Somewhere behind, she was positive, the danger was lurking, growing ever closer no matter how fast or hard they rode. Then she shook off her goose bumps and looked again ahead, this time at the reassuring figures of Ramagar and the haj. Both men sat impassive and unspeaking, their right hands fondling the hilts of their weapons.

At the base of a steeply inclined mound the haj called the band to a halt. He worked his way alone up the tricky slope and dismounted when he reached the crest. There he wet a finger, put it to the wind, and nodded with satisfaction. Then he called his companions to join him at the top.

The crest was far wider than it seemed from below, and to Mariana's surprise she saw that a few scrubs and trees stood well concealed by boulders. There was even some weedy, yellow grass.

"This will be a perfect lookout for us," said the haj, stretching out his arms and moving them in a broad circle to indicate the vast field of vision the mound afforded. "From here we'll be able to see anything moving at us for leagues in every direction. We can sleep peacefully knowing the baboons won't be able to sneak up and kill us in our beds."

143

Saddles were hastily untied, and the mules began to buck joyously with their new freedom. Burlu began the task of watering them down and preparing to stand the first watch. Everyone else groaned, rubbed at sore muscles, and, spreading out blankets, fell thankfully to the ground. They curled up in a semicircle close beside the trees, too tired to speak or even eat, and there they went to sleep.

The sun came up, hot and sultry. All the day they dozed and rested, tended to their various aches and pains. By the evening they were all wide awake again, fully refreshed and ready to continue. Spirits markedly lifted while they ate their cold breakfast/supper of salted beef and biscuits, and then in what had become humdrum routine, they rolled up the blankets, resaddled the mules, and eagerly looked forward to putting more distance between themselves and the searching baboons.

It was a mild desert evening, pleasant for riding, with only the softest of breezes stirring. The moon was full and bright, and to Mariana it seemed larger and more luminous than ever. A thin layer of cloud dulled the dazzle of the stars into a pale bluish glow. Mariana found herself feeling calmed and relaxed after yesterday's adventures.

Pulling aside the veil from her face, she reached for the goatskin water bag, popped the cork, and took a long swallow. Ramagar reined in and pulled up close. He leaned over and kissed her quickly on the cheek. The girl blushed. "What was that for?" she asked.

"For being so brave and so valiant," he replied teasingly. "Next time you—"

His thought remained unfinished. Mariana stared dumbly up at the cliffs overlooking the hills and concealed her gasp. Ramagar fixed his gaze steadily higher and gripped tighter at the reins. The cliffs were crawling with them, dark, shadowy creatures, scrambling in endless procession to the ledges and boulders below.

The haj whirled his mule around, his face masked to hide his fear. "Ride back!" he shouted. "They've seen us! It's an ambush!"

The mules dashed back for the dunes, but it was too late. Ahead came racing a phalanx of baboons, screaming at the top of their lungs, sinewy arms flailing in the air, teeth bared like poison fangs. Again the riders turned, but again they came to abrupt desperate halts. The crazed screaming was

144

growing louder and louder, coming at them from every direction. And there was no safety to be found.

Ramagar slapped his mule and pushed her forward toward the hills. "Take cover at the rocks!" he cried. "It's our only chance!" And in reckless abandon the others followed.

Thundering along the gorge between the hills they ran headlong into a small group of concealed warrior baboons waiting to pounce. As Mariana and Ramagar wheeled to turn, the haj and the Prince drew their blades and began to deliver shattering blows. Dark blood spouted, and the baboons started to wail and leap high into the air like frogs hopping from lily pad to lily pad. Homer cried out in terror. A large hairy arm squeezed at his throat and he felt a rush of putrid breath zip up his nostrils as the baboon's teeth made ready to bear down.

The Prince's dagger flashed, slashing and slashing again, cutting the monkey's belly. The fierce beast let loose his hold of the urchin and, leaping to his feet on the mule's back, dived straight for the stunned Prince. It was Burlu's blade that caught him mid-flight. The knife dug up from the stomach, deep and straight into the black heart. The baboon shrieked so horribly that even its unharmed comrades shuddered.

It fell in a heap to the ground, knocking over three other charging baboons as it did. Madness took over. As a well-schooled group of warriors tore up from behind the rocks, Ramagar let loose. He heaved his long knife this way and that, thrashing faces, dismembering limbs. Baboons slammed into his mule, reeling, staggering, clawing and clutching at the matted mane. For a moment it seemed as though the thief would fall. Mariana saw the tumult and screamed, her own knife bearing down as she fought to wade through the crowd and reach her lover.

Suddenly the haj was at Ramagar's side. Then the Prince as well. But the baboons were forming into a solid wall of monkey flesh and escape became impossible. The three men continued their relentless barrage of blows. The mules felt the sting of monkey nails digging and ripping into their flanks. Ramagar knew they would soon fall. With a mighty leap he bounded from the saddle and onto the top of a high boulder. Two monkeys lurched; his fist slammed out, catching one in the jaw and sending it sprawling, the other squarely on its squatted nose and beating its soft flesh to pulp.

Finding courage where none had been before, faithful Homer dodged his own assailants and somehow managed to clear a path for Mariana. The girl lost no time in reaching the others and then doing as Ramagar had, jumping for better safety among the rocks.

Next it was the Prince who made it away from the fray. While Homer struggled to complete the jump, the haj boldly charged into the baboon midsts and dealt a series of shattering blows. If there had been any question of the old man's prowess, it was soon dispelled. Even Ramagar, surely no slouch when it came to a fight, had to marvel at the way the aging haj twisted his blade this way and that and made chattering idiots of the baboon army.

Then just as Burlu's mule buckled, the haj kicked from the saddle, landed on the ground, knocked a baboon out cold, and successfully scrambled up the steep slope to the cheers of his companions.

But the fight was not yet over—not by a long shot. Seeing their forces in disarray in the gorge, the baboon generals screeched commands and brought forth the charging phalanx. From the cliffs opposite the hill another brigade appeared, some racing down the incline at top speed, others flinging rocks, pebbles, sticks, and anything else they could get their devilish hands on.

Mariana and Ramagar hit the dirt, the barrage flying above their heads. The haj took a blow from a sharp stone and angrily shook a fearsome fist. Baboons were climbing now, inching their way to higher ground on the hill and causing the travelers to hastily retreat up toward the crest.

A group of monkeys grasped for Burlu's legs; up went the haj's boot, striking a powerful blow in the grabber's face and heaving it backward into the arms of its confused friends. Another baboon sprang from the side. The haj ducked a blow, grasped the monkey by the arm, twisted it, and spun it around, then banged his fist evenly on the top of its head. The baboon sank in a daze to its knees. Then Burlu picked it up, lifted it over his head, and tossed it clumsily into the fast-approaching crowd.

The dazed ape screamed as it went flying through the air. Other baboons looked up in horror and dove helter-skelter to avoid the soaring weight. For many of them, though, it made little difference. When the hapless baboon crashed you could hear the crunching of bone, the snapping of limbs like twigs. A half-dozen warriors lost their footing on the precarious

146

sand, tumbled backward, and created a small landslide of monkey flesh, gathering the oncoming baboons and rolling them down back into the gorge.

Taking a cue from the monkey army, Ramagar and the others quickly picked up the largest rocks they could lift. The thief hurled his with all the strength he could muster; the heavy rock crashed, crumpling some staggering baboons and splitting skulls like logs. The next rock hit a split second later. The haj had found one as heavy as he was. It smashed with such furied force against the boulders that it broke into a hundred whizzing missiles which cut and slashed through the ranks of the reeling enemy, rendering deep, ugly gashes across a dozen hairy faces.

The Prince, meanwhile, was up to tricks of his own. At the top of the hill he found a large stick; he wrapped it with dried weed and moss, struck his flints, and smiled grimly as the tinder caught. The dried shrub burst into blazes, weed catching like sulphur.

Fire was strange to the baboons—and all the more terrifying as the Prince fanned the flames against the black sky and threw the torch high into the air. The monkey army broke in panic, tearing along the gorge. The torch hit the earth, igniting nearby patches of weeds which in turn set off yet other, more distant patches. In this waterless land it took only moments for the entire gorge to erupt into something of a furnace. Hopping, yelping, moaning, and cavorting, the baboons desperately tried to dodge the ever-growing flames.

All regimentation was gone; senselessly they rolled in the sand and wailed while their hairy coats smoldered and blazed. Torch after torch came hurtling through the night. It was not long before the gorge was completely devoid of any baboon who could yet run for its life. Those left behind hobbled and cried over the corpses of comrades long since broiled.

Panting, hands on their hips, the five travelers looked at the grisly scene below and smiled thankfully at their fortune. Mariana stared blankly at the cliffs and watched as what was left of the phalanx clambered among the ledges and over the top, running wildly for their very lives in any direction their legs would carry them. Even the dire shouts for order issued by their generals went unheeded. The troops were oblivious to commands; if the fight was to continue, then their leaders would have to carry it themselves.

The battle of the gorge was a total rout. And to this very

147

day, as a matter of fact, it is still spoken of in baboon land with whispers and shudders.

"Run, you cowards!" hollered the haj, shaking an imperious fist as the last crippled stragglers dragged themselves into the night.

"And don't ever come back!" chimed in Homer, his face black with grime and soot, but his teeth gleaming with his grin. "Unless you want some more of the same!"

Soon the flames were dying, and the travelers deemed it safe to climb down the hill and look over the wreckage of the battlefield.

"Will they attack us again?" Ramagar asked the haj.

Burlu wiped a grimy hand across his mouth and spat. "We taught them a lesson, this time," he growled. "But the baboons' king won't rest so easily. If he can, he'll send another army as soon as he can raise one."

The Prince shook his head and sighed. "In that case, we'd better get out of their domain with all the speed we can make . . ."

Mariana nodded. But then she looked around at the carnage and tallied their losses. Of the seven mules, three lay dead at the edge of the gorge. Two more had run off the moment they saw the fire. That left two mules, two mules for the five of them. And to make matters worse, one of the absconded mules had carried the extra water bags. The little water left would have to be rationed, rationed while they walked to the sea.

At Kalimar's northernmost border, nestled along a fertile plain at the foot of the mountain range known as the Great Divide, lay the port city of Palava. A free port, visited by ships from every maritime nation among the Eastern Kingdoms and from across many seas, it stood as Kalimar's greatest contact with the world outside her desert borders. And because of its free trade, there came to it men and women from every walk of life: foreign merchants and sailors, traders from both the desert and the hills, opportunists, fanatics, religious sects of dubious worth, and a host of nameless others who made the port a melting pot of cultures, some strange, some exotic, some as secretive as the Druids themselves.

Much has been told of Palava; hardly a traveler to its walls did not return home filled with tales to whet the imagination. Its marketplaces and bazaars were like none others in all of the East. A visitor could wander through its maze of shabby streets and see a new wonder at virtually every corner. Once seen, Palava would never be forgotten. It was a city of the unusual, a city of mimes, fire-eaters, magicians, and contortionists, dancers and strong men, flutists, animal trainers, lute players, and poets. Of head-shaven Karshi fanatics gathering to pay homage at the sight of the hovel where their leader was born. Of scholars and lunatics, of holy men who pierced their flesh with pins and needles and then lay down upon beds of broken glass, all to the amusement (and sometimes revulsion) of their audiences.

Whatever the visitors' opinions, all agreed it was a city you would never erase from your thoughts.

Captain Osari, of the merchant ship *Vulture*, sat glumly at the inn, staring into his half-filled flagon of black Palavi beer. A hefty fellow, with prominent jowls and thick, slanting brows above keen, intense eyes, he made no pretense of hiding his moroseness on this particular evening. His cargo of furs and quarried marble had been delivered to its buyers in Palava more than two weeks before. His cargo for the return trip, cinnamon and other spices, sat in bags and crates at dockside ready to be loaded. His vouchers had been stamped by the proper authorities, his sailing permit had been issued without any problem. Now all he needed was to find a new crew.

Captain Osari put his head in his hands and groaned. A new crew! Where in this forsaken backward land of Kalimar would he find the caliber of men needed for the *Vulture?* Of his twenty hands only three remained, the others having run off the moment they berthed and their wages were paid. Osari knew he should never have taken such men on in the first place. It would have been better to have sailed on to Cenulam and signed on a crew of trustworthy hands. Men from his own land whom he could count on. True seafarers; not a bunch of swaggering misfits from the East. But time had pressed. The cargo was urgently required. So, he had done the expedient thing and hired on in the first port he reached. A very foolish mistake. Oh, the slouches had made it to Palava all right. Problem was, where would he get the men he needed for the return voyage? A voyage that would take them a thousand leagues from home across some of the most violent seas the world had ever seen.

Ah, to be back in Cenulam now. Among real civilization

again. Far away from places like Kalimar. Osari shook his head sadly. Within three days' time his permits would no longer be valid. His cargo would find another ship, while the *Vulture* would be forced to lie languid and rot upon this uncivilized shore.

It was with these thoughts in mind that the captain ordered another round of the bitter beer and blotted out the noise of the rowdy crowd of sailors milling about the inn's tavern. Sailors indeed, he mused. They were nothing but dregs of the lowest kind. A poor substitute for honest seafaring men. Only sheer desperation had brought him here tonight; that, and an urgent need to get the *Vulture* away from Kalimarian waters before the corrupt military authorities took a mind to impound it.

Amid the flute music and the dancing girl's cavorting and the raucous laughter that accompanied them both, the Cenulamian captain hardly saw the two hooded figures who had briskly entered and asked questions of the landlord. It was only when the proprietor pointed his hand in his direction that Osari took notice. One was a man, tall and rugged; the other a woman, well tanned and pretty, with fire in her eyes.

The man approached the table first. "Is the *Vulture* your ship?" he asked.

"Are you Captain Osari from Cenulam?" quizzed the girl.

The seafarer looked slowly from one face to the other before answering. "I am Captain Osari," he said at last. "What of it?"

Mariana glanced to Ramagar and sighed. Then she turned with a smile to the captain, saying, "At last we've found you. We've been searching all day. Your first mate told us he hadn't the slightest notion where you were . . ."

"And now you know where I am," observed the captain dryly.

Ramagar leaned his forearm against the table and met the captain's questioning gaze. "We would like to speak with you, Captain. A few moments of your time is all we ask."

Sensing a business proposition in the offing, Osari gestured for them to take chairs. Then he snapped his fingers to catch the barmaid's attention and shouted for a small bottle of sweet wine to be brought.

When the wine was served he leaned forward, his hands clasped together, and said, "What's this all about? There must be a hundred captains in Palava. What is it that brings you to see me?"

150

"We understand that your ship is scheduled to leave for Cenulam," said Mariana, wasting no time. "We want to book passage and sail with you."

The captain nodded, thoughtfully wondering why these obvious Kalimarians seemed so eager to reach a land so alien to them. "Have you business to conduct in Cenulam?"

"Not in Cenulam itself," replied Ramagar mysteriously. "But in waters nearby. We've queried every captain we could find. Only you are sailing across the Western Sea."

Osari frowned. "It is a very long voyage, my friends. And a difficult one to boot."

"We understand," said Mariana. "We have some money; will this be enough?" She spilled the contents of a small purse onto the table. Osari stared at the glittering coins, a few gold, but mostly silver.

"More than enough for two," said the captain.

Ramagar shook his head. "We are five. Five passengers—"

"And we're willing to work to make up any difference," added Mariana. "What do you say? Will you take us on your ship?"

Osari scratched his head. This was a most baffling offer. His companions certainly were not merchants, nor even traders, if he had sized them up properly. From the looks of it they were offering every penny they had in the world to make the journey. Curious, as most Cenulamians are, Captain Osari wondered why. Still, it wasn't his affair, and he had need of the offered money to help defray the cost of a new crew.

"Have we a bargain?" pressed the thief.

The mariner nodded, but as his companions smiled he said, "There's just one problem. My crew, you see, has seen fit to desert me. And unless I can find another one within three days' time I'm afraid none of us will sail. Already the authorities are fining me for each day the *Vulture* stays berthed. And pretty soon they'll confiscate the ship. Likely as not I'll be as stranded in Palava as you are."

Ramagar groaned. "There must be sailors about?" he questioned. "What about the men here?"

"Rabble," Osari said honestly. "Murderers and cutthroats fled from their own lands to a free port. I wouldn't trust a single one with a penny, if you want to know the truth." Here he sighed. "And I have to warn you that even should some agree to sign on with me, I can't vouch for your safety ... Such is the nature of Palava's sailors."

Mariana looked at him evenly, with a small smile working

151

around the corners of her mouth. "Captain Osari," she said slowly, "my companions and I have just come from the desert. Nearly two weeks of facing one danger after another. The last fifty leagues we were forced to walk—with an army of baboons following every step of the way—"

Osari stared with disbelief. "Baboon Land? You two have traveled through Baboon Land?" He shuddered.

Ramagar nodded darkly. "And lucky we are to be sitting here with you tonight. But that's a tale for another time. My companions and I are used to facing risk and danger. The dilemma of putting up with a thieving crew is a small matter. We can take care of ourselves, I assure you. All we ask is that you take your ship directly to Cenulam as quickly as possible."

Osari downed the last of his drink. "So do I," he groaned. "Believe me, so do I."

"Perhaps there might be something we can do to help you," said Mariana.

The seasoned sailor glanced about at the motley bunch of mariners for hire and shook his head. "I think not, my lady. Leave finding the best up to me. Be on the south quay at dawn on the day after tomorrow. By then I should be ready. You'll not have any trouble in finding the *Vulture*; she flies the brown banners of the North. As soon as my spice is loaded and the inspectors have weighed the cargo, we'll be on our way."

The mention of inspectors caused both Mariana and the thief to wince—which did not go unnoticed by the captain's sharp eyes. Ramagar looked briefly at the girl and they shared an unspoken thought: mingled with the inspectors was certain to be no small number of Kalimarian soldiers, who by this time would have received word from the capital city and would be on the lookout for the fugitive thief and his lover. If only a single soldier caught sight of them and suspected . . .

It was a sobering thought, one that Ramagar was not in the mood to deal with now. A smile returning to his face, he rose from his chair and clasped Captain Osari's hand, shaking it firmly. "Until we sail, goodbye. Thank you, Captain, our bargain has been more than fair."

Osari stood and bowed politely. "Mutually fair, sir. I'm looking forward to seeing you both again." He turned to Mariana. "And maybe the next time we chat you'll tell me more of your adventures in Baboon Land."

The girl flushed. It was hard not to like the company of

the easygoing sailor. "A pleasure, Captain," she said. "But for now I think we should all just pray for a quick and successful journey."

Osari grinned, adding thoughtfully, "Believe it or not, I'm every bit as eager to leave Kalimar forever as you are."

With one full day to spend before Captain Osari's ship was set to leave, the travelers decided to leave their clandestine lodgings and spend their time in seeing some of Palava's colorful sights. Heading first to the major pavilions, they all laughed at the antics of street clowns and assorted acrobats, stood dumbfounded while a pipe player's melodious tune somehow caused a lumbering viper to uncoil from its basket and weave its scaly body upward in a parody of a dance. Amazed, they watched a strong man break his chains, laughed at a puppet show, and cried at a tragic drama at the city's huge amphitheater. The five farers enjoyed every moment of it all; even the usually sober-faced Prince was forced to admit he was having a good time. So unlike the capital city of Kalimar was Palava, that only the occasional sight of grim-faced soldiers reminded them that they had not left her borders at all.

But amid this merriment Mariana found herself feeling quite uneasy. It wasn't the first time, either. Although she had not brought it up, ever since that first night in the desert when the haj had found tracks of a man and proven her suspicions, she had felt that somehow her every movement was being observed. There was nothing she could point to, nothing she coud prove, even to herself. No shadowy figures peered from dark alleys or lurked at the ends of the streets. It was just an unrest, a disquiet that was nagging her constantly and wouldn't leave.

She had not mentioned it to Ramagar, positive that he would only smile and assure her it was imagination, tell her she was becoming too jumpy. Nor had she spoke of her fears to the haj, although she knew that he alone might give her thoughts the credence they deserved. After all, this was their last day upon shore, their last day ever in Kalimar. By tomorrow all her concerns would be gone.

It was early evening when they returned to their rooms at the inn. Restless for time to pass, they decided to enjoy the best supper the inn could provide. Gathering in the dining accommodations of the tavern, they ate a splendid feast of rare roasted beef that even Burlu had to grudgingly acknowledge

153

was among the finest he had ever sampled. There was no shortage of wine, both domestic and imported, lots of music, and even more song. The haj, of course, frowned upon receipt of the bill, thinking that city ways were far too expensive for a hill man's tastes; but he was fully aware, as they all were, that after tonight, money would have little meaning for them, and in any case there would be no place to spend it. It was best to make the most of it now, while they still could, momentarily allowing themselves to forget the monumental journey about to unfold.

One by one, groggy-eyed and weary, they all returned to their rooms, bellies filled and heads considerably lightened. Mariana kissed Ramagar goodnight and lit the candle beside the bed. At first glance everything seemed completely normal; but then she noticed the open window.

Walking to it slowly, she saw that the dust on the outside sill had been disturbed. And more than that, she was positive that a fleeting shadow of a man or a boy had just swept quickly past her vision in the alley below.

Losing no time, she woke Ramagar told her tale, and frowned while he looked at her and grinned. "Don't be so upset," he told her, cradling her in his arms. "Palava is filled with rogues, just like the Jandari. Are you so surprised that a thief came in and tried to find something of value?"

Mariana looked away, unsatisfied. "I think it's more than that," she confided. "I think someone was looking for something. Oh, Ramagar, I'm frightened."

His eyes grew cold as he propped himself up, tossing aside the blanket. "Looking for what?"

She shrugged. "I—don't know. But more than just a purse or a piece of jewelry . . ."

"Could it have been soldiers? Inquisitors come up from the capital?"

Mariana shook her head firmly. "No, an Inquisitor wouldn't bother to come through a window. More likely he'd break down the door."

The thief drew her closer to him and ran his fingers through her dark hair. "Then it was only a thief. Hush, Mariana, don't be scared. If you like you can spend the night here, with me."

She nodded, smiling like a child, and nestled herself against the crook of his shoulder as he leaned back and closed his eyes. "I'll be all right," she whispered. "Maybe I am just

154

a little too tense. You try to sleep, I'll just stay by your side . . ."

Ramagar had fallen asleep even before her thought was finished. Mariana kissed him and lay still and silent, listening to the sound of his breathing. And soon her fears were gone. Ramagar had been right, she was sure. It was only a thief; a common thief. Nothing more. And then she laughed to herself. Less than a month before Ramagar was such a thief; the master rogue of the Jandari. And she had been what? A dancing girl, with no future, no hope of ever attaining any of the things a woman dreams about. Now, though, because of the Prince's dagger, all that had irreversibly changed. They had fled Kalimar; crossed an inhospitable desert and beaten a formidable foe. Joined forces with a prince, come to love a kindly old haj. Even seen the wonders of Palava. Hard to believe that all this was only the beginning.

Suddenly she felt no fear of this night or of the days ahead. It crossed her mind that if she could live her whole life over again she would not change a thing. Bridges were meant to be crossed, no matter how high or how fearful. It was her good fortune, she reasoned, that she would always have Ramagar at her side to cross them with her.

The thief smiled in his sleep as she put her head beside his and gently kissed him. Then closing her eyes and yawning, she eagerly anticipated the coming of dawn.

11

Homer was kneeling, tying as securely as he could the last strap around their meager baggage. Then, when it was drawn as tight as he could pull, he looked up at his waiting companions and grinned. "All set," he announced.

The haj munched on a freshly baked biscuit and nodded. "Good," he said, brushing his hands of leftover crumbs. "Then we can get going."

Ramagar drew himself up from the cushioned chair and glanced out the large bay window. While Burlu paid the landlord he stared at the predawn Palava skyline. Here and there above the roofs a soft gray hue was pushing back the black, tickling the edges of the domes and obelisks and thinly spreading higher against the waning stars. From somewhere distant came the cry to morning prayer, and down a quiet avenue a handful of robed holy men hurried on their way to answer the call.

For a moment the thief felt a twinge of terrible sadness overtake him. Tears began to well in his dark, cold eyes. Never again would he come back to Palava. Never again would he set foot upon the sandy desert shores of Kalimar. As harsh and as cruel as the land may have been, it still was, after all, his home. And leaving one's home, never to return, is the hardest thing a man can do.

Mariana knew what was in his mind; in many ways her thoughts were identical. She came quietly to his side and drew him away slowly, knowing that for them to wallow in regret would only make leaving that much worse.

Ramagar took her hand, and smiled. The past was past, it could never be altered. Now they must look to the future. Drawing his hood over his head, he left the inn and walked briskly into the street to join his friends, determined never to think of Kalimar again. Like the Prince, he was now a man without a country.

The walk to the docks was completely uneventful. They were all just another band of robed hill folk visiting the city. Even the occasional passing soldier never even turned his head.

At last they reached the south quay where the *Vulture* was already loaded and busy with sailors scrambling about the deck and checking the rigging. Ramagar gazed with interest at the boat, taking note of her sharp, arching head and her slim bow running along her convex sides all the way down to the rounded graceful stern.

The *Vulture* was a large ship, worn and ragged in places, but as sturdy and fit for duty as any you would ever find. Perhaps eighty meters long from stem to stern, twelve in breadth, she seemed as well fitted as the finest Kalimarian vessel ever constructed. There were two masts, iron banded, taut, and well tapered. From the furled lower crimson sails to the upper yellows, her spars were long and graceful, and Ramagar knew that within an hour's time these latticeworks would be stretching a skyful of colored canvas into the strong sea winds.

With some fear and trepidation the band passed the milling pursers and Palava inspectors and walked the gangplank onto the main deck. A silver coin or two cleverly placed into the

156

right hands by the haj ensured that no questions would be asked of the passengers.

Captain Osari stood at the quarterdeck, hands folded behind his back. As his passengers stepped on board he grinned and saluted. "Welcome to the *Vulture*," he told them. "You arrived just in time. We're ready to hoist anchor."

"And not a moment too soon," mumbled Ramagar. As he looked down to the end of the pier he saw a patrol of dark-tunicked soldiers heading straight for the ship.

Osari saw them, too, and frowned. "It's probably a trivial matter," he said distastefully. "Nothing to be concerned about."

"Ahoy, captain of this vessel!" shouted a hawk-nosed commander, rushing to reach the gangplank before it was lifted.

Osari leaned over the rail and eyed the man carefully. "I'm the captain," he called down. "What do you want?"

The soldier saluted him respectfully, but adroitly kept one hand clutched at the hilt of his long dangling sword. "I'm under orders to inspect your crew, Captain—"

The *Vulture*'s wily commander grimaced. "I'm afraid you can't. You should have come earlier. We're almost under way."

But the soldier was as firm as the man he addressed. "You have no choice, Captain Osari. No ship is to leave Palava without being thoroughly searched."

The captain grew red. "Searched? What in heaven or hell are you talking about, man? My ship's already been inspected. All my cargoes have been checked through and through."

"It's not cargo I'm concerned with, Captain Osari . . ."

Ramagar looked quickly to the Prince and the haj. He felt his body tense; his mind began to click, looking for quick avenues of escape, if it came to that.

"What's this all about?" demanded Osari. "By what right do you dare stop a free ship in a free port?"

The soldier drew a hand inside his tunic and came up holding a small, rolled piece of parchment. "These orders have just come from the capital," he said. "No ship can leave unless she's been checked by me and my men. I'm sorry if this will be an inconvenience, but . . ." He sighed and gestured to his men, who had all drawn their swords. "But neither one of us has any choice. If you try to refuse me boarding rights, I'm afraid I'll have to do it by force."

Mariana glanced at the dozen or so rugged soldiers and shuddered. It was plain they meant business; she knew they wouldn't hesitate to follow their orders even if it meant bloodshed.

Captain Osari seethed, but relented, knowing there was nothing he could do. "Very well," he said sharply to the waiting captain. "Come aboard, but make it quick. I've lost too much time in this stinking country already."

The soldier ignored the remark and made his way to the main deck. "We're looking for a fugitive," he said, glancing around. "A murderer escaped from the capital and believed to have fled to Palava."

Osari knitted his brows. "You won't find any fugitives on my ship," he assured the man. "I chose my crew as carefully as I could. They're all honest seamen."

The soldier smiled thinly. "Let me be the judge of that, Captain. The man I seek is a master criminal, the most wanted soul in Kalimar. He's as clever and as dangerous as any we've ever known." Here he leaned in close to the sea captain and whispered, "He's killed in cold blood before. Mark my words, if he's on your ship, he'll do it again. Now, assemble your crew."

Osari nodded, and the first mate, a trusted man from Cenulam, rounded up everyone on deck. And what a surly bunch they were, even Ramagar had to admit. Stiff-necked, growling men. Some bore scars of knife fights along their faces, others showed the marks of the whip upon their shirtless backs. They scowled and grimaced as the tight-lipped soldier walked among them, checking their descriptions against the one he had written on his orders.

The crew stood sullenly while the captain completed his chore. It was as obvious as their scars that each and every one of them was a known criminal, a wanted man either in Kalimar or some other land. But it was equally plain that none of them was the man being sought, the master rogue, the thief of thieves: Ramagar.

"Are there any others among your crew?" questioned the soldier as he turned away from the brigands, leaving the grim line of renegade sailors smirking among themselves.

"Two others," replied Captain Osari truthfully. "One is my personal cabin boy, brought with me from Cenulam. The other is a cook I hired. A hunchback, seeking to work for his passage across the sea. Shall I have them brought topside?"

The soldier deliberated for a second, then frowned and shook his head. "No, I don't think that will be necessary, Captain." Then, catching sight of the five passengers standing
158

mutely at the steps of the quarterdeck, he said, "And who are they?"

Osari shrugged. "Paying passengers," he said. "I know little about them, but surely you don't suspect one of them to be your fugitive—"

"Let me decide that, Captain Osari." He walked over, eyeing them one and all suspiciously. The message from Kalimar had not gone into much detail, but it did say that the thief Ramagar would probably be found traveling with a woman, a woman not at all unlike the pretty girl he was looking at now.

Mariana thought she was going to die right then and there. Her heart was pounding so loudly that she couldn't understand why the soldier didn't seem to hear it.

"Who are all of you?" the captain asked at last.

The haj stepped forward quickly, partially shielding his friends from observation; he bowed graciously before the doubtful-looking soldier, and said, "I am haj Burlu, of the hill country in the south. I travel on board the *Vulture* to reach Cenulam, where I am told I can purchase the world's finest stallions. Stallions for breeding . . ."

"I see," replied the soldier, rubbing his thumb along the side of his thick jowls. He narrowed his eyes. "And who are your companions?"

The haj gestured grandly to Mariana. "She's my granddaughter," he beamed, squeezing her hand. "The jewel of my life. And beside her is her husband . . ."

At the feel of the soldier's steely glance Ramagar bowed his head in a respectful fashion and lowered his gaze to the freshly scrubbed deck.

"Take down your hood," said the captain sternly. "Let me see your face."

Ramagar did as asked, but he still kept his stare firmly fixed on the damp planks.

Once again the haj interceded to cut off trouble before it began. "My granddaughter's husband is a slow-witted fellow," he said in an apologetic tone. "But as you can see, his brawn and muscles more than make up for what he lacks in the head."

Ramagar fumed, but he didn't move and didn't say a word.

The soldier took a step closer, looking at the written description. "What is your name?" he asked. Before the thief could reply, Mariana said, "We call him Ishi. Among hill folk it means the Foolish One. My husband does not speak very

159

much, as he rarely has anything intelligent to say. But he enjoys making up poems, and he also likes to sing on occasion . . ."

At this Ramagar lifted his head and smiled in the fashion of a buffoon. "Shall I s-s-sing for you, sir?" he stuttered. "I kn-kn-know many pretty tunes."

The soldier grimaced, feeling slightly sickened. Ramagar broke into a loud, grim tune extolling the virtues of farm work and shoveling manure for fertilizer. "Can't you shut him up?" rasped the soldier in total exasperation.

"It isn't easy once he gets going," admitted the girl with a sigh. "But for you," she smiled, "I'll do my best." Then, catching the thief off guard, she delivered a quick boot to his rump. Ramagar looked up at her sharply, then, returning to his slow-witted grin, ended his song.

The commander, relieved, looked away and shook his head. It was a mystery to him how such a lovely young woman, granddaughter of a haj, could have allowed herself to be wed to a dimwit like this. It was really a terrible waste. But then hill people were known to be a peculiar lot, and there was just no accounting for a woman's tastes.

He looked next to the Prince, who lost no time in pulling off his own hood so the soldier could get a better look at him. The blue eyes and yellow hair immediately removed him from suspicion and the need for any questions. Likewise with Homer; there wasn't much point in interrogating a mere boy.

Captain Osari drummed his fingers impatiently against the side of the railing. "Well?" he said. "Are you satisfied? Do I have your permission to sail my ship?" His tone and manner were gruff and angry, but inside it was all he could do to stop from bursting into laughter.

The soldier put his written orders back into his tunic, took another fast look at the foul crew the *Vulture*'s skipper had been forced to hire, and nodded. "My apologies, Captain Osari," he said, saluting smartly. "Of course you are free to be on your way whenever you like. I'm sorry for this delay. Please allow me to wish you and all your passengers," he glanced admiringly at Mariana, "a pleasant and satisfying voyage. Perhaps the next time you sail to Palava we'll meet again on better terms." And with that, he spun around and made his way down the gangplank, signaling waiting troops to put away their weapons.

When he was gone, Ramagar and the others breathed a long sigh of relief, as did the captain himself. "I owe you a

160

debt of gratitude," said the thief. "Thank you for not speaking up. I suppose that you know—"

"Know what?" laughed the Cenulamian sailor. "That you are indeed the man the soldiers were seeking? It makes no difference to me. I am neither judge nor jury."

"Perhaps. But I want you to know that I never committed the murder they accuse me of."

The sea captain tightened his eyes and stared at his ragtag crew. "See those men?" he asked. Ramagar nodded. "They're thieves and liars every one. I'd wager each man among them is a scourge on the face of the earth. I'll have my hands full enough with the likes of them to have to concern myself with the deeds of a paying passenger."

Ramagar nodded with understanding. They did seem a rebellious bunch, filled with swagger and bravado. And desperate men sometimes will take desperate actions. "Are you expecting trouble, then?"

The captain's face grew stern and impassive. "Nothing I can't handle."

"You've been a friend to me," said Ramagar. "So if at any time during the voyage I can repay you in any way, don't hesitate to ask."

Osari smiled grimly. "I'll remember that, Ramagar. Let's both hope, though, it doesn't come to that." He clasped the thief on the shoulder and nodded politely to all his passengers. "We'll all talk again later at supper," he said. "But for now I'll have to ask you to excuse me. I'll have the cabin boy show you to your quarters and give you a chance to settle in. As for me, the tide is with us and I've got too much to do." Then he shouted an order to his helmsman, and another to the first mate, who in turn bellowed the command down the line to the crew.

Every sailor quickly scuttled to his post. The morning sun by now was blazing; a flock of gulls flew high above the masts, racing out to sea. Mariana, her baggage in her hand, watched in wonder as the birds soared, then glided, and squawking, dived down to the water.

Hand over hand the thick iron chain was hoisted, the black shell- and moss-covered anchor pulled aboard. Lines were untied, shirtless sailors grappled at the halyards. The lumbering ship groaned and bobbed as it slowly began to pull from the pier. Then with a rush the lower sails were unfurled, swelling in sudden crimson majesty against the salted wind. Mariana watched from the stern as the sprawling city of Palava, its

161

towers and minarets shimmering in the light, became toy miniatures along the near horizon. Beyond the city the desert sparkled with golden sands and blood-red dunes and mounds of clay. Turning, she gazed at the vastness of the ocean ahead: the Great Western Sea, now calm and placid, deepening in its tones of blue with every forward surge of the mighty ship. Bow raising and dipping, the *Vulture* cut a wide swath of foaming white froth whose waves rippled endlessly on for as far as Mariana could see.

And at last the voyage they had all dreamed of was under way, setting its course for the far North, the seafaring land of Cenulam not too far from the coasts of Speca. Kalimar and all of the Eastern Kingdoms became but a haze to her, a fragile memory slipping away as fast as the shoreline itself. And by evening all sight of land was gone.

As the sun dropped away and the sky glowed in a dark azure, Mariana spent a few moments of solitude on deck, watching the stars appear one by one until the sky was lit as she had never seen it before. She felt the wind rushing through her hair and salt spray gently splashing against her face. This would be a long voyage, she knew, with a new world waiting for her at its conclusion. But for the duration of the journey she and Ramagar would at last share some peaceful time together; a few weeks of quiet happiness and tranquility until the stark mountains of Cenulam were in sight.

Or so she thought.

12

The first few days of the voyage were completely uneventful, save for the mild discomforts the passengers felt at being at sea for the first time in their lives.

But it was pleasant company they shared; supper at night with Captain Osari and his jovial first mate and cabin boy; long evenings of recounting longer tales of both the ancient Eastern Kingdoms and those of the mysterious North.

Osari proved to be an affable fellow, eager to speak of many subjects, especially of his homeland. The only times he seemed to grow quiet were when the name of Speca was mentioned. Needless to say, the passengers never once told him or anyone else of their true mission or their urgency in reaching Cenulam.

In addition to Captain Osari, three others of the crew were from Cenulam: the first mate, the cabin boy, and the helmsman. All were excellent sailors, all were completely trustworthy. As for the rest of the crew, though, they proved to be every bit as surly and ·cantankerous as the captain had feared. Many had to be badgered or threatened into performing even the simplest of tasks. And many of them seemed to show a strange interest in the passengers. More than once Mariana had been frightened by the sight of several of them milling about in the evening and watching her and Ramagar closely. The Prince noticed it, too. They seemed to follow him everywhere, without reason, be it day or night. Once he found two of them posting themselves outside his cabin. And though his cabin seemed in proper order, he was sure that it had been secretly rifled.

Strangest of all, though, was the behavior of the little man Osari had taken on as ship's cook. He prepared his food at night and never stepped on deck at any time. Hardly anyone had ever seen the fellow. He kept to himself like a hermit. There had been one occasion when Ramagar, returning below after an afternoon of exercise, had seen him lurking in the dark shadows of the hold. The thief tried to approach the little man, but the cook caught sight of him and ran away as fast as a lizard, slamming and bolting the galley door behind.

After one week out and perhaps a third of the voyage done, there was no longer doubt in anyone's mind: there were peculiar doings on board the *Vulture*, doings that bode only ill.

And then the problems began, a series of minor misfortunes that constantly plagued them and severely cut into the ship's carefully planned running time. A small fire in the hold. A broken boom that was not discovered until the sail had ripped and was left slatting in the wind. Broken tools. Spoiled meats. Leaks in the water barrels. There was only one word to describe what was going on: sabotage.

Making matters worse was that with the onset of spring, the terrible gales and tempests that troubled the Western Sea were about to begin. Captain Osari had hoped to avoid the season at all costs. He had reasoned that, by plotting every track with utmost care, they would make Cenulam or one of its close neighbors just in time. But now because of these nagging problems, his hopes were dashed. Already the weather

163

was beginning to change. Cloud formations massed on the horizon every morn, ever thicker, ever darker. Each day he would watch them closely and take notes. The rains were coming, swept down from the frigid north by brutal gale-force winds. By now the hurricanes would be approaching Cenulam. Given a few days more they would reach the *Vulture*, and the ship would face the last week of its journey battling the fiercest wrath of the sea.

Yet why the crew, even these rogues, would be so intent on forcing delays and creating difficulties was a mystery beyond his comprehension. What had any of them to gain by this behavior? Certainly any levelheaded, intelligent sailor would be trying to do everything he could to avoid such confrontations with the storms. But these men didn't seem to care. In fact, at times he could only assume that the opposite was true. But why? For what reason would they welcome such havoc? What was their motive for slowing the ship down and making her journey to Cenulam needlessly treacherous?

Captain Osari shuddered. He had discussed the matter with his mate and helmsman. They had drawn as many blanks as he had. Cornering the bosun and one or two other slouches, he had tried to get some information out of them. But when questioned they grew silent and sullen. Osari had felt the burn of their eyes upon him and the snickers on their lips when he turned his back. If answers were to be provided, he could only bide his time and be alert for what might turn up elsewhere.

It was the evening of the fifteenth day; the captain went topside as usual to record his sextant sightings. Mariana was on the quarterdeck, alone, staring in fascination out at the eternal sea.

"A beautiful evening, isn't it?" he said, coming beside her and saluting. Mariana glanced up and smiled. "Magnificent, Captain." She turned and faced him with her back leaning against the railing and the wind rushing through her hair. "The sea is an enchanting mistress, especially at this time of day. I'm beginning to understand how it lures men from home and makes them sailors."

Osari grinned, gazing out at the northern horizon. Low dark clouds, turned violet in the waning light, were scudding across the sky. "You should have a shawl," he said. "It gets chilly at night."

Mariana shook her head. "I like it like this." Her hand

164

grasped at the rail and she sighed. "So calm, so peaceful . . ."

The captain nodded with understanding. "Once you've been at sea you'll always want to return," he told her. "And the more you sail, the more you want to come back. When a sailor's out, like we are, he always looks forward to reaching port. But once he's back on land all he thinks about is returning, sailing the ocean again . . ." He looked at her and frowned. "Pardon me, Mariana. I didn't mean to get sentimental."

The girl laughed briefly, but then her face turned more serious. The look in her eyes only hinted at the worry she was concealing. "I've been wanting to have a few words with you, Captain," she said soberly.

"Is anything wrong? Has the crew been bothering you?"

She shook her head. "Not that. But about our reaching Cenulam—we all know something's wrong. What's going on, Captain? Ramagar says we're running several days behind schedule—"

Captain Osari rested his arms on the rail and stared at the choppy water for a long time before answering. "Then . . . you know," he said at last.

Mariana shivered and rubbed her sleeveless arms, searching Osari's face. A strong gust blew her hair across her eyes as she said, "It's hard not to know. It's the crew's doing, isn't it? This sabotage, I mean."

Osari's features remained impassive even as his face darkened. "They're a strange lot, Mariana. Defiant, sneaky. A sad bunch of wretches. And I won't lie to you; I'm deeply worried. The way things are going now we won't be able to reach Cenulam until the storm season passes. I'll be forced to seek the first and closest shelter I can, to berth the ship until the weather changes for the better." He looked away, tensely clenching his hands into fists. "I just don't understand it," he mumbled, as much to himself as to her. "Why would they want to sabotage the ship? My cargo isn't gold or silver. Just spices, a hold full of cinnamon. What do they have to gain by forcing me to alter course?"

"Perhaps that's exactly what they want; to force you to reach a closer port."

The captain's eyes slitted like a cat's; he stared at the girl with unguarded puzzlement. "You could be right," he said. "Frankly, I hadn't thought of it like that. But I still don't understand why."

The wind was growing colder; Mariana glanced down at the poop deck, where two burly sailors stood watching and grinning as she and the captain spoke.

"I don't have any answers, either," she admitted, turning her attention back to Osari. "I only wish I did. I only wish that someone could explain to me what's going on." Then she leaned in closer to avoid any prying eyes. "I saw something very peculiar last night, Captain. I was just getting ready to go to sleep when I heard some muffled noises outside the door. Opening it just a crack, I saw at least six of your crew, including the bosun, sneaking down the hall and into the galley." She looked at Osari sharply. "What would they be doing in the kitchen at midnight?"

It was an interesting question; the captain rubbed a hand at the side of his clean-shaven face and pondered. Whatever they were doing was certainly a mystery; but one thing was certain—there were no meals being served at that hour of night.

"Then you think that the cook might be involved in all this?"

"Seems more than likely. If you ask me, I have a hunch that your galley is being used as some kind of headquarters for the crew to plot whatever they're up to. And this cook, whoever he is, could well be the mastermind."

The captain seemed incredulous. "Him? No, Mariana. It's impossible. Anyone but him. Why, the man's a virtual hermit. He has nothing to do with any of the crew—or anyone else for that matter. Why, he hardly comes out of the galley for air. The cabin boy does the serving and returns the empty bowls. No one sees the cook. Not even me."

"All the more reason to suspect him," growled Mariana. "Why is he so secretive? I've been on board the *Vulture* for over two weeks now. *Two weeks.* And I don't even know what he looks like. Don't you find that rather odd?"

Osari was forced to agree; it certainly was.

"Who is he?" she asked. "What name did he give you? What does he look like? And where does he come from? I have a feeling that if you question him he'll provide some pieces to fill in the puzzle. What do you know about him?"

Captain Osari shook his head and sighed. "Very little, I'm afraid," he replied. "I needed a cook urgently, so I just took on the first man that asked . . ."

"*Asked?*" mimicked Mariana, stunned. "He *asked* to sail aboard this ship? Isn't that strange by itself? From everything

166

you've told me, just about every sailor had to be prodded and bribed to make the journey to Cenulam. Why do you suppose he volunteered?"

Osari snapped his fingers and bit his lip. "You know, you're right! I never really gave it much thought. I guess I was too relieved to get someone to question his motives . . ."

"I think we'd better rectify that," said the girl. "Let's start from the first peg. What's he like, where's he from?"

The captain of the *Vulture* thought hard, trying to recall everything he could. "He's a small man," he said at last. "Slightly deformed, poor fellow. A hunchback . . ."

Mariana tensed. "Go on," she urged.

"He told me he was from the south. Didn't say which city. Only that it was urgent for him to find a ship to take him to Cenulam. At first I was skeptical, but then he offered to work in any capacity I had available. Once he knew that I had taken passengers for the voyage, he wouldn't take no for an answer. He gave me a gold doubloon and promised more—anything I asked, in fact—if I'd just let him sail . . ."

Mariana felt goose bumps rising and her hands began to tremble.

"What's the matter?" said Osari, suddenly concerned. "Has anything I said upset you? Have I—"

She shook her head briskly. "No, no. It's all right. It's nothing. But you just reminded me of something, someone I'd hoped never to see or hear of again . . ."

The skipper seemed confused. Then the girl faced him again, and this time her smile returned. "Do me a favor, Captain Osari," she asked. "Don't mention our conversation to anyone. Not just yet. Not until I have a few things straightened out."

"But why? I thought it would be best if I called all the passengers together, to see if we could get some of this cleared up—"

"Please, Captain," she pressed. "Wait a day. Give me until tomorrow to find some answers of my own. Will you do that for me?"

Osari nodded reluctantly. "All right, Mariana. If that's what you want—"

Her dark eyes flashed. "It's what I want. Thank you. You're right, it is getting cold up here. Will you excuse me? I think I'll go back below."

And without waiting for a reply, she turned and hurried

167

down the steps to the poop deck. Osari stood and watched her go. He felt bewildered—and more than a little bit worried.

It was late, close to midnight. By ten bells all the other passengers had returned to their cabins and were fast asleep. As Mariana slipped from her door into the dim passageway she could hear a deep snoring coming from the haj's cabin. She put her ear to the door of the cabin that Ramagar and the Prince were sharing. There wasn't a sound or a stir. Then she smiled. Ramagar would be furious if he knew about her little escapade. But she didn't want to tell him—at least not until her frightening suspicions were either proved or disproved. And right now, with her knees quivering like jelly and her hands as cold as ice, she hoped more than anything that she would be wrong.

A dim oil lamp swayed in the distance at the end of the passage. The merchant ship groaned softly with the noises of aging wood. Step by step, wearing her moccasins to muffle any sound, she inched her way to the end of the passage and around the corner.

Back hard against the wall, hands clenched at her side, she held her breath and strained her ears to hear. The door to the galley was a needle of light ajar. There came a steady stream of dim whispers from inside, then a laugh, a shared laugh of several men. Low, and mean, and ugly.

It took all her courage to go any farther. But go she did. Some meters away from the galley entrance she saw an open door to one of the storerooms. Mariana tiptoed for it and quickly slipped inside. There, amid the weighted crates and sacks of flour and grain, she took her first full breath. It was almost black inside the storeroom. The only light was from the closed porthole at the far side, where a trickle of moonlight worked its way inside the edges of the bolted wooden shutter.

Half leaning over a dusty pile of mealie bags, she listened again to the muffled voices. This time, though, they were clearer. Much clearer.

"Aye," said a thick, guttural voice which she knew belonged to the bosun. "We can do it tomorrow. Best get this matter dealt with as quickly as we can."

There was a long pause, then: "You'll tell your lads?"

The bosun chuckled. "They've been itchin' for it as much as me, matey. 'Bout time we got a bit o' our own say 'round

168

here. Cenulam, indeed!" The bosun spit, and Mariana could hear it clang into the bottom of an empty spittoon.

"What about the captain?" came a whisper. A familiar voice that made her flesh crawl.

A low laugh. "Ha! Leave that Northern pasty-faced canary to me. Him and 'is first mate both. Once I've dealt with those passengers—"

"Remember what I told you!" snapped the whispered voice. "Don't get any ideas in that head of yours. The girl is mine!"

Again the bosun spit. "Think yer man enough for her, do ya?"

"We made a bargain, friend. You get the ship and my gold. I get the scimitar and the girl . . ."

Mariana turned white with fear. Now she knew: she was listening to the plans for a mutiny.

Desperate to run out of there, to warn Ramagar and the captain, she tripped over a small wooden bucket placed beside the crates, causing a clatter like the beating of a drum.

"What was that?" gasped the bosun.

"I don't know—let's have us a look-see . . ."

Perspiration poured down Mariana's face as she peeked through the crack of the storeroom door's hinges and saw the galley door swing wide open. She watched the grim-faced bosun and one of his henchmen striding toward her, and then her heart skipped a beat. Following behind, a sneer on his face and a look of hate in his eyes, came the cook, the hunchback weasel of a man she knew to be Oro.

It all became painfully clear in her mind and she hated herself for not realizing it sooner. The evil trader had left Kalimar—left the moment he realized that Ramagar and somehow eluded the Inquisitors and escaped with the precious dagger. Oro had wanted the blade, coveted it at any price. And Mariana was now positive that he had known all along its true secret. No wonder that he wanted Ramagar dead. The dagger meant far more than mere money to him—it was the key to the throne of Speca. An ambition worth any risk.

He must have followed them every step of the way, caught sight of her and Ramagar on the road and trailed them until they sought shelter at the tents of the haj. Then he had pursued them into Baboon Land; there was no doubt in her mind that it was Oro's shadow she had seen that night at Alasi oasis. By the time they reached Palava, he was already there—waiting, looking to see which ship would carry them

169

across the sea. As Captain Osari's ship was the only vessel in harbor heading for the far North, it made it that much easier. All he needed to do was arrange his own passage, keep out of everyone's sight, and hatch his devious scheme. And what better cronies could he ask for than a bunch of shiftless cutthroat sailors who would sell their souls for a purse of gold?

It was a perfect plan; Mariana knew she had to give him credit for at least that. And if Oro had his way, by this time tomorrow all her companions, including Captain Osari and his Cenulamian sailors, would be dead. The renegades would own the ship and a bagful of gold—while the evil hunchback would take both her and the scimitar for his own.

Mariana ducked behind a large crate of boxed spices just as the bosun cautiously stepped inside the storeroom. Shadows bounced malevolently as the treacherous sailor struck a match and peered about. His glowering eyes scanned the room from one side to the other, poring over every inch of darkness.

Oro was paces behind. "Well?" he rasped impatiently. "See anything?"

The bucket stopped rolling at the bosun's feet; he watched it rock from side to side for a moment, and then he smiled.

"*Someone's* been hiding here," he said with assurance.

Oro was shaken. "Who? The first mate? Surely not the captain—"

The bosun shook his head, scratched at his matted beard. The tiny jeweled ring in his left ear glittered as he lit a second match. Mariana snuck a fast look between the slats and shuddered at the cruelty of his face. His shoulders lifted from a stoop and he brazenly took a few quick steps forward.

"I know yer in here, somewhere," he growled. "So ya might as well come out now and make it easier on yerself . . ." His hand slid down to the hilt of the twin-edged knife strapped at his waist. "I ain't got no time for little games, mousey. Stand up."

Mariana swallowed hard and crouched lower. The bosun circled around one side while his henchman grabbed a loose board like a club and covered the opposite end. Oro, meanwhile, backstepped to the door, rubbing his hands one over the other as he glowered in anticipation.

"Better come out, little mouse," warned the bosun. He stepped between the bags of meal and came frighteningly close to where the girl had hidden. A third match blazed like a torch, and Mariana's shadow bounced across the low ceil-

170

ing. As the bosun stared she slipped behind another crate, closer to the wall.

The sailor roared with laughter, his firm belly quivering slightly with merriment. "Think ya can still hide from me, do ya? Hide from old Bucky-boy, eh? Well, Bucky got a little surprise of his own, mousey. Oh, yes. A surprise of his own." He blew out the flickering match and drew his knife.

Mariana panted. He had her cornered; she had to get away. But how? The second sailor stood waiting along the other wall, while Oro had the door well covered. The only chance she had, she knew, was to make a fast dash for the doorway and somehow hope to knock over the hunchback before he could grab her. Then with luck she could be at Ramagar's door before they caught up . . .

Mariana leaped to her feet; spinning, ducking, she fled as fast as she could toward the dim light.

"Get her!" barked the bosun.

His crony flew across the storeroom, diving for her and barely missing. She sidestepped his tumbling hulk and bolted to the entrance. Oro drew to his full height; when they collided they both fell tumbling to the floor.

"Quick!" called the bosun. "Gag her!"

Mariana wriggled and squirmed, trying to free herself from Oro's tight grip. She tried to scream but it was too late. The bosun and his mate were all over her, pulling out a sweaty scarf and tying it tightly between her teeth. She kicked wildly as they dragged her to her feet, again tried to run but stopped frozen at the feel of the knife positioned sharply at the small of her back.

"Just do as we say, mousey," growled the bosun in a low, panting voice. And pushing and shoving, they threw her into the galley and closed the door behind.

Oro was sweating. He glanced at the girl and wiped his brow with his sleeve. "What do we do now?" he asked the bosun.

The sailor spat into the spittoon. "Get rid of her. It's all we can do . . ."

"Aye," chimed in his grisly henchman, and Mariana's eyes widened in terror.

"You can't do that!" wheezed Oro. "The girl is mine—part of the bargain, remember?"

The bosun scowled. "Sure, little man. Sure. But that was before we caught her spying, right? Now things is different.

Very different. She knows what we're up to. Don't tell me ya think we should let her go?"

Oro shook his head nervously. "No, no. Of course not. She'll have the captain after us in a minute. But maybe we can hide her somewhere . . ."

"Hide her? Not likely! You want to have that bloody lover of hers tearing the ship apart plank by plank? No, little man. She has to be disposed of—right away."

The hunchback gulped and shuddered. The thought of losing the dancing girl at the whim of this lout made him bristle with anger. He had spent so much time, so much effort in finding her, he wasn't about to give her up now. But what could he do about it? Clearly the bosun was far too gruesome a character to cross.

"Well, little man? Do you agree or not? Or maybe you place a higher value on the woman than you do on the dagger?"

As Oro flushed the bosun turned to his foul friend, saying, "We'll take her up on deck after first watch. Then we'll dump her over . . ."

Mariana screamed a gurgled scream and fought with all her strength against the two sailors who laughed grimly as they bound her hands and feet with rope.

"Wait, wait!" pleaded the hunchback. "Listen to me, both of you. The girl needn't die—"

The bosun looked at him with one eye cocked. "Oh? You have a better plan?"

"I do. Alert all your men now, tonight. Why must we wait for dawn to take over the ship? Do it tonight, while the captain's still asleep. We can get him and all the others out of the way and have done with it. By morning the ship can be in your hands. Sail her where you like, along with all the gold I promised. Well, what do you say?"

Oro was sweating profusely as he waited for the answer. While Mariana stood trembling she watched the bosun rub his chin and consider the change in plan. Then he smiled, glancing lecherously at the girl.

"Would be a shame, wouldn't it, mousey?" he chortled to her disgust. Mariana looked away as he said, "Tell you what, little man. I'll consider going along with your idea—but only if you want to sweeten the offer a bit."

Oro's jaw hung; Mariana could see his beady eyes narrow as they began to bulge. "Sweeten it how?" he stammered.

"Like with more gold, that's how! Lookie here, little man.

172

I been watching you, and I seen that hidden chest of yours. Every man aboard knows you're paying us just a pittance of what you're hiding."

"But you'll be getting the ship!" cried the dismayed hunchback. "Isn't that enough? It's worth a fortune by itself."

The bosun laughed with an evil fire burning in his eyes. "Maybe so, little man," he drawled, looking at him sharply. "But now me and me mate here, we decided that we want more—much more. For everyone. Unless . . ." He wielded his knife and grinned. "So make up your mind. How much does mousey here really mean, eh? Alive, that is. Dead, I can let you have her for free." The bosun chuckled meanly and his friend howled.

"No, no," pleaded Oro. "D-Don't hurt her. You win, I'll pay you more. Double what I promised."

"Well, now. You're getting closer, little man." He pressed the point of the gleaming knife against Mariana's soft throat. "A prize like her should bring a better offer from a rich man like you . . ."

Oro was shaking. "Triple, then! I'll pay you triple!"

The bosun exchanged a quick glance with his companion and both men grinned. "Ya made yerself a deal, little man. Triple it is." Then he looked back at his companion and said, "Let's get on with it." He ordered his crony to wake up the rest of the conspirators and sat Mariana down in the corner, threatening to cut her throat, deal or no deal, if she so much as batted an eye.

Seconds ticked by slowly; Mariana lifted her head and stared contemptuously at the nervously pacing hunchback. A minute later she could hear whispered voices from the nearby crew's quarters and bare feet shuffling as the crew roused themselves from their slumber.

The rest came swiftly. There was shouting; the haj must have been giving a terrific fight, she knew, hearing him bellow as a handful of sailors scrambled to subdue him. Doors banged, the shouting became louder and louder. She could hear Ramagar curse and Captain Osari's deep voice sternly commanding his crewmen to let him go. All to no avail. One by one the passengers and the few trusted sailors were hustled topside to meet their fate.

"Okay, mousey," growled the bosun. "Get up. Now it's your turn."

He pulled her roughly to her feet, cut the bonds around

her ankles, and forced her through the door and up the darkened steps to the poop deck.

The ship was suddenly swaying horribly and Mariana struggled to keep her balance. As she climbed into the night she could see no stars, only a thick black mass of low clouds scudding their way from the northern horizon. And the ocean was becoming turbulent, tossing waves more violent than she had ever seen before.

Ramagar and the others had been forced to stand in a single line, hands bound behind their backs, prodding knives and billy clubs assuring they kept in their places. Across from them, forming another line, also with their hands firmly tied behind, were the Cenulamians: the cabin boy, the helmsman, the first mate, and the Captain.

Three men gruffly pushed the captain forward when they saw the bosun appear on the scene.

"You! You scum!" shouted Osari lividly. "You'll pay for this! I promise you'll pay! Every last one of you!"

"Shaddup!" barked one of his captors. And with an ugly sneer on his lips the sailor belted the captain in the back of the head with his fist.

Ramagar tried to break loose; his foot kicked high and caught one of the nearby sailors in the groin. As the man staggered, another sailor delivered a pounding blow to Ramagar's stomach, doubling the thief over and forcing him to gasp for breath.

Mariana tried to run to his side, but the bosun grabbed her arm and swung her back viciously. "Not yet, mousey," he said. "Don't worry. If little man here doesn't mind, I'll let you say goodbye."

Osari shook himself out of his daze and glared at the leering bosun. Mountainous waves were increasingly breaking over the bridge, splashing spray down to the poop. "What do you intend to do with us?" he asked.

"Tell him, little man," chortled the bosun.

When Oro appeared from the hatchway Ramagar's veins popped from his neck. It didn't take very long to put two and two together, and he rued the day he had left Kalimar without first paying the hunchback a visit.

"Well?" said the captain.

The diminutive foreigner paced up and down before the prisoners with a silly grin on his face. "The dagger, thief!" he demanded. "Where is it?"

Ramagar spit in his face for reply.

174

The hunchback began to rave. "You've taunted me once too often, thief! Throwing you into the sea is too good for you. Maybe we should give you a good lashing first."

"Or have him keelhauled," laughed the bosun, much to the delight and agreement of his friends.

Osari scowled. "Have your fun with us, if you like," he warned. "It won't much matter. By tomorrow we may well all be dead."

"And what's that supposed to mean?" derided the bosun.

Captain Osari smiled grimly. "The weather, you fool. Take a look. Can't you see what's coming? Look at that storm—she'll rip the *Vulture* to shreds."

The bosun glanced at the advancing swirl of clouds and turned back to the skipper. "We ain't afraid o' bad weather," he rattled. "We been in storms before."

Osari laughed. "Not like this one you haven't. These are Northern climes, my scummy friend. Ever been in a hurricane? Ever fought one out for three, four days at a time?"

The bosun shook his head.

"Aye, looks like a bad 'un," someone called.

"You need me," said Osari triumphantly. "Me and my first mate and my helmsman. Without us to help you, you'll never make it through tomorrow."

And as if for emphasis to what was said, a huge wave slammed fiercely against the port side of the ship, sending the boat tilting hard to starboard and straining every board. Slipping and sliding, the crew and the passengers grabbed for anything that was bolted down.

The first rain slanted harshly in the rising wind, and Captain Osari regained his stance, glaring eyeball to eyeball with the hesitant bosun. "Do you believe me now?" he said.

The bosun gritted his teeth, wiping salt water from his eyes. "All right, then," he conceded. "Maybe me lads do need some help. I'll spare your life, as well as your crew's—"

"Not good enough," replied the captain stoutly.

The bosun stepped back a pace and studied the skipper's resolute features. "What's that supposed to mean?"

"You heard me. Your offer's not good enough. I want freedom for us all. My crewmates as well as all the passengers. Either we're all set free—or we die together." And he glared up at the thunderous sky.

"I'll set your crew free," said the bosun hastily. "But the others will still have to be dealt with—" Just as he spoke a tremendous blue-charged flash of lightning lit up the black-

175

ened sky, swiftly followed by three deafening claps of thunder. The rain began to whip furiously in the wind.

Captain Osari looked at his adversary evenly and shook his head. "No compromises, bosun," he said. "All or none."

"Don't listen to him!" cried Oro, growing frantic. The very thought of seeing Ramagar set free from his bonds left the hunchback shaking with terror. "It—it's a trick! They'll try and win back the ship!"

Osari scowled. "The hunchback talks like a fool," he said, his voice regaining its vitality. He knew he had played his hand well; the bosun would have to make a decision quickly. The storm was bearing down too fast for any debate.

With an untried sailor now at the helm, the twin-masted ship was already steering badly, yawing beneath the punishing blows. The bosun bit tensely at his lower lip and glanced about at his increasingly anxious companions.

"The storm's a killer, for sure," sighed his crony. "And she's overtaking us faster than I've ever seen. If we're hit with the stern to the wind she'll tear us apart . . ."

"Make up your mind," said the captain. "While you still can."

The bosun drew his knife and freed the captain's hands. "All right," he rasped. "You win. Get us through this weather and I promise to set the lot of you down at the nearest land." Then he turned into the wind and faced the crew. "Untie them all, and get them below."

"You can't!" screamed Oro. His beady eyes focused intensely on the thief, and Ramagar smiled grimly. "I order you to throw them over!"

The bosun glared at the little man who stood at his side shaking from limb to limb, and grabbed him by the collar. "You what?" he shouted. "You *order* me? I'm in charge of the *Vulture* now," he reminded. "And I make the rules. Understood?" And he dug his knife lightly into the hunchback's exposed throat. "Bucky-boy don't play no more games . . ."

Oro's face drained of any remaining color. He nodded submissively, knowing the bosun would kill him without a second thought if he gave him any more trouble.

"All right, Captain," said the bosun. "I'll keep my part of the bargain. See that you keep yours. Any false moves and the passengers die—the girl first."

Captain Osari rubbed at the rope burns on his wrists and agreed. He didn't trust the bosun's word for a minute, sure that the treacherous sailor would do him and the others in as

176

planned the moment the ship was out of danger. But any counterplan would have to wait. The storm would have to be dealt with first.

"Every man to his post," he called. And as the crew dashed to their places and the passengers were shuttled below, he turned to face the coming wrath of the Northern hurricane—the most dreaded tempest a mariner could battle.

The sea raged all around like a battering ram, dealing blow after blow after blow. "Two points into the wind!" shouted the captain, and slowly his sure-handed helmsman battled to bring the lumbering vessel closer to the wind. Cold, icy waves exploded over the decks time and time again. Every man, even these misfits, though waist-deep at times in the frigid water, fought deftly with the lines and strained to keep the sails trimmed. They yanked at the lines, spared no effort in turning every wheel, even as ice-crusted water sprayed their hands and faces and left their skin raw and bleeding.

For hours they clung to their tasks, while the lightning flashed and the constantly shifting winds tossed the boat like a hapless cork. Captain Osari ordered the ship rounded-to first on the starboard side, then on the port. Again and again the angry sea lashed out, smashing them broadside and pounding in frenzy. The bow dipped and rose, dipped and rose; planks and pins and barrels went flying, shattering like tinder above their heads. And still the storm grew worse.

"We're being pulled deeper into it, Cap'n," called the helmsman.

Osari, lashed to a line at the bridge, nodded darkly. "We're running across her face," he replied. "And we'll be lucky to make the eye by night."

It was a gloomy dawn, the sky colored in shades of gray and blacks, broken only by the hideous lightning and the white-foamed rolling waves. As the ship canted with a sickening blow, the loft masts strained. Lines tore loose, a section of rigging flapped about furiously. Osari screamed a warning to the handful of sailors working at the block. When the lash lines parallel to the quarterdeck broke, they hit whip-like into everything in their path. It was a horrible sight. Frightened men tried to run, sliding, feeling the weight of the tearing waves crush over them, screaming hollowly as flying spray choked them and filled their lungs. Then over the side a handful were carried, hurled into the air like toys until they disappeared completely.

The rain became tiny pellets of ice, limbs became numbed.

177

The captain knew that a few more hours of this and every man topside would freeze to death. But neither he nor anyone else faltered for a single moment. They were going to fight their way through like mariners, match the weather until it passed—or die in the effort.

Down below, meanwhile, the passengers had been huddled together in a single spartan cabin, the door bolted with an armed crewman posted outside. Helplessly they sat waiting while the tremor-wracked vessel fought for its life.

The beamed ceiling groaned under the weight of rushing water and Mariana looked up in trepidation. The *Vulture* was a sturdy ship, a fine ship, but it was plain that she could not take much more.

Ramagar sat at her side sullenly watching the steady trickle of dripping water pour through the cracks; he rubbed sourly at his whitened knuckles and prayed for the chance to get his hands on the hunchback for just a single moment before the end.

The haj stood leaning beside the porthole. He listened to the crash of the waves and the howls of the wind, lost in thought. Homer restlessly paced back and forth, from time to time putting his ear to the door and trying to determine if their guard was still posted.

Of them all, it was only the tall, yellow-haired Prince who sat calm and controlled.

The cabin shook from a tremendous blow above; the ship heaved heavily to port. Everything in the cabin that was not firmly bolted suddenly flew pell-mell from one wall to the other. The passengers grappled to grasp anything solid to break their awkward slide. The *Vulture* strained, slowly righted, and everyone regained his footing.

The thief wiped salt water from his eyes and scowled. "We're pinned like worms in a bucket," he complained. "I'd rather take my chances above, on deck with the others. At least we'd die in the open, not drowning like rats."

The haj pulled a long face, deep worry lines cracking across his tanned features. "If only there were some way to get ourselves out of here," he said. "Once the storm breaks . . ."

Ramagar's shoulders sagged as he stared at the triple-locked door, impossible for them to break. "It seems," he sighed, "that we are all trapped. Caught between the raging of the sea and a band of ruthless cutthroats. What chance do we have?"

Mariana looked about uneasily. "But what about the promise to set us free? The bosun gave his word. Surely if Captain Osari pulls the ship through this weather—"

"That will be one promise never kept," interrupted the thief. He rapped a fist into an open palm and cursed under his breath. "One way or another they will have us dead. I'm afraid this time we're sunk."

"Doomed to the ocean's cold floor," agreed the haj, tapping a nervous foot against the sodden planks. Then he raised and shook an imperious fist. "By the Seven Hells," he growled. "If only we still had our weapons!"

In the heated discussion everyone was too preoccupied to see when the Prince shifted his posture and closed his eyes as if in deep meditation. He crossed his legs, bowed his head low against his chest, and began to rock slowly back and forth, oblivious to both his companions and the surging sea.

"What are you doing?" said the thief, suddenly taking notice of his puzzling behavior. That their companion and leader was a strange sort of man they all knew; but now Ramagar wondered if he had begun to take complete leave of his senses.

"Shh . . . Don't speak," whispered the Prince. "Stand back and leave me to my thoughts." And as everyone stared bewildered, he reached inside his tunic and drew the scimitar—the Blue Fire.

A single oil lamp swung wildly from the ceiling as the cabin heaved and rocked. At best its light had been dull; now, though, Mariana saw that it was growing steadily dimmer—until the flame was all but extinguished.

Something was afoot, she knew. Something strange and unexplainable. She felt the short hairs on the back of her neck rise and she shuddered. Staring at the blade, held lightly in the Prince's open palms, she saw it begin to change color, change from its glittering gold and slowly pale into new hues. The cabin was almost black; she could see nothing except the dagger itself. She blinked her eyes and gaped, thinking that her mind must be playing tricks. But no—Ramagar, the haj, and Homer all stood equally entranced, their faces tight and motionless. They had seen what she had seen.

The blade glimmered in the darkness for a time and then it began to glow. Deep, deep blue, then lighter and lighter until it took on a blue-white pall. "*Az'il!*" she gasped. "What's happening?"

"Quiet!" snapped the Prince tensely. And he clutched the

179

scimitar tighter, holding it before his shut eyes. He slipped off the scabbard, let it clang to the floor. The tiny rubies and emeralds dazzled in white heat, sending speckled prisms dancing up and down and along the grim, bare walls. The blue of the dagger itself became a brilliant tiny sun, burning intensely, and now it was not merely glowing as before, but burning, raging in terrible shimmering light.

Mariana's mouth opened involuntarily, forming the soundless words: "Blue Fire . . ."

Flickering shadows cascaded eerily over the dumbfounded companions, spreading bit by bit until everyone in the cabin had been encased within the pall. At that moment time seemed to stand still, as if there were no storm around them, as if the sea were as calm and as quiet as a sheet of glass. No pounding of waves, no rocking of the ship. Only an extraordinary, incomprehensible silence overtaking everyone and everything in the cabin.

And then, very gradually, the blue shadows started to fade; the room was no longer shrouded as before. The walls slowly changed back to their normal colors of brown and yellow; the oil lamp was burning again and swaying; the crashing of waves filled their ears. But still the dagger kept its mysterious bizarre glow, softer, yet still intense, its effect holding the onlookers totally transfixed.

Mariana was the first to shake out of her daze. Her dark eyes continued to reflect the blue-white tones of the blade. "It's alive," she whispered aloud. "The scimitar is alive!"

The Prince still sat cross-legged and rigid. He opened his eyes and stared at the glow, and then he smiled. "No, Mariana," he said, sounding drained of all energy. "Don't be frightened. The blade is not alive. All I've done is call upon the Blue Fire to help us. Its powers are limited, but they are strong enough to free us from this prison."

The haj swallowed tensely and stared at the knife. "Then it's bewitched, cast with spells—Druid spells."

"No," flared the Prince. He glanced at each of his friends one by one, his eyes glowing with the same ice-blue fire as the dagger he held. "You must trust me," he said. "The Blue Fire can do no evil. It can only aid us. There are no spells upon it. Although perhaps it would be to our benefit if there were. You see, the scimitar was blended with a rare alloy, as I once told you, an alloy discovered in Speca a thousand years ago. Its powers and abilities are dormant—unless you know the secret of bringing them into focus, as I do."

180

"And how can your glowing blade help us escape?" queried Ramagar, as he knelt down beside the Prince and reached out to touch the scimitar.

"Don't!" cried the Prince, recoiling. "You must never touch it when it glows."

At this frantic warning, the stunned thief quickly pulled back his hand. "But why?" he asked, shaken. "Will it harm me?"

"The Blue Fire may be our ally, good thief, but it is also dangerous. It will harm, nay kill, anyone who knows not the secret of using it. See how the blade glows? Do not let the blue color fool you," he explained severely. "The dagger burns as fiercely as any fire ever made by men. No one but the rightful owner may touch it in this state. Yet, even I must be careful. Look." He stood cautiously, sweeping the blade above his head, and put the tip close to an overhead beam. Without even being touched, the dampened wood sent off a charge of tiny flames—blue flames—scattering the breadth of the cabin. The beam crackled and sparkled until the blade was pulled away. And even then it continued to smolder, with a thick cloud of dark blue vapor billowing across the ceiling.

"Now we understand," said Mariana, watching in awe.

"Yes," agreed the Prince darkly. "Now you understand. No more of this alloy exists, and Blue Fire was the only weapon ever forged with it. The blade has the ability to burn through a wall of solid iron, when properly used. There is no prison that can hold it—or us." He glanced to the lock-encumbered door. "Not even this one."

A cunning smile broke across Ramagar's rugged features. "This blade of yours becomes more of a mystery to me every day," he admitted. "Tell me, are there other *tricks* it can perform?"

"A few," replied the Prince. "Never fear. They will be there when we need them. But for now . . ."

Ramagar's eyes twinkled excitedly; his hands tingled excitedly with the idea of escape. Again the Specian Prince moved his eyes to the door and said, "We have to move fast; there's not a moment to lose. The guard outside must not get a chance to warn the others."

"Leave him to me," snorted the thief.

"And I'm ready too," added the haj. Burlu rubbed his hands in anticipation. "What is the plan?"

The Prince signaled for Ramagar to cover one side of the

doorway and the haj the other. "The moment the locks burn we strike," he said. Then without another word he slipped across the cabin and kneeled at the base of the heavy oaken door. His fingers ran gently along the locks, inspecting them, noting the thickness of the aging, rusted iron.

"Stay back," he whispered to Mariana and Homer; then he raised the blue-fired scimitar and placed the tip lightly against the heavy metal. Slowly the black iron began to smoke, making popping and sputtering noises. The locks turned color as they began to melt misshapenly and grotesquely, dripping hot blue flame.

Suddenly the door was burning. "Now!" cried the Prince. Ramagar and the haj set their shoulders and heaved with all their weight, crashing against the wood. The iron hinges groaned and gave, the door burst open dramatically, a slab of blue-hot timber still clinging haphazardly to the melted locks and bolts.

The crewman on duty at the edge of the dim corridor gasped in horror at the sight of the terrible flames and the two men charging from the room. He drew his knife, then turned and ran in fear, heading for the small stairwell leading to the forward hatch.

Ramagar was after him like a swift panther. The thief lunged and grabbed the sailor by the legs. Spinning around, the mutineer slashed at empty air as the cunning rogue lithely ducked the swinging arm and slammed the sailor against the wall. Ramagar pinned him savagely, drew back his fist, and thrust it with all his might. The crewman caught the blow directly on the mouth. Sputtering blood, he gurgled incoherently, eyes rolling, and slid to the bottom of the slippery steps. Panting, the thief adroitly scooped up the sailor's fallen knife, tucked it safely in his belt, and went back to the corridor to beckon the others.

The ship was still rocking violently, taking a fearsome beating at the hands of the Northern winds. "Come on!" the thief shouted above the din of the sea. "The way's clear."

Mariana and the rest scrambled out of the cabin, over the burning door, and into the waterlogged passage. They reeled and fell sharply against the opposite wall as the *Vulture* pitched with a new broadside onslaught. The corridor was already permeated with clouds of thick, swirling blue smoke, and coughing and wheezing they made their way to the hatchway steps.

Suddenly the hatch banged open. A rush of water came

182

tearing down with brutal force, swilling over Ramagar and the writhing sailor and flooding the passage waist-deep in ice-cold frothing liquid.

The haj fought to pick himself up, and with Mariana at his side, clinging to his flowing robe, he managed to push his way forward to Ramagar's outstretched hand. Mariana barely held her balance as a new oceantide slammed through the hatch, tearing the door off its hinges and sending it flying. She peered bravely up the flight of stairs and gasped at the sight of the grim morning sky: a foggy black sky, as turbulent as it was frightening.

Hand over hand Ramagar grasped his way up the railing with frozen fingers. The hyperborean wind was blowing mercilessly, pushing him backward. His eyes were clogged with rain, his mouth continuously spat frigid seawater. But on he pressed, until at last he had climbed his way to the entrance.

Dark forms of running sailors crossed his line of vision briefly. Electric-charged flashes of blinding light exploded furiously above. And then the brightness was gone, obliterated in a rush of grays and blacks that swirled directly atop the ship.

A cold wind nearly crushed the life out of him as he crawled onto the deck. Amid the tumult no one noticed his presence—and for that much at least he was glad. Regaining his feet, he glanced to the bridge, sheltering his eyes with his arm, and caught sight of able Captain Osari lashed with his helmsman beside the wheel, both men struggling valiantly to keep the ship aright for just a while longer.

A voice was shouting from behind. "You there! You there!" Ramagar spun to face a heavyset bear of a man he recognized at once as the third mate.

The sailor's eyes flickered with recognition; he glanced down at the blown hatch and immediately understood. Ramagar gave no time for thought. The ship rolled and he leaped at the man, feeling the sting of rain on his face as they grappled and rolled across the deck.

"It's the thief!" came a dim scream of someone at the quarterdeck. "He's escaped—catch him!"

The cunning master rogue leaped to his feet, grasping for the lash line, and kicked his boot at the third mate's face. The sailor took the blow and tumbled back with his arms flying out to reach the rope. But as he did, another wave hit broadside, catching him off guard. Choking water, the mate slipped helplessly, sliding between Ramagar's open legs, roll-

183

ing over barrel-like until he came to a crushing halt at the block of the second mast.

At that point another member of the mutinous gang battled from his station at the halyards and made toward the crouching thief at the lower portion of the deck. A small single-edged knife was set between his teeth and he carried a thin, weighted pin in his hand. Ramagar saw the club come flying, tearing down against the wind in his direction. He twisted to avoid it, but not quite in time. The pin hit a powerful blow against his shoulder and the thief winced, fighting off the stinging hurt and adeptly swinging himself under the lash line and grabbing for another. Desperately he tried to make for the bridge.

A salvo of roaring thunder shook every plank and board from stem to stern, and the battered vessel staggered yet another time as a mountainous wave crashed over the bow and came tearing down the main deck, splintering spars and railing and masts alike. Screams of drowning men filled the air and Ramagar, water high over his head, swam up from the deluge in time to fill his bursting lungs with air. His assailant also had managed to survive the wave. A companion cried out to him for help, but he shook off the man and came lunging at Ramagar with the knife firmly in hand.

Holding onto the line with all his energy, the injured thief lashed out, yanking the oncoming sailor by his tunic and sending him spinning. The quartering seas caused the ship to cant with a sickening heave. Driven rain fell like pricking nails. Ramagar shoved at the dazed sailor and sent him tumbling over the buckling planks. The crewman staggered only as far as his knees before he started sliding backward. And when the *Vulture* rocked with the ensuing pounding, he lost all control and fell headfirst over the steeply angled broken foremast, down into the sea.

Straining with every step, the haj, too, had managed to climb from the hatch. He swung himself up and around barely in time; a sailor jumped directly for him from his place at the quarterdeck and sent both of them tumbling into the rolling froth. The haj's leg tangled in the lash line. As the sailor's knife came up, the haj shifted his weight and swung his clenched hands powerfully into the mutineer's face. The sailor tottered with surprise. The haj barreled forward, caught him by the wrist, and wrenched loose the knife. Both men lunged for it as it slid by, the haj straining to keep it in sight. Both touched the blade at the same moment. Then they be-

184

came a tangle of bodies, flesh so closely mingled that it was impossible to determine who was who.

A low groan was the only sound; slowly the sailor righted himself, clutching his hands to his belly. Then he doubled over and slid, Burlu watching in fascination as dark blood swilled and blended with the foaming water.

The Prince reached the bridge, fighting his way to the startled captain and helmsman. All around them was mayhem; the two mariners from Cenulam battled evenly at the out-of-control wheel and desperately made every effort to stop the ship from spinning dizzily into the vortex.

From the block of the mainmast the bosun and his henchman looked on in biting terror as they saw the ship begin to flounder and the handful of passengers wage a distressful conflict with the remaining mutineers. The ship was unable to right itself as they half-crawled, half-stumbled their way along the slippery lash line to the bridge.

Icy waves came exploding into the hull, over the battered sails. The pressure of the wind was terrific; the yardarms had all but broken and were slashing into the crests while the ripped sails flapped torturously.

"It's no good," cried the frantic helmsman to the captain. "We're falling off to starboard and ready to capsize!"

"We're not done yet!" replied the captain with resolve. And though his hands were numbed and bloody, he pushed his weight against the immobile wheel with all his might, point by agonizing point turning it until the *Vulture* returned to a precarious balance while it tore through the vengeful waves.

"See there!" shouted Osari, waving his hand toward the high cirrus clouds suddenly appearing to the west. It was a curious sight that the helmsman strained to see; a patch of near blue surrounded by thick gray and black.

"It's the eye!" called the helmsman with glee.

"Aye, that it is," flared Osari. "And if we can reach its calm the ship still has a chance!"

Muscles taut and aching, veins popping, the two mariners struggled to bring the ship around hard enough to let the eye of the hurricane pass directly above them. The bosun, meanwhile, and several others had crept closer to the bridge and the bold men determined to save the ship from total destruction. One sailor agilely clambered up, a long knife held loosely in his right hand. The Prince, who had been securing the ropes from behind for Ramagar, caught sight of the man

185

from the corner of his eye and turned as the sailor daringly leaped to cut the lash line.

The Prince crouched, blue fire flaming from his hand. At the sight of the dagger the seaman hesitated, debating whether to attack or run; but anger burned in his eyes and hatred smoldered in his heart. With a loud cry on his lips he scrambled forward, slashing out wildly and forcing the Prince to backstep dangerously close to the shattered railing. The Prince dodged the whistling knife and thrust the dagger. The blade touched wet flesh and everything that followed happened so quickly that all became a blur.

The sailor dropped his knife and put his hands to his face as he screamed. Blue fire ignited and exploded, his tunic becoming a flaming torch, his skin charred and blackened. Crying for mercy and insanely running across the bridge, the hapless mutineer tumbled down to the main deck, where the flames caught the block of the forward hatch and set the entrance to the hold raging in blue-tinted conflagration. Men called to heaven to help them as the lash lines, soaking as they were, burned like heavy fuses up and down the length of the ship. Out of control, the fire was spreading swiftly, fanned by the hostile winds and unhampered by the deluge of pouring rain.

The bosun shouted for his men to follow, but few heard, and those who did were either too frightened or were themselves being encompassed by the fire.

Ramagar had no feeling in his frozen fingers as he climbed to the wooden guard railing and hoisted himself onto the bridge. The bosun had lunged for Captain Osari, eyes glowing madly, aware that his plot had been spoiled, and now determined to kill the brave captain before the ship keeled over for the final time and smashed into ten thousand raging embers. Ramagar made it to his feet, shaking off fatigue, and slid his way between the lashed captain and the racing mutineer.

The mizzen and topsails burst into glorious color, dancing fingers of fire rising ever higher and lighting up the black sky. Relentless winds rocked the mainmast until it split and fell, crushing a few cowering crewmen taking shelter beneath the lifeboat. The fires were burning more freely now, dousing momentarily with every wave that crashed over the deck, only to fan again when the cold water subsided.

The bosun trembled in horror as chunks of flying mast came bounding over his head. Ramagar forced his body up

186

and slammed himself clumsily into the sailor's ribs. The bosun wheezed with the blow and a savage gush of freezing water; pushing forward, groping for the slipping thief, he kept firm control of his knife and swung out wildly. Ramagar rolled in the bracing salt water, fighting off the sharply growing pain inflaming his shoulder. Through the driven rain the bosun grinned acidly; he knew the thief was hurt, knew he could no longer give him much of a fight.

Charging into the flying sprays, he wielded his weapon at arm's length, cutting against the air with quick, slashing movements and forcing Ramagar to huddle beside the rail-guard overhanging the bulwark. His eyes stinging so painfully that he could barely see, the salted water adding punishment to the already swollen and raw wound, the thief of Kalimar shielded his body, twisting and turning to avoid the oncoming thrusts.

Licking flames rose all about the bridge, great tongues of blue fire, scorching everything in their wake and throwing off terrible heat. A thick swirling pall of bluish smoke hung low above their heads.

Metal clashed on metal as Ramagar's knife met the flat edge of his adversary's vicious thrust. Angrily the two men parried and stalked while the captain and his helmsman watched helplessly, lashed to the wheel and daring not to lift a finger while the ship yet pitched. But the eye of the hurricane was drawing closer; the shattering winds had already begun to slacken. Straight ahead the sea was strangely calm, and the burning ship was inching its way toward it.

Ramagar slipped again, this time just before the white froth slammed over the side. His knees buckled and he tumbled, knife flying from his hand. The bosun held his balance, whipping his own knife in frenzy. Ramagar was cornered, caught between the still flaming lash lines and the fractured rail. Face and beard drenched and dripping, lips blue and unfeeling, he dodged this way and that, constantly moving, seeking only the slightest opening to topple the bosun and send him crashing over the side. But the excruciating pain only worsened, spreading down his arm, and he could barely find the strength to shift fast enough to skirt the bosun's well-delivered thrusts.

The sailor saw this and laughed cruelly. The bent and staggering thief was at his mercy, waiting to die at his whim. Pacing now in a semicircle, careful to avoid the lash line, he glared callously at the thief, taunting him to attack. "Say a prayer, if you know any," he hissed to Ramagar. "And remember that you'll never touch that whore of yours again!"

In the wind and the rain Ramagar could not see clearly what happened. A dark form slipped behind the bosun, slowly moving between lines and crossing the bridge. But the blue flame in his hand told all there was to know—it was the Prince, finished with his own skirmish and coming to the thief's rescue.

Blue Fire plunged into the sailor's back. The mutinous bosun bolted upright, jerking in spasms, trembling witlessly. Then his tunic burst into flame, his hair a mass of bluish coils, stinking as it singed like brushfire and the flame ate into his scalp. His face distorted horribly, a death mask of contorted misery, fire rotting him to the bone before the thief's startled eyes. And his scream was a scream no man who heard it would ever forget. Ramagar put his hands to his ears to stifle the pain of it. He shuddered; no man should die like this, he thought. No man—not even the cruel, spiteful leader of the mutineers.

Another wave crashed and the bosun was lifted up and hurled from the ship. The blue flames carried far and wide; both the Prince and Ramagar stared in wonder at the bright glow from the water which lasted long after the charred corpse had sunk into the bottomless bowels of the sea.

Ramagar pulled himself up, gratefully looking at the man who had saved his life. But before a word could be passed between them, they turned abruptly at the helmsman's cry: "The eye! We've reached the eye!"

And suddenly there was a strange quiet. Looking beyond the shattered ship, Ramagar could clearly see the terrible storm dealing thunderous blows at every side—every side, that is, except where the sky glistened above them in soft blue and the rain had ceased.

"We made it!" called the helmsman happily. "We made it!"

"Aye," growled Captain Osari as he surveyed the incredible damage done and the fires nipping at the edges of every sail. "But what good will it do? The *Vulture* is doomed. She cannot survive the fires. We'll burn to ashes."

And so it seemed. In the swiftest of glances it was obvious that the vessel would be lost long before the eye was passed and the storm began anew.

The Prince looked about at his friends, aware of the fear and anger in their eyes. The haj and Mariana stood together below, the old man virtually encompassed by spreading flame and holding the anguished girl in his powerful arms. Young Homer stood bravely beside the lifeboat, which also had begun to spark. The Prince looked on motionlessly as the thief sighed a long sigh and hung his head. Even Captain Osari and the helmsman seemed to accept their fate. They had given it a good fight, one and all, each of them doing his share. But now the battle was lost; it would take a miracle to save them. And none of them believed in miracles.

Scattered across the deck lay the still bodies of a few mutineers, drowned or burned to ghastly deaths. Among them was also the Cenulamian first mate, close beside the smoldering corpse of the cabin boy, who had given his life while bravely entering the fray.

It was a sad sight that the Prince gazed upon: a handful of dejected survivors helplessly waiting for the fire to flare out of control and consume them all.

"How far to the nearest land?" asked the Prince, turning to Captain Osari. "Can your ship hold through the storm to get us there?"

Osari looked at him as though he was mad. "We're burning to cinders," he said with bewilderment. "We're days from land—any land. But what matter? The ship will be a total ball of flame in less than an hour."

The Prince shook his head. "No, Captain. It won't," he replied mysteriously. "Believe me, it won't. Just tell me, is the ship too badly damaged to make it to shore?"

Osari couldn't believe his ears. By now he was thoroughly convinced that his passenger was a raving lunatic. But still, even though demented, the man would have an answer.

"No," he drawled slowly. "If the fires could be put out, and *if* we all fought together to keep ourselves afloat, maybe, just maybe, we could hobble to some safe harbor."

The Prince smiled. "Then do it, Captain Osari. Guide your ship to land."

Osari glanced at Ramagar and the thief shrugged.

The Prince held out his dagger for all to see, and laughed. The blue fire had begun to dull, diminish to the point that it was all but extinguished. "Look to the sails," he said.

The survivors raised their heads wearily, and each peered at the shattered yardarms, cracked masts, tattered sails. To their amazement they could see the fires begin to blow themselves out, one by one, slowly and deliberately. There was no

189

rain to douse them, no waves to smother them. They were extinguishing themselves.

Mariana stared incredulously; she turned her gaze up toward the bridge and the mirthful Prince, saying, "I don't understand . . ."

The Prince laughed merrily, his eyes dancing, taking in the mystified looks on their faces and enjoying their confusion.

"But don't you see?" he called to them all. "The solution is simple. When the scimitar returns to its natural state, as it must after a single hour's time, all fires it has caused will cease. If the dagger does not glow, the blue fire cannot breathe. The two are inseparable."

And even as he was speaking, the uncanny glow ebbed and vanished. The dagger once again returned to its normal state, gold blade glittering, rubies and emeralds dazzling profoundly along the hilt.

"By the Seven Hells!" gasped the haj. "The ship no longer burns!"

"Nor will it again," answered the Prince as he bounded from the bridge and joined his companions on the main deck. "Set your course, Captain Osari," he called. "We've no time to lose."

The captain nodded, glancing at the other side of the hurricane, now moving dangerously close off the starboard bow. The helmsman looked at him wide-eyed and baffled, and Captain Osari, in no small bafflement himself, merely shrugged, as if to say that such things as they had seen were a common occurrence and he would treat them as such.

"It takes a crew to fight through a storm, my friend," he called at last to the Prince. Then he peered at the lonely corpses. "Mine is dead. Who will replace it?"

"I sailed the sea once, when I was young," offered the haj.

"Nor am I a stranger to the sea," added the Prince. "So you see, you already have the beginnings of a new crew—small in number perhaps, but willing and eager."

"And loyal, at least," chimed in Ramagar. "We'll all help in every way we can. What about it, Captain? Shall we fight our way to land? Or give up now for lost?"

Captain Osari scowled, though inwardly his heart was bounding with joy. They were only a handful, to be sure. But with the helmsman at the wheel, and himself to direct the others and show them what to do, well, his ship just might have a chance. And compared to his feelings of only a few minutes earlier, that in itself was a miracle.

190

"No," he said at last, in response to Ramagar's question, "we do *not* give up for lost. No true sailor would ever yield and lose hope."

"Then we fight?"

Osari laughed. "We never stopped."

13

The flickering oil lamp swung slowly in its davits above the table in Captain Osari's cluttered cabin. Exhausted and aching, the fatigued mariner looked briefly at sleeping Mariana, cuddled in his bunk and wrapped tightly in a quilted blanket. In the corner Ramagar was waking from his doze; the haj snored quietly, sprawled out beside him on the polished floor.

These past eighteen hours had been the hardest of his life, Osari mused as he glanced down at the plethora of navigational charts scattered across the tabletop. But Fortune had been with them, there was no question of that. Time and again the damaged ship had nearly floundered and sunk, yet time and again the *Vulture* managed to raise her bow and resume the fight. Now, the terrible storm had passed and the broken ship was limping its way toward land. Osari knew he had lost everything. His spice cargo, so carefully stored, was in ruins, worthless. His creditors in Cenulam would demand recompense for their loss; no new crew could be found without at least some cash, which the captain did not have; and perhaps worst of all, the cost of repairing the *Vulture* would be staggering. There was just no way he could raise the money; he was already in deep enough debt as it was. No, on this tranquil night, with his companions catching some well-deserved rest and only the helmsman up on deck, Osari was sure his captain's days were over. The best he might now hope for was to sign on as first officer on some other ship, and thank the Fates that at least he was alive.

Ramagar yawned, rubbed at his tired eyes. "Haven't you slept yet?" he asked, looking at the captain slouched over his table, his brow furrowed with his work.

"Not yet, Ramagar. Later. I haven't time to rest now; at least not until I set our new course and make certain of just where we're heading."

The thief stood up moodily, scratching at his matted beard, feeling the burning sensation come back to his shoulder. Looking about, he took note for the first time of the stacks of delicate equipment the sailor kept: tools housed in a leather chest, books stacked in boxes and atop wooden shelves, specially constructed brass casings for his more private possessions.

"And where does it seem like we are?" asked the thief, breaking a long silence in which Osari had eagerly returned to his charts. The captain replied by running his finger along the crude but easily recognizable lines of the coast far north of Kalimar and the East.

"See this?" said Osari, tapping his finger at some peninsula wedged between two large islands. "With a good wind, and if our single remaining mast holds, we can make Tarta by week's end."

Ramagar pursed his dry lips and nodded. "I've heard of it," he said. "A rugged land, they say. Poor and backward—"

"Yes," the captain agreed. "But Tarta has a port. A good one, if I recall. There we can at least berth and," he shrugged, "I can sell my ship for scrap. As for you and your companions, I'm afraid you'll have to find another ship to take you on to Cenulam. As much as I hate to say it, I fear I cannot complete the journey. But you'll have no trouble. Tarta abounds with vessels headed for Cenulam. In fact, I have many friends there. I'll have you placed aboard a fine boat. One better than mine, at any rate." He sighed wistfully and frowned.

Ramagar felt the silence between them, a silence often found when friends are forced to part and never see one another again. He peered at the map beneath Osari's hand, glanced at the numerous charts placed at either side. "And what land is this?" he asked suddenly, referring to a coast hundreds of leagues from where Cenulam lay.

"That? Oh, it has no name anymore, Ramagar. It's nothing but desolate waste. Once, a long, long time ago, men called it Brittany, I believe. What became of it, I cannot say. But why do you ask? Your aim was to reach Cenulam, and that forsaken place is nowhere near . . ."

The two men looked at each other evenly, and Ramagar sighed. "May I be honest with you, Captain? In all truth I must tell that Cenulam is not, nor has it ever been, our true destination. Only a stopping place in the North from where our true goal can be reached."

192

The captain looked at the thief with some surprise. "Then you're not traveling with the haj to purchase stallions for breeding?"

Ramagar smiled thinly. "Hardly," he replied. "Our real adventure barely begins at Cenulam. Or Tarta. Or any place for that matter."

Captain Osari scratched his hair and shook his head. "Then where?"

"Have you ever heard of . . . Speca?"

The stare Ramagar received was one of astonishment. And then the mariner began to laugh. "My dear fellow, you must be joking! Speca? The Lost Kingdom?"

Ramagar moved his head slowly from side to side, eyes narrowed and face taut. "No, Captain. I'm not . . ."

"But there's no such place, man! Surely you know that! It —it's a fable. Like Atlantis, like so many other mysterious isles that men speak of at night to while away the hours."

"You're wrong," said Ramagar firmly. "It does exist. As surely as Cenulam exists. As real as Kalimar."

Captain Osari threw up his hands. "All right, you can believe it if you want—but listen to me, Ramagar. You're wasting your time on a fool's errand. Look here—" And he pulled out a different map from under the others, old and well worn around the edges. It claimed to show all of the Northern lands, indeed all of the globe in the Northern Hemisphere. "Here is Cenulam," said Captain Osari, pointing to a finger-shaped peninsula set at the top of a broad continent. "And here is the waste of Brittany to the west. See?"

Ramagar nodded. "I follow you. What about it?"

Osari moved his hand swiftly to the extreme North. "These are the Ice Lands," he said, sweeping the pole of the top of the world. "Speca is said to be somewhere in between. But as you can see for yourself, there is nothing. Only the frozen sea for a thousand leagues on either side. Barren, Ramagar. No land at all, save perhaps for a few uncharted small islands inhabited by pelicans and seals. Cenulamian fishermen used to chart these waters often. Believe me, I know. My own father was such a fisherman . . ." He stopped his speech abruptly and frowned.

"What's the matter?" said Ramagar.

The captain closed his eyes, a saddened look upon his weatherbeaten features. "My father," he said slowly, measuring his words. "My father used to sail those waters as I said.

193

And they tell me he died in them during an expedition twenty years ago."

"I'm sorry," said Ramagar, moved by Captain Osari's grief. "You must have loved him very dearly."

The mariner nodded. "I did. But why even mention it? It bears no import to what I've been telling you."

"Perhaps it does," came a voice, and they both turned to see the yellow-haired Prince standing in the open doorway. "Forgive me," he said. "I did not mean to overhear, but I woke up and came to look for you."

The captain dismissed the matter with a quick gesture. "Come in, please," he said. "You may as well listen to what I've been saying. This quest of yours to Speca—"

"How did your father die?" asked the Prince, cutting the captain off curtly and making the mariner feel somehow uncomfortable.

"When the other ships came home they said my father's ship was lost," said Osari. "They searched for a week, I'm told. But the ice was thickening and winter was near; they had to return. In the black they could see nothing . . ."

Ramagar's eyes widened; he shared a knowing look with the Prince. "What do you mean by 'the black'?" he asked.

The sailor from Cenulam shrugged. "No mariner can properly explain it," he conceded. "But in those waters, some hundreds of leagues from Brittany, there is a vast unknown darkness. Some ships have tried to master it, sail past to the Western Continents, but none have ever succeeded." Osari tugged nervously at his earlobe. "It's as if, as if . . ."

"As if the night never recedes?" questioned the Prince. "As if even in summer that place remains cold and dismal and a ship cannot see past its own bow?"

"Why, yes!" Captain Osari was both startled and shaken at what the Prince had said. "But how did you know. Surely you've never been there—?"

"No man can go there," replied the Prince darkly. "Those who try will never return. It is obvious to me now that your father must have tried."

Osari nodded sadly. "Tried and failed, yes. You're right. But I still don't understand how you know all this. Who told you of this darkness in the middle of the ocean? This abyss where the boldest sea captain will not dare to trespass?"

The Prince folded his arms and gazed at the small pools of dark water which still lay at his feet. "I know because it is my home—the home to which I must return."

194

Osari was incredulous. But then he recalled the flaming blue dagger and its secret powers, and knew that the man who possessed it was no common man. He was either a devil or a saint, and the captain had frankly not yet decided which.

"Home?" he queried at last. "You would call that misbegotten black ocean your home?"

The Prince shifted his gaze to the map, saying, "Point out the area of black ocean." The captain was quick to comply with the request, circling a broad area with the palm of his hand, an area that encompassed virtually a quarter of the Western Sea. "All this," he said soberly, "is where even our best ships must circumnavigate. Where, as you said a moment ago, the night never recedes."

"And this is the very place where I and my companions are compelled to journey," the Prince told him sharply. "You see, your maps cannot detail it because no mapmaker has been able to chart it—nor will it be charted until the Dark is forever removed and the evil it brings destroyed once and for all. Under those grim tides of Darkness lies the fair and gentle land of my fathers: the Lost Kingdom of Speca."

The captain noticeably paled. "It can't be!" he protested. "It—it isn't possible. Our ships would have found it!"

The Prince shook his head. "The conquerors of Speca will not allow it. They will destroy any who try."

"But Speca cannot exist! Maybe once—"

"Scholars never denied its existence," the Prince was quick to point out. "And ancient artifacts believed to be Specian are highly valued throughout the world."

The captain fell silent, reflecting on these truths. The broken ship was creaking, but creaking with the soft reassurance of its sturdiness. This, the wind against the sails, and the lapping of waves against the prow were all that could be heard as the Prince drew the scimitar and held it out in his open hand. "Here is Speca," he whispered. "Here is the very embodiment of a proud nation bound by chains that must at last be broken." He looked down at the map the captain had provided and stared gloomily at the configuration of emptiness set west of the isle called Brittany. "The sailing directions for Speca are quite clear," he observed. "First west, then north. Past Cenulam, past Brittany. Until the cold prevailing winds are reached and the eternal night shrouds our ship like a blanket."

Captain Osari drew a breath. "Then you really are serious about this venture?" he asked. For a moment he studied the stern faces of the men beside him and realized that his question need never have been asked. "Of course you know that finding a ship to take you there will not be easy," he added. "None that I know of, either from Cenulam or other faring lands, will dare the risk."

The Prince clasped his hands behind his back and nodded glumly. "Unfortunately, you're probably right, even though I would offer every single sailor who accompanied us a healthy share of Speca's great wealth."

It was then that Ramagar put his hand on the captain's shoulder, and said, "My friend and I discussed the matter earlier, Captain Osari, and we are agreed. We want to ask you to join forces with us; help guide us to this foul blackness that slowly spreads over the world. Make our quest your own . . ."

Osari's jaw hung. "Me?" he stammered. "Come with you to Speca?"

Both men noddded seriously as the mariner stared. And then the captain broke into loud laughter. "Gentlemen, gentlemen! Please! I am flattered you would ask—but look about you. I am a ruined man. My ship could never make such a voyage, and even if she were repaired, where will I find a crew to sail her? A dozen creditors already demand all I have—if not my head. You see, going with you, even if I wanted to, is totally out of the question."

"Think," said the Prince, "what you could do with the fortune I offer for your help. You would have enough for a fleet of ships, Captain. A port full of them. And I do not ask you to die for my cause; only take us there and wait for our return."

Osari seemed to mull it over for a time, then he shook his head. "It . . . wouldn't be possible. I am a mariner, gentlemen. I know the sea and the wind. I navigate by the stars at night and the azimuth of the sun by day. And I also know that certain death awaits anyone who enters the blackness of the Western Sea."

"Yet your own father was bold enough to try," said the Prince. "Daring enough to sail where few men have been before, to win both fame and glory, honor to his name and wealth enough to make a king envious."

"My father is dead," remarked the sailor dryly.

Ramagar's face tightened. "Then aid us if only to avenge him. Believe me, he died an untimely death, murdered no

196

doubt by those who possess the very evil we seek to destroy. Would not your father want as much?"

There was quiet as Captain Osari slowly lifted his gaze heavenward, his eyes smoldering with bitter memory of the day he received the shattering news. "Yes," he whispered. "My father would want it so, I think . . ." Then he frowned and shook his head again. "But how can I even consider it? The *Vulture* is a broken ship. It would take a king's ransom right now to repair her properly for such a monumental voyage. And frankly, my friends, I haven't a single copper to my name. Not to mention the difficulty I would have in enlisting a crew with no money to offer."

"Your ship will be repaired to your satisfaction," assured the Prince. "We'll see to it in Tarta."

Osari looked at him curiously. "How? With what? A hold full of spoiled spices?"

Ramagar smiled, gaining great satisfaction from what he was about to say. "Have you forgotten your cook, Captain?" he said. "Oro left a small chest filled with gold on board, to pay for the mutineers. But now the hunchback must be as dead as the others, swept away during the storm, I assume. But his gold remains intact somewhere near his quarters. All we have to do is find it and it will be ours for the taking."

The captain from Cenulam was amazed. As mad as this whole scheme seemed, he was on the verge of agreeing heart and soul. The thought of a newly fitted ship excited him as much as the chance for adventure—the kind he had never known. Add to that a full crew of the best sailors, Cenulamian mariners, the finest in the world, and how could he refuse?

He sucked in air and grinned. "Count me in," he said. "We'll lay anchor at Tarta and have the ship repaired there. Then we'll be on our way."

Ramagar pursed his lips and nodded. "Fine. Then it's agreed. But first, I think we had better locate that gold."

It was close to dawn and the sky in the east was turning from a soft shade of wine to a golden crown capped with red. The seas were smooth, a few morning stars still shining in the west. The only sounds were those of mild breezes against the sails and the soft lapping of white-capped waves. It was Ramagar's turn to stand watch over the helm, and he did so sleepily, thinking of days to come with Mariana, peaceful days of sharing their lives, when all this was finally

197

behind. He glanced up at the waning stars, recognized a few of the signs that Captain Osari had taught him: Orion, Polaris, landmarks to a sailor, well-greeted friends to help show the way. Ramagar stood fascinated and transfixed, with the wind rushing warmly against him and the taste of salt mildly upon his lips. On such a glorious and peaceful morning nothing disturbed him, not the throbbing in his bandaged shoulder nor the dreaded threat of Druid black magic. At this moment he was unafraid, in love, content to sail forever if need be with his good friends and constant companions.

Yes, on a morning like this, what could go wrong? What could possibly ruin his day? Ramagar tingled with the feel of the breeze and chuckled to himself, certain that the answer was nothing.

And then the helmsman suddenly appeared, making his way from the smashed hatchway and climbing to the bridge. He waved at young Homer, who was tackling with the halyards, then turned to greet the thief. "I'm to relieve you, Ramagar," he said.

"Why? What's the matter? I was supposed to be on duty until eight bells . . ."

The helmsman, a stout good-natured fellow with bright, intelligent eyes that attracted many a wench, pulled a face. "Captain's orders. He wants you to report below right away."

Ramagar's brows furrowed deeply. "Is something wrong?"

"Not wrong," replied the sailor with a shrug. "But maybe you'd better see for yourself. You'll find everyone in the galley." And with that, he took over the wheel, leaving the thief puzzled and a bit perturbed.

Ramagar made his way quickly down the splintery steps, splashing into shallow pools of seawater left over from the storm. At length he came to the end of the narrow corridor and found his companions gathered together as the helmsman had said. They stood in a half-circle, speaking in low, subdued tones. His first thought was that they had discovered the hidden gold. For two days they had turned the ship upside down in search of the chest, but all their efforts had been fruitless. Oro's riches remained as elusive as ever. And there were few places left to look.

As he reached the door he heard the sound of sniveling, a familiar sound that unbalanced his calm. Bursting into the kitchen, he tripped over a disarray of pots and pans, then regained his balance and stood transfixed. To his total shock and chagrin he found himself face to face with Oro—the

198

little hunchback standing rigid, his knees knocking together and his mouth twitching uncontrollably. At the sight of the thief, the cunning trader of stolen goods almost fainted. He cringed toward Captain Osari, tugging harshly at the mariner's sleeve. "Please," he wailed. "Don't let him kill me! Don't let the thief kill me!"

Ramagar stood livid, his face darkening and his eyes glowing like a cat's.

"We found him hiding behind a wall," muttered the haj distastefully, gesturing to the spot. "Evidently he fled and hid when the fight began and hoped we'd think him dead."

Ramagar sneered bemusedly at the ragged little man. "Playing possum, eh?"

Captain Osari sighed. "He's posed a dilemma for us, Ramagar. By the laws of the sea I could have him hanged for his mutiny." Here the hunchback began to whimper. "But seeing as he's caused you more trouble than he has me, I thought I would let you decide what we should do."

Ramagar's reply was brief and curt. "Kill him. Slowly . . ."

Oro's shoulders shook and tears formed in his beady eyes. He looked to Mariana, who was standing quietly against the counter, and pleaded, "Don't let them do this! It's not fair!"

"Fair?" growled the thief. "Was it fair for you to accuse me of murder in Kalimar? To plot to steal the scimitar from my corpse? Why, you little weasel!" He clenched his hands into menacing fists and addressed the captain: "Turn him over to me—just for a few minutes . . ."

Oro's fear of the thief was apparent to all. He would rather face anything, it was clear, anything at all, than have to deal man to man with the master rogue.

"No!" he cried, still looking at the impassive girl. "Tell him, Mariana. Tell him that I saved your life!"

Mariana sighed, folded her arms, and gazed up at Ramagar.

"What's he talking about?" demanded the thief.

"It's true," admitted the girl, although she hated to do so. "When the bosun caught me listening he was ready to kill me on the spot, throw me overboard right then and there. But Oro stopped him, bargained with him for my life, even offered to pay any price they demanded."

Ramagar was clearly taken aback. He rubbed disconsolately at his beard, falling silent. How much he hated the hunchback! How very much it would delight him to strangle

199

the man slowly with his own two hands. Yet in his blind love for the dancing girl Oro had saved the only person the thief had ever loved. If not for him Mariana would be dead.

"What do you say, Ramagar?" said the captain, growing impatient. "Give the word. His life is in your hands."

As the thief thought, Oro lowered his gaze to the floor and stood shivering.

"I should pluck out your eyes, little man," grumbled Ramagar. "Tear out your limbs, one by one. Watch you squirm and squeal like a stuck pig. Maybe cut out your tongue and slice off your ears . . ."

Oro could hardly stand, so terrified was he of Kalimar's master thief. "If—if you do," he stammered, "then you'll *never* find my gold . . ."

The point hit home. Mariana stepped forward, glaring at the hunchback. "And if," she hissed, "I persuade Ramagar to let you get away with your miserable life, will you turn your riches over to us now?"

Oro nodded wretchedly. "I swear it! I'll take you to it right now. What do you say?" And he looked from Mariana to Ramagar to Captain Osari and the mute Prince.

Mariana locked her gaze with Ramagar's, her eyes pleading with him to show mercy. Ramagar looked away and scowled. "Very well," he said. "It's your bargain. Your life for your gold." Then he pointed a threatening finger at the quivering hunchback, saying, "But no tricks, mind you! Otherwise I'll throw you into the sea."

The hunchback smiled. "No tricks, I promise."

"Then what do we do with him?" said the Prince, speaking up for the first time. "Surely we can't leave him in Tarta. If we do he'll probably wrangle his way to another ship and follow us again."

Ramagar sighed. "I know. We can't trust him for a minute. He's a snake, the meanest viper I've ever known. But we gave our word to spare his life . . ."

Mariana looked at them all and closed the argument in the only way it could posssibly be concluded. "It seems," she said craftily, "that Oro is only a threat when he's out of sight. So I guess we have no choice." She smiled wanly. "We'll have to take him with us. With us to Speca."

IV

On to Aran

———————◆———————

14

The decks of the *Vulture* were cluttered with carefully lashed stores of equipment tightly fastened to the new railing and the bulwark. New canvas gleamed in the soft Tartanian morning light; new and sturdily fitted masts glimmered dully over the freshly mopped decks.

It was a warm day, bright and fair, almost cloudless. Spring had come to Tarta and the North. Once bleak hills now glowed with thick grass, abounding with multicolored wildflowers. Mariana tugged gently at the shawl over her shoulders as she eagerly awaited the ship's long-delayed departure. Six full weeks they had berthed in Tarta, waiting restlessly for the repairs to be completed. Now, at last, the day had arrived. The spanking ship was as seaworthy as any in the world. Captain Osari himself had overseen the work, watched sternly as every plank and pin was fitted. His new crew was one of which he could be more than proud: good, fine sailors all. Some from Cenulam, a few from Tarta, all from seafaring lands. They were the best, the best Oro's gold could buy, and perhaps as adventurous and eager to conquer the lost black lands as she and her companions.

Mariana glowed with exhilaration, though it was hard to believe all this was really happening. She glanced to the starboard side of the gently bobbing ship and gazed across the open sea; a dark Northern blue, crested with magnificent whitecaps that smashed majestically against the long rocky breakers beyond the tiny harbor. Then she glanced to port, recalling fondly the small city nestled at the base of the endlesss hills. A quiet town, peaceful and serene. Perhaps a good place to settle down one day, she mused. A place where she and Ramagar could live simple and happy lives, raise their family, and remember fondly this grand adventure each time they gazed out to the beautiful sea.

Looking up to the sky, smiling, Mariana caught sight of a seagull, a large bird with enormous wings fluttering and reflecting sunlight. The gull squawked harshly and flew in a figure-eight pattern as it buzzed the topsail. The sailor in the crow's nest tried to shoo it, but the pesky bird paid him no heed and continued its little dance above the ship.

Mariana laughed with bright eyes. A good sign, she told herself. A good sign for sure! An omen that the *Vulture*'s journey would begin on a sound note.

Captain Osari saw the bird from his post on the bridge. Looking to Mariana he grinned, sharing her thoughts. Then to their surprise, and that of the sailors scrambling to their posts, the bird dived and glided its way slowly to the deck. Having landed, it moved about brazenly in tiny circles inspecting this and that with its beak. The new first mate gave chase with the back of his hand, but the bird merely flapped its wings, flew a few paces, and resumed its curious walk a bit further away.

"Leave him be, mister," shouted Osari bemusedly.

"Sir?" said the bewildered sailor.

Osari laughed. "I won't mind one more passenger. Let him stay as long as he likes."

And then to Mariana's delight, the speckled bird flew to her feet and perched itself comfortably between a coil of rope and her boots.

Around the deck the ship's activity increased. All packing done, all stores accounted for, the *Vulture* was ready to be on her way. She bobbed and weaved impatiently at anchor while smaller craft plied in and out of harbor all around her.

Captain Osari paced back and forth for a few moments longer, then curving his hands around the sides of his mouth, he called to the first mate, "Hoist the anchor!"

A group of men lost no time in obeying. "Aye, aye!" came the reply, and the crusty, moss-dripping weight was lifted.

Next the mainsail was unfurled, wind filling it with a *whoosh* and yellow canvas spilling like gold as it obliterated great chunks of clear blue sky. And the ship began to move smoothly through the choppy waters.

The bow dipped; the deck slanted sharply. Winds rushed at Mariana and her heartbeat quickened. To her side came running Ramagar and the haj; they stood at the edge of the afterdeck rails and watched with some sadness while the pleasant harbor of Tarta slipped away.

The captain stared briefly at the compass in his hand and looked to his helmsman. "Sail for Brittany," he said. "And the unknown waters beyond."

And so they began the last leg of a journey started so long before. As Tarta faded on the eastern horizon all on board, passengers and crew alike, thought only of their homes. Cenulam, Palava, yes, even Kalimar. From here on out the dangers they had shared would increase a hundredfold; and there could be no turning back.

"We reach the coast of Brittany sometime before dawn," said Captain Osari, unfolding his finest map across the table and waiting for his passengers to look.

The Prince drew in a deep breath of air. It had been twenty days since they had left Tarta, twenty restless, uneventful days in which the ship had bypassed Cenulam completely, taken a westerly course, and now came at last into the turbulent waters of the Western Sea. According to his own calculations, the Prince knew they could reach the Darkness in less than ten days of sailing at top speed.

"Is there any reason we have to drop anchor at Brittany?" asked Ramagar.

"Only to bring aboard fresh water," replied the captain. "Then it should be a clear path to here . . ." He pointed his finger to an area some three hundred leagues to the west. "At approximately this spot the weather will change. Spring or no, we'll come upon ice. Great, lumbering bergs as tall as the highest tower. The winds will chill to the bone. They say it's frigid even at the height of summer. And unless I miss my mark, about then we'll begin to see the eternal night show itself in the west."

Mariana shivered involuntarily. "Speca," she whispered.

Captain Osari nodded. "Speca—or whatever. Remember, no man has lived to say what he's seen."

"There is another island in those climes," said the Prince. "We call it Aran; do you know of it?"

Captain Osari scanned the map, his eyes pinpointing a small marking set perilously close to the void. "There is such an island," he conceded. "But Northern mariners have a different name for it. Is this the one you mean?"

The Prince peered closer. "Yes. That's the one. That's Aran."

"What of it?" said the captain. "It's not on our course."

"It will have to be," the Prince told him. "Aran was once an ally of my land. Its kings were fair and just men. We must stop there before reaching the Darkness, and try to enlist Aran's support."

The mariner drummed his fingers atop the table. The Prince had mentioned these allies while unfolding his tale, Osari recalled. But expecting its people to fight Speca's battles after so many years seemed foolish, to say the least. All the

205

more so when you considered that Aran lay at the very door of the eternal night.

"It would be a waste of time," he said at length. "These men of Aran, why should they risk their necks? Besides, setting anchor there could very well mean allowing some Druid spy to spot us and warn the magicians of our arrival. Why give them that advantage? We have enough against us as it is."

But the Prince was firm. "Aran must be consulted," he insisted stubbornly. "We have need of them, of their fighting ships. At any rate, the knowledge of the Druids they can give us will more than balance any risk we run by harboring there." He drew out his scimitar, eyes lowered toward it. "Much would have changed in these many years," he added sadly. "And only at Aran might we learn what has occurred. I need their guidance as surely as I need your own. Each and every one of you." He looked at them all. "But if there are still doubts, if some regret the bargains we made, please say so now while there is yet time for the good captain to take you back . . ."

Mariana clasped Ramagar by the hand and stood poised and erect. In the soft yellow light of the lantern she looked more beautiful than ever: her face cleaned and darkened by the winds of the sea, her eyes as bewitching and fiery as always, yet somehow matured by the ordeals of these last months.

"We trusted you in Kalimar," she told him directly, "and that faith has never been broken. You know that both Ramagar and I have come to love you as we would a brother . . ."

"And to me as a son," added the haj poignantly.

As for Homer, the look of adoration in his eyes left no need for mere words.

"I would think that settles matters," said Captain Osari with an air of finality. "Aran it is. We'll be there in seven days' time."

Mariana tightened her heavy shawl about her shoulders, pushed long strands of dark, wavy hair from her face, and realized suddenly that her teeth were beginning to chatter.

"It gets colder every day," snorted the haj, standing in his warmest robe, leaning against the rail at her side. He rubbed his hands together, to keep the stiffness out of his fingers, while keeping his gaze fixed on the slashing, chalky seas ahead.

"I know," said the girl with a small shiver. She tilted her head upward and gazed through shaded eyes at the weak late afternoon sun. "This isn't like the East at all, is it?"

Burlu scowled. "What manner of men would choose to live in climates like this, I'll never know. They say Cenulam is very much the same. Not to mention these other strange lands we've passed. As for me, though, I'll take the desert anytime."

Mariana looked up at him and smiled. "Then you should have stayed in Kalimar," she teased. "In your tents beside the fire, with your pigs to keep you company."

The haj seemed offended. "My women are *not* pigs," he retorted. Mariana laughed. "Good haj, I was referring to your swine . . ."

"Oh."

He turned away with a sour expression, hiding his embarrassment. "Anyway," he said, clearing his throat, "if it gets much colder than this I think I'll be as frozen as a board. You'll probably have to hang me over the cooking fire until the icicles melt."

Mariana sighed moodily, her soft features losing their gentility. "The captain says it's going to get worse," she said seriously. "And that by the time we do reach Aran, likely as not we'll all have to dress in furs."

And to her distress, Captain Osari's prediction proved more than right. Warm winds and sun came late to these climes, months later than they did to the fair lands of the South, where by early spring flowers bloomed and sand burned. Here, summer was still far away, and the ship found itself upon an ocean of desolation, bleak and forlorn, yet strangely beautiful in its own way. A pale sun reflected across an endless panorama of grayish-blue water and stark peaks of ice, standing like mountains along the horizon.

The North. The far North. It was a fascinating world to Mariana: grim, inhospitable, and awesome. And to reach Aran, they were forced to head even closer to the Northern extremities than was needed to reach the Eternal Dark.

Two days' sailing from Aran the sun became little more than a reddish sliver against a mauve horizon. When they did see the moon it was fog-veiled, peering myopically back at them as it hung low, clinging to the valleys between the bergs.

Great sledges of ice filled the sea, broken off from these arctic monstrosities and slowly floating south with the strong current, where eventually they would melt and cease to be forms. Icy winds bit harshly into flesh; no clothes the crew or the passengers could find, mend, or weave seemed to serve well against the brutality of nature. Building fires on deck was the only way the crew could keep enough heat to perform routine tasks.

Nights were intolerable. It was so frigid on one occasion that the sand in the hourglass ceased to trickle. It stuck frozen against the glass, waiting for the morning sun to dispel the crusts of ice that blocked the passage.

But never once did the ship or the captain flinch. Never once. No matter what the hardship or peril, day in, day out, they pressed ahead, closer and closer to bleak Aran at the northern edge of the Darkness, plowing forward with terrible effort against ice packs. And through all this Captain Osari remained resolute, with but one goal in mind: to find Aran, and then swing south where the waters would warm.

"Ahoy, Captain!" called the lookout perched precariously atop the crow's nest. He pulled the fur of his jacket more tightly about his ears and signaled with his hand into the western night sky.

Captain Osari clutched at the ropes, half sliding across the frosted deck. Cupping his mittened hands, he shouted back, asking the sailor what he saw.

"Straight ahead, sir! Straight ahead!"

Osari squinted into the dismal midnight sky and shuddered. As some of the mist dissipated, twin peaks of ice assembled before his vision.

The slowly drifing bergs were like jagged volcanoes, walls smooth and reflective, made that way by the constant pounding of the wind. Yet at their base they were pointed and ragged like razors, ready to shred anything that rubbed against them. And they were high, far higher than the topsail, virtual towers lighting up the night, obstructing the horizon as boldly as any mountain range the captain ever saw.

The handful of sailors on duty glanced at one another and felt their heartbeats quicken. They saw right away that the ship's position was treacherous. Strewn on either side of the frozen nightmares was an endless barrage of lesser packs—it would be impossible for the ship to pick its way among them. No, there was only one way the *Vulture* could proceed:

straight ahead, right through the narrow artificial valley the slumbering giants created.

Captain Osari felt his palms moisten, even in this great cold. Rubbing icy fingers over his scarf-covered mouth, he darted back to his post, instructing the helmsman to veer two points more to port where the awesome entrance to the valley began.

A small floe ground loudly against the hull; the ship rocked and pulled away from the raw chunk, spraying tiny fragments over the main deck.

The jolt awoke Mariana from an uneasy sleep. Rushing to her porthole, she gasped with her hand to her mouth as the mountains came into view. Above her head she heard the scramble of more sailors rushing onto the deck, also awakened, ready to do whatever they could to help.

Bundling into her furs, she made her way from the silent cabin and hurried topside, panting with dismay as her skin felt the bite of the cold. She stood in the shadow of the open hatch, out of the crew's way and careful not to let her presence be known lest the captain order her back down below.

Thus the treacherous passage began. The rough sea calmed a bit, due to the barrier imposed by the fantastic blockages of ice at both sides. For some time Mariana held her breath as if bewitched by the white-blue spectacle rising misshapenly away from the masts.

The ship lurched sharply, sails momentarily losing their swell and flapping. "Steady . . ." came the assuring voice of the captain. "Keep her steady . . ."

A low rumble sounded from behind; Mariana whirled, almost losing her footing on the slippery planks. A hefty chunk was sliding clumsily from its place near the jagged crest. It cracked as it rolled, shattering into a half-dozen deadly boulders that came crashing fiercely into the water and sent huge sprays swelling knee-deep over the afterdeck.

Ramagar had also been awakened; he lumbered his way up the steps toward the hatch. Finding Mariana startled and also angered him; but the sight of the incredible bergs left him so transfixed that he just stood by her side speechless, unable to convey his thoughts.

Moments later Osari called for the ship to adjust for the wind, but the command came a hairsbreadth too late. A second ice pack ground against the hull's thin wood; the ship jerked, the bow dipped, slowly pushing away. But the deck remained slanted at its incline with a definite bias to the starboard side. Lumber crunched, a brittle snapping sound in the cold, and rushing water heaved through the hole.

"She's damaged us, sir," called the first mate calmly. "We're taking on water."

"Damn," growled the captain, and he kicked his boot savagely onto the floor. Then he quickly regained his composure, barking for the first mate and a handful of sailors to get below and inspect the damage.

The *Vulture* heeled, and it was obvious that the gash was a bad one, allowing the sea to flood wildly in at least one section of the hold. Normally such a tear could be repaired in a matter of hours—but not now, not here between these all-powerful monsters where even the slightest miscalculation could send them roaring into the mountain's face.

"More trouble ahead, Cap'n," shouted the lookout.

Captain Osari clenched his teeth and stared. From some distant edge of the closer peak the ice wall cracked and split; a section of the mountain was breaking away, ripping itself like sackcloth and pulling toward the center of the valley. Rocking horribly as it broke loose and free, it celebrated its birth by causing a tremendous upheaval before them, displacing water in rivers and splashing it up along the smooth walls.

The captain expertly calculated the needed adjustments, and gave precise directions to the helmsman. The sturdy little ship, sleek and proud, seemed to him now to be like a tiny matchstick, fragile and helpless, next to the awesome forces nature had set against them.

The helmsman was at his very best, calling long years of experience to the fore. He maneuvered the craft like an eel, slipping the ship between lumbering floes with barely inches to spare. The cliffs of white hovered over their heads, pale sheets of solid ice, trembling and ready to crumble.

The wind slackened as they reached the center of the canyon, and the new prevailing silence made them shudder. Save for the occasional command the captain issued, no one uttered a word. Crew and passengers stood by breathlessly, watching the hideous walls slowly slide by, and anxiously keeping an eye on those yet to come. Mariana bit at her frozen lips and clung to the arm of the thief.

The ship was tilting more sharply as it sliced ahead through the frozen debris. There were muffled noises coming from below, where the first mate and his hands were frantically trying to plug up the yawning hole in their side. The

210

clang and clatter of hammers became louder and Captain Osari tensed. Then suddenly the rush of swelling water against the hull eased; inch by inch the ship began to right itself and he smiled grimly. A shipwreck here was certain death for them all, he knew. A man would last maybe three minutes in the freezing water, or even less; but in such a dreaded circumstance, less was probably better.

A heavy fog had begun to swirl above. Thick and clammy, it shrouded the peaks of the bergs, then gradually moved lower. "Steady as she goes," Osari whispered, straining his vision to peer beyond the exit of the valley. He brushed his ice-flecked hood and clasped his hands behind his back. He saw that the fog would make further progress impossible. Although he was doing everything he could to guide the *Vulture* through, he knew it would take far more than a sailor's ability to push safely out of this mess.

The mist descended faster, at an alarming rate. Soon they could hardly even make out the walls of the bergs at their sides, even though in places they were only meters away.

With all but the mainsail furled, the ship seemed to halt abruptly, then continue its movement forward at a snail's pace. A dozen lookouts were placed along the prow, each man holding a torch and measuring with careful counts the pitiful distance that could be seen ahead.

Blocks of ice danced before the bow, bobbing and weaving, clumsily knocking into the straining ship. The cold fog had settled above the waterline, totally shrouding the ship and covering it from yardarm to deck, stem to stern, with a thin veneer of frost.

By this time no one was still asleep. Every man aboard had come topside to see. They gasped and they groaned, understanding the fate they faced if the *Vulture* veered from her precarious course and came into contact with the jagged mounds strewn on either side.

The mists writhed demonically across the high and ragged scape. As the ship wallowed, Captain Osari stepped from the bridge and worked his way to the prow, following the burning light of the torches and watching the deep shadows the flames cast on the faces of his men.

"What are we going to do?" asked a distraught Burlu as the mariner passed.

Osari turned sharply, a look of anxiety etched into his sea

211

rover's features. "I suggest we pray," he replied dourly. "I fear there is little else we *can* do."

Mariana swallowed. "You mean we're trapped until the fog clears?"

The mariner smiled thinly. "Yes—if we can make it that long. But we're as blind as a ship can ever be. Chances are we'll smash up long before the mist rises . . ."

"Our torches won't help?" asked Ramagar.

Osari shook his head. "See for yourself. The only hope we have is to anchor, stay put in a single place, and hope we don't find ourselves embedded in ice . . ."

"Or have the bergs come crashing atop our heads," Mariana added gloomily.

They stood in silence. Captain Osari had been frank with them, and the picture he painted would only grow more dismal as the night wore on. Mariana envisioned what would happen if the ship couldn't keep moving; and the image of the *Vulture* encrusted in solid ice made her shudder. In a day, two at the most, they would all have been frozen to death. And a grim monument would stand forever in the far North—a monument warning all other ships: Keep away! Or share the same fate.

Ramagar rubbed at his whitened knuckles, blowing large volumes of smoky frost from his mouth. "Isn't there *anything* we can do?"

The captain sighed. "If you know of something, I'd love to hear it."

"Maybe I can help." It was the Prince who spoke, and all eyes quickly turned toward him. With bitterly cold hands he reached inside his heavy fur jacket and pulled out the scimitar.

Mariana shuddered. "Blue Fire," she whispered.

"Yes," said the Prince. "Blue Fire. Perhaps the glow can cut through the fog—" His eyes darted to the prow and the huddled sailors still holding their torches high in the air. "But we must be careful," he cautioned. "You've all seen the strength of its flame. If the blade touches the ice, even fleetingly, it could set off a terrible explosion—an explosion which would melt the bergs in an instant and send an ocean of water flooding down from above."

"We'd be drowned in seconds," gulped the haj. And the Prince nodded darkly.

Oro moved out from the shadows, trembling. Since Tarta he had never ventured from his cabin, and his sulking

212

presence had hardly been missed. But now, with this new threat to them all, he had come onto the deck, as worry-filled and frightened as any.

"You can't use the magic!" he blurted out. "You saw what happened the last time! We'll be engulfed!"

The captain stepped into a circle of melted snow formed at his feet and glanced up and down barely visible ice walls on the port side. "It will be dangerous," he agreed. "A very tricky business . . ."

"Is it better to wallow until we freeze?" snapped Mariana. She looked at the Prince. "Use it," she said. "Use your blade. Call forth the power of the alloy and light up the night."

The Prince looked at her evenly. "Then you're not afraid like the others?"

She laughed hollowly. "My dear Prince, I am petrified. My flesh is crawling. But what alternative do we have? Anchoring is only begging for our deaths. At least the Blue Fire gives us a chance—no matter how slim it may be."

"Mariana's right," said Ramagar. "We must act. The more time we lose debating, the faster these bergs will close in."

The Prince turned to the captain. "This is your ship," he said to Osari respectfully. "Only you can give the command. Shall I use the dagger? Or not?"

It was a dilemma with no easy solution. Captain Osari thought long and hard to make his decision. But in the end he realized that Mariana had been right. The scimitar was the only way. And in any case, if the bergs exploded, the water would drown them so quickly that they would never know what happened. If they *were* to die, that would be the best way.

"All right," he said at length. "We've nothing to lose. Do what must be done while the rest of us pray for your success."

The Prince sat down cross-legged on the open deck, oblivious to the stares of incredulous sailors, oblivious to the tiny particles of frozen snow rushing against his exposed hands and face. Then with his eyes tightly shut, he once more went into his trance, calling forth the strange secrets of the unknown alloy. Careful not to touch anything solid, he lifted the dagger in his open hands, bowed his head, and concentrated as hard as he could.

Oro gazed intently at his first demonstration of the dagger's power brought to life. As the blade lost its golden aura he gasped, then watched raptly as the first tones of swirling blue

213

glowed above the gold and reflected across the Prince's clean-shaven face.

Suddenly the wondrous blade began to burn, as before, sending tiny slivers of blue light scattering into the night. Crewmen doused their flimsy torches; the lamp swinging freely from the bridge sputtered and went out. Bathed totally in the peculiar blue light, the Prince slowly rose to his feet, holding the scimitar now in one hand high above his head, and made his way slowly and cautiously across the deck to the prow. And everywhere the blade met the mist, the fog was pushed back. Not far, but enough for everyone to see clearly the walls of ice that surrounded them.

The Prince reached the prow and grasped the iced-over lash line. The dumbfounded sailors scurried aside and left him to stand alone. Holding out his arm, the Prince slashed the dagger through the air. Tiny flakes of ice buzzed wildly, like sparks from a firecracker, burning up and plummeting dizzily into the sea.

And the fog itself recoiled, drifting eagerly out of harm's way as the blue flame licked upward into the shroud. The sailors cheered loudly.

"Full ahead," called the captain, gazing with astonishment as the path before the ship cleared. No time was to be lost, no effort spared. The *Vulture* crunched over a blockage that had already formed off the prow and lurched forward.

Like a statue the Prince stood, fixed in his place, holding Blue Fire aloft. Here and there the monumental ice packs thinned or lowered, only to regain their height and thickness suddenly. The ship weaved in and out, dodging floes with regularity.

But as Blue Fire singed, much of the loose snow along the edges of the cliffs began to dislodge. A low malevolent rumbling filled their ears before they could understand what was happening. The mist had turned hot, its vapor rushing madly against the packed walls in its frenzy to escape the flames. In so doing, it was melting some of the ice, causing great fissures to burst and boulder-like chunks to slide from the mountains. And as they rolled they picked up speed and even more ice, dislodging other chunks as they fell.

The ship rocked; Mariana screamed. A huge misshaped block came crashing onto the bridge, nearly crushing the helmsman. Then came another from the opposite side. The melting slab thundered from the cliff, splitting into two and hitting beside the afterdeck. Two sailors scrambled for

214

cover—but not in time. Their terrible wails pierced the frigid air; the ice hit with such impact that both men were sent flying over the side, sucked down into the water right before the eyes of their stunned companions.

Lines were thrown, a dozen men raced to help, but nothing could be done. Mariana looked on in horror as a lonely hand rose from beneath the murk, splashing about and causing tremendous ripples before it slid below again, never to reappear.

"Off the prow!" came a howling cry.

And there, a huge slab, a virtual berg by itself, began to totter. Then it tipped to its side and rolled over. The bottom of the berg rose, larger than the top had been, displacing incredible amounts of icy water and spilling it violently across the prow. The Prince slipped with the swell, holding onto the line for his very life. For an instant it seemed the dagger would fall. Mariana's eyes grew wide with panic. One touch to the wood, the barest glance, and the entire prow would shoot up into roaring blue fire. But the Prince lost control only fleetingly. Finding his feet, he let go of the line and reasserted his control over the blade. The scimitar glowed brighter under the hovering mountains and the Prince drew back his arm slightly when he saw the smoothed wall of ice at his side slowly begin to melt.

All through this period of uncertainty and fear the *Vulture* never wavered from its course. More slabs crashed and submerged, rose again. Sailors came running with pikes and axes and deftly pounded the closest of them until their razor edges were dulled and could no longer pose a threat if they struck the tender wood of the hull.

Suddenly thunder echoed behind, and Mariana turned aghast to see the far side of one mountain fall with frightful slow motion into the black water. A rush of sea swelled and slammed against the stern. Wind was rushing at them once more, cold and harsh. But Captain Osari grinned and clapped his hands. "We're breaking free!" he shouted gleefully. "We're passing the valley!"

And in the weird blue of the dagger's glow they could all see the way ahead beyond the bergs: dark, choppy seas, menacing and stormy—but at last they were in the open.

The sails filled with a *whomp!* The *Vulture* pitched and lurched forward. The mist above the masts began to fall back in a rush. Stars began to glitter, a bright half-moon now brightened the sky.

Laughter, tears, and merriment filled the ship. The haj scooped up Mariana in his arms and smothered her with kisses. The crew danced, sang, complimented each other, and congratulated the weary captain and helmsman. Homer and Ramagar rushed to the prow, glowing with gratitude to the Prince. Exhausted from his feat, still holding the ebbing Blue Fire, he sighed deeply and smiled.

"That's the second time you've saved us," exclaimed Ramagar.

Dark shadows flickered from the Prince's worn face. The dagger's magic had its price—and it was beginning to show. "How far to Aran?" he asked the beaming captain.

Osari glanced at the stars, reckoning. "A day and a half."

The Prince let his shoulders sag. "Good," he replied. And while the others continued their frolicking, he placed the scimitar carefully away under his jacket and slowly climbed down the hatchway steps to his cabin.

"Land to port!" cried the lookout, waving madly from his post in the crow's nest.

The main deck suddenly teemed with life, passengers and crew eagerly racing topside and straining their bodies over the rails to catch a glimpse. Shading eyes from the glaring afternoon sun, they stared intently at the distant range of tall, brooding mountains that spanned the horizon. Snowcapped near the tops, they glistened with hints of rich green grass steadily creeping up the slopes. As the ship moved closer through the choppy waters the watchers could make out the vast forests of spruce and aspen that cut sharply away from the hills and covered the landscape in every direction. Where rivers and fjords watered the land, wide expanses of fertile plain could be seen. A stunning array of beautiful wild heather dotted the dales and valleys.

There were birds as well, great flocks of them everywhere: grouse, ravens, wrens, and jays—and of course the ever-present seagulls, who had massed themselves by the thousands beyond the rocky reefs, waddling in the roaring surf between flights.

After the grueling adventures the companions had endured the sight of land—any land—was joyous indeed. Yet there was a strange character about the land, one that only dawned as the *Vulture* drew close to the coastline. Mariana grasped the railing with both her hands, the wind blowing through her hair, and stared out at the grazing lands along the range of low hills at the base of the mountains. She could plainly make out a large herd of caribou feeding peacefully beside the banks of a river. There were other animals as well, moose, and deer, in plain sight. But as for human inhabitants, there seemed to be none.

"Where are the people?" Mariana wondered aloud as the ship furled sails and slipped into a tiny inlet. "The ports? The towns?"

"Aran must be deserted," said Ramagar. The thief looked at the haj and saw that he was as perplexed as the rest of them.

The Prince filled his lungs with the pleasant, warm air, and bowed his head. Eyes closed, he said a silent prayer for his fortune in having at least reached this island. Then he said, "Aran has no cities, my friend. Nor any ports. At least not the type of ports I think you mean . . ."

"Then where is everyone?" asked Mariana. "Do they hide from us? Are the inhabitants hill folk and shepherds?"

At this the Prince smiled. "You will see them all, Mariana, when they are ready. Be assured they have already seen us. First they will ascertain whether we be friends or enemies. Then they will come."

"A mistrustful lot," grumbled Oro, pulling a face and nervously tapping his foot against the freshly swabbed deck. "They must be cowards to hide from a merchant ship."

The Prince's brows angled down sharply. He glared at the hunchback. "You will not feel that way for long, little man," he said. And he stretched out his arm to the west. "Look!"

The lookout had also seen what the Prince saw. "Warship approaching off the starboard side!" he shouted, recognizing the manner of vessel at once. Captain Osari spun from his place, shading his eyes and peering intently where a long *knaar* raised its oars, and by the swell of its single crimson sail came slashing through the dark water toward them.

The passengers stared wide-eyed. It was a ship, a long ship, the likes of which they had never seen before.

"Hoist our flag!" boomed the captain, and the Cenulamian colors fluttered in the wind. The Aranian vessel approached cautiously, and Mariana gasped at the sight of the rugged seamen who had put down their oars and picked up shields and weapons. They were tall and rugged men, yellow-haired as was the Prince, broad-shouldered and burly. Upon their heads they wore helmets like barbarians, many made of hide,

217

others of metal, some with twin pointed horns protruding from the sides.

As for the ship itself, its prow was swan-necked, thrust sharply upward almost as high at the mast. Perhaps forty meters long, its beam was extraordinarily broad, built clearly of oak and pine, yet seeming supple enough to withstand the hardest beatings of a pitching sea. Sixteen oars flashed from the black-shielded portholes at either side; she had no wheel, only a well-fitted rudderboard placed along the starboard side of the stern. A multitude of weapons ranging from axes to longswords, clubs, and knives were in evidence in open crates.

Mariana watched breathlessly as the *knaar* plowed to a safe distance from the *Vulture* and stopped dead. "They look like savages!" she concluded, seeing the man she assumed to be the captain of the curious vessel move to the prow and hold up a great battle-ax with both his hands.

"No, not savages," corrected the Prince. "Warriors. Brave and daring seamen—forced to live under the shadow of the Eternal Darkness. They are fierce and reckless fighters, but we need not fear them. To us they are friends."

"Some friends," sighed the girl as the Aranian captain signaled for his crew to raise their weapons.

Osari's crew stood shivering and terrified. The men of the *knaar* seemed awesome indeed—if it came to a fight, the *Vulture* would stand no chance.

The burly warrior commanding the fighting ship narrowed his blue eyes at the intruder and tightened the grip of his ax. His yellow beard, flecked with gray and black, hung almost to his stomach; his long yellow hair fell from beneath the imposing horned helmet, over his shoulders, and tossed gently in the wind.

"Who are you?" he called in the language of the North, a language that both Captain Osari and the Prince readily understood.

Captain Osari pointed toward the flapping banner. "A peaceful ship, Captain. From Cenulam—"

It was obvious that the warrior knew of Cenulam. He glanced at the flag, let his gaze drift to the crew, and nodded. "What do you want here?"

At this question the Prince bounded onto the prow and held out his arms in the recognized peaceful gesture common to these lands. "To seek your shelter," he replied, shouting across the void of water. "And to speak with your Council."

218

It was an odd request, and one that the warrior would not consider. "Turn your ship around!" he barked. "If you came in peace, then go in peace. You cannot land."

"Just as well with me," said the captain to the Prince. Knowing something of Aran from the stories told by unfortunate sailors who happened by there, he was in no mood to argue. To try and impose his will on these people was sheer madness.

But the Prince was adamant. "They must let us berth," he said. "We need them." Then he turned from Captain Osari and back to the *knaar*'s captain. "In the name of Freydis the Bloodax, in the name of Lito the Sword—I beseech you to change your mind!"

The warrior seafarer winced. The stranger had called the names of the two most revered kings Aran had ever had, bold, wise men whose stature had only increased in the long centuries since their deaths—but men whose names meant nothing in Cenulam or other lands. That this stranger knew of them was astonishing.

He put down his ax slowly, signaling for his crew to do the same. Then he took off his helmet and fixed his gaze on the stranger who had spoken. "By what right do you invoke the names of our kings?"

The Prince lifted his shoulders, meeting the captain's eyes. "By the right of every free man. By the right of all Friends who come to Aran in friendship."

"And you . . . are such a Friend?" he called back.

The Prince nodded. "I am and have always been. And I vouch as much for my companions, one and all."

The opposing captain was in a quandary. A Friend of Aran was always to be welcomed; it was foremost in their ancient law. Yet times had changed. Aran no longer accepted strangers, and a true Friend had not come in more lifetimes than he could count. Still . . .

"What is your purpose?"

"As I have said, to meet with your Council. A small request, my good captain. Would you deny so little to one who has come so far?"

The able seafarer scowled and grunted. He signaled for his men to take their places and pick up the oars. "Follow me," he called to Captain Osari, and then to the Prince: "If you truly are a Friend, as you claim, then you are welcome." But here his blue eyes turned steely cold and he warned, "But if you are not, be assured you shall pay the price." On that note

219

he placed his helmet back on his head and gave the commands for the ship to sail.

"What do you suppose he meant by that?" said Osari, his eyes keenly following the *knaar* as it sliced easily through the rough waters.

The Prince frowned. "It's better you don't ask," he replied. "But know that men of Aran are not to be toyed with."

The *Vulture*, its own sails trimmed, stayed close behind the warship, as they sailed west into the setting sun. The sky had turned a blood-red at the horizon; the moon, crescent and low, hung between the valleys of the mountains on the port side. And finally another destination was in sight. The *knaar* slipped into its harbor, and glided next to a well-sheltered quay.

The quay was crowded with fishing vessels of all sizes. There, Mariana could feel the mistrustful stares of the rugged, yellow-haired fishermen who looked up at the foreign ship with trepidation.

There was something of a village spread out before them, the first they had seen in all their hours of navigating the island. A few hundred small homes lay scattered at random along the base of the harbor's gently sloping hills. The houses were made of stone, with timber and thatched roofs. She could see few windows, but chimneys rose above every room, grimly attesting to the cold nights and long winters which made fireplaces a constant necessity.

Away from the village she could see orchards. Apple trees and wild berry bushes abounded. Vegetable gardens were behind each house; there were a few barns about, and she saw cows and goats grazing in a distant pasture. Beyond them all, she could not fail to notice again the vast forests that rose magnificently up the snowcapped mountains.

It was a harsh land. But there were children playing and laughing in the muddy streets; pretty blue-eyed girls and beautiful women, all in thick fur jackets, greeting their returning husbands and fathers with kisses and smiles, and holding their hands as they led them home. Smoke puffed up from the chimneys; the windows glowed brightly from the cooking fires. Suddenly Mariana could feel much of her fear vanish. She saw that Aran was not the hostile and gruesome place she had believed it to be; rather, it seemed quiet and peaceful, and she wondered how much of its barbarian exterior was a charade.

As the passengers prepared to debark under the watchful

eye of the *knaar* captain and some of his burliest men, Mariana turned to the Prince. "What will they do with us now that we're here?"

"Probably keep us under guard until the Council has gathered," he replied soberly. "They'll not trust us until I've proven who I am."

"And then?"

The Prince sighed as he walked down the gangplank, gazing edgily at the gathering crowd of women and children standing back from the ship. "And then we'll know just where we stand. Look at the horizon, Mariana."

She did so dutifully, peering into the splendorous sunset in the west. But then she tensed at a curious sight. Although the sky was yet bright, a portion of it, at the rim of the horizon, was already as black as night. And even though the sun was dipping into the darkness, it would not penetrate.

"Speca," she whispered.

The Prince nodded gloomily. "Yes, Speca. We are almost there. Almost close enough to reach out and touch it. Aran lives with her shadow constantly; and her men are every bit as frightened of what lies beyond as we are."

The girl chewed at her lip and looked away. "Then they'll help us?"

He shook his head pensively. "I don't know. But I pray I can convince them that they must. For without the ships of Aran, I fear we are surely doomed."

15

Word of the foreign vessel's arrival did not take long to spread; messengers traveled to the farthest reaches of Aran, saying that a stranger had come—one who claimed to be a Friend. He had known how to invoke the land's ancient customs and hospitality, and had requested that the *Sklar*, the Council of Elders, be called at once and all the many Clans bidden to attend.

Many long days and longer nights passed before everyone had gathered. Normally this group of Clan leaders, Sages, and battle-wise sea rovers would meet for but a single week once every fifth year, to air and debate all disputes among them and to satisfy just grievances. Then the *Sklar* would disband, members returning to their disparate fiefs. But now it was claimed that a Friend had come, so very many years since the last. Each leader accepted the news with wonder, doubting if it could truly be so. Yet a Friend's plea to be heard could not go unanswered; Aran's law was firm on the matter. So the *Sklar* must be held, and the stranger must be heard.

Some journeyed from the Hinterlands, harsh and secretive places deep within Aran's mighty forests; others made their way overland from the northern coasts called the Rock Shores, bleak and barren lands on the northern frontiers, where life was dismal and only the strongest and fittest could survive. Yet others of the Clans traveled in sledges drawn by wolfhounds, across a wilderness of frozen tundra called the Ice Lake, whose very name attested to the lives these rugged men led.

Mostly, though, it was by ship that they came, long, sleek *knaars* that carried them from their homes along the coasts, tartan colors of their Clan flying grandly above the masts. Intricately carved images of dragons, some spitting fire, adorned the spitheads; the ships bore sails of crimson and gold, ocher and blue, all tones chosen by their ancestors long before, when Aran was young and first settled by other tribes of the North.

The meeting place of the *Sklar* was and always had been a huge amphitheater carved out of solid rock, built deep within the hollow of a mountain. Since time immemorial the members had been free to speak openly here, to argue their causes as free men, and to await the *Sklar*'s binding judgments. It had been in this very place that brave Rond the Princeling, son of Ash, tore out the foul heart of the king of the Banes with his knife, and forever rid Aran of its last vestiges of Druid influence. Also at this spot had noble Tule banished the Hawliis by beheading the evil Clanmaster of Skule who had plotted Aran's defeat. And yes, it had also been here that courageous Rik the Lonely had brought Aran the news of Speca's fall, pleading with his peers for ships and men to come to their neighbor's rescue. But Druid magic had cast a fearful pall over the *Sklar* that sleepless night, and when Rik at last did set out, he was forced to do so virtually alone. The Clans had watched silently as his ships set sail into the Eternal Darkness—and no man of Aran ever saw Rik or his men again.

These sagas and a thousand more were told of the *Sklar*

and of Aran itself, but tales of the past made little difference now, as the Elders came one by one to hear and see the supposed Friend. They could not think of glories gone by; their only concern was for the strangers in their midst and what their arrival might herald for Aran.

During the handful of days while the *Sklar* was yet being prepared, the Prince and the other passengers were kept carefully guarded in a stone castle close to the meeting place. As for Captain Osari and his brave crew, they had not once been allowed to set foot off the ship. Virtual prisoners themselves, they watched and trembled while a fleet of warships kept them surrounded, blocking the entrance to the inlet and brandishing fearsome weaponry as a warning lest the foreigners prove inhospitable guests.

And then, on the fourth day after the *Vulture* reached Aran, in the cool of the evening, the *Sklar* was ready to sit.

Mariana stepped across the narrow drawbridge, bundled tightly, and waited as stern-faced Aranian guards brought her companions from their separate rooms. She gazed about at the darkening landscape, the high mountains rising majestically above the crenellated walls of the castle. A tall soldier prodded her gently, pointing toward the grim hill. Then they were all led single file to a set of wide stone steps that began far from the walls at the base of the mountain. From the base it was impossible to see the top, and the stairway she was being told to climb seemed to twist and wind ceaselessly as it skirted the rocky slope, disappearing at times behind the ledges and the shadows, only to reappear again and again at distant points.

Two of the guards took the lead, unspeaking and somber, holding their torches well above their heads. The Prince followed close behind, beginning the treacherous ascent. Next came another guard, then Ramagar and the haj. Young Homer was next, and then it was Mariana's turn. Two more Aranians brought up the rear.

It was a starry evening, and the wind became more and more blustery the higher they climbed. Yet even with the wind the weather had turned considerably milder than on previous days, and Mariana wondered if at last the long winter was drawing to a close, even here in the far North. Some of the steps were crumbling and Mariana allowed one of the guards to help her hold her balance. Then to her surprise she saw that there were handholds embedded into the rock walls, quite a number of them, all of ancient iron, still as strong and as sturdy as the day they were placed.

Mica in the rocks glittered as torchlight briefly reflected along the surface. Lumbering dark shadows danced above and behind her, and she found herself struggling to catch her breath when the steps became sharply steeper. Pausing momentarily, she glanced below and was startled to see just how far she had actually come. Thick forests stretched out before her, ending abruptly at the edge of the fields and pastures. She could easily make out the sweep of the sea, listen to the roar of the surf breaking smoothly against the reefs beyond the cove. The houses of the village glowed with pinpricks of light, appearing so tiny that she was sure a single scoop of her hand could pick them all up.

The guard at her side nudged her, breaking her from her musings. She looked ahead and saw that she had fallen behind the others; Ramagar waited for her at the edge of what seemed to be a narrow plateau set beneath voluminous overhanging ledges. There was also the sound of water coming from somewhere, cascading water. When she finally reached the plateau herself she stared amazed at the sight of a waterfall of melting snow, pouring down from the ledges and over the rocks, and splashing into some unseen pool or lake close to the bottom.

"This way," said one of the guards, gesturing for them all to step into a cavern easily overlooked in the darkness. The torches lit the granite brightly; the Aranian led them to a hidden flights of steps. These, far narrower than the others, formed a tricky passage right through the walls of the mountain and up to the amphitheater.

Entering the meeting place the small group was greeted by a sudden swell of bright silver moonlight which beamed eerily down upon the hundred or so somber and tight-faced men seated on a wide semicircle of stone benches. Mariana held her breath and swept her glance across them, shuddering as their own gazes fixed upon her and her companions.

The Elders of the *Sklar* sat rigidly in their places, each man dressed in the traditional dark robes of Aran, each with flowing beard and hair, each silently studying the group of strangers set before them.

A guard nudged Mariana gently and she took her place in a single-file line with the others, Ramagar to her right, the haj to her left. The leader of the stern soldiers bowed sweepingly before the august body and gestured the presence of the

224

guests and then of the Prince, the stranger who claimed to be a Friend.

The Sages of the *Sklar*, older than their peers by a generation's and set apart from the rest along a wide rock slab in the front, nodded severly, several dropping their gaze momentarily as they conferred among themselves in whispers.

Two guards gestured for the Prince to leave the others and brought him to stand before the bench of Sages.

"This is the man, my lords," the first soldier told them. Then he bowed again and stepped slowly backward into the shadows, his long cloak fluttering behind.

The Prince drew a deep breath as he scanned his questioners, then he set straight his shoulders and stood to his full height. His eyes met the stares he received evenly, returning their obvious skepticism with a look of honesty.

One of the Sages stood, a lumbering, broad-shouldered man, very old, very powerful, and, by the keen look in his gray-steel eyes, very wise.

"You have come to Aran claiming to be a Friend," he said to the Prince. "And we have received you as a guest. But now we are gathered, and we ask that you prove your worthiness of the title you claim."

At this the Prince smiled a thin smile and bowed graciously with his hands cupped in a pyramid and his body arching forward.

"Who are you, stranger?" came another voice from the row of Sages. Mariana looked up to see who had spoken but was greeted only by the grim silent faces as before.

"I am who I am," replied the Prince coolly. "The son of my father and his father before him."

The standing Sage gripped tightly at his walking stick, his eyes growing wider and ablaze at the guest. He lifted his chin and tossed back a shock of white hair from his craggy face. Mariana could see that this man, whoever he was, was more than a mere spokesman for the others.

The elderly Sage remained fixed in his position, studying the man before him carefully. "And your fathers before you," he said, "were they, too, Friends of Aran?"

The Prince nodded, looking his grim questioner straight in the eye. "For a thousand years and more, my lord," he whispered.

This reply caused a slight stir among the members of the *Sklar*. Muffled whispering rippled along the benches, and there was much shaking of heads and scratching of beards.

225

"Aran has few such Friends remaining," countered the Sage coyly. "By what right do you make such a claim?"

A slight sneer, mocking and cold, crossed the Prince's lips. "Has mighty Aran forgotten so swiftly?" he retorted. "What has become of the noble Elders of my father's father's time? Where are those among the *Sklar* who would recognize a Friend without the need to first make him their prisoner?"

This caused an even greater stir than before; the members of the *Sklar* were clearly incensed, some clenching their hands into fists and glaring at the brazen stranger with open anger.

It had been difficult for Mariana to follow these curious proceedings, but from this sudden reaction it was apparent that the Prince had insulted them one and all—insulted them purposely—and for what reason she could not imagine. Her companions were also aware of what had happened.

"By the Seven Hells," growled the haj beneath his breath. "What's the fellow up to? Infuriating these barbarians will only make matters worse for us. And from everything I've seen of this dismal land so far, none of them would lose very much sleep if their axes were sharpened on our throats."

Mariana deftly hushed the haj with a jab of her elbow and meekly resumed her stance to listen. The Prince, meanwhile, made no gesture to apologize for his rashness; on the contrary, he now stood with his hands on his hips, a smile upon his face, and defiance in his eyes.

At that moment Mariana expected someone to call for the immediate executions of them all, but much to her surprise the band of rugged lords and Sages did nothing. They resumed their silence and their rigid expressions, clearly content to let the Sage do their speaking for them. They folded their arms and leaned forward, weather-burned faces bathed in silver light and blue shadows.

The Sage's eyes again met the Prince's and the two men glared at one another in some unspoken form of combat in which neither flinched for a single moment. Then the Sage lifted his hand and beckoned with a bony finger for the stranger to come closer to him.

The Prince did as commanded; his form glowed for a moment, then darkened, as a low, fast-moving cloud crossed the face of the moon.

"You have spoken boldly," said the Sage, his voice impassive, showing no trace of anger or suspicion. "And rightly so—*if* you are indeed a Friend. But these are grim times for

Aran, aye, for all the lands of the North. We can no longer afford the luxury of hospitality such as you ask of us. Aran stands upon the threshold of terrible peril; our fate is yet undetermined, be it good or ill. And alas we must be careful, trusting in no man until his worth has been proven. Can you understand this?"

The Prince lowered his gaze toward the stone floor and sighed. "I know the things you speak of, my lord," he said in response, this time with humility in his voice. "Perhaps I have asked too much. If so, I beg the *Sklar*'s indulgence with me. For I am just a man—a man who has traveled many years and many roads to be here with you now, and my heart has been saddened to see what I have seen." He lifted his head and scanned the rows of Elders slowly, noting the pride in every eye, the heroism etched into every face. And he shook his head sadly, truly sorry for his outburst. These brave men had lived under the terrible shadow every day of their lives, lived with the threat of Druid magic without cessation. Who was he, a prince of Speca or no, to come before them and berate them for their mistrust?

"I am no stranger to the Eternal Dark that threatens the world," he added. "Nor to any of the dangers that Aran must contend with each morning of her existence. Yet . . ." and here he tilted his head and gazed up at the stars, "yet Aran knows the sun by day, as surely as she knows these very stars by night. In my own home there is neither. Only blackness."

The old Sage shuffled his feet restlessly and cast a long troubled glance toward his guest. "You have come to us from Speca?" he asked.

The Prince shook his head. "No, lord. I return to Speca. I return to the land of my father and his father before him. I return home."

The air was as still as ever it becomes upon the windy scapes of Aran. Each member of the all-powerful *Sklar* stared with disbelief as the Prince hung his head low to hide the soft tears falling down his face.

For a long while there was total silence; the Sage leaned heavily on his walking stick, his eyes tightly shut. At last he straightened himself again, and with a deep sigh, he said, "The time has come, Friend, for you to tell us who you are."

The Prince stood motionless only for a brief moment, then he placed his hand inside his tunic and took out the dagger. Jaws gaped, eyes stared in wonder. The Prince's hand trembled slightly as he held the blade out for all to see, and

227

the august Sages gasped as Blue Fire began to dance before their eyes; slowly at first, as always, but then more intensely, searing flame crackling out in every direction in the pulsing hues of deepening blue that colored every inch of the mountain's surface, every nook and every cranny, every recess and every crevice, creeping up and down along the sheer walls, bounding over the ridges and the distant trunks of dark Northern trees, reaching far beyond the huge amphitheater and up into the sky, right across the face of the moon and above and beyond the stars themselves. It was a sight that men of Aran had not dared to dream they would ever behold—a magnificent sight, as frightening as it was compelling, as mystifying as it was awesome. Speechlessly they watched, tongues lolling in their mouths, eyes fixed to the dazzling display, as it bounded to and fro, catching their vision and transfixing them. It was overpowering, shattering, terrible yet beautiful. The knowledge of its power dazzled their minds and fogged their vision. Blue Fire. Yes, the men of Aran knew its name. *Blue Fire!* The golden scimitar of the throne of Speca, the power and the glory of the land that once Aran loved as a brother.

Blue Fire!

Cold fire. Burning fire. Vengeful fire.

And here it was, before them tonight—not a magician's trick, for such majesty could never be recreated; nor was it the passing illusion of Druid magic, that malevolent force that kept Aran at bay and powerless to stand against it.

Never could this be duplicated—though for countless years the black-souled Druids had tried. Oh, how they had tried. They had blended every alloy known to man to recreate it; forged each element time and again in futile effort to possess it. Even as alchemists seek to blend gold from dross, so had the conquerors of Speca sought to regain the lost power of the glittering scimitar.

Blue Fire!

Never had Aran dreamed that it might come again.

In due course the mysterious dagger began to lose its glow; gradually the face of the mountain and the sky returned to normal, silver stars glimmering brightly above as before. The men of Aran, the *Sklar*, stood dumbfounded, panting to catch lost breath and beginning to gaze at one another in wonder and amazement.

The Prince's shoulders sagged, heavy with the weight of his

228

burden. At length he managed to look once again to the row of Sages and the wizened leader who stood in stunned silence.

The aged lord drew a deep breath and nodded his head. "You are indeed your father's son," he rasped, clearing his throat. Then he turned from the Prince and peered at his companions, slowly lifting his arms toward the sky. "A Friend has indeed come," he proclaimed for one and all to hear, and, glancing back to the stranger, he added, "Aran indeed welcomes you, and the return of the Blade of the Throne."

Again the Prince bowed before them, this time with a small smile of satisfaction apparent on his face.

"Speak, Friend," called the Sage. "Tell us why you have come to us, and how we may be of aid to you."

Mariana was certain there was a twinkle in the Prince's eyes as shook off his exhaustion and with a look of determination replied, "I, and my companions, have traveled half a world and more to reach the *Sklar* and the allies of Aran. We have faced peril and danger time and time again in our quest to reach Speca's shores. Now," here he sighed, "we must face perhaps the greatest danger of all—the regaining of my throne."

Gasps rippled across the cold stone benches in the hollow of the mountain. The old Sage, wisest of the wise, looked at the yellow-haired Prince aghast. "No man—no mortal man—can enter the Eternal Darkness and live," he stated flatly. "You journey to your deaths." He glanced briefly at Mariana and Ramagar, then looked sternly at the Prince. "You have all come on a fool's errand."

The Prince shook his head. "No, my lord. Not a fool's errand. I have come to regain what is rightly mine; to free my people and my land, to find a way to rid the world of Druid power for once and for all."

"Noble thoughts," came a deep voice from the back, and a tall muscular man, a fearsome fighter by his looks, stood from his place and glared down the sloping amphitheater at the Prince. "Many men would rid the North of this scourge, even give their own lives gladly. But we of Aran live beneath the shadow of the Darkness, and we alone know what awesome perils must be faced. How can you and your handful of friends possibly hope to succeed when even Aran's fleet cannot?"

"Have you an army of magicians to send against the Druids?" came another deriding voice. "Or a thousand long

229

ships indestructible against the Night-Watchers who prowl the black waters?"

"I know not of these 'Night-Watchers,'" admitted the Prince.

The fierce lord looked at him with unmasked scorn. "Know you of the Dragon Ships whose armor cannot be pierced even by swords of steel? Or the Black Mists that descend on all ships that dare to pass below the clouds? Know you of the hideous tortures of their Dwarf-king and the wizard who rules in his stead?"

The Prince shook his head, forced to admit that he had heard of none of it.

"Then you must be told. No ship, no man, has ever returned from the Eternal Dark. Aran knows, for once we tried. But no longer. Your throne can never be recovered. Sail your ship back to the land you came from. Speca has met her doom, now Aran must wait for her own. Nothing can save either one."

Startled, the Prince stared inquisitively at the Sage. The old man sighed and bent his head. " 'Tis true, I fear," he said in a low voice. "Slowly the Darkness spreads, encroaches upon us like a silent, evil bird in flight. Year by year the sky turns blacker before our eyes. I am old and will not live to see the day that it reaches our shores. So for myself I do not weep. But for the young of Aran, for the children and their children after them, I grieve every moment of my existence. Druid magic is upon us, upon all the lands of the North. And one by one we must succumb, until there is nothing left, nothing at all."

Ramagar listened incredulously. "If this is true," he called, stepping forward from his place and drawing closer to the Sage, "then why don't you fight? Why don't you gather your ships and meet this enemy head-on?"

The Sage smiled thinly, sadly amused by the young foreigner's belief that no power is too great to match.

"You are the companion of a Friend," he told the thief with understanding, "and therefore Aran shall consider you a Friend as well. But you speak of matters which you know so little of. Neither you nor your companions have seen what we have seen." He shook his head slowly. "Ten thousand ships of Aran would be useless. Don't you see? Druid magic comes not from the strength of their armies, nor even their grisly apparitions which prowl like beasts upon the black waters.

No, we would face all this and more. But first the key to their power must be broken. Until then, we can do nothing."

"But what is the key to this terrible Druid power?" questioned the thief. "Is it the spells themselves that these wizards cast?"

The Sage could not hide his sneer. "Aran does not hide from the conjuring of magicians," he answered contemptuously. "What we fear is the hopelessness that the Druid coming has brought." He drew a long breath of the chilled air and tightened his hold on his walking stick. "What we fear," he repeated, "is that which has taken men's very souls and condemned them forever, crushed them of will, stolen from them all that a man cherishes and left only despair in its place. What civilization would not cringe at the knowledge that to live is to be sapped of strength, rendered helpless, forlorn, and devoid of belief. Alas," he sighed, "under such conditions we can only accept . . ."

"Accept?" chimed Ramagar. "Accept what?"

"Our fate," replied the Sage sadly.

The thief of Kalimar was clearly confused by the strange and fatalistic soliloquy he had just heard. "Exactly what is this evil you speak of that so misshapes men? Above all else, what magic weighs so heavily that you fear it worse than death?"

There was a pause, and Mariana shuddered; she alone among her companions had understood the Sage's words; she alone had realized the terrible threat looming against Aran and the North.

"It is the night," she whispered, the words almost too painful to speak aloud.

The Sage looked up suddenly and cast his glance toward the young girl before him. With widened eyes he studied her briefly and then beckoned for her to come closer.

Mariana let go of the haj's strong hand and softly stepped toward the speaker's place where both the Prince and Ramagar stood silently. Silver beams of moonlight caressing her dark, flowing hair, she lifted her chin and gazed evenly at the Sage.

"Repeat your thoughts, child," he told her gently, and Mariana swallowed as she nodded.

"The blackness, my lord," she said meekly. "It can only be the Eternal Dark itself that causes Speca to lie in her dormant and enslaved state. A malevolent cloak across the sky enshrouding one land and slowly descending upon Aran . . ."

231

The wise man continued to study her; he noted her youth, her beauty, her dark eyes and golden skin so very different from that of the women of the North.

"You have spoken wisely and correctly, child," he said at last. "It is only the Darkness that we fear, for we know the madness it can bring. It creeps inside a man's soul like a fog, cold and damp, severe and relentless. It brings a world without stars, a world without moonlight, a world without the warmth of the sun. And it is this knowledge above all else that we cannot defeat. Only the blackness defeated Speca so long ago; Aran, try though she may, cannot hope to best it. And now it spreads insidiously eastward to subjugate us. This then is the true strength of Druid power. This and only this. Without the Eternal Night against us Aran would surely fight, even as the slaves of Speca themselves would lift off their yokes and rise to rid themselves of their conquerors."

Ramagar looked away painfully as the Sage ended his words. The thief quickly recalled his own brief encounter with the Eternal Dark, that fleeting glimpse he had had from the *Vulture*'s deck when the ship had first approached Aran. The fearful blackness had spread across the entire western horizon, and even at his safe distance the mere sight of it had sent chills up and down Ramagar's spine. He had seen the sun itself, a blazing ball of crimson in the evening sky, descend into nothingness before his startled eyes as it dipped lower and lower, unable to penetrate the dim pall lowly settling beneath the clouds. So frightening had this first view been that he had been forced to look away and try to block the thought of it from his mind. No wonder it drove men to madness!

"But surely there must be some way to dispel the Dark," protested Mariana.

The old Sage smiled a thin kind smile at her, one that was most warm and generous considering the poor circumstances of the discussion. "Ah, so many times we have tried to find such a way," he lamented bitterly. "And each time we have failed completely. The best of Aran's efforts have been futile; the terror we face cannot be dispelled, nor even pushed back from our shores. We know what we can expect, and that is no less than the worst." He glanced back to the Prince and the two men locked stares. "Aran is doomed," he continued, "although outside of the *Sklar* our peoples do not yet know it. Each day brings the Eternal Dark that much closer; already our fighting ships have sighted the grim vessels of the

Night-Watchers sailing closer to our harbors. I fear that the North is lost forever, and nothing can be done to alter this distressing destiny."

For a long while there was no further talk, as all reflected on what had been said. The wind began to pick up again, making eerie noises as it gusted down over the quiet amphitheater, whipping and whistling between the cracks and crevices along the mountain's jagged ridges.

It was Mariana's voice that finally broke the silence. "Then our true enemy is but the Darkness," she observed. "And if that much could be conquered then we might stand a chance . . ."

The Sage laughed a short hollow laugh, the bitterness of his mirth apparent to all. "Yes, child. As simple a matter as that. For then we would know that Druid magic has been defeated." He hung his shoulders dejectedly and pinched the bridge of his nose. "But such a welcome happening can never be. No man, no woman, on the face of the world possesses such a power."

"Perhaps you are wrong," said the Prince with an air of mystery. "Perhaps a way can yet be found to dispel the Darkness, to scatter the blackness across a thousand winds and render it harmless."

Steely eyes tightened and glowered questioningly at the Friend of Aran, son of kings long since vanquished from their home. "Do you truly believe what you say?" said the Sage. "After all you have been told here tonight? After all you have learned? The greatest minds of Speca herself could not regain the sky, nor even the bold fighting ships of Aran."

The Prince nodded glumly. All this was true; indeed the picture the Sage had painted was even bleaker than the one he had expected to find. Yet now he was all the more determined to go forward in his task, to defeat the Druids before their power encompassed the world.

"But you have forgotten one thing, my lord," he said to the Sage, folding his arms and smiling slyly. "My fathers have entrusted me with a tool—a single tool to be sure—but with its aid, and perhaps your own as well, I shall defeat our enemies."

"The scimitar!" cried Mariana, having momentarily forgotten all about it.

The Prince nodded gravely. "Blue Fire. The one weapon we possess that the Druids with all their magic cannot duplicate."

233

"The Blade of the Throne is a mighty power," conceded the Sage. "Yet how can it possibly defeat all that we face?"

The Prince shook his head slowly. "For now your question cannot be answered. But this much I do know—a way must be found for my companions and myself to slip past these Night-Watchers you have spoken of and reach Speca's darkened shores. Unless we can penetrate within the world of blackness ourselves, live with it and breathe of it, Blue Fire will be of no value to either Speca or Aran."

"The Night-Watchers cannot be passed, Friend," called the burly warlord darkly, again rising from his place at the *Sklar* and addressing all the visitors. "Your ship knows not these waters. You will be caught—and punished for it. Tortured in ways that no man dares to speak of."

"Argyle speaks the truth," added the Sage glumly. "His own ships have tried . . ."

The Prince shot the awesome warrior a long, hard glance. "Then you have seen Speca?" he asked.

Argyle's cold eyes showed no fear with the memory of his experiences, only the grim sailor's knowledge and respect for an adversary that had been responsible for the deaths of his brothers and his crew; he had escaped with his own life only by the thinnest thread of fortune.

"I have seen the Dark Lands," he said at last, scratching at his red flowing beard and feeling the scars of battle etched into his face. "But no man can reach her shores. At least not without Druid chains. Only a fool would even try."

"Yet you tried," pressed Ramagar, the thief's keen eyes quickly appraising the warrior and realizing him to be as brave as he was brawny.

Argyle pursed his lips in a grim smile. "When I was young, I too was a fool."

The Prince felt his heartbeat begin to quicken; here before him was a sailor of Aran who had actually dared the waters of the Lost Kingdom, a man who could be of enormous value in his quest. It was an unexpected opportunity that could not be lost.

"My ship has need of you, Argyle," he said honestly. "Will you join us and guide the way to Speca?"

The thick-necked lord of Aran scowled. "And join you in death? No, Friend. I have told you, the way cannot be found. Not I nor any other man of Aran would dare to try. Go yourselves if you must—but I share no responsibility for your fate."

234

And Argyle's words were joined by the agreeing calls of all the other lords of the *Sklar*, save for the Sage, who stood his ground and remained silent.

"Then you are still a fool, Argyle," snapped Mariana, the words skipping off her tongue before she could stop them.

The warrior's face grew crimson; he put his hands on his hips and stared down at the slight young girl who had dared to speak to him in such a manner.

Mariana defiantly stared back, then swept her glance over all the members. "All of you are fools," she declared. "You yourselves have told us the danger Aran faces. Yet you are unwilling to do anything about it!"

"Nothing can be done," said the Sage. "All efforts are useless."

"And how do you know?" she flared, spinning to face the wise man. "I and my friends have dared to risk all in reaching Speca; to save it and to save the North as well. We know our chances are slight at best. We know that we may die. But at least we want to *try*. The *Sklar* ponders and debates, weighs and measures, thinks only of the dangers. And when the records of history are written, and these pages are looked back upon a thousand years hence, who will be remembered? You who have debated? Or we who have tried?"

Her words stung the august body; the lords of the *Sklar* looked at each other in amazement.

The Sage sighed deeply and hung his head. "You have shamed us, child," he said in a whisper. "But try and understand us. We have lived beneath the shadows for so long . . ."

"Then it's time to do something about it," said Ramagar, eager to put forth his own views but not wanting to chide them as Mariana had.

The Sage limply turned to face the row of his peers and looked into their eyes one by one. And in each and every face he saw the same thoughts of concern and despair. Then he nodded slightly and focused his gaze back on the Prince.

"Exactly what is it that you want of us, Friend?" he asked.

"Your help," replied the Prince. "The assistance of Argyle to lead us through the black waters, and Aran's fighting ships to defeat the Druid fleets."

"You ask much, Friend, perhaps more than we can give you. Before the *Sklar* can commit its sons to your cause we

235

must first be assured that your own part in the matter has been played."

The Prince nodded slowly. "What are your terms?"

The Sage looked to his peers for their approval before he began. Then, when it was plain that to a man they agreed to let him set the demands, he turned to the Prince and said, "If Argyle is willing, then certainly we shall permit him to lead you into the Eternal Dark. But as for our ships, that is another matter. Aran cannot risk all she has on the thread of your blade. Our *knaars* will be gathered and prepared, as you asked, and we shall sail to the very limits of the Darkness itself. But not one ship shall sail within the blackness—not until we have seen some sign that you have found the key to dispelling the Druid magic."

"And what would such a sign have to be?" queried Ramagar.

The Sage rolled his eyes toward the heavens. "The Eternal Dark itself. Blue Fire, by whatever means it can, must first dispel the clouds. The sun must shine over Speca. Then, and only then, will the ships of Aran complete their part of the bargain and attack the powerful forces against us."

Ramagar sucked in a long, deep breath. The terms were harsh, indeed, he saw. The Sage had decided his strategy most carefully. Aran would bide her time and wait before committing herself fully; she would ask the Prince to do more than any one man could possibly hope to accomplish alone.

"Are these terms acceptable?" asked the Sage.

The Prince smiled shrewdly. "More than acceptable, my lord." And he glanced across the amphitheater at Argyle, who stood with fists clenched at his thighs.

"Will you share my burden, Lord Argyle?" he asked in a strong and clear voice.

The sea warrior thought for a moment and then nodded. "I give my pledge, both to you as a Friend and to the *Sklar*. All my knowledge of the Darkness will be at your command." Then he peered down at Mariana and the thief, looked briefly to the silent haj and the tense Homer beside him. "You are a brave band of souls," he told them all. "But with all my heart I pray that when I have told you all I know of the Dark Lands, you will take my warnings more seriously and change your minds."

Mariana threw back her head and grinned. "Not a chance,

236

my lord. We have come too far. And there are too many wrongs yet left unrighted."

The Sage seemed impressed. "Then you actually believe it can be done?"

Mariana's dark eyes burned with dancing moonlight softly reflected. "My lord, all things are possible—if you believe."

V

. . . And into the Lost Kingdom

and passengers could and, finally...

well against the brutality of nature. Building ... es on deck
was the only way the crew could keep enough ... ... to perform routine tasks.

16

"Dead ahead, sir!" cried the lookout from his lonely perch atop the mast. "Three points off the starboard bow!"

Captain Osari turned from his place and grasped at the bridge railing with both his hands. All around him passengers and crew scrambled to the bulwark to see for themselves.

Ramagar tightened his arm around Mariana's shoulder and she nudged herself closer against him. Breathless and unspeaking, the two of them stood and stared at the unreal sight looming ever closer, only leagues away.

The bow of the *Vulture* dipped gracefully and easily through the choppy waters as it plowed its way toward the gruesome scene. From far away the Darkness had seemed like thick, black hovering clouds. But the nearer the ship came to it, the more the Eternal Dark showed itself to be a mist; thin and cold, gently swirling in the gusty winds, tauntingly daring them to enter the place from which few had returned.

Above their heads the sun was shining; puffs of gentle white clouds drifted slowly by. Mariana glanced briefly behind her and realized she could still make out the distant peaks of Aran poking like tiny fingers in the east. Thinking fondly of that peculiar land, she felt herself shudder and tightly drew her shawl around her, again forcing her gaze to the alien fog silently pulling them nearer.

The haj gulped; for the first time since joining the expedition he felt queasiness knot in his belly. He drew a step closer to Mariana and her lover, hardly aware of Oro, who stood on his toes shivering from head to foot as he peered with unguarded alarm at what lay ahead.

"Trim the sails," called Captain Osari to his mate, and seconds later the well-trimmed ship slowed sharply in its tack. Osari swallowed hard and bit at his lip, realizing that if they did not turn back now they would never again be able to.

"Not much to look at, is it?" the Prince commented with a frown.

The sea captain grunted in reply. The more he stared into the mist, the more foul it seemed to become. It danced malevolently only centimeters above the waterline and rose as

241

high as he could see. Beyond its entrance there was nothing; it was like staring at an empty hole, a vast and endless void of nothingness. No bottom, no top, no form or substance. Only the dank and grim Darkness itself, covering everything. Ancient mariners had told tales of the Pits of Hell, Osari recalled, and right now he was sure that here was where they began. And his ship was heading straight for them.

The huge lord of Aran lifted his shoulders and fondled the hilt of his long sheathed sword. Argyle had spent half his life trying to forget his first visit to the Darkness; except for the nightmares where he still saw his brothers' ghastly deaths at the hands of the prowling Night-Watchers, he had almost succeeded in putting it from his mind. Now, though, the bold sea warrior saw his memories streaming back at him in a rush and so disturbing his thoughts that it was all he could do to put down the impulse to scream.

Realizing what he must be going through, the Prince came to the lord's side and clasped him firmly on the shoulder, saying, "Be at ease, Friend Argyle, and bear in mind that what we do today shall soon free men everywhere from the suffering Speca has known for an eternity."

The brawny lord cast his gaze down at the youthful Prince and nodded, tears welling in his icy eyes. But now was not a time for crying, he knew. Now was the time for gathering strength. And with a sigh of resolve he, too, looked deeply into the mist, which now seemed so close that outstretched fingertips would touch it.

"What shall our course be?" asked Osari, ready to give his instructions to the helmsman.

"A quarter to port," replied Lord Argyle, his eyes still fixed ahead. "Once we enter there shall be no need of charts or instruments. Speca herself lies directly before us. Our only fear is of the Night-Watchers; once they sight us, we can only fight." With that, Argyle fell silent again; he shut his eyes and lifted his gaze skyward, a small prayer to the Fates for guidance and protection soundless upon his lips.

As Mariana looked about she saw that other sailors were doing the same. A religious lot are mariners, she thought, whatever land they come from. Turning to speak with Ramagar she saw that the thief was doing the same. Eyes lidded, he was softly mumbling a sacred song of the East. Mariana watched him, smiled, and blew a kiss he would never feel. It was the first time she had seen him pray, and she realized how much he had changed since leaving Kali-

242

mar, indeed how much they had all changed since the strange beggar of a prince had touched their lives.

Mariana smiled and sighed. She was painfully aware that this day could well be the last they would spend together. She squeezed Ramagar's hand tightly and closed her eyes as the dismal Darkness closed in, thinking now only of the true happiness they had shared in days past and the contentment that had come from their shared love. Mariana knew she was at peace, with herself and with the world. In her own prayer that moment she asked only that if the end for them must come, then let it be swift and silent.

Then slowly, very slowly, the *Vulture* quietly entered within the cloak of the mist.

The strong winds of the North died, and the ship groaned under its own weight as it drifted with the rippling undercurrent. Captain Osari was the first to reopen his eyes; he stared about in wonder and disbelief as the black world of the Druids became reality all around him.

There was nothing to be seen, save for black water gently bobbing against the hull of his ship. All around was silence, grim and foreboding solitude. "As quiet as a grave," Argyle was heard to whisper.

"Light the torch," called Osari, and from somewhere aft dim sparks flashed, oil-soaked rags burst into orange dancing flame. The sailor holding the torch shakily inched his way closer to the bowsprit and poked the burning light at arm's length into the fog. Mist swirled around his arm and above the fire, gray-black mist that thickly coated the surfaces of everything it touched.

"Caravans of Kalimar!" wheezed the haj, eyes transfixed on the awesome sight. He glanced to the mast; he could no longer see the topsail, nor even the lookout still perched in the crow's nest. Above, the abysmal fog seemed to be lowering itself, slowly creeping down the sturdy wood of the mast, sticking to it and wetly glowing in the dim reflection of the torch.

"Hold your course true, Captain," advised Argyle, his features growing stern again and his mind clicking with a mariner's sense of navigation. He could not see the sky, nor the stars, nor the horizon. But the sea was second nature to him, be it in calm or tempest, and upon the water he felt a sailor's confidence in the ability to face any peril.

The helmsman held tight on the wheel and the ship crept ahead like a snail. Mariana looked on in trepidation at this new world where all life seemed to cease. There were no birds in the sky, no wind or breeze, no chatter or banter from either crew or passengers. There was no up, no down, no sideways, only the lasting stillness that made her cringe, and the awful blackness that only deepened. That, and the frightful thumping of her heart.

"How far do you reckon until we might reach some shore?" asked the Prince, breaking the grim mood and fondling the scimitar nervously as he turned to their guide.

Argyle frowned, then shrugged; then folded his powerful arms. "Some say a day's journey, some say less," he replied. "No one can know for certain. Soon, though, we shall be hearing the signs of land . . ."

"Signs?" said Ramagar. "You mean the Night-Watchers?"

The lord of Aran shook his head glumly. "Neither they nor their Dragon Ships. But the Calling. The Calling of the Sirens."

The thief narrowed his eyes and stared at his enigmatic new companion; he quickly saw that Argyle's hands had balled into tightly clenched fists, so tight that his knuckles showed white even in the shadows.

The Prince glanced at him sharply. "What are you talking about?"

It was a dark smile that crossed Argyle's rugged features. "You will know when you hear it," he answered, his shoulders shaking with a small shudder as he recalled the first time he himself had heard it, so long before. "It begins as a distant cry," he went on. "Low, and mournful, as if some poor wounded creature were slowly dying in pain. But then the sounds increase, building to such a terrible pitch and fervor that mortal men can no longer bear it. Some will recoil at the sound and press their hands over their ears, others will scream in desperation to try and blot it out; all, though, will fear for their sanity, for many have been driven to madness. And then, the Sirens will laugh . . ."

Mariana, Ramagar, and the haj all exchanged quick, fretful glances. "What are these Sirens?" Mariana asked. "What causes them?"

"No one can say," Argyle told her with a long shake of his head. A dark shadow crossed his eyes. "But the mariners of old claim it to be the weeping of lost souls bound forever in Black Hell, begging to be freed from their torment." He sighed and shifted his great weight so that he leaned squarely against the lashed rope secured along the railing. "The wise

244

men of Aran say another thing; that it is a warning wail to any passing ship. A warning from sorrowful beings calling to the living to flee these waters while there might yet be time . . ."

The Prince scoffed, saying, "I have heard of these 'Sirens,' and I believe them to be no more than noises made by the strong winds of the North as they blow down between Speca's mountains. Such natural occurrences would be common in these climes during the warm months of the year."

"You think so?" quizzed the haj, relieved to hear this benign explanation.

"I am convinced of it."

Argyle grimaced. "Think what you will, all of you," he replied gruffly. "Perhaps it is no magic. But be assured of this: never has any sailor of the North heard anything more ghastly and terrible." He tightened his glare at his companions and added, "It is in no man's interests to deride until he has heard for himself." With that the lord of Aran turned and faced the all-encumbering fog hovering above the waterline.

Mariana tried hard not to shiver; she realized that the temperature was swiftly dropping.

"Well, whether these Sirens are a natural occurrence or not," she said thoughtfully, "it's easy to understand how anyone would be terrified by them while forced to travel in *this* . . ." She gestured sweepingly at the mist and frowned.

Captain Osari nodded in full agreement. "Our ship is like a sightless child forced to grope its way without direction. Without our vision to guide us it becomes easier for the mind to play tricks."

Argyle did not turn around; he laughed soundlessly in his place and said, "Listen well, Friends, for the time is upon us. Soon we will know."

And on that note of despair they heard the first dim whines. So faint and soft were they that Mariana had to strain her ears to hear anything. But there it was, just as Argyle had described it.

The haj licked his tongue over dry lips and gulped. The sound of the Sirens was like a moan. He thought of an injured stallion he once owned whose leg had broken while on a run. The poor animal had cried in a similar way, pitiful and pleading, until the haj's knife had slit the horse's throat and put it out of misery.

The ship was moving faster now with a strong current, which pulled it deeper and deeper into the fog. The Sirens'

245

cry, meanwhile, was becoming steadily more intense. It was now a humming akin to a ship's horn, powerful and resilient. The crew were becoming uneasy, many fidgeting in their places, others restlessly moving from their posts, pulling anxious faces as they stared bleakly out into the nothingness, trying to pinpoint the source of the sound.

The bow of the *Vulture* had begun to rise and dip, rise and dip, the foreboding waters becoming more turbulent at an alarming rate.

"We're being pulled pretty fast, Cap'n," called the helmsman, trying his best to hold a steady course.

Osari needn't have been told. He could feel the dramatic change for himself, and the suddenness of it all disturbed him greatly. He knew well just how swift and treacherous undercurrents could be, but never could he recall one that had come on quite as fast as this. Rubbing his mouth tensely with a sweaty hand, he shouted for the first mate to take the wheel. Then he ordered all unnecessary crewmen below and set his ship several points more off to starboard in a desperate effort to counteract the violent pull.

Mariana cupped her hands and pressed them tightly over her ears; all across the deck she could see the crew doing the same. The pitch of the wail rose, and while not deafening, it clearly had begun to take its effect.

As Mariana began to groan, Ramagar pulled her closer to him and tightened his arms around her. But the dancing girl could easily tell from his pained expression that the Sirens were having a far worse effect on him than on her. By virtue of his trade as a thief of the night Ramagar's hearing had become finely attuned to sound, and Mariana wondered how much longer he would be able to tolerate the noise.

Suddenly there was a loud cry from the forecastle, followed by another and still another. Looking up in horror Mariana saw several sailors, numbed by the ravishing pain dizzily spinning inside their heads, bolt from their posts and run screaming along the deck.

"Grab them!" cried the captain, his own face contorting from the terrible pounding. Other sailors boldly took their hands from their ears and tried to hold down their frantic comrades. The stricken men cavorted and moaned, one gurgling and whimpering like an infant as strong arms held him down, stuffed his ears with cotton, and bound his hands and feet with cord.

And the call of the Sirens rose again. It was precisely as

Argyle had predicted. Mariana watched brave and resolute men suddenly become reduced to sniveling half-wits as the pressure on their eardrums increased.

"Sing!" shouted Argyle, frantically doing his best to stem the tide. "Sing at the top of your lungs!"

Amid the screams and anguished prayers Captain Osari's resonant voice sounded. The words were familiar to all, a sailors' song, renowned throughout the North and also in much of the East. Quickly the helmsman and first mate joined in, followed by the haj and the Prince. As their voices lifted the shattering violence of the Sirens was blunted. From every corner of the deck the crew, hands yet to their ears, added in harmony to the pitiful chorus until virtually everyone had taken part.

Over and over the verses were repeated, fervor diminishing the monotony, even as the Sirens' own shrill tune continued to unfold. For a time the battle of matched strength went on, the men of the *Vulture* doing all they could to counteract the fearsome wail. Soon, though, as men's throats grew parched and their vocal cords cracked, the hopelessness of their situation became all too clear. One by one some of the sailors began to fall, first crumpling to their knees where they moaned and cried, then banging the decks with clenched fists, finally baying like jackals at the moon.

The ship's wheel was spinning out of control; the helmsman and the first mate, hands clasping their ears, looked on in hapless desperation as their lips continued to force out the lyrics of Osari's sea chanty.

Ramagar spun in writhing torment, his body wracked with growing pain. "When will it stop?" he cried, reeling from side to side and pressing so hard against the sides of his head that tiny veins had begun to bulge from his forehead.

"The only chance we have is to ride it through," rejoined Argyle, equally tormented as he experienced the ordeal for the second time in his life. Then he shouted that dire warning to all the others, raising his voice above the din to make sure that everyone could hear.

The ship itself had begun to reel now, tossing wildly as though in a terrible storm. It was reminiscent to Mariana of the frightful tempest they had battled the night of the mutiny. Her own ears were bursting, but she could think only of Ramagar, who suddenly had begun to pale and shake uncontrollably, his misted silhouette doing a grisly dance before her worried eyes. And the moan of the Sirens, the foreboding

247

Calling, was still growing louder; she knew the worst was yet to come.

Sailors were openly weeping now, sobbing like small children, some in frantic prayer, others tearing at their hair. She watched the scene in near panic, observing them become madder and madder, fighting among themselves, hurling each other in furious and insane rage—and she realized the truth in Argyle's scorned warnings.

Captain Osari himself had fallen to the deck, his senses wrenched from him, and now mindless and witless. The words of Argyle's song still formed at his lips though no sound would venture forth. Then she saw the Prince grasp for Homer; the youth was staggering beside the flimsy railing at the quarterdeck and it seemed that he was intent on throwing himself overboard. It was all the Prince could do to hurl the lad away in time and wrestle him to the deck while both screamed for the shrilling to cease.

The *Vulture*, meanwhile, was lurching ahead on its own at what seemed to be breathtaking speed, dragging them all to Fates knew what strange Hell, while insanity took over completely. Men were dragging themselves toward the open hatches, seeking some refuge from the din in the stores and cabins below. But there was no shelter to be found. The Calling of the Sirens proved all-pervasive, whining through the moaning pine and oak, reverberating along the walls from floor to ceiling, shaking the decks until planks literally began to quiver, nails and pins and bolts flying loose, popping from sockets like bursting bubbles.

Ramagar pitched forward upon the deck and Mariana screamed. Then he blacked out into unconsciousness, blissfully unaware of everything around him. Mariana threw herself over him, to shelter him with her body, oblivious to her own cries and the tears pouring down her face.

Argyle kneeled beside Captain Osari, tugging at his tunic and wetting his mouth with fresh water in a futile effort to draw him out of his crazed state. Deranged sailors were running up and down along the deck; a few, no longer able to cope with the Song of Death, blindly flung themselves over the side, where their limp corpses were greedily swallowed by the fog-enshrouded waters.

Mariana could feel her mind slipping from her; she gazed about in a trance, no longer able to think coherent thoughts. Looking on at the whimpering sailors her brain swam with dark dreams—hideous and shapeless discolorations pranced before her, formless images somehow reaching out for her, tormenting her, laughing at her. Yes, laughing, and that was the worst.

Around the edges of her mind thought played: something about the last verse of the Sirens' song, something about laughter. But then even that was gone, and she fell over, sobbing wildly . . .

A voice was shouting at her, she was sure. Strong, persistent, it wouldn't go away. She was dimly aware it was Argyle's voice, but what he was trying to say she couldn't tell.

" 'Tis the laughter of the Sirens!" he was shouting frantically to any who could hear. "We've passed! The worst is done! The worst is done!"

Dizzily, the dancing girl lifted her heavy head and stared at him uncomprehendingly as he repeated his words over and over. Slowly her eyes regained focus and her nightmares shattered. Consciousness returned and she could hear him clearly.

"Listen!" he was shouting. "Can you hear?"

Mariana strained her ears. The Sirens' moan *had* changed. Though still as loud and strong as before, it was somehow different. The pitch had lowered; it was no longer the shrill sameness that had dulled her brain, but rather an intense drone that came in spurts, indeed sounding strangely like laughter, low and mocking laughter, coming from somewhere distant.

Excitedly she bent over Ramagar and nudged him gently, taking his cold hands into her own and rubbing them, soothing his brow and whispering soft words. The thief slowly began to rouse; his eyes opened and he stared up at her blankly. Then they filled with recognition, and he smiled.

Tears flooded through her long lashes as she closed her eyes with a thankful prayer. "It's over," she whispered. "The Sirens' song has passed."

The thief put a hand to his throbbing temple and sighed. After a moment's pause he managed to prop himself up on one elbow, casting a brief glance over the main deck. On all sides fallen sailors were lifting themselves from their stupors, trying to collect jumbled thoughts and piece together what had happened while the madness had overtaken them.

Captain Osari responded to Argyle's aid and bolted back to his feet, ignoring his own throbbing head pains and tending to his crew. The haj dunked his head inside a water barrel and cleared a foggy mind. Nearby, Homer was sitting dumbly, spindly legs crossed, chin hung low on his chest and his face turned a sickly white. Behind him, still crouched beside the store of lashed provisions where he had lain prostrate and quivering, was Oro. The Prince pulled a distasteful face as he lent the glum hunchback a helping hand, then it was off to young Homer's side to see how badly the boy had been injured. The youth smiled broadly, although wanly, at the sight of his friend; he accepted the Prince's outstretched hand and stood wobbly to his feet. "We made it," he rasped, and the two of them exchanged cheerful grins.

As the effects of the Sirens' call wore off the mood of the crew became one of elation. The last vestiges of the terrible drone faded rapidly into nothingness, and suddenly all fears were vanished. Together they had faced the first test of Speca's dark waters and come through with hardly a scratch. Osari held a moment of silence for the poor hands who had flung themselves into the sea and then resumed his normal stance, barking commands and setting his men back to their posts.

Surprised and pleased at their good fortunes, every man happily went back to his duties, eager to face the next task. Only brooding Argyle, lord of Aran, remained dour. He lost no time in studying the ship's new position. Of them all, only he had realized that with the end of the Sirens, the mysterious current had also passed. No longer was the *Vulture* carried deeper into the fog; rather, the ship was now motionless upon a glassy sea.

Mariana left Ramagar's side momentarily; she stood gazing out into the gloom, her small, slim hands clutching at the rails. It did not take very long to realize the new predicament they were all facing, for with neither wind to swell the sails nor a current to pull them forward, the ship was trapped, a prisoner, in these eerie waters.

Had the powerful undercurrent dragged them to this particular spot by mere happenstance, she wondered. Or had they been brought here by some unknown Druid force? Were they nearer to Speca's shores? Or farther away than ever? These were questions without answers, she knew, and there was little time to ponder.

"What's our plan, Captain?" asked the Prince, glumly noting the ship's stationary stance.

Osari frowned and bit down at his lip. "We'll have to row."

He shouted to the first mate, who in turn called for the two small skiffs to be lowered. Osari's best and hardiest sailors climbed aboard, and as the boats hit the waterline with a soft splash long twine ropes were securely fastened from the skiffs to the ship's prow. The rowing commenced; the lines became taut and the sailors stroked in unison, straining to the limits. The *Vulture* groaned with its first lurch forward. It was a slow and painful venture, pressing onward without direction, hoping that soon a breeze might rise and swell the sails.

Hours passed; murky waters swilled all around. The oaken oars dipped, cutting through the placid depths cleanly, stroke after stroke. It was grueling work, futile work, for after what should have been the end of a long night, the ship found itself as lost and as helpless as before the rowing began. A man could barely see as far as the end of his outstretched hand, and even were land close, there was no way for anyone to know it.

Ship's routine, though, never wavered. Six bells rang, signaling the coming of dawn. But of course there was no dawn, not even a shade of light to break through the black sky. "If this be dawn then indeed it's a grim one," Osari was heard to remark. And Mariana listened in silence.

"It's no use," said Argyle, after some time. "We might as well bring our skiffs back aboard."

Captain Osari shook his head and reluctantly agreed. "Then what do we do next?" he asked.

Argyle put his hands on his hips and glared beyond the bridge. His awesome shadow loomed over half the deck as he set his powerful jaw and pressed cold lips together. "We wait," was his only answer.

17

In Kalimar it would have been evening, Mariana thought, a beautiful summer's evening with a purple sky and a blazing crimson sun setting majestically at the horizon. But here there was only increasing cold, and dampness from the mist that malevolently invaded her bones.

Most of the crew sat shivering and sullen, not speaking, with blankets tossed over their shoulders. A single torch burned like the herald of a wraith from its brace near the prow.

Ramagar was sleeping peacefully beside her. Homer was quietly dozing, and beside him sat the Prince, awake but with eyes shut and head bowed.

Mariana knew they were close, perhaps only a few leagues from shore, yet it might as well have been a million. There was no way they could move without the aid of some wind or current.

And the chill deepened; a thin veneer of frost formed over the masts and the railing and along the deck, caking the halyards and the braces. The men's hands grew numb and stiff. It was like going through the icebergs again, only this time with no assurance that all would be well once the perilous passage was complete.

Mariana huddled closer to her lover and managed to close her eyes for some well-deserved rest. She did not know how long she had been asleep when a wild shout from the lookout brought her half leaping to her feet.

She rubbed at her red eyes and stared. Sailors were madly dashing to and fro, lines were being tugged, canvas beginning to flap, the ship bobbing and the deck slanting.

Looking about in confusion, she caught sight of the bulky form of the haj, laughing and calling to her. "Wind, Mariana!" he shouted gleefully. "Can you feel it?"

Billowing sails spread open with a *whump*. Mariana stared up in wonder and disbelief. Wind! Real wind! The ship was moving again; plying the cold, dark waters like an eel, streaming into the mist like an agile cat prowling the dim alleys of Kalimar.

Captain Osari was beside himself with delight. Out of nowhere it had come, for how long he could not tell. But he was determined to take as much advantage of it as he could. An able mariner from Cenulam needed far less wind than this to make up for lost time.

Ramagar sprang to his feet and shared the mirth. Hugging the dancing girl, he forgot the bitter cold and the dangerous trials still ahead. Again there was hope, and more than that he could not ask.

The flame of the torch swayed dizzily as the ship plunged on to the west. Captain Osari took the wheel, relieving the helmsman, and from his post set the *Vulture* onto her new tack, a true course this time, straight for the coves of Speca.

Even Argyle seemed pleased; he had expected a wind to rise sooner or later, but not one so strong, and certainly not so soon. He glanced at the beaming silhouette of the Prince

252

and pondered, wondering if the man were indeed charmed. For a moment he even believed that perhaps Speca could be taken—wrenched away from her conquerors by the stolid belief and determination of this single man whose mission was his life.

For half a day's time by the hourglass in the captain's cabin the *Vulture* moved on steadily. If anything, the wind continued to rise all the more. This, according to the Prince, was due to the closeness of Speca's shores, where gales were said to sweep down frequently between her majestic peaks and spill into the natural harbors and the open sea.

Lord Argyle stood at the prow, contemplating the land they were certain to reach within hours. His long cape swirled behind him, and he buried his frigid fingers deep within the folds of the woolen scarf wrapped around his face. Gray eyes narrowed, then blinked. A shudder ran down his spine. Jagged rocks had begun to appear spottily in the near distance; he knew they were approaching the treacherous reefs that fishermen used to speak of. Many a vessel had been wrecked upon these awesome rocks, some as large as mountains hidden beneath the waterline with edges as sharp as blades. Even with starlight to guide them such a passage was tricky at best. But in the gloom of the Eternal Dark, it was all the more difficult, and if it wasn't for his belief in Captain Osari's expert seamanship, he would have doubted their chances.

Yet it was not sight of the reefs that disturbed the lord of Aran now. It was something far more dangerous than was evident. Something wicked and evil, and it played at the edges of his mind. His only prayer was that what he had just glimpsed, fleeting as it was, had been nothing more than illusion. But if it wasn't . . .

"Is something wrong?" asked Mariana, rubbing her mittened hands as she approached the lonely figure.

Argyle did not turn or speak to her. He kept his stare fixed, features frozen in a mask of study. At length, while the girl stood watching him doubtfully, he said, "Look deeply into the fog. Tell me what you see."

Mariana shrugged and leaned slightly beyond the frosty rail. Her dark eyes simmered, dancing from the mist to the sea and the tips of glistening rocks pushing back the waves.

"What should I be seeing?" she asked.

Argyle sighed. "Best that you see little or nothing," he reflected. "But look again, Mariana. Tell me if you can detect any light . . ."

Assuming that he meant some light from shore, a torch perhaps or a candle flickering in a window, she did as he asked and swept her glance from one end of the Darkness to the other.

"Well?" queried the burly sea warrior.

The girl hesitated. "I . . . No, nothing. I couldn't see a thing."

Argyle tilted his head and peered down at her. "But you think you might have seen . . . something?"

"I don't know. Just for an instant, though, I thought I saw a flash of some kind. Very far off," she pointed in the direction, "but it was so fast—"

"Like a glow, perhaps? A red glow?"

They stared at each other. Mariana slowly nodded her head. She saw Argyle grimace and the look in his eyes harden.

"What was it?" she asked breathlessly, but the fiery lord turned from her and gruffly ordered a nearby sailor to put out the torch. The sailor hesitated at the odd request, and Argyle strode past him, yanked the leaping light from its brace, and tossed it into the sea.

All eyes concentrated on him, as the only brightness in their black world was quickly extinguished beneath the waves.

"Are you mad?" cried Osari, dashing from the bridge and confronting the hefty Aranian. "Why did you do that? Don't you know—"

Argyle lifted his right arm and stretched it out toward the gloom. Captain Osari's mouth hung open, his thought unfinished. There was a dim reddish tint, almost circular in form, glowing from afar, a faint light that flickered in the distance, nearly obliterated by the mist.

"A beacon," whispered Mariana as the others looked on. "It must be a beacon."

Argyle shook his head. "There are no beacons in these strange waters," he replied.

Osari eyed him nervously. "Then what?"

"A Dragon Ship."

The captain gasped. He lifted his shoulders and unconsciously let his hand slip toward the hilt of the double-edged sailor's knife strapped at his waist. "Night-Watchers," he rasped.

Argyle nodded darkly. "They must not sight us, my friend, or we'll find hell itself a better place to be . . ."

"Can we hope to elude them before they come any closer?"

"It depends how good a sailor you are," replied the seasoned warrior. "It will take a strong hand to lead us safely between these reefs while a Dragon Ship follows in pursuit."

Captain Osari gritted his teeth, aware that he was about to face the most difficult task of his life, a grim test of wits against the sea and the dreaded Night-Watchers. He glanced up at the swelled sails, studying the strength of the wind and its direction. Then with hands on hips, he said, "We have our work cut out for us, Friend Argyle. We're both men of the North, are we not?" He spun around, not waiting for a reply, shouting the order for battle stations.

All around men scurried. Some, crossbows in hand, took up fighting positions along the bulwark and the raised deck of the bridge; others scampered to emergency posts where they would manipulate the lines under siege conditions.

"I want every stitch we can draw," Osari shouted to the startled first mate.

"But, sir! We can't handle any more speed—not while we're caught between the reefs—"

"Every stitch!" repeated the captain. And, while he ran to the wheel to instruct the helmsman, a smile of satisfaction crossed Argyle's somber face. His intuition had been right; Osari of Cenulam was the best, and if they were all to die, they would do so in good company.

Behind the rank of archers beside the prow both Ramagar and the haj drew their own weapons. Across the deck the Prince drew Blue Fire, not to summon her terrible flame, which would only alert the nearby Dragon Ship, but to thumb the razor-sharp blade in anticipation of a head-on clash with the finest Druid fighters the Dwarf-king of Speca had to throw against them.

Mariana ignored the thief's pleas and remained steadfast at his side. The haj stood to protect her at her left, and from the corner of her eye she saw mighty Argyle raise his ax, ready to heave it the moment that Druid flesh came within range.

The sails fluttered briefly as the *Vulture* shifted tack and glided easily between a ragged bed of jutting rock. In the distance the red glow had become brighter; it was plain to all that the Dragon Ship was pressing in, heading straight for them, whether by chance or by design.

These were tense moments. To a man, the crew and passengers stood steadfast and ready, come what may. All, of course, except for Oro, who by devious design of his own had hidden himself in an empty water barrel with all the gold he still possessed, prepared to barter for his miserable life if worst came to worst and he found himself at the wrong edge of a Druid sword.

"The wind is shifting!" shouted the lookout.

Osari called for the ship to be swung ten points off starboard. As the helmsman complied, the waves sent a crushing spray falling over the deck. Deeper into the treacherous reefs Captain Osari negotiated the *Vulture*, knowingly playing a most dangerous game of cat and mouse.

"Closing in!" cried the lookout.

Mariana looked behind them; the red glow was larger and brighter, and it seemed to be spreading from a fixed place to encompass everything around it.

"Steady as she goes!" called Osari. He balled his hands and kept them firmly on his hips as he watched the glow of the Dragon Ship rapidly close in. Damn fast, that ship must be, he thought to himself in grudging admiration. Too bad he couldn't command her himself.

Mariana squinted into the Darkness, straining for a clear first sight of the enemy ship. Though mostly formless, it already showed itself to be massive in size, easily twice as large as the *Vulture*. This of course was what Captain Osari was hoping for: a vessel too cumbersome to maneuver at top speed in these tricky lanes.

"I can see her!" the lookout bellowed, fear apparent in his voice.

Osari swallowed hard. "What does she look like?"

The lookout shaded his eyes and peered again. "Huge, sir. And . . . mastless . . ."

"Mastless?" The captain shared a fretful glance with Ramagar. "Are you certain, boy? She carries no canvas?"

"None at all, sir! Not a stitch!"

This was indeed ominous and distressing news. Argyle caught Osari's troubled look and shook his head with worry. If the Dragon Ship carried no sails, then what powered her? What force gave her the ability to plow these forbidden waters with such ease and speed?

Apart from the whistling of the wind, all grew silent. The red glare moved in steadily, blindingly. Suddenly the rock and the waves began to reflect the glow; for the first time

Osari was able to get a good look at what lay beyond the prow of his ship. And the sight was not one to gladden the heart; scattered hither and yon, poking up from the murk for as far as he could discern, were numberless rising, jagged rocks, all protruding in grisly array from the red-tinted water.

The captain saw that the *Vulture* would have to veer and twist precisely through these obstructions—one slip in her navigation would send the ship's hull crunching into knife-sharp walls. But an equal threat loomed from behind.

"I think she's seen us, skipper!" came the frantic cry of the lookout.

Argyle heard and spun around with the speed of a man half his size. One hand clutched at the hilt of the great broadsword he always wore, the other closed upon the handle of his ax. He leaned forward and stared at the vessel which was bearing down upon the *Vulture* like a demonic wingless bird.

It was then that Mariana put her hand to her mouth to stifle a cry. The Dragon Ship was not really a ship at all; it was a floating fortress the likes of which no mariner had ever seen. Slowly the image took form as it rolled out from the mist. Burning in red light, its bulwark and prow made of metal encased with armor, the Dragon Ship now cast fantastic shadows over the water, setting everything aglow like burning coals, causing every silhouette to glimmer in dark hues of crimson.

Gradually the crew of the Dragon Ship came also into view. These Night-Watchers of the Eternal Dark stood dressed in plated armor, plumed helmets adorning their heads, fierce images of dragons embroidered into their black tunics and painted onto their metallic shields.

Huge men they were, beardless, broad-shouldered men with curling lips and cruel mouths, a sinewy, hairless lot, all grim and silent. They sought no identity of the intruders, swore no foul oaths, sang no chants, uttered no war cries. It was plain to all that the Night-Watchers would give no quarter, nor ask for any.

Mariana peered at the line of steely faces and shuddered, for she looked into their eyes and knew true terror. From deep sockets red pupils glowed back at her; the eyes were malevolent, trance-like, and crazed, as cunning as they were savage. It was then that she fully respected Argyle's fear, for these were like no other men she had ever seen.

Again the winds were shifting, causing the Cenulamian

ship to toss wildly about. "Run with the wind!" Osari bellowed, his mind racing to formulate a quick strategy. The *Vulture* swerved twenty points off to port, and hurtled down an increasingly narrowed path, trying to avoid solid granite and the Dragon Ship, which bore down on them with all haste.

The air filled with strange staccato churnings, as great and terrible wheels chopped through waves, propelling the Night-Watcher vessel forward at speeds Captain Osari could not believe.

And then the sky was alight; metal missiles, arrows and javelins, all twisting and whistling with flame, came sailing gracefully through the air, over the water, with tremendous billows of dark smoke pouring away from the rushing shafts. Steel-tipped missiles stabbed into the *Vulture*'s frame, slamming into the bulwark, crashing against the hull. Others sailed into the water, sinking untold fathoms before the flames had died.

New and furious gusts struck the *Vulture*; mountainous waves smashed over reefs and came tearing down upon the heaving ship, dousing many of the arrow-borne fires.

Mariana jerked her gaze up as a horrible scream sounded from the mainsail. She recoiled in shock as the young lookout in the crow's nest fell with his body aflame, a metal arrow sunk straight through his neck.

And closer in the fearsome Dragon Ship pressed, so close that Ramagar and those beside him could actually see the snickers of delight parting the lips of the enemy Druids. Ghostly shadows swam helter-skelter before them as the massive body of the Dragon Ship parted the waters at the entrance between the reefs. Osari looked on in despair, forcing down his own terror and desperately trying to stick to his job as navigator, leaving the fighting to Argyle and the others.

"To starboard! To starboard!" he shouted, blinking at the sight of a gigantic boulder sticking up from the dark in front of the bowsprit. And even before the masterful helmsman had time to raise a hand, the captain had knocked him out of the way and with all his strength had spun the wheel a full ninety degrees. The sails flapped helplessly, the ship itself groaned with the sudden turn. Half in a spin, the ship tilted, righted itself, and turned on a dangerous sideward course barely in time to miss the threatening mountain.

The maneuver had barely been completed when a second

tremendous volley was loosed from the Dragon Ship. The sky brightened for a second time as roaring fire arced down upon them. The Prince, incensed and not to be cowered, wrenched the crossbow away from a dazed sailor at his side and took dead aim at the Druid soldiers standing firmly in their places on the bridge.

Let my mark be true! he hissed, and *twang!* went the taut bowstring, the dart shooting in a straight and deadly line.

The arrow struck home; a Druid clutched both hands to his flimsy breastplate and pitched forward, his orange-plumed helmet toppling from his head and bouncing over the deck.

Panic grabbed those at his side; the Prince smiled with satisfaction as his companions ran to aid him. For a moment the Dragon Ship came to a complete halt, then it began the charge anew, this time with greater speed than ever.

"We'll meet in hell for that little deed," grunted Argyle.

"Why?" asked a panting Mariana.

The Prince's smile deepened. "I just killed their admiral."

The pressure of the wind was terrific; the *Vulture* swayed this way and that as Captain Osari drew on every trick he knew—and some he didn't—to negotiate her safely through the rocks.

A third volley roared above their heads, this time with the dull moan of catapults adding to the din. Sailing balls of granite smashed with clumsy force fore and aft; arrows of fire cast out wave upon wave of sickening heat, whizzing through the air, sticking into masts and deck, occasionally catching some poor lad unaware and sending him reeling over the side.

The *Vulture*'s sailors responded in kind. Under Argyle's steady command, they directed a fearful barrage against the oncoming hulk. But many of their arrows were thwarted; some glanced off the metal protectors, others fell short, and still others were deflected by Druid shields. Through all this, the Dragon Ship continued to gain.

"We're lost," groaned the haj, beginning to despair for the first time. He stood directly beneath the lumbering red shadows and watched while Druid steel flashed before his eyes. A line of fearsome warriors had now taken places up and down the Dragon Ship's main deck; they stood poised and silent, defiant in the face of *Vulture* arrows, biding their time until they were close enough for grappling chains to be thrown. Then they would clamber aboard the puny ship, seal their victims' deaths, and begin the search for loot.

259

By this time fully a third of Captain Osari's men had been either wounded or killed; the situation was growing grimmer with each passing second.

As fire arrows sparked above, Ramagar pulled Mariana away from the fray, shielding her with his body so they could steal a minute together. He was certain that the way events were turning for the worse they would soon find themselves parted. Although he dreaded to think about it, he knew that Mariana must not be taken captive; he shivered when he recalled grim tales the Prince had recounted. Mariana must not fall into Druid hands.

As the girl stood meek and frightened in his arms, Ramagar looked again at the Dragon Ship, bearing down faster and faster, and resolved to do what he must. The first grappling chains had been hurled from the enemy deck, although one had fallen short and the second had been cleaved loose by a single swing of mighty Argyle's ax. But the end was near; they could not hope to hold out much longer.

Mariana gazed into the thief's eyes and locked them in love. She put a hand to his face and touched him tenderly; Ramagar swallowed to clear the thickness in his throat. "It seems to be the end," he whispered.

Mariana sighed, closing her eyes, and tried to smile bravely. "I love you, thief," she said.

He put one hand on her shoulder and let the other secretly slip toward his knife. "If—if the worst happens, you know what I must do," he told her.

The girl nodded slowly. "I know. Then there is no chance?"

He shook his head; she sniffed and drew a deep breath. Terrible screaming was coming from behind; Ramagar's dark eyes drifted to the Dragon Ship, now so close that he could almost touch its steel-plated prow. He could hear commands for boarding being issued by Druid officers, see the looks of horror etched on the races of Cenulamian sailors still holding their positions. Only minutes remained before the ship would be overrun and taken. As for himself, it was a small matter. He would fight to the end, of course, dying beside his good friends. Death did not frighten him, nor even capture and torture, at least not as long as he knew that Mariana would not be made to suffer. His own pain was of absolutely no consequence; life without the dancing girl was meaningless anyway.

Mariana threw her arms around him and kissed him. She

shut her eyes and tasted the salt of her tears upon her lips. "We almost made it, didn't we?" she whispered.

The thief of Kalimar held back a sob. It was true; they had come so close, so close to having a life together. He wanted to say something to her, something to explain the way he felt—had always felt—but the words would not come.

She put a hand to his lips. "If you must do it, Ramagar," she said, "do it now. Swiftly. Don't make me wait . . ."

His hand clutched the hilt of his knife and he drew it from the sheath. He raised it, trembling, poised to plunge the blade deep into her heart. Mariana pressed herself closer, clinging to him like a frightened child while the madness of battle filled her ears.

"I love you, Mariana," he cried. "Remember that, even now. I love you more than life—"

"Land ahoy!" came the croaking cry.

The girl opened her eyes and wrenched herself away, staring out into the blackness; Ramagar spun and let the knife fall to the deck. Beyond the railing of the forecastle they could both make out a dim, swelling form beyond the mist, far beyond the glow of the Dragon Ship, well away from the treacherous reefs. And there was the sound of surf crashing upon a shore.

"Land!" gasped the girl. Ramagar took her hand and looked on in absolute amazement.

"We've reached Speca!" cried the Prince, leaping down from the bridge, ducking his head to avoid whistling projectiles as he ran.

But all around them sailors were still staggering and falling under the assault of Druid arrows. The Dragon Ship had moved in with a vengeance, the chains so close that each link of steel could be discerned. Then suddenly the *Vulture* lurched, nearly sending all aboard flying over the side. Two massive triangular rocks poked up mere meters from the railing. The ship strained to right itself, and turning sharply upwind headed toward the land. The Dragon Ship stayed close, like a dog snapping at an intruder's heels.

There was a loud crunching noise, then a soft grinding that sounded like a moan. "We've struck!" shouted Ramagar, positive that the *Vulture* was now aground and totally helpless against the onslaught.

"Gates of hell!" came the haj's voice rising above the din. "Not us, man! Them! It's the Dragon Ship! Look!"

It was then that Mariana saw a sight she would never for-

261

get. The Dragon Ship had come to a total stop, and was sinking like a leaden weight.

"She's struck the reefs and can't keep afloat!" cried a jubilant Captain Osari. "Just look at her! She can't float!"

Slowly, painfully slowly, the monster ship had begun to tilt. Mariana could clearly see her sailors rushing about frantically, their red eyes flaming, panic-stricken as they realized what had happened.

Osari had proved the master. He had purposely taken the larger vessel on a chase through the least navigable channel available, hoping against all hope that the massive craft would run aground somewhere along the way. And that was exactly what had happened. The Dragon Ship's awesome bulk had hit a canyon of hidden rock beneath the waterline, shattering its hull. For all of its speed, for all of its terrible war machines, the ship had proved vulnerable after all. Now she was floundering, taking on water like a bloated barrel, leaking it like a sieve, while her frame cracked and broke before her crew's astonished eyes.

"Trim the sails!" called Osari to his stunned sailors. The Vulture lurched forward, zigging and zagging between the reefs, cleanly pulling away from the stranded vessel. Osari laughed boisterously while grim Night-Watchers stared and shook angry fists.

Soon all that could be seen of the indestructible Druid ship was its quivering red glow; that would finally be extinguished when the boat slipped beneath the murky waters.

Captain Osari came bounding from the bridge, a delighted grin on his face.

"Incredible!" wheezed the haj, scratching his head in wonder. "A minute more and we'd have been done for!"

Osari chuckled good-naturedly. "A sailor never gives up my friend. Especially a mariner from the North. Eh, Argyle?" And he winked at the dour lord of Aran.

"Never mind," chided Mariana, recalling just how close to death they had all come. "You didn't look so confident ten minutes ago."

"Well, maybe not," conceded the captain with a shrug. "Still, it was a merry fight while it lasted." His eyes crinkled with his mirth while he glanced behind at the dimming glow. Then suddenly his smile had faded, replaced by a frown. "It's not going to be very long before another Dragon Ship heads this way on patrol," he said. "And next time we might not be as fortunate."

262

Ramagar set his gaze toward land. "Then we'd better get a move on," he said.

The Prince nodded gloomily and stuck out his hand to the captain. "You have more than fulfilled your part of the bargain," he said. "We are grateful. But there isn't much time to spare . . ."

"Aye," Osari replied thoughtfully. "We'd best be quick." And he shouted for his men to ready one of the skiffs.

"What will you do after we leave?" asked Mariana.

The mariner smiled. "Run back into the mist as fast as we can, I should think. The same way we came in, if possible."

The haj furrowed his brow. "And you'll wait for our signal?"

"Precisely as we discussed. You have my word on it. We'll stand in these waters as long as we can, waiting for your beacon. Then we'll come to shore and get you out," he looked to Argyle, "perhaps with a fleet of Aran's ships behind."

"Once the black clouds begin to swirl, Aran will know of your success," Argyle told them all. "And my people won't let you down. You can count on that as well . . ."

"Good," said the Prince, and after a few words of parting he made his way toward the skiff, where supplies were already being loaded.

Mariana stood on her toes and kissed Captain Osari warmly. "Goodbyes are too tearful," she said. "So for now, good friend, farewell. We'll meet again soon."

The sailor flushed and grinned. "I'm certain of it, Mariana. Good luck." He pinched her cheek, and turning to Ramagar, took the thief's hand with a powerful grasp. "Take good care of her, my friend. She's priceless."

Ramagar smiled, hiding his sorrow at the parting. "I will. And take good care of yourself. We'll have need of your services again."

Captain Osari's own smile deepened. "I hope so. Now hurry, time is pressing."

The Prince and Homer had already taken their places on the farthest of roughly hewn slat benches; the haj lent a hand to Mariana, and with his arm around her sat down on the second. Just as Ramagar was about to take his own place a hand grasped firm hold of his shoulder. It was Argyle.

"I am coming also," said the burly lord of Aran.

The tiny band of adventurers stared at him with surprise. "But your part of the bargain is done," said Mariana. "You

263

have successfully guided us to shore. Now isn't your wish to return to Aran?"

The sea warrior smiled thinly. "Aran needs me far less than you, my friends. And I think perhaps I can be of special value." He fondled the handle of his great ax.

"You will be of invaluable service," said the Prince, as he stood to make a place for the Aranian to sit. "Come, Argyle, share our company and our fortunes."

Argyle grinned, and tossing his cloak behind with a quick turn of his hand, sat and took hold of the oars.

The skiff was silently lowered into the dark, forebidding waters. Slowly Argyle rowed them away from the *Vulture*. From his post Captain Osari watched until they had disappeared. Then with a deep sigh he turned his back and made ready to sail. His heart was with them in that leaky skiff, his heart and all his thoughts. But the knowledge of what they must face, the trials they would surely endure, made him certain that he would never see any of them again.

18

A small, half-moon-shaped inlet loomed straight ahead as Argyle's strong strokes swiftly took them to shore. High cliffs hung menacingly on one side; deadened stumps of what had once been mighty and proud trees dotted the low, sharply slanting hills on the other.

There was no grass growing anywhere, only clumps of weed and moss, twisted and colorless, that had somehow managed to grow without benefit of sunlight. Beyond the inlet a broad sweep of mountains fanned one end of the horizon to the other, beautiful mountains, high and stoic, capped with thin layers of snow near the summits. But in the pervasive gloom of the Eternal Dark the mountains seemed to sag, as though they had been weighted down by the burden of night never to breathe again, never to feel their soil enriched by the warmth of the sun. They stood dormant in a land without color.

The sky itself was a canvas of darkness. Low-hanging clouds, thick and threatening, varying in shades from gray to charcoal, scudded rapidly across the peaks and down into the valleys. And above them were more clouds, equally as heavy equally as depressing. The overall sight was one of total gloom, so depressing that even the Prince cringed as his gaze swept the rugged scape. It was a place like no other, destitute and forlorn, with the only sound that of the wind, a low and mournful howl creeping down from distant dales, crying, begging to see the light of day just once more. It was a grim and unhappy land, and it tore at the hearts of the strangers about to set foot on its soil.

The sea wind still had a bite to it, although the inlet's protection sharply curtailed its ferocity. Mariana sucked in her breath as the skiff grated against an arc of sand at the base of the hills. Her breasts rose and fell rapidly as with a mixture of excitement and fear she stared up at the racing banks of black clouds hurrying inland. From the distance came a low rumble of thunder, and she knew that their landing would soon be marred by rain.

While Argyle silently drew in the oars, the Prince leaped from the boat and secured her fragile line beneath a rock. Then one by one they all got up and looked about.

"Any idea where we are?" asked the thief.

Argyle's eyes narrowed; he stared hard beyond the broad, barren fields set on a long plain nestled between the hills and the mountains. "Speca's walls will be found to the east," he grunted.

"And the palace of the Druid king?" asked the girl.

"We shall come to it soon enough. The Devil's Tower can be sighted from leagues away."

The haj cleared his throat. "What, may I ask, is the Devil's Tower?"

"I can answer that," said the Prince. "Long ago the Specian kings built a temple in reverence to the Fates. Unfinished at the time of Speca's demise, the tower had already risen to heights undreamed of by the world's architects. Fully completed, it would have been a monument so colossal that the highest mountain would have seemed small by comparison . . ."

Mariana blew the air out of her mouth in contemplation of such an awesome structure. "It would rise right into the sky itself!" she exclaimed in wonder.

The Prince nodded darkly. "Yes, and into the black clouds themselves. Into the Eternal Dark."

The dancing girl shivered. "Let's stay as far away from that as we can," she said.

The Prince shook his head. "If I am right," he told them

265

all, "then the Devil's Tower is precisely the place we mus
find. For there may rest our only chance of dispelling th
night."

Ramagar sighed. "Well, wherever we have to go, there's n
point in staying here." He put out the palm of his hand and
raindrop splashed. "Come on, let's collect our gear."

Homer leaned over the side of the skiff to pick up th
bundles of blankets and provisions.

"AH-CHOO!"

Mariana heard the sneeze. Looking at Homer, she said
"Bless you!"

The youth stared back at her, perplexed. "But I didn'
sneeze," he protested.

Mariana smiled. "Of course you did. I heard you."

Homer shook his head. "It wasn't me . . ."

The girl looked sharply at her companions, and one by on
they all shook their heads.

"AH-CHOO!"

Homer's hand tugged the blanket away from the stores
and he gasped at what he saw. Huddled beside the boxes o
food and weapons a slight figure of a man drew away, seem
ingly trying to slither unnoticed under the nearest slat bench.

Mariana groaned. "It's Oro!"

The hunchback lifted his head and smiled wanly at the an
gry faces pressing in at him.

"And what are *you* doing here?" demanded the thief.

Oro stood meekly, with his knees shaking. "I—I was hidin
from the Dragon Ship," he said unconvincingly. "I thought i
would be the only way I could escape—"

"He's lying," growled Ramagar. "More likely he still think
he can wrest the scimitar away from us and do some double
dealing with the Druids himself."

Oro stuck out his hands, palms upward, and shook then
nervously. "No, no! Please, believe me!"

"Let me have him," growled the haj. "I'll get the truth ou
of him yet!" He turned to Argyle and reached for the ax
"May I?"

The lord of Aran smiled wickedly. "My pleasure, goo
haj."

The hunchback paled and backed up, tripping as h
stumbled into the provisions. The haj drew menacingly closer
holding the weapon with both hands. *"Well?"* he asked.

Oro was shaking all over. "All right! All right! You win!
was plotting to steal the blade . . ."

266

"As usual," commented Mariana dryly. Then she looked at the thief and the Prince.

Ramagar threw up his hands in exasperation.

"Shall I remove his head, and settle the matter once and for all?" said the haj.

Although as angry as the others, the Prince was also somewhat bemused. Oro's gall and tenacity had been a thorn in their sides for so long that life without him would somehow seem lacking.

"We might as well let him alone," he said.

"And leave him here to scheme against us?" rattled Ramagar, aghast. "The sneak's been listening to every word we've been saying!"

"It seems to be either that or taking him along with us again," observed the dancing girl.

The thief heaved a sigh and looked to the Prince, who merely shrugged in reply. "All right," Ramagar grunted after a hasty moment's decision making. "Perhaps it is best if we do take him with us. Just so that we can keep our eyes on him."

With a mutter and a frown the haj returned the ax to Argyle. Then he shook an angry finger at the trembling hunchback. "None of your tricks, mind you," he warned severely. "Remember, we can always see to it that the Druids use you for target practice." And the look in his eyes warned Oro that this was no empty threat.

"I agree," mumbled Oro.

"*Now* can we get moving?" said the thief, scooping up supplies and stuffing them into the knapsacks Captain Osari had provided.

The rain had begun as the small band gathered up their belongings, dragged the skiff safely out of sight behind some nearby rocks, then slowly began the trek, making their way first along the base of the hills and heading in the direction of the barren plain that would lead them to their destination.

They had been on the move for less than an hour when Argyle, who had taken the lead, stopped, kneeled, and ran his fingers across scattered pebbles and mud. The tracks discovered were plain enough; horses had passed this way only recently. Druid soldiers, it was a fair bet, and an even better one that they would sooner or later pass this way again.

Pressing on with growing concern, they skirted the path of the tracks and took a long route across a wide dale. Skeletons of trees, branches twisted and broken, swayed slowly in the

267

wind. Shadows greeted them everywhere, enormous and shapeless, harmless perhaps, but a glum reminder of where they were and what the rest of the world could one day expect should the Druids grow restless.

Whether the hour was day or night no one could tell; but they felt as though they had walked forever, and unless shelter were soon found they might well drop in the mud from exhaustion.

Keen-eyed Argyle saved them from that fate. Cunningly surveying the land, he caught sight of a small grotto halfway up the face of a boulder-infested hillock. He led the way up the mound and everyone followed eagerly. Right now even a hole in the wall seemed a palace.

The cavern proved low and narrow, but large enough to accommodate them all. Everyone stretched out wearily and amid long sighs prepared for a good rest. They could not build a fire for fear of its being seen by nearby patrols. Yet the grotto was warm and dry. That was enough. So here sheltered from the starless sky of the Eternal Dark, they spent their first night in Speca.

Mariana knew she was dreaming, but what a marvelous dream it was. There were golden sands beneath a hot summer sun, blue sky, the laughter of children running barefoot along the beach. Palm and date trees swayed in a gentle eastern breeze, and cool waves of an aquamarine sea swept softly onto the shore. She was walking along the beach, with Ramagar at her side holding her hand. Far away domes and spires glimmered in the morning light. She felt the rush of sea wind against her face and glowed with contentment. This place, wherever it was, could only be home. And she was safe at last.

Home, she thought. *Home!*

She woke abruptly, and the illusions shattered like glass. It was very cold in the bleak grotto and she rubbed at her arm as she sat up. Her companions were still fast asleep, Ramagar close by her side, his hand resting on her thigh.

For a few minutes she sat motionless, listening to the strange noises caused by the ever-howling Northern wind outside. She mulled over recent events and wished to herself that this adventure would soon be over. Oh, it was not that she was unhappy with her new friends; quite the contrary. Nor even that her brushes with death made her question her reasons for coming in the first place. It was just that she was ired. Tired of running, tired of living from day to day. All he wanted was all she had ever wanted. A home, a family, and Ramagar. And right now, all of that seemed farther away than ever.

A small cough made her snap from these thoughts and cast her glance toward the mouth of the cavern. She had not noticed before, but the haj was also awake. He sat with his back resting lightly against the rough wall, his knees slightly up, and his arms buried within the folds of his flowing Eastern robe. He seemed as deeply lost in his own thoughts as Mariana had been in hers.

The haj heard her soft shuffle as the girl got up quietly and, careful not to disturb the others, made her way over to sit by his side.

"Is something the matter, Mariana?" he asked in a whisper. "Why aren't you asleep?"

"Nothing's wrong," she told him, smiling. "I woke up, that's all." She shifted her weight and made herself comfortable on the pebbly dirt. "But what about you? Why aren't you fast asleep like the others?"

"I rarely sleep much these days," he replied with a sigh, and Mariana was sure she saw sorrow flicker in his eyes. "Perhaps it is because of age," he went on after a moment of reflection. "At least some would say so."

Mariana dismissed the idea with a wave of her hand. "Don't be silly. You're not so old—"

The haj smiled. "Old enough, at any rate. But you, Mariana, are so young. So very young . . ."

"Over twenty," she admitted.

The haj's smile deepened. "Ah, twenty. Yes, a good age. Let me see." He leaned back and closed his eyes. "At your age, if I recall properly, my own wife had already delivered my second child. My second son . . ." Burlu inhaled deeply and bobbed his head up and down as if to confirm his memory.

"You must have been very proud of your sons."

The bejeweled haj twirled his finger ring and nodded. "Yes, very proud of them all. The first left home to sail the seas, you know. And never have I heard from him since. My third died while yet a youth, gored to death by a wild beast. He was a brave lad." He shrugged, grew silent.

Mariana looked at him curiously. The haj had spoken of his first son, and of his third. The middle son had purposely been omitted, and she wondered why.

269

"And what of the second?" she asked.

At this the haj frowned. "Another sad tale, Mariana. Wh[y] speak of it?" He took her small hand in his own and presse[d] it gently. "It's time you had children of your own," he tol[d] her in a fatherly tone. "Your *own* family and sons . . ."

Mariana flushed. "I hope to," she confided. "As soon a[s] this *business* is ended."

He squeezed her hand harder. "Promise me, child, that yo[u] will. I must know it before . . . before I die. Promise me!"

She was startled by him. With a gasp, she said, "Die? Wha[t] do you mean? What is this morbid talk? Why are you sayin[g] such things?"

Burlu sighed again. "Because I suspect what lies ahead fo[r] us, and I know I am old . . ." His smile returned; he touche[d] her cheek, brushing his fingertips toward her mouth. "But yo[u] shall live, Mariana. I vowed it long ago. Even should ever[y] man among us be lost to the Druids, you shall live." H[e] leaned in closer and looked at her sternly. "Now promise m[e] you'll keep your word."

"Of course I promise," she replied, taken aback and feelin[g] frightened. "But why even ask it?"

"Because it's important to me. Very important." He shu[t] his eyes, and she watched in surprise as a single tear rolle[d] down his face. She wondered why he was telling all this t[o] her now.

His eyes opened again; he gazed at her fondly. "You sti[ll] have no idea of why I say these things, do you?"

Dark curls fell over her eyes as she shook her head.

The haj smiled. "Then perhaps it it time we spoke, Mar[i]ana. And when we are done, many mysteries will be e[x]plained."

She hadn't an inkling of what he meant; she began to won[n]der if some fever had overtaken him. In all the time she ha[d] known haj Burlu, she had never seen him act or speak s[o] strangely. This sudden change left her feeling uneasy.

"Where were you born, child?" he asked suddenly.

"In Kalimar. Outside of the city, somewhere. Or so I ha[ve] been told."

"And your parents?"

Mariana sniffed. "Both dead. My father when I was an in[n]fant, my mother when I was four. It was then that I w[as] taken to the Jandari and raised by an old woman I called m[y] aunt, though she really was no family at all. In fact, exce[pt] for Ramagar, I have never had any family to call my own."

270

"None?" questioned the haj.

Mariana shrugged. "At least none that I knew of. Why?"

Burlu made no attempt to answer her question, only asked another of his own. "Your mother, what was her name?"

"Rhia. Those who knew her say she was a very beautiful woman."

"She must have been," reflected the haj. "Very beautiful indeed. And you very much like her. Except for the eyes, those could only be his. I would know them anywhere . . ."

A strange sensation was growing and spreading through Mariana's body. She shivered as goose bumps rose down her neck. "I don't . . . understand. What—what are you saying?"

The haj's eyes were wet with tears now; he could not stop the flow, nor did he want to. "Do you still not know?"

She shook her head.

"I have known it since the first night you came to my tents," he admitted. "Known for certain since the very instant I saw you. There could be no question of it. Now now, not then."

She was staring blankly, and the haj gently ran his fingers through her silky hair. "Your father, Mariana. Do you know his name? Did your mother tell you that much?"

The girl swallowed and nodded.

"And that name, was it . . . Etron?"

Her heart leaped to her throat and she gasped. "Yes! How did you know?"

The old haj lifted his shoulders, putting his hands to his face while he cried. "Etron was my son, Mariana. My second son, gone to Kalimar to seek his fortunes." Then he looked up at the astounded girl and tried to smile. "And you are my . . . granddaughter."

Mariana opened her mouth to speak but could find no words. It could not be true! But then, she hoped it was, for she had already come to love the haj as if he were her grandfather. Yet the news was so sudden, so unreal, that it left her head swimming.

"Is . . . is all this really true?" she asked with a sniff, her eyes wide and bright. "Or . . . are you just teasing me?"

The haj drew her close, cradling her against him as they both shed tears. "Never would I lie to you, Mariana," he said. "I swear it by all I hold dear. The blood that flowed through Etron's veins flows through your own. You are my granddaughter . . ."

For a time they both sat in silence. Mariana's heart was

271

filled with joy, yet also with sorrow for the father she ha
never known.

"What was he like? My father, I mean," she said after
while.

The haj sighed; he gently toyed with her dark locks, twis
ing little curls around his finger. "Etron was a . . . a fathe
you would have been proud of, child. Tall, handsome, va
iant. Even as Ramagar is. It broke my heart to see him leav
home and set out for Kalimar. Yet, young men must follo
their destinies, be they for good or ill. Alas, after he left m
tents I never saw him again . . ."

"What happened to him?" asked the girl.

"A trader from the city sought shelter one night, sever
years after Etron had gone. By chance he had heard of m
son, and he told me that the lad had taken a wife and bee
given a daughter. But then my guest's eyes grew dull, and h
cast his glance away, reluctant to speak further. But I en
treated him until he told me how Etron had died, died n
more than three weeks before of a terrible fever that ha
swept the city." Here the haj paused to reflect on that crus)
ing hour, to relive the pain that had never quite ceased.

"Not long after," he began anew, "I sent to the city two
my most trusted and able servants. They combed Kalima
high and low for Etron's wife and their baby daughter. B
the city is so vast, and there are countless thousands to
found there with tales equally as sad. At last my servan
came home. As I waited with eagerness beside my tents I sa
the long faces they wore, and I had no need to hear the
speak the words. Etron's widow was lost, never to be foun
And likewise the young daughter whose name I did not ev
know . . ."

"If only my mother had stayed," whispered Mariana.

"Yes, child. If only. But fate often plays cruel games wi
mortals. Heartbroken, I was forced to give up the searc
though the desire to seek them forever remained. But then
and here his old eyes brightened like stars, "that starless ev
ning when Ramagar came to my tents seeking shelter, I re
ized that the Fates had not betrayed me. For when I saw yo
from the very first moment, something within me alread
knew, although I dared not let myself admit it. Before n
stood a lovely woman, yet still a child. And her eyes we
his—Etron's—her smile, her gestures. It was almost li
seeing my son reborn.

"At first I could not believe; I wondered if perhaps n

272

mind was slipping from me, as it frequently does to old men. But when we spoke, you and I, and I listened and watched, I knew I had not been wrong. I dared not tell you of it, certain you would think me demented. Indeed I doubted if I would ever tell you, knowing that only pain and bitter memories would come of it. Yet now, when we face such dangers on the morrow, I could hold back no longer. I had to say it while there was still time, so that should I . . . not return with you . . . you will know that I loved you, and that all I have is yours."

Mariana looked into his eyes and saw the glow of truth. And she too thought back to the evening when they had first met, recalling her own strange affinity for the old haj. Perhaps in some way she had known of their bond as well. But that no longer mattered. What did matter was that now, a thousand leagues from home, she had found the family she'd been seeking all her life.

"Do you believe what I've told you?" the haj asked at length.

Tears welled again, as she said, "I do believe you . . . Grandfather." And as her voice cracked, she fell into his strong waiting arms and sobbed.

19

Deeper and deeper into Speca's curious landscape the band of adventurers marched, ever mindful of the lengthening distance between themselves and the sea, constantly oppressed by the darkness that swirled above their heads.

After hours of making their way over barren hills and into a valley, they paused to consider the best route to follow. On one side lay a shallow wisp of a stream, whose waters seemed tinted yellow in the subdued light; on the other, a sharply sloping trail appeared to lead to the blackened forests where deadened trunks stood limb to limb, taller than houses, as foreboding as they were dense.

Argyle and the Prince debated heatedly for a few moments over which direction they should follow. It seemed likely that both led sooner or later to the walled city where the Devil's Tower stood as a grim monument for all Speca's subjugated peoples to see.

Mariana stood quietly at the edge of the gathered group, sweeping her gaze along the stream, gloomily noting vast stretches of crushed rock strewn in jumbled masses on either side. It mattered little to her which of the two choices was finally agreed upon; each seemed inhospitable enough. Like everything else in this barbaric wilderness, the selection was of one clump of rot over another.

While the discussion continued—Ramagar and the haj agreeing with the lord of Aran and the others siding with the Prince—Mariana first caught sight of a cloud of dust suddenly rising from the edge of the plain beyond the dale. The source of the dust was hidden by a line of broken ridges and cliffs set in the valley, but now it was beginning to swirl and thicken and a faint rumbling sound rose with it.

The girl stood frozen; against the backdrop of the Darkness it was too difficult to ascertain what was going on, but the rumble was steadily growing in intensity, starting to shake the ground beneath her feet, and sounding more and more like the clamor of racing horses.

"Druids!" she cried.

Argyle spun like a cat, his sword drawn in the blink of an eye. As everybody hit the dirt, Ramagar grabbed the girl by her tunic and yanked her down into the damp soil beside him.

The horses were growing closer, hoofbeats shattering the stilled air like cannon. Slowly, the thief and Argyle inched their way to the crest and, poking their heads between two enormous rocks, peered uneasily out at the plain.

Far away, crossing the empty flat with deranged speed, came a grim procession of fine black stallions, blue manes flowing in the wind, coats sleek and shiny with perspiration. Magnificent horses, Ramagar noted, perhaps the best he had ever seen. Riding low in the leather saddles were the soldiers, tall, lean men, not as burly perhaps as the gruesome Night-Watchers, but equally as alien, and equally as intimidating. Brutish fellows from the looks of them, dour and cruel. At least twenty in number, they all wore silver and black tunics, crimson cloaks curling behind. Upon their heads were plumed helmets, thin mail across their chests. They rode their steeds with expertise, clearly masters of Speca's wild trails. Never once did they halt or even pause as they crossed the treacherous flat and disappeared inside the Black Forest.

"They seem to be in quite a hurry to get where they're going," Ramagar observed dryly.

Argyle spit into the wind as response.

The thief tapped a finger against his teeth warily. "Do you suppose they've had wind of us?"

The brooding lord shrugged. "Best we don't stop to ask," was all he said.

Ramagar slid back down to his waiting companions, careful to keep his body low, even though now the Druid troops were gone.

The band gathered closer, kneeling and listening uneasily as the thief explained what he had seen. "We were fortunate this time," he told them all. "I doubt many patrols will pass while we're still in this *wilderness*." His eyes scanned the surrounding scape briefly, his hand grandly gesturing as if to add emphasis to his words.

"But there'll be plenty about the closer we get to the city," added the Prince gloomily. "We'll have to be more alert. Between the soldiers and the Death-Stalkers our hands are going to be full . . ."

Mariana shuddered, recalling Argyle's warning while they were still on Aran. The Death-Stalkers! Hideous birds of prey, trained to swoop down and kill, they combed the skies of Darkness at will, ready and eager to do the bidding of their Druid masters. They were said to attack in frightful numbers, shrieking as they dived upon their hapless prey, be it man or beast. And when they were done, only bones were left to give testimony to the deed.

It was a sobering reminder to everyone—and they trembled to ponder what other horrors yet unknown they might encounter in this land.

Heaving a sigh, Ramagar picked up his knapsack, fitted the straps, and easily slung it back over his shoulder. "Sitting here and worrying isn't going to help us any," he said. "Let's get moving again. Now, which route shall we take?"

"It seems our Druid friends have already decided that for us," the Prince replied. "Since they rode toward the forest, our best bet is to follow the stream after all."

He glanced around at his companions one by one. There was no dissent; everybody seemed eager to avoid the soldiers at all costs. As they made ready to leave each pair of eyes drifted occasionally toward the sky, this time not with concern for the dismal array of clouds, but rather in anxious fear of the flying enemy who could be swooping unseen upon them at this very moment.

After a last-second check of weapons and gear, Argyle as

275

before took the lead, beginning the eastward trek anew. The moss-filled yellow waters reflected an eerie night pall as the band followed the stream, which coiled snake-like, this way and that, up sharp inclines and down steeper ones. Worn boots tramped first over mud, then over coarse and hard sand, grated and pebble-strewn, lifeless except for scattered blue-tinted shoots that shot up like stunted trees, their grotesque roots bending awkwardly to suck every bit of moisture in the way a spider devours a fly.

Up and down, over hills and dales, ridges and hillocks, the band of adventurers marched, teeth gritted, eyes ever straight ahead on the treacherous path, their flesh becoming numbed by the bitter bite of the mountain wind. The gusts blew with more vicious force than before as the mountains loomed ever closer; whipping and whistling along the chalky cliff set to the north, tearing down the craggy drops in the west, the wind increased dramatically as the band came closer to the valley's end and the vast plain that spread out from there like a blanket.

By normal reckoning, the time should have been close to evening when Argyle called for a brief rest. Thankfully, they spread out along the grainy banks of the water and sighed with pleasure as they rubbed aching feet and shut stinging eyes.

As a cold meal of biscuits and dried beef was passed around, the haj restlessly got up to take a closer look at an interesting sight. Among the crushed rock and rubble of the hill beyond their resting place, set against the base of twin hillocks, there was a clump of scant vegetation that had somehow managed to break through the hard ground and nurture itself without benefit of sunlight. He waved to Mariana, who had strayed farther upstream from the others so that she could wash, and beckoned the girl to put down her bar of soap and join him.

With a smile and a shrug she eagerly came to his side, and without the need for words they climbed partway up the face to get a better look at what seemed to be a small vegetable garden.

The haj yanked out a herb, studied the root, and took a bite. "Tastes like squash to me," he said, smacking his lips.

Mariana looked at him. "Squash? But that's not possible!"

"And look!" added the haj, pointing to a tiny clump of shrubbery. "Those are berry bushes!" He ran to inspect, nimble fingers plucking, teeth biting, tongue tasting.

276

"I don't believe it! Look, Mariana!" he held out a handful. "These are cranberry. Wild, to be sure, but cranberry! And these," he stuck out his other hand, "are without question bunchberry . . ."

"Are you sure?" asked the startled girl, taking one and hesitantly biting. "How could berries—how could anything—grow in a climate like this?" But then she tasted the berry and stared at the haj.

"Well?" the swineherd asked.

"Mmmm! They're good!"

"Delicious, Mariana! Ravishingly delicious! Come on, let's get back and call the others! Like as I would to hoard all of this for ourselves, my conscience won't allow me to be such a glutton."

He belched, swallowing a mouthful; the girl grinned. "Won't everybody by surprised!" And her skirt swirled as she hurried to go. A lumbering shadow cast darkly from atop the hill, and they both froze in their tracks.

It was a man, a towering figure of a man. Hands on hips, he stood sternly glaring down at the two intruders, his form a powerful silhouette in the pervasive dark.

Mariana gulped; the haj stepped in front of her, ready to field any blows the frightful figure might deliver.

"Is he a Druid?" Mariana whispered faintly.

"He wears no uniform," observed the haj. "But he's frightening enough all the same . . ." His hand inched its way toward the hidden dagger beneath his robe and his fingers toyed for the hilt. "When I say," he told her, "run as fast as you can. Bring Argyle—"

The thought went unfinished as another grim silhouette appeared along the crest. And then another, quickly followed by another. The haj turned slowly, his eyes sweeping the terrain for avenues of escape—there were none.

From among the group a thick-set man, dressed in various skins, the skull of some wild beast adorning his head, came slowly walking down the slope. Long blond hair, unkempt and stringy, fell over his shoulders. He sported a long blond beard, much in the fashion of Argyle's, and stared at the strangers from a deeply set pair of cold blue eyes. Thin lips folded back in a curious expression; he examined the strangers close up, a scowl deepening. In his hand he carried a long shaft of wood, the tip finely honed into a razor-sharp point.

This is no Druid, thought Mariana. More like a barbarian. A wildman.

The wildman screwed his eyes, fluidly taking note of the haj's curious garb. He had never seen a man of the East, it was plain, nor a girl with skin bronzed by the sun. It dawned on Mariana as he gaped at her that he had probably never seen the sun either.

"We . . . we are not enemies," she said, gathering her courage and speaking in her broken understanding of Northern tongues.

The wildman stepped back a pace, mistrust written all over his rugged features.

"We are friends," the haj quickly added, and he put up his hands palms first to show his intent was peaceful.

At that, the wildman raised his spear, prodding the tip at the haj's belly. He shouted something to his companions, and two more wildmen came bolting down the hill with rope in their hands.

"They mean to take us prisoner!" gasped Burlu, beside himself with fear. He now realized how stupid it had been for him to have wandered off from the others like this. What would happen to them now? What would Ramagar do when he realized Mariana was missing?

The haj shuddered involuntarily. A fine mess of matters he had made of things, all right. But maybe if he could catch his guards off balance . . . make a quick run toward the others . . .

The tip of the spear pressed in tighter, and the wildman indicated for them both to hold out their hands. Submissively they did, wincing as the bonds were strapped about their wrists.

As the points of other spears dug into their backs, the first wildman gestured his hand in a direction far behind the berry bushes and toward a rocky cluster of mounds at the edge of the valley.

"I think he wants us to walk that way," said Mariana.

Burlu groaned, lamenting their fate. Prisoners. Caught like rank amateurs by a handful of barbarians. And as he began to shuffle along, he wondered if perhaps they would have fared better coming face to face with the Druids. Compared to these wildmen, even they had seemed civilized.

Shoved and badgered, not a word or a glance allowed between them, Mariana and the haj were mercilessly forced

278

along a path of treacherous shale, until at last they came to a spot where the valley narrowed before them to a twisting defile barely wide enough for the two of them to pass side by side. Mariana saw other wildmen about keeping stoic watch from the bluffs and ridges above.

Their captor gestured and they followed him along a smooth rock wall through the defile. A thin trickle of fresh water flowed down one side of the rock, indicating either a pool or a catch basin somewhere below. There was no vegetation to be seen in these parts, save for the long green shoots they had encountered earlier, which here grew far taller than before, with stems stout and firm, unbending in the mountain wind. An odd sight, thought Mariana, as if these plants were declaring their defiance of the bleak world around them by their very growth.

The wildman in the lead suddenly and gruffly signaled for them to halt. Ahead by some meters the defile opened into a spacious basin, dark, hard soil surrounded on all sides by jutting peaks of rock. Ragged men carrying spears and other simple weapons stood silently at scattered points along the heights, obviously serving as lookouts both at the valley and the plain beyond. What startled Mariana, though, was not these barbaric soldiers, but the sight of children. Set against the inner walls of the hills stood small groups of wide-eyed youngsters, stopped abruptly in their games by the sight of the intruders, and now staring in wonder as their mothers hastily began tugging them away.

"Don't be frightened," said the girl, calling to them. But before she could finish she was pulled away by one of the guards and pushed onto another path, this one winding at a slight incline away from the basin.

Deadened stumps and fierce boulders cast dark shadows over her; she winced when she saw where they were being led. Well concealed by huge rocks was a small opening in the wall of the hill, an entrance leading downward inside the mound itself. Without having to ask, Mariana could see that this place was to be their prison—perhaps even their permanent home if the wildmen decided not to kill them.

As she was pushed inside she stifled a cry of panic. This place, this whole basin, was so forlorn and secluded that no one was likely to find it. Ramagar could search endlessly, scouring the valley, but never locate it—and even if he did, a wildman's spear was the only contact he was likely to make.

And it was down, down into the shaft they were led,

sightless and stumbling. Mariana could only make a comparison with the dreaded sewers of Kalimar, equally as black and as foul. Only from here, she knew, there could be no escape.

A rabbit warren of tunnels crisscrossed beneath the hill, some leading upward, others down, still others off to the side. For a time their captors seemed to debate among themselves where their prisoners should be placed. Then it was decided and they were taken to a small secret chamber, where their captors pushed them inside and forced them to seat themselves upon the hard ground.

Mariana clutched tightly at the haj's sleeve while the wildmen exchanged a few words. Suddenly there was a dim light; a young woman, little more than a child, lithely stepped inside carrying a tiny oil lamp. Eyes downcast, flowing yellow hair falling below her spine, she placed the light on a recess, quickly withdrawing before Mariana could try and speak to her.

"Food will be brought," mumbled the leading wildman, and with that, he and his companions withdrew, leaving the captives completely alone.

The haj bounded to his feet, inspecting the entrance, running his hands along the walls in search of some hidden exit. There was none; only a constant mild downward draft rushing from above, assuring them of fresh air. Save for that, the closeness of the grotto was like being in a grave.

"Think they mean to do us in?" asked Mariana.

The haj growled. Then cold and hungry they huddled together to await their uncertain fate.

Hours passed. Mariana put her head in Burlu's lap, crying softly while her grandfather ran his fingers through her hair. Still cursing himself for this predicament, he wracked his brain to devise some scheme for escape. But with wildmen posted at the entrance and no way to gain access to the downward corridors it seemed an impossible task. All they could do was wait, and hope for some reprieve from their desperate situation.

How many hours had elapsed since they had been brought to their cell Mariana couldn't tell, as she suddenly found herself being gently roused from sleep by the same young woman who had brought the lamp. Behind the woman stood a brute of a wildman, a grimace on his face and a sharpened spear in his hand, waiting impatiently for the prisoners to be brought to their feet.

The girl jabbered something in the language of the North, and Mariana understood that she and the haj were to be taken from the cave. Thankfully she nodded her understanding and raised herself slowly, still feeling the aches and cramps from a most uncomfortable night.

The haj was already up; he lent a helping hand, and forced a thin smile of reassurance. Then the brute grunted and pointed to the chiseled rock doorway, now wide open.

"Where do you suppose they're taking us?" Mariana whispered as she smoothed the skirt of her soiled tunic.

The haj frowned in response; wherever it was, it would be a relief to get out of this place.

With the brute taking the lead and the silent servant girl in the rear they made their way back into the winding corridor and up the incline to the entrance. In the distant opening Mariana could see the swirling patterns of black clouds looming low over the valley, and she began to feel the bite of the bitter wind howling from the range of peaks down into the lowland basin. It was a grim reminder of the harrowing world outside.

She could hear noises coming from the village. Someone— a wildman by his tone—was addressing a crowd, occasionally pausing while his listeners murmured among themselves. This whole episode was making Mariana uneasy; she slowed purposely in her gait, wondering if the crowd had not been gathered to witness her execution.

The brute glanced back over his shoulder, grunting a few angry words and rattling his weapon to display his annoyance at his reluctant charges. In no mood to show defiance, the haj pulled the girl sharply, and quickstepping they found themselves steps from the cave's mouth.

Mariana drew up all the remaining courage she could muster and took Burlu's hand. Together they marched out into the stillness and dim light of Speca's day.

The entire village must have been out for the occasion, Mariana mused, sweeping her gaze across the large crowd in the craggy basin, a hundred pairs of staring eyes—men, women, and children—all curious and eager to gaze at the peculiarly garbed strangers. Mariana threw back her hair and lifted her shoulders, feeling that whatever was in store, she was determined to face it without showing her fear.

It took a moment or two for her to realize that, though some in the crowd were still watching her, many were showing far more interest in another group of men coming

281

through the narrow defile. She held her breath, looked to the equally surprised haj, then turned her gaze back to this new cause of excitement.

Into the basin came a severe bunch of wildmen, all carrying spears, all wearing grim smiles of satisfaction on their faces. Behind them, tied together by a single rope that looped around the ankles, came Ramagar and the others—all with heads downcast and hands tightly bound behind their backs.

"They've been captured!" cried the girl.

The old haj sadly nodded and looked away, his small hopes of rescue utterly dashed. It was a forlorn sight: the bold Argyle, his fists balled, cursing loudly as he maneuvered to break free; the Prince sullen and heavyhearted behind him; Homer walking in a daze; and little Oro sniveling while wildman spears jabbed at his ribs to make him keep up.

It was more than Mariana could stand; "Ramagar!" she shouted, bolting from her own guard and pushing her way through the gathering to reach her lover.

Ramager lifted his head in amazement; then he too tried to break free, but his own guards acted more quickly than hers had. They pushed the thief from sight and grabbed the pleading girl as she fell onto the gravelly soil.

In a rage, the lord of Aran burst his bonds with a single thrust, snapping the rope like string. He rushed forward, knocking two wildmen off balance, grabbed the first spear he saw, and aimed it at the leader of the wildmen, the straggly yellow-haired man who had been addressing the crowd.

The leader did not raise a finger in his own protection; he didn't have to. On every ridge, from behind every boulder along the awesome heights, more warrior wildmen showed themselves, all armed with deadly weapons, all poised to throw the instant Argyle let loose. And every spear was aimed at the heart of the dancing girl.

"Throw down your weapon, my powerful friend," commanded the wildman chieftain.

For a moment Argyle wavered, debating his choices, but there was really no choice to be made. The moment he threw the spear Mariana would die. The chieftain was offering him a cunning choice—two lives, his own and hers, or death for them both.

Reluctantly, Argyle threw down his spear. One of the fallen wildmen scampered to his feet and scooped the weapon up, looking to his chief for direction.

The stocky chief studied Argyle's face carefully, his eyes

taking a long, slow measure of his adversary. Then he set his gaze on the others one by one, focusing finally on the Prince with the instinctive knowledge that this one, the quiet one, was the leader of the alien band.

"What shall we do with them, lord?" one of the guards asked.

The chieftain pursed his lips; from folded arms he put a finger to his mouth and ran it gently along the sides of his brush moustache.

"Bring them all to the Hall," he said at last. Then he turned his back and disappeared into a small stone house with a thatched roof that stood beside the near mountain wall.

Another wildman snapped his fingers and his men shoved the band forward across the basin. The crowd huddled back as they passed, the women and children shuddering as mighty Argyle strode by.

Mariana and the haj were the last to enter; the dancing girl threw herself into the arms of the shaken Ramagar and clung to him fiercely. A deep cut showed along the side of his temple, another near his shoulder. It was plain to see that a powerful fight had been given by all her companions—a fight that left each of them bruised and far more disheveled than when she had seen them last.

The "Hall," as the chieftain had called it, proved to be little more than a large room in a stone edifice with nothing but packed earth for a floor. There was no light inside, save for a single torch set in the wall near the front, and a tiny window close to the beamed ceiling that allowed only a sliver of the dim Specian daylight to filter through. There were no chairs, no cushions, no tables—only a semicircle of smoothed rock to serve as seats—a configuration that left Argyle and the Prince exchanging puzzled glances. Somehow, as primitive as it was, it all seemed vaguely familiar.

Wildmen at the entrance quickly stepped to the side as their leader came into the Hall. Unarmed, escorted by two young women, one who was the same girl Mariana already knew, the chieftain crossed the floor and sat himself atop the tallest stone.

"We demand to be released!" barked the haj, feeling his oats now that it was certain they would not be put to an immediate death.

The wildman slanted a curious brow and stared at the

283

brazen swineherd. "Oh?" he said softly. "And who are you to make such demands?"

"Haj Burlu of Kalimar," he replied, slapping dirt from his robe and bowing politely if not graciously.

"Kalimar?" repeated the chieftain.

"A faraway land of the East," the Prince told him.

The chieftain nodded. "Ah, yes. The East . . ."

Ramagar glanced at Argyle. This wildman, this chieftain of wildmen, was acting as though he had heard of Kalimar. A most curious development, considering that as a Specian, and a barbarian to boot, there was no possible way he could have known of it.

"Are you all of . . . Kalimar?" questioned the chieftain further.

"All but two," replied the Prince.

"You and," he glanced to Argyle, "the big fellow?"

The lord of Aran fumed, incensed at the attitude of the seated man. He put his fists to his hips, and said, "By what right have we been taken prisoner by you? We meant you no harm—"

The chieftain frowned and cut him off with a flippant gesture. "On these shores, *all* are our enemies. Tell me, how came you here?"

"See here," said the haj. "We need not answer all these questions. We are your prisoners, and you may kill us if you will." He waved an imperious finger in the chieftain's face, adding, "But know this: my companions and I have come here to free Speca of its misery. Slay us and you only harm yourselves."

The chieftain mulled over his words and then leaned back with folded arms. "You are a peculiar lot, invading our lands like this, then making demands."

The chieftain leaned forward again. Argyle restlessly shifted his weight and continued to glare. "Well?" he said. "What are you going to do with us?"

It was a wry and knowing smile that crossed the chieftain's rugged face. He turned to the lord of Aran and shook his head. "You're still as impatient as ever, Argyle. Even after all this time . . ."

Argyle's mouth dropped so low it looked as though his jaw would fall off. "You . . . you know my name?"

The chieftain grinned; then he stood and confronted Argyle face to face. "Yes, I know your name—as surely as you know mine."

284

The lord of Aran narrowed his eyes and scrutinized the barbarian leader, shaking his head.

The chieftain sighed. "Have I changed that much?" he asked rhetorically. Then he sagged his shoulders and lifted his gaze heavenward. "Nearly twenty years now in this forsaken land," he mumbled. "Twenty years! I suppose it would alter any man . . ."

"Who . . . who are you?" questioned Argyle, suddenly dimly aware of a vague familiarity in the chieftain's features.

"Have you forgotten the hunts we once shared, Argyle? Or the warmth of the fires as we camped beneath summer stars? Or even how we once were rivals for Griselda's hand . . . ?"

"Thorhall!" whispered Argyle. "*Thorhall!*"

And the wildman laughed. "Yes, it is I—doomed to spend my life under the skies of Eternal Darkness."

"But you were slain! I myself saw your ship sink in the dreaded waters, a flaming torch beneath the fire arrows of the Dragon Ships! You and my brother both!"

Thorhall answered sadly. "It is a long story. A very long story—and not a happy one." The memory of that long ago battle was still strong and powerful, and the aging leader of the wildmen returned to his seat, his long face marked with his dejection.

"Then you're not one of these . . . barbarians?" said Mariana.

Thorhall smiled. "No," he answered, turning his head toward her, his long, stringy hair falling freely over his shoulders. "Merely one who found himself a place to hide from the devils."

"But how did you manage to elude the Druids?" asked Argyle.

"And who are these people you now lead?" added the girl.

Thorhall put out his palms in a patient gesture. "So many questions," he said. "Sit down, all of you. Everything will be explained to your satisfaction, I promise."

They took seats upon the smoothed stones of the Hall, which all now realized was fashioned after the meeting place of Aran's *Sklar*. Thorhall looked to the two young girls at his side. "My daughters will bring us some food," he said. "You all must be very hungry."

"Famished," Mariana admitted, "especially after that long night in your prison."

"Forgive me. But you see, I had to be certain that you were not an enemy . . ."

285

"No need for apologies," said the haj, feeling his belly growl with hunger. "You did what you had to do, and now let's let bygones be bygones."

"Agreed," chimed in Ramagar, scratching at the raw wound he had received in the morning's battle. "Needless to say, I hope those wildmen I knocked unconscious won't hold a grudge . . ."

Thorhall laughed boisterously. Moments later his two daughters came into the room carrying trays laden with food. It was plain fare, a porridge of herbs mixed with mutton, and a pitcher of berry wine that sweetly rinsed down the salt of the meal. When it was done, Argyle clasped his hand on his friend's shoulder, and said, "Tell us your tale, Thorhall. Tell us all you can about these Dark Lands. For in truth, my own coming here was no accident. And what you have to say could prove of invaluable import to us all."

"Very well," sighed the weary chieftain. With his daughters kneeling at either side, Thorhall began.

"Three ships of Aran had sailed into the Darkness that gloomy night," he said. "Argyle's, his bold brother's, and my own. Once past the dreaded Calling of the Sirens we had hoped to slip easily upon Speca's shore. Alas, it was not to be. From nowhere came the red glow of Dragon Ships. Our own *knaars* were trimmed and stout—and men of Aran have never been eager to run. It was a brave fight, with Argyle and his brother pinning down one Dragon Ship while my own craft engaged another approaching from the opposite direction. The fight lasted for hours on end, with one side and then the other gaining the upper hand.

"My spirits had never been higher; for innumerable years we had feared these Druid vessels, and now our *knaars* had almost tasted victory. Am I not right, Argyle?"

The lord of Aran nodded glumly. That was indeed as it had been—at least as it had seemed.

"But then," continued Thorhall in a quiet, almost respectful voice, "matters began to change. We found ourselves in the midst of a terrible maelstrom; the sea had become a whirlpool. I saw from my bow Argyle's ship reel, pushed back by the sea, helplessly looking on while the Dragon Ship bore down upon his brother's, tearing that vessel asunder. The cries of drowning men filled my ears until I could no longer bear it. Bold Rhyn, Argyle's brother, stood at the shattered prow and waved defiant fists at the laughing enemy. Stout and tall he remained, even as arrow after arrow tore hrough his flesh and his blood washed across the deck. Then he *knaar* was gone; sucked from sight, down, down deep nto the black waters. And all around me, men stood in horror. Who among my own crew did not have a brother or a close friend on that stricken ship?"

Here Thorhall was forced to pause; he shuddered at the vivid recollection while Argyle thought of his lost brother and cried. Then he continued.

"But perhaps Rhyn and his men were really the lucky ones. As the battle raged, I saw that my own ship no longer had a chance of winning the fight. Rhyn was gone, and Argyle's craft was smoldering with fires, too far away to come to my aid. The Dragon Ship steadily pressed on, even as the whirlpool tossed us about in a frenzy. Amid the turbulence we were rammed. My sails sputtered with flames, Druid sea fighters attacked our decks at will. To a man we fought them, hand to hand, our decks a river of dark Druid blood. But their numbers prevailed. Those of us yet alive were shackled and dragged aboard the enemy vessel, our fates to be sealed for all time. I watched with terror as my *knaar* sank, good ship that she was, and I shut my eyes and whispered a farewell to Aran—for I knew I would never see my home or my friends again. My ship was swallowed by the murk to join Rhyn's. Only Argyle's remained afloat, yet until this day I had no way of knowing what his fate had been. Although I freely admit I wept as I prayed for his successful escape."

Thorhall stopped, and there was a long silence, not broken until Mariana said, "What happened to you when you were captured?"

Thorhall winced. "A destiny that I hope no one of you will ever have to share. Drugged by strange herbs, we were carried ashore in our sleep and brought to the walled citadel where once the noble kings of Speca governed in majesty. Kings yet rule from there, but never has the world known blacker ones. For the injured or ill among us, it was a slow and painful death; the Druid magicians used them for experiments in casting new spells. As for the rest of us, we were sent to the mines, to the darkest pits imaginable, where sightlessly we toiled sixteen hours a day, digging with spade and pick, loading for our masters unimaginable wealth, gold and diamonds, rubies and silver, marble from the quarries, each day adding more and more bounty to the overflowing storehouses and vaults of the Druid king. Our own shelters were hovels;

287

we slept beside filth, forced to endure our fate side by side with the once proud Specian people . . ."

The Prince swallowed to remove the lump in his throat. "And what has happened to the people?" he asked in a weak voice.

Thorhall frowned. "They suffer more than any race deserves. The men are beasts of burden under the taskmasters' whips, their bodies poisoned by an unknown spell that keeps them docile and submissive. They have no will, they have no minds of their own. The Druids have taken everything—including their sanity. They live in a trance, a perpetual dream world where they know nothing save Druid commands.

"As for the women, they are chattel. Druid lords and masters use them as they will. Only at breeding time are they permitted to be brought to the men . . ."

Mariana squirmed uneasily, the image of such a life making her mind reel.

Ramagar leaned forward. "Tell me, Thorhall," he said, "is there an explanation to this 'poison' that keeps the people in bondage?"

"It is believed that the poison is spread through the very air itself," Thorhall replied gloomily. "Spawned somewhere in the vile citadel, thrown to the sky, and borne by the wind across the length and breadth of Speca—the farther away from the source you travel, the less potent the effects."

"If that is so," said Mariana thoughtfully, "then why aren't you yourself affected? Or even us, for that matter."

"Ah, but to some extent we all are," countered the chieftain. "I myself was far more affected while I was still in bondage."

"How did you ever manage to escape from those pits?" asked Argyle.

"Another long tale, old friend. I was in bondage for more than two full years, down in the bowels of the earth and never once coming into the light of day. My mind, and those of my companions, had already begun to warp; my thought became blurred, at times I no longer could remember who was. In such a dreadful state I knew that life was hardly worth the living. Yes, better to be dead like Rhyn and the others than to endure any more. While I yet held onto some sanity I and a few others plotted our escape, not caring what tortures we would endure should our plan fail and we be caught.

"With the edge of a sharpened rock I little by little

288

loosened the shackles around my legs, careful to work only during the sleep periods when no one would notice. In the black of the pits I feigned sudden illness—the fits, we call them—where men mindlessly convulse. When the overseer came to see, I slit his throat and robbed his corpse of his keys. Swiftly I released my companions from bondage and broke the shackles of the poor Specians as well. Then I donned the overseer's clothes and made my way toward the top, behind me an entire gang of mindless slaves ready to follow any shouted command.

"My ploy worked well; the chain bosses, seeing my uniform, let me pass, and right up to the surface we marched. There things became more difficult. Druid guards spotted me at once; I ordered the slaves to run and a melee began. From everywhere came the guards, dashing hither and yon to round up their work gangs. But during the fray my companions and I slipped out toward the hills—the faraway steppes where fugitives have managed to hide and keep away from danger.

"For weeks we were hunted like animals; one night we were set upon by a large patrol. In the fight all of my companions were slain; I wrenched the blade from a fallen Druid, and like a savage I fought them off. With neither wit nor reason, I fled the scene with my life, scrambling for shelter in these very hills. So barren, so desolate, a place where safety is sometimes found but only at the expense of human contact.

"Few men can survive this place; when I came, some eighteen years ago, its only inhabitants were semicrazed nomads—wildmen you call them—plus the odd fugitive, hiding out in the canyons, eating nothing but weed to sustain him. A curious existence, to say the least. Half insane myself, I stumbled upon an old blind man and his daughter, who also had managed to escape bondage. The girl became my wife; this place our home. From time to time other nomads wandered by and stayed. I organized them as best I could, showed them that even soil such as this could be tilled to some extent, and tried to make the beginnings of a new civilization. Because of our isolation, we knew we were fairly safe from Druid intrusion. Even the fierce devilish birds called Death-Stalkers have never come upon us. And over the years we have developed as you see: a tiny village of sorts, living off our meager gardens and the few beasts that still roam these hills. Until yesterday," and here he smiled at Mariana, "this place had never been found. It was sheer chance that you strayed from your path and came upon our shrubs, a chance that could have cost you your lives had my orders to my men been to kill on sight rather than to take prisoners."

"I see," said Argyle, sadly reflecting on the harsh life his childhood friend had been forced to lead. "Then because we are all now some safe distance from the source of the poison, those here are barely affected."

"Something like that," agreed Thorhall. "Although as I said, the closer you trespass . . ."

Mariana frowned. It was this very source she and her band hoped to locate. "By what process or spell do these Druid magicians manage to spread the poison?" she asked.

Thorhall could provide no ready answer. "As I said, they scatter it in the sky. Probably from some very high place."

"The Devil's Tower?" asked the Prince looking up.

Thorhall stared at the bedraggled young man oddly. "Perhaps," he agreed. "What of it?"

"My good man," replied the Prince, "we are here for that very purpose. To rid Speca of its poisons—all its poisons."

Thorhall stared at him as though he were a madman. "But what are you saying? No power can defeat them! Many have tried, from the Specian kings of old down to my own foolish venture twenty years ago. There is nothing to be done. Nothing."

"My companions feel otherwise," said Argyle to his astounded friend. He put his hand to Thorhall's shoulder, saying simply, "Perhaps it's time for us to tell you our own story."

So the Prince began, sparing no detail, recounting the long series of adventures the band had encountered since leaving Kalimar.

"So you see," said Argyle when the Prince had finished, "we are not to be deterred. The information you can provide is of tremendous value. Any small detail might give us the very clues we are looking for."

Mariana leaned forward, a worried look furrowing her brows and the soft features of her face. "Is there anything else you can think of? Anything that might have been overlooked?"

Thorhall shrugged. "I can't think of a thing," he admitted. "But even if I knew more, what then? All right, so you will have the knowledge of how the poison is spread. Then what? What powers have you to destroy it? What magic of your own?"

Thorhall's cynicism was easy to understand; after all he

290

had been through, it did seem a hopeless task. But the Prince made the chieftain's eyes widen in wonder. Placing a hand inside his dirtied shirt he pulled out the glittering scimitar.

"We have no magic," he said. "But we do have this. Do you know what it is?"

Thorhall's breath swept from his chest. His eyes studied the dazzling scabbard, focusing at last on the tiny inscribed runes—the telltale engraver's mark of which there could be no doubt.

"The Blade of the Throne," he whispered.

Ramagar nodded severely. "The only one in the world. Blue Fire, my friend Thorhall. Blue Fire—our only advantage—and hope—in finding a way to defeat the enemy."

"It cannot be so!" gasped the chieftain.

Argyle looked him straight in the eye. "I have seen the blade burn myself," he said. "At the *Sklar*, where all men could bear witness. Both the blade and the man who carries it are authentic. The Prince of Speca has come to claim the throne that is rightfully his—and Aran has committed herself to help."

"You mean—?"

Ramagar nodded. "The *Sklar* has agreed; once we find the way to disperse the Darkness her ships will enter the Black Waters. Already her fleet masses and waits from the moment. Every *knaar*, every Clan, every sea warrior has made this promise."

"The evil of Speca spreads daily," added Mariana. "Soon the Darkness will reach Aran itself, and your fair land will also be overtaken. There is not much time left." She leaned in closer, forcing the hesitant chieftain to meet her gaze. "We must act now, Thorhall. Don't hold back on us. In the name of Rhyn and all those others whose memory you hold dear, avenge them if you can. Tell us everything you know and help us to save the North from the coming holocaust."

Thorhall could find no words; he lowered his head and shut his eyes, slowly rocking back and forth as he contemplated his course of action.

"But what if I help you and you fail?" he said at last. "Such a circumstance will hasten the Druids to sweep down upon my people." He glanced sadly at the two silent girls still standing at his sides. "My daughters will be captured—ravished and forced into a life of—"

"I know," said Argyle, trying to comfort his friend. "And you are right. Our failure will indeed cause the enemy to seek

291

your door, the door you so carefully sealed from the world. But think, old friend: this life you lead is daily fraught with danger. Sooner or later you will be found in any case. Death-Stalkers will one day spy you from the sky, and then . . ." His thoughts needed no conclusion.

"You cannot hope to hide away forever," reminded Mariana. "Your situation is little better than our own."

"But I cannot risk my daughters!" protested the chieftain. "They are all I have."

Mariana nodded with a woman's understanding. "If you love them as much as you claim," she told him, "then give them a chance to live, live freely as they were meant to. Let them know the meaning of sunlight. Let them gaze upon the stars . . ."

Thorhall glanced up toward the window, a sigh emphasizing his wistful expression. He thought upon the stars, those shining baubles he held so dear and had not seen for more than half a lifetime. How very much he missed them. But how very much everyone here in this hall missed them.

"If I could protect my family," he said after a time, "then I would do anything for you . . ."

"Perhaps there is a way." It was Ramagar who had spoken. He knelt beside Thorhall, placing a hand on the chieftain's shoulder. "We have a ship waiting for us. A Cenulamian merchant vessel hiding near the coves in the shallow waters of the coast. Just one signal from us, a beacon flashed three times, will bring our ship to the inlet."

"A ship!" rasped Thorhall, amazed. And hope, long extinguished, flickered anew in his face.

"I propose a bargain," Ramagar went on. "We give you our pledge that if you help us now, win or lose in our quest, that beacon will shine and Captain Osari will come. Your daughters can be waiting for him, whether any of us make it out of here alive or not. And be assured that Osari will find the way out of the Darkness the same way he guided us in. His ship will make for Aran with your daughters as passengers, and they will be safe. What do you say to that?"

Thorhall put his head in his hands. "If only it could be so!"

"It can be," Argyle assured him.

Thorhall searched all their faces. "Do I have your words on this matter?"

The Prince nodded gravely. "You do."

"And mine as well," added the lord of Aran.

292

Thorhall wet his lips and thought for a moment. Then he beckoned his lovely daughters to him and hugged each girl in turn. All three had tears in their eyes.

"I once made a promise to you both that freedom would come," he said. "And now it seems that my dream may have come true. Go now, both of you, and collect whatever belongings you must take. Then wait until we send for you, and follow any instructions that Ramagar gives."

The girls nodded meekly and kissed their father before they hurried from the hall.

"I will do all I can to help," Thorhall vowed when his daughters had gone.

"Then you *do* know more of this magic than you told?"

The chieftain looked at Mariana and nodded. "I fear I have not been completely honest. Further information can indeed be provided, although I was being truthful when I told you I didn't know of it personally."

"Speak plainly, man," growled the Prince with impatience. "If you can't help us, who can?"

Thorhall smiled. "Remember that I spoke of a blind man whose daughter I married?"

Everyone nodded.

"Well, that man, my wife's father, yet lives. Once he was a servant within the unholy citadel itself. He has seen these magicians, even been forced to aid them in their spells. He knows more of the Druids than any man in Speca. His masters burned his eyes out for his knowledge; they would have killed him had his daughter not stolen from the brothels and found a way for them to escape . . ."

Mariana's heart was racing. "We must speak with him at once!"

"And so you shall," promised Thorhall. "But bear in mind that the man is very old. He has seen many horrors and they have sometimes deranged his mind. Often he speaks in riddles . . ."

"Then we will decipher them," said the Prince flatly. "Be quick, Thorhall. Time is short; we must be on our way."

The chieftain of the wildmen clapped his hands and commanded the guards to bring Old Man at once. A long minute later a bent and shriveled shell of a man shuffled slowly into the hall. His face was wrinkled and sagged; he held tightly onto a walking stick, tapping it gently a pace or two before him, and made his way to the semicircle of stone seats. Then

293

sensing the presence of many, he stopped in his place, empty
sockets directed at the leader of the clan.

"Good tidings to you, Old Man," said Thorhall with reverence. "Did you sleep well?"

Old Man cracked a slight smile. "My dreams were of yesterday," he replied enigmatically. "Or of tomorrows yet to
come."

"There are strangers in the Hall, Old Man. Friends from
Aran and the East who have come to save our land. They
wish to speak to you, ask you many questions of your young-
er days . . ."

The man nodded. "I am ready for their questions. They
may ask what they will."

Then, refusing the offer of a seat, he leaned heavily on his
cane and waited in silence.

The Prince was the first to speak, and Old Man turned his
sightless gaze in his direction.

"How do the Druids keep the people of Speca in subjuga-
tion?" the Prince asked.

"By the Stones," came the reply without hesitation. "By the
Seeds of Destruction that are tossed to the winds and blown
from the hills. By this do my people wither and die. By this
are they robbed of minds and wills both."

"What are these Stones?" asked Mariana. "These Seeds of
Destruction you speak of?"

The elderly Specian sucked in his breath and shivered. "A
ghastly potion are they, a magician's concoction harmless
against the Druids, but deadly to all others. From evil is it
spawned, spreading further evil upon evil and closing in the
Darkness."

Mariana glanced at the Prince. "What do you mean?" she
asked.

"From the sky!" cried Old Man. "The Seeds and the sky
are one!"

Ramagar scratched at his chin. Obviously Old Man was
telling them of some connection between the Eternal Dark
and the poison, but what that connection was he could not
understand.

"From where are these Seeds scattered?" asked the Prince.

Old Man lifted his face skyward. "From the highest of the
highest. From the very pinnacle of stone that rests within the
clouds."

Mariana beat a fist into an open palm. "The Devil's

294

Tower!" she cried. "It must be! The highest edifice of the land—where stone walls reach up inside the mists!"

"Aye," wheezed Old Man. And his face tightened with fear and contempt as he continued. "High, high among the clouds, where the winds howl and the world freezes. Up from the labyrinth, winding through the tunnel across the devilish shrines and altars, up the Thirty Thousand Steps until the zenith is reached. From there, aye, from there, do the black-hearted men of magic, these unholy wizards, spawn their brew and their vileness. Up, up in the Tower, up, up, where no man can go, where no man can bear the agony, where no man can see all this and live . . ."

"Yet you have seen these things," reminded the girl. "And you still survive."

Old Man hung his head. "Survive? Do I? Do I yet live? If this be life, then surely death is to be preferred. Like thieves in the night did they steal my mind, like scavengers did they rob me of all I had, like grim vultures did they pluck my eyes from their sockets and render me useless before all those who knew and loved me. Nay, girl, this is not life. My mind knows no peace, no rest. My dreams haunt me with memories I cannot dare to speak of. Eternal damnation is my fate, to have seen what I have seen, to have witnessed the unspeakable and never be able to wipe it from memory." His entire body sagged; he pressed his weight so heavily against his cane that it seemed he would topple over. "Doom is waiting, doom is waiting. Would that I had eyes so that I might cry!"

"All the world sheds tears in your place," said the Prince. "But harden your heart and regain your resolve, for we, Old Man, have come to battle these forces. Speca shall be freed!"

Old Man sighed deeply, his ears hearing these bold promises but his heart too broken to have any faith. Again he fell silent, waiting for the next question to be posed.

Mariana turned to her companions. "If the Druids must continually seed the clouds," she said, "then the effects of the poison must be short-lasting. What we must do is find something certain to counteract these effects . . ."

"Easily said," grumbled the haj, crossing his legs and drumming his fingers on the stone. "But how?"

The dancing girl chewed at her lip, then to Thorhall's father-in-law she said, "The antidote, Old Man! Do you know of one?"

"The world can gather a thousand alchemists and still there

would be no solution. The poison cannot be stopped. How can one hope to defeat the epitome of Evil?"

"With the epitome of Good." It was the Prince who had spoken.

Old Man turned to him sharply. "Have you such a thing?"

"Only this." And he placed the golden scimitar in the old man's hand, waiting as the sightless philosopher ran his fingers over the engraver's mark.

"Will Blue Fire dispel the magic?" asked Mariana breathlessly. "Can the blade's flame defeat the Seeds spawned in the Black Sky?"

"The forces of Good against the forces of Evil," contemplated Old Man. "I cannot say. But this I am sure of: the Druids fear Blue Fire as nothing else. For centuries they have toiled to duplicate it . . ."

"So we have been told," said Ramagar. "But its powers must not be wasted. Tell us what we must do, Old Man. Tell us how to use our weapon against theirs."

Silver hair tumbled across his shoulders as the philosopher bent his head and pondered. The thief fidgeted uncomfortably while they waited for the answer. It was not long in coming.

"On the first day of the full moon, Moon Time, the magicians in holy procession carry the Seeds for the new month into the clouds. To the Devil's Tower your blade must be brought. The Thirty Thousand Steps must be climbed—but in secret, lest you be caught—and then, while aflame, the dagger must be hurled from the zenith into the Eternal Dark itself . . ."

"Throw away the dagger?" gasped Oro, who had listened in disbelief.

Old Man nodded darkly. "It is the only way. The Blue Flame must then battle on its own against the very Blackness and the poisons within. And a terrible battle it shall be; the world itself shall seem to go mad. But if Blue Fire succeeds, and I fear the chances are slight after so many centuries, then the cloud will swirl and shatter, the light of the sun shall pour across Speca, and the Druids will be devoid of their powers . . ."

"As I suspected," sighed the Prince. "The clouds themselves hold the key."

"Aye. And the Evil will consume the Good. Blue Fire will be lost to mankind forever. Yet if we are fortunate, so shall Good destroy Evil. The Specian people shall awake from

296

heir trances and overthrow their tyrannical masters. The cimitar shall be lost, but the North shall be saved."

"But we cannot destroy the blade!" cried Oro frantically.

"You are a fool," snapped the Prince. "The safety of the world is at stake and must be preserved. It grieves me to hink that the scepter of my fathers should be consumed—yet o save my land, to save the North, there is no price I would ot pay."

"Then to this Devil's Tower we must hasten," said the haj. By the calendar, if my calculations are correct, Moon Time omes in three days."

The Prince pounded a fist. "Can the Tower be reached in o short a period?" he asked.

Old Man looked at him worriedly. "Only if your travel is nhampered. You will have to walk the Valley of Morose, he place where Death-Stalkers nest, where the birds of prey cour the skies and keep careful watch over the road to the itadel."

"We are armed," reminded Argyle.

A grim laugh sifted from between the philosopher's racked lips. "Axes and swords do not frighten Death-Stalkrs. If you are set upon, many of you will not live to reach he Tower."

The group of adventurers exchanged sour expressions. Ramagar took Mariana's hand and held it tightly. "We have o choice," he said quietly. "We'll have to take our chances nd do the best we can."

"No more than that can be asked," replied Old Man in vise observance.

Argyle turned to his friend Thorhall. "Your aid has been f great value to us," he said. "And our part of the bargain hall be kept. But there is one last favor we would ask before ve depart on our journey."

Thorhall nodded. "Ask anything. It shall be granted."

Argyle smiled. "We need you to lead us into the Valley of Morose."

20

Several leagues past Thorhall's village and the defile, at the very foot of the hideous Black Forest where only the ghost of the dead can be heard, the band came to the heinous Valley of Morose.

High atop a craggy hillock the adventurers stood, their cloaks tossing wildly amid the vicious winds that screamed around them. Wordlessly they looked across, hardly aware of the open plain to the south and its meandering riverbeds long since turned to stone and chalky powders.

The Valley of Morose seemed to be the eye of a tempest of bedrock. At either side, bleak walls of gray swept up toward the sky a thousand meters and more, looming over their heads like malevolent breakers ready to come crashing down at any moment. Mist, white as soft clouds, shredded eerily among the fingers of slate and rock, silently rising from the bogs below to greet the dim brightness of Specian day. In parts the valley showed hints of the palest green, places where weed and tussock poked from between cracks in gravel and caked soils. Overall, though, it was easy to understand why the place had been named Morose; grimly the valley maintained its dulled brown sameness, a monotonous stretch of grisly marsh and bogs and fog punctuated occasionally by the remains of decayed bones—bones of unknown creatures who had dared to chance a crossing and who now rotted along the ruts and ridges.

Thorhall sighed at the sight, shaking his head. "Once this valley had been a refuge for forest life," he commented sadly. "They say that herds of caribou and elk roamed these hills by the thousands . . ."

"And mighty redwoods grew as tall as the mountains," added the Prince, recalling his father's teachings. "There were brooks, and fields of sweet grass. Birds sang in the morning and a traveler could spy the smoke rising from farm chimneys and be sure of a welcome breakfast."

Ramagar put his arm around his friend's shoulder and smiled wistfully. "It will be so again," he promised. "The soil will be fertile as before, and there will be flowers, wildflowers in abundance."

298

Wishing it could be, the Prince hung his head and nodded. It would take a lifetime to recreate what had been lost, to renew the barren wastes that covered the land from shore to shore.

A cruel wind whipped savagely down from the mountains and across the shadowy cliffs as they prepared to enter the valley.

"Best we should not stay put in one place for too long," Thorhall told them all. "A sitting target is easy prey for Death-Stalkers."

And the stranded Aranian led them on, among the great tapering rocks, until they came upon a hard path of packed dirt. The twists of the path were reasonably clear, but at each side the clinging white mist thickened.

"This trail remains for some way," Thorhall said. "With any luck we can stay on it all day and perhaps come within sight of the Devil's Tower itself."

Mariana rubbed at her arms, feeling the chill quicken to her weary bones. Treading carefully over sharp pebbles, she glanced nervously at both sides of the trail. She knew that if any one of them happened to step more than a few meters off the road, they would quickly be lost from sight in the mist. With a shiver she turned her gaze ahead, thankful that Ramagar and the haj were both close by. Otherwise, she would probably have taken Thorhall's advice and turned back long before.

After hiking for a while they began to gain altitude. The narrow path was winding its way higher on an increasingly steep incline. For the first time, the travelers were able to look far past the mists, and they could see that the climb was leading them along the valley's edge toward the reaches of the cliffs and ridges—a happenstance, they were soon to realize, not without importance.

It was while they crossed over an extremely treacherous edge of cracked shale set along a craggy peak that the haj, blinking as he stopped dead in his tracks, mumbled aloud in disbelief. "Dungeons of the Caliph! Look at that!"

Mariana spun and stared. Nestled at the edge of the gray chalk cliff stood a nest, carefully woven, made of weed and moss and broken bits of branch. Half buried among various niches, well concealed from the bite of the wind, were two unhatched eggs beneath the lip of moss. They were brownish-yellow in color, each as big as an oversized melon.

299

The haj reached out his hand to inspect. "Don't touch them!" warned Thorhall with a grimace.

Burlu adroitly pulled back his hand. "Why? What's the matter?"

"These are nestlings. Hideous offspring of our enemy, the Death-Stalkers . . ."

Ramagar ran his fingertips over the hilt of his dagger. "These are bird eggs?" he asked incredulously. "Look at the size of them!"

The nearer of the two eggs suddenly showed a crack. Mariana put a hand to her mouth, and her eyes widened in wonder. First came a scraping and then a crunching, and before any of them knew it, a piece of shell had been tossed aside and a long, hawk-like black beak protruded from the opening.

"It's hatching!" cried Oro.

The Prince pushed the staring hunchback aside and stepped in closer to examine. At first glance the bird seemed much like a vulture or any other carrion, what with its long thin neck and dark, intense beaded eyes. The nestling pushed its beak toward the sky and rolled its infant eyes until they came to rest on the agog strangers. Colorless and bald, it tilted its misshapen head and peered curiously.

The Prince moved in closer; instinctively the nestling drew back. Powerfully the carrion hunched its body and rose up splitting more chunks of shell and scattering them to the wind. Then it howled its high-pitched wail, a shrill cry for its mother.

"We'd better move away from here quickly," urged Thorhall, already looking skyward for sight of its parent Death-Stalker.

Argyle also scanned the clouded heavens. "You mean you want us to let this . . . this . . . monster live?"

"It can't harm us; not yet, anyway—"

But Thorhall's words went unheeded. Before anyone could move fast enough to stop him, the lord of Aran lifted his mighty ax with both hands, swung it above his head, and heaved again and again. The fragile shell smashed into a thousand bits. The dying bird screamed an awful scream, so ghastly that Mariana was sure it was the worst sound she had ever heard.

His tunic and cloak both splattered with dark blood, Argyle commenced to smash the yet unbroken egg. As the a

300

...ll, a slimy yellow liquid oozed from within the rupture, ringing with it a foul and putrid smell.

Sickened, everyone looked away while Argyle cleaned his weapon on the rocks and moved away from the deepening pool of blood and mucus. "At least those two won't fly these dreaded skies," he commented sourly.

Thorhall shook his head. "Perhaps not, but their mother will. And she'll be looking for the slayer of her young."

Argyle scoffed. "Be this bird devil or no, let her come." He lifted his ax again. "I am prepared . . ."

A distant cry caused Mariana to raise her head sharply. A shapeless dark form suddenly appeared from behind the swirling clouds, moving across the sky with lightning speed. As yet it showed no form, but one fact was singularly apparent: the gliding bird was huge, its wingspan as long as a horse. And the carrion was shrieking at the top of its lungs in an inane, witless moan of grief.

"Quick!" shouted Ramagar, yanking Mariana by the arm and pulling her off her feet. "Get to the bluffs! It's attacking!"

Helter-skelter the small band dashed, bounding for cover among the grainy and broken ridges that slanted along the side of the cliff. The bird was coming head-on, blazing fury in her red slotted eyes. Her nest ravished, her unborn dead, she sought no reason to her anger, only the heat of unleashed rage seeking retribution.

Huge, gleaming talons spread malevolently as the great bird began her rapid descent. Peering down at the heights and her shattered nest, she caught sight of the scampering adventurers and with a terrific wail came charging upon them.

Mariana screamed as talons *whooshed* inches from her scalp; the dancing girl rolled over barely in time, gazing straight into the hideous face as the bird spread her black feathers and darted up to the sky.

Eyes burning with frenzy, the soaring Death-Stalker closed in again. On one knee, Argyle swung his ax; tattered feathers danced before his anguished eyes while the bird squawked and glided up, unharmed. Then down again she was flying, flapping wildly and crying, beak parted to emit her deathly screech.

Thorhall leaped to his feet, brandishing his spear in a desperate attempt to parry the thrust of the talons. As the bird circled and dived, his heart began to pound in further agitation. The calls of the mother had not been lost on empty air;

301

fanned by the gusty winds, her wail had carried the length and breadth of the valley, and now, from every point in th dark sky came more of the menacing carrion. Perhaps dozen more in all, each as fearsome, each as frenzied.

Ramagar's twin-edged dagger slashed wildly as the host o Death-Stalkers tore at his body; the haj reeled with the stin of claws slashing along the side of his throat. Marian screamed as young Homer drew back against a boulder an with both hands flaying vainly tried to ward off the terribl blows.

A piercing cry filled the air; Mariana saw one of the car rion twist in a tizzy as Argyle's ax broadsided the beast an severed a wing from its haunch. The bird twisted an moaned, blood spouting like an evil fountain, then it smashe against a crevice and plummeted to its death in the bogs be low.

The Prince swung his blade with all his might; the ne mother yanked back her head, but not in time. The slash wa deep, running down from her throat to her plumed breas For an instant the mighty bird wavered, then forward sh toppled, clawing and scratching as life ebbed out of her. Th Prince spun and fended off the blows, then again Blue Fir struck, deep, deep into her black heart. And there, pinne against the edge of the ridge, the carrion mother gasped fc breath and futilely tried to lift her wings once more to fly.

Her demise cheered the hearts of the adventurers, yet th fight was far from its conclusion. More birds had entered th fray, some even larger than those yet encountered. Rank k rank they swooped in unison, well trained by their Drui masters, and intent on slaughtering the invaders of the lands.

The haj's knife hacked and slashed and cut and stabbe while three carrion tore at his robe, ripping the garment shreds. When Argyle had finished with his latest victim I made a mad dash to the Easterner's side, and together the managed to draw themselves back until the overhanging ledg gave protection from the scraping claws.

Overhead the sky had begun to rumble. Flashes of terrif ing lightning filled the heavens with unholy light. Ramaga panting to catch his breath, looked up and shuddered. Fa far away, he could see another scourge coming this way: low black mass, an uncountable number of Death-Stalkers overwhelming, unstoppable force.

302

And the harsh rain began to fall, slanting sharply and painfully in the angry wind.

"Away from the heights!" cried Thorhall in desperation. He made a quick, lurching motion to lead the way back down. But in midstride he staggered as a vicious carrion cackled and swept in low, screeching horribly. Thorhall swung around but the blow of the weighty bird toppled him completely.

Like hell's fire itself three more hideous Death-Stalkers were upon him. Thorhall tossed about in a frenzy, bellowing as he struggled to regain his feet. Bloodied hands covered a bloodied face, and the birds closed in to tear at his flesh.

Argyle and Ramagar raced from the others, wielding their weapons. Carrion hovered every inch of the way. Thorhall, barely conscious, started to crawl as best he could to reach his rescuers. Slashing claws cut through air to keep the newcomers at bay, but Argyle, nearly crazed at the sight of his wounded friend, stood boldly before them, swinging his weapon, whistling it above his head with such force and fury that the carrion had to retreat.

Ramagar deftly took hold of the injured Aranian amid the thunder of Argyle's war cries and the exultant song of the birds who spread their wings toward the sky with small shreads of Thorhall's flesh hanging from their mouths.

It took a very long time before everyone made it under the lip of an overhanging ledge. There, Mariana threw herself into Ramagar's arms, sobbing and not able to look down at the writhing body of their latest companion. The haj kneeled beside Thorhall and examined his wounds. Then with a dour face, he said, "He's been badly gored, and lost too much blood. But if we can get him to safety—"

"He'll live?" asked Argyle.

Burlu nodded hesitantly.

Silently they all stood beneath the ledge's lip, staring again at the massing horde and pondering their fate. Bruised and injured as they were, they knew that as long as they stayed away from the open, they would be safe from immediate attack.

"Scavengers!" cried Argyle, shaking his hairy fist. It was only the strong grip of the thief that stopped the lord of Aran from bolting into the open and challenging the birds to come down and fight.

Above, the winged enemy had begun a grisly dance; their appetites partially sated by the battle, they seemed for the

moment to be content to bide their time and watch the whi
their prey contemplated the next move.

Thunder was crashing everywhere in terrible volume, a
the wind's howl sounded more and more like a laugh, a cru
and vengeful laugh, as it roared its way from one end of tl
valley to the other.

"What do we do now?" groaned Oro, lips quivering as l
huddled close to the ledge wall for shelter.

The Prince glanced down at Thorhall and sighed. "O
friend was right about one thing," he said glumly. "We wo
stand much of a chance while still on these damned heights
He wiped rainwater from his brow and grimaced at the ci
cling carrion.

"A wise observation," said the haj grumpily as he tended
cut on his leg. "But what are we to do about it? Surely Tho
hall proved we'll never be able to make our way back dow
We dare not even try." Thorhall whined softly in his pa
and Burlu shuddered.

Hands on hips, Ramagar sighed. The haj was absolute
right, he saw, peering down from the ledge to the tricky op
path they had climbed. Even contemplating trying to rea
the dubious safety of the bogs was foolish. Yet staying pı
here in the middle of the Death-Stalkers' nesting lands, w
even more fraught with danger. Only the Fates themselv
knew how many other horrid carrion might soon be comi
to join their cackling comrades. It was a sad predicamer
leaving at best only one possible choice.

"We'll have to go forward," said Ramagar with determin
tion.

Oro looked up, aghast. "What? Go forward, you say? Yc
expect us to climb over these cliffs in rain like this? Wi
those, those *beasts* waiting for us?"

The Prince beat a fist against his thigh. His sharp ey
quickly scanned the local terrain. "It doesn't look to me li
we'd have a chance," he said at length.

A sly smile cracked Ramagar's lips. "Ah, but you may l
wrong. Look again, my friends; note the formations of tl
ridges and ledges. If we could cling close to the walls, stay
all times beneath overhanging bluffs, we'll be given excelle
protection. Our carrion friends won't be able to swoc
directly down on top of us—they'll be forced to dive in lov
swoop up from the defiles, attack only from the front . . ."

"So?"

"So that means they can only try and get at us one at

304

time, two at best. And with the wind against them to boot. If we can only hold them off until the hills descend again, we can make it all the way."

"We'll have to jump some pretty wide chasms," mumbled the haj.

Ramagar and Homer exchanged bemused glances and smiled. "In the Jandari jumping roofs is not much easier," observed Homer. "We can do it with no trouble."

"Perhaps you can," conceded the haj, rubbing his chin. "But what about the rest of us?"

"Using rope," said the thief with a wink. "Homer will jump first, lash our line on the other side. Those who can't make the leap can ford the chasms hand over hand, one at a time . . ."

"Sounds like a tricky exploit," said Argyle.

"But the only chance of escape open to us. Now what do you say?"

The Prince wiped his face and shook off excess water with a flip of his hand. "It's not exactly the way we planned, but . . ." He looked at the thief and grinned. "Lead on, Ramagar. The sooner we get away from here, the better."

The haj and Homer helped Thorhall to stand. Mariana had been busily dressing his wounds, and with the bleeding now stopped, the Aranian was slowly coming back to his senses.

Argyle stoutly lifted his ax and stood side by side with Ramagar. "We'll go first together," he grunted.

Then both men took a few cautious steps out from the overhanging ledge and stood with held breath. A carrion spied them immediately and sailed in low. Mighty Argyle tilted his weapon and raised it high; the blade still dripped with blood, and at first sight of the cumbersome ax the carrion flapped its black-feathered wings and darted upward in a beeline.

Argyle laughed. Then he and Ramagar began to slink carefully, measuring their footing on the slippery wet stones, until they had covered the distance from the open space and reached the shelter of the overhanging ledge on the higher landing.

"Come on!" cried the thief, beckoning frantically, and one by one everyone stealthily crossed, under the watchful eyes of wary Death-Stalkers.

It took nearly an hour for them to inch their way along the new ledge. Pelting rain made it almost impossible to see anything; the incessant cackle of the carrion and the mocking wind reverberated in their ears. Still, they were making progress, away from the crest where Thorhall had fallen, and up along the only route leading to their destination.

Mariana sucked in air and held it as the first in a series of crevices was reached. Ramagar knelt down and with narrowed eyes expertly examined the length of the jump, taking special note not to peer below into the chasm, where a fall of a hundred meters led to a pile of jagged rock.

Homer nodded as the thief signaled, and then Ramagar leaped, stumbling to the other side. "Not so bad," he called back, hands cupped over his mouth. "We should all make it without the line."

Argyle swallowed hard and pushed his body forward; for a man his size the jump proved to be little more than a stride. For Oro, though, it was a very different matter. The hunchback stepped a few paces backward, closed his eyes, and charged forward with all his speed. His spindly legs knocked together as he tumbled across and shook as he landed roughly on his knees. Mariana shut her eyes; then she, too, made the leap, eager to reach the thief's waiting arms. Thorhall clung fiercely to the haj's back, and together the two of them crossed the chasm with surprising ease. Homer watched as the Prince jumped, then he himself danced gleefully across, thinking this leap a piece of pie compared to many he had been forced to make back home.

Above, the carrion were watching still. Darting this way and that, several times they had almost dived to the chasm. None had missed a single step the adventurers had taken, and now they formed as eager as ever waiting for the first, inevitable mistake.

Below them, the intrepid band pressed onward, protected by the bluff above. As they trod, an occasional carrion zoomed in close by, but as before, the sight of Argyle and his menacing ax deterred any sneak attack.

Thunderclouds scudded directly above; the deluge became awesome. All along the heights lightning rippled, crashing into peaks and cliffs and shattering rock into powder. Frequently, the roll of the thunder itself proved devastating enough to make the ledges quiver. Here and there, chunks of slate and chalk actually did slide, and Mariana could only gulp with fear when the tumbling rock smashed below.

"It can't be very much farther until the descent begins," said Argyle.

"Let's hope it's soon," rejoined the haj, putting a hand to

306

Thorhall's brow while the injured man leaned heavily against him. "He's burning up with fever."

Ramagar searched the skies and slowly cast his gaze to the peak ahead. It was a craggy bluff, filled with dangerous shale and loosened boulders. The way over it was precarious, the ledges narrow and badly spaced. It would be the most difficult climb yet, and at the end of it, he could see another chasm, this one at least three times the length of the last.

". . . Cave . . . Cave . . ." mumbled Thorhall in his delirium.

"What's that you say?" asked the haj. But the Aranian had passed out again, and Burlu was forced to slap him to revive him. Thorhall rolled his eyes briefly, trying his best to focus on the intent faces around him, and straining to get the words from his lips. But again he fell into his stupor before having given his thought.

"What do you suppose he's been trying to tell us?" said Mariana as the haj let the limp body down and pulled a face. Shrugging, he replied, "I think it was something about caves—"

"Caves?" repeated Ramagar. And the thief looked about inquisitively. "Maybe there's one near here. A shelter . . ."

"Or a hidden shaft to take us down off the heights," added Argyle. "Remember, Thorhall's been a fugitive for almost half a lifetime. He must have learned the secrets of this valley very well just to have led us as far as he did."

The Prince shaded his eyes from the rain and strained his neck away from the ledge to get a better glimpse of the next peak. He stared for a long moment and then nudged the thief in the ribs. "What do you make of that?" he asked.

"What?"

"There. Can you see it?"

Ramagar focused on the craggy bluffs, cursing under his breath as the wind drove the rain more harshly against his flesh. His glance swept from rim to rim, studying the angular formations and observing the many shadowed crevices leading on an upward spiral. But then something caught his attention. Up from the ridge, set away beyond a pinnacle of jagged rock shaped curiously like the head of a demon, he could see a dark hole in the side of the mountain, a grotto of some kind beside the natural rampart.

"That must be it," whispered the thief. Argyle nodded solemnly, and with his ax tightly clenched led the way, his powerful form so well sheathed in its envelope of sinewy flesh

307

and muscle that he might have seemed a deity himself as he boldly strode toward the open.

Everyone else huddled closely together as lightning crashed. A huge carrion suddenly descended, its silhouette flashing before them. The adventurers recoiled in fear as the bird wildly flapped its black-feathered wings and projected its talons. A shudder shook Mariana's soul; Argyle's blade glinted in the instant of light, and she heard the monstrous bird wail as its vitals were ripped by the cut. And then the lightning struck again, this time smashing with heavenly fury against the very ledge on which they stood.

Screams, terrible screams, filled the air. Mariana reeled and tumbled, her eyes catching fleeting glimpses of flying rock and diving carrion obliterating the sky above her. She was rolling now, rolling and clumsily banging into stone and boulders, sliding downward endlessly into a dark abyss. A dozen times she cried out her lover's name, a dozen times to be drowned out by the terrific claps of thunder and the shrieking of unholy birds.

The world was spinning madly, the wind pounding, and the rain curdling. And suddenly she had stopped, bruised and pain-wracked as she hit forcefully against an unknown object. Her eyelids were too heavy to keep open; slowly soft black lashes closed on her cheeks and all consciousness was lost. It was the end, she knew. The sudden and brutal end that had been somehow always expected.

21

The rain had stopped. That was all Ramagar was aware of as he came around, that and the awful ache in his injured shoulder. Gradually he lifted himself to his knees and put his hands to his head. The dizziness eased, and he was able to remember who and where he was. But what had happened took a good deal longer to reconstruct.

The ledge was still there, at least most of it. Enormous chunks both before and behind gave grim evidence of the charge of electricity that had struck. Staring expressionlessly, he looked to the sky. The birds were gone. Great swirling clouds hung above his head, and he knew that day was past. This was the middle of Specian night.

A gurgling groan caught his attention. Peering to the edge of the cliff, he saw the haj. Burlu had been tossed to the very precipice of a lightning-caused chasm, and even as he groaned one arm and one leg were dangling limply over the side. Ramagar cleared his thoughts and pulled him to safety.

"What . . . what happened?" wheezed the haj.

The thief shook his head. "I don't . . . I don't know—"

The haj propped himself on his elbow and grabbed Ramagar by the collar. "The girl, man!" he panted. "Where's Mariana? Is she safe?"

Ramagar gulped, his heart beating wildly. He jumped to his feet and frantically looked about. It was then that he caught sight of Homer and Argyle lying sprawled and gasping for air, and Thorhall prostrate and unconscious. But of Mariana or the Prince there was no sign at all.

Burlu put his hands to his face and wailed. "She's gone!" And he peered down into the dark abyss, his mind flooding with the image of Mariana lying smashed and lifeless somewhere upon the rocks below.

Ramagar crumpled to his knees in disbelief. "Maybe she's still here somewhere," he said, clinging to hope against all reason.

The haj sadly shook his head. "Where? Where could she be?" And he glanced back and forth across the ledge. It was then that Argyle roused from his own blows. He managed to stand, and groggily made his way toward his two distraught companions.

"The lightning," he mumbled, fingertips to his temples. "It must have hit directly above us and scared the carrion off—"

"Aye," agreed the haj. "And more than that, my friend." He moved away from the others and picked up a piece of dark cloth, squeezing it in his hand and putting it against his breast. That it had belonged to Mariana there was no doubt.

"She's gone," the haj whispered. "She and the Prince, both. Oro as well. When the ledge gave way they must have fallen." He gestured to the chasm and the littered path downward. "And I fear we'll never find any of them—"

"You can't be sure!" snapped Ramagar. "Maybe they didn't all die. Maybe they're only injured, and waiting for us to find them . . ."

Argyle sighed. "We must look and be certain," he agreed.

"I'll not leave this damned valley until I am!" Ramagar bellowed. "I'll seek a lifetime, if need be. I'll spend my

309

days searching until one way or another we find her. I don't care if we never——"

Argyle put his arm around the troubled thief and nodded with emotion. "We will find them, friend," he said. "And I give my word not to stop trying. We owe them both at least that much."

The haj stirred, bitterly glancing around at the grotesque scape. "The Druids will pay for this," he promised in deep anger. "Woe be unto those responsible for her untimely death. Though I shall certainly die in the effort, I vow to find this Druid king and single-handedly squeeze the life out of him." He clutched harder at the torn shred of cloth. "My granddaughter's blood is on his hands—and I shan't rest until I have avenged her death."

A cupped hand poured droplets of sweet water between her open lips. Mariana coughed, then swallowed. Her eyes forced themselves open and she waited long moments for some recognition to come.

"Are you all right?" It was a soft and soothing voice. The Prince's voice.

Unable to talk, she nodded. She drew a long breath and dispelled foggy images playing at the edges of her mind. Clearing her throat, she whispered, "Where are we? What happened?"

"We fell," replied the Prince. "But we were very fortunate. We seem to have tumbled back down the way we came. It could have been worse; we might have been thrown off into the chasms."

A simple turn of the head assured her that he was right. On either side were the bogs, just as before they attained the heights. Only now, they were not on the path; indeed they must be far from it, for the white mist swirled about them everywhere. And suddenly Mariana felt very frightened. "Where are the others?" she gasped.

The Prince put a gentle hand to her brow. "Back up there," he replied. "Where we left them. Safe and sound, I'm sure."

A small laugh from behind broke into the conversation. Oro stepped from the fog, a hand rubbing at the bruises on his crooked shoulder. "You really expect to find them alive?" he said caustically, his brow furrowing in a sharp downward slant. "Have you forgotten those birds, eh? Likely as not the

310

carrion have whisked everyone away and into the hands of the Druids."

"I won't believe it!" cried the girl.

Oro snickered. "Oh, no?"

Ignoring the irritating hunchback, the Prince tried to smile. "Don't listen to him, Mariana. He's only trying to confuse you while he plans a way to wrestle the dagger from me. Ramagar's as safe as we are, I promise. They're all safe, and probably looking for us at this very moment."

The dancing girl sat up. "Maybe we can find them first," she said hopefully. "Maybe we can meet them on the heights—"

The Prince frowned. "Perhaps," he sighed. "But . . ."

Something was bothering him, she saw, something that suddenly made her feel very cold and alone, as if her companion were a stranger again and no longer a friend. "What's the matter?" she asked, shaken, forcing his reluctant eyes to meet her own.

The Prince took her hand and held it firmly. "Listen to me, Mariana," he said. "For now, at least for a while, we have to forget about the others . . ."

Mariana was aghast. "*Forget?* What are you talking about?"

The Prince leaned in closer and lowered his voice to a harsh whisper. "By my reckoning there are only two days left until Moon Time. Two days until the wizards will have to seed the clouds for another month. We can't allow that ritual to take place. We have to stop it, and stop it now. Free Speca while there's time. Our allies are waiting, but they won't hold still much longer. Aran's ships can't be asked to wait another month. There is too much danger."

Mariana drew back. "What are you *saying?*" she gasped. "You mean we should abandon them? Leave them on their own, to die?"

The Prince bit tensely at his lip, struggling to find a way to make the girl understand the gravity of the situation facing them.

"It's not that I want to," he insisted. "Rather that we have no other choice. We *must* press on at all costs. We must reach the Devil's Tower and put an end to these insidious deeds. Won't you understand that, Mariana? Won't you listen and see that too much is at stake?"

She shook her head, tears coming to her eyes. She could picture Ramagar and the haj at this very moment, in a frenzy

311

with worry, doing anything, risking anything, to find her. They would be easy prey for the Death-Stalkers and the cohorts of Druid troops searching for them high and low.

"Two days, Mariana," repeated the Prince. "That's all the time we need. Then, we can come back . . ."

She sniffed, childlike eyes wide and sad. "By then it may be too late."

The Prince nodded darkly. "Perhaps. But think of this poor, wretched land. Think of how long she has suffered. And think of the North—how long will even Aran remain free while the Darkness spreads across the sky? We must not fail . . ."

Although her heart was breaking, she had to acknowledge that everything the Prince had said was true. "What . . . what do we have to do?" she asked at last.

"Continue on. East. Try and stay to the lower grounds, if we can. And find our destination before it's too late."

Oro cackled; he rubbed his hands together one over the other. "And how long do you think we'd last, eh? Have you a map to show us the way? Or fast horses to carry us there?"

"We'll find the way," replied the Prince with defiance. He stood, holding out a hand for the girl to come by his side. Forgetting her sorrows and pains, Mariana drew on her courage and wiped away her tears. "All right," she said. "I gave my word long ago, and I won't break it now."

The Prince smiled.

"Fools!" barked Oro, standing before them and glaring. "Look about you. Just how long do you think you'll last, eh? It's hopeless, I tell you. Hopeless. Take my advice and give up. Maybe we can work our way back toward the coast, give Osari the signal, and at least get out of here with our lives."

The dancing girl glowered at him. "You go back," she hissed. "Save your skin if that's what you want. As for me—"

Oro's jaw hung. "You mean you're actually going on? Listening to this, this . . ." He gazed in astonishment at them both. "Bah. You're both mad! And you'll pay the price for it!"

The hunchback continued to rant as the two companions stepped away from him and wandered off into the fog. Oro's face beaded with sweat from fear at being left alone, but no one paid any attention.

"You'll be sorry!" Mariana heard him call, his voice already sounding dim and distant as they marched deeper into the mists. "And you'll rue the day you didn't listen to me!"

312

Mariana said nothing, and was not surprised after a short while to hear shuffling footsteps behind. Without bothering to turn around she knew it was Oro, his cowardly mind changed, now racing to catch up with them before it was too late.

VI

The Devil's Tower

22

Hallooo!" called Ramagar, his hands cupped tightly around
his mouth as he stood mired in ankle-deep muck.

From the distance he could hear his echo reverberate off
the mountain walls.

"Mariana! Can you hear me?" came the haj's furtive cry.
Again and again the swineherd called, while the band stopped
and waited for a reply. Nothing. Nothing at all, save for the
dull, mournful moan of wind through the swirling mist.

"Let's keep going," said Argyle doggedly. He flung his tattered cloak over his shoulders and stiffened his resolve. They
were almost at the end of the line, he knew, having searched
for their missing companions all the way down from the
heights, negotiating the tricky path back to the bottom, and
once this morning, tramping right through the damnable fog
that seemed never to go away.

To make matters worse, they had no way of knowing that
their chosen course through the bogs was the right one; everything so far only led to the conclusion that it was not.

Ramagar wiped his sweaty brow with his sleeve and
clenched his teeth. The mist engulfing them was so overwhelming that, should Mariana and the Prince indeed be
alive somewhere close by, finding them was a million-to-one
chance. The very thought of them lying helpless and stricken
in this mire made him physically sick, all the more so because there was so little he could do.

The haj walked on ahead of the others, sullen and quiet,
his head bowed in despair. Although it was unspoken, they
all shared the knowledge that each passing futile hour only
lessened their chances that much more.

All through the night they had searched, and all through
this dismal Specian day. Slime and mud clung underfoot; at
times the terrain of the bogs was like quicksand, so they sank
knee- and even thigh-deep as they passed from one barren
patch to the next.

At the end of one swampy field, where the landscape rose
high enough for them to get glimpses of the sky, they paused
to rest.

Argyle sat apart from the others with his head gloomily in

317

his hands. Homer and Ramagar shared a lichen-infested boulder, while the haj settled himself beside the stump of a long deadened tree. Thorhall, still quite ill but at least conscious, huddled beside him.

"We're almost at the beginning of the Black Forest," said the injured Aranian glumly.

Ramagar sighed. "What do we do now?" he asked.

"Double back," offered the haj wearily. "What else can we do?"

"Is it possible that the Prince could have lost direction and wandered into the forest with Mariana?" wondered Homer. "After all, they'd be just as directionless as we are . . ."

Ramagar was afraid even to speculate; it dawned on him that it really didn't make very much difference; in these for climes all roads seemed to lead to the same place: nowhere.

"We have nothing to lose if we try," observed the haj. "We can always return to the bogs."

The thief hunched his shoulders. It all seemed so pointless. But he mustn't lose hope, he told himself. Better to keep going, search anywhere, no matter how dim the chance. "What do you say, Thorhall?" he asked at last.

The wounded guide sucked in a breath of dank air and let it out in a slow hiss between his teeth. "Whichever way," he replied, "it won't do us any good to sit here and moan."

"I agree," said Argyle, joining in the conversation for the first time. He got up from his place and swung his weapon over his shoulder. "Point the way, Thorhall," he said.

And one by one they all stood, cold and hungry, dejected and as pessimistic as they could be. Thorhall shivered; rubbed at his arms and gestured with his head toward the thin line of black trees already apparent past the misty field. "Straight ahead," he told them, and without another word spoken they marched on again.

The foliage of the Black Forest was a sight to sadden even the cheeriest of hearts. Where once mighty redwoods had risen halfway to the clouds, there were now only row upon row of thick, ugly trunks, with gnarled and rotting roots hideously twisting up from the coarse soil and grotesquely wrapping into the air. Heavy branches clung like lifeless appendages to the trunks, intertwining, intermingling in an overall effect so unnatural that the sight caused every member of the band to avert his eyes. And the trees rolled on as far as they could see, the occasional clearing they came to no more than a gutted mat of caked, crumbling dirt, brittle

318

e touch but ready to crumble like powder at the slightest
ressure.

At various spots chosen at random both Argyle and Thor-
all would stop, kneel down, and run their fingers through
he dirt. Their eyes searched with true hunters' guile for any
gn of tracks or pieces of fallen fabric. But as before there
ere no clues to be found.

The dark Specian sky was becoming bleaker, and they
ew that the night was about to set in. At length they
opped to rest and debate whether they should go on or turn
ack.

It was then that they first noticed a new sound. Ramagar
ushed the others and put a hand to his ear. From some-
here not too far off he could hear a low pounding noise, a
eady rhythm that reminded him of beating drums.

"What do you make of it?" asked the thief.

Argyle shook his head; he turned to Thorhall. Thorhall lis-
ned in silence and took a few steps toward the constant
eating. "Perhaps we'd better go see," he said.

Slinking cautiously, the adventurers closed in on the noise,
hich became steadily louder. At the base of a low hill they
opped. The sound was coming from just over the other side;
ey could hear it quite loudly now, and it began to sound
ore and more like the swinging of hammers.

They inched up the hill crouching, careful not to stumble
er the multitude of twisting roots and fallen branches.
oward the crest they lowered into a belly crawl, each man
ushing himself forward by his elbows, keeping his head no
ore than a few inches above the ground. As they reached
e top and peered over, they held their breath and looked on
credulously.

Down below they could see a vast patch of cleared forest,
rricaded with barbed wire. Huge mounds of recently dug
il were piled near a large man-made shaft leading straight
wn into the bowels of the earth. Close by stood what ap-
ared to be great vats of steel, their contents boiling over
aring fires.

Ramagar gasped at the sight of a squad of Druids, all with
eapons in hand, marching away from the vats and toward
e entrance of the shaft. And from somewhere deep inside
e shaft came that pounding of sledgehammers and picks.

"It's a mine!" cried the thief.

Thorhall hushed him, then shook his head while the others
oved in for a better view. His face broke into a cold sweat,

319

as the memory of such a place as this came flooding ba⋯
over him.

Just then the stillness of the scene was abruptly broken ⋯
a shrill whistle whose blast nearly shattered their eardrum⋯
The pounding of the hammers ceased and the adventure⋯
watched in wonder while a shackled group of pitiful souls b⋯
gan to file out from the mine. Unspeaking, the ill-clothed, e⋯
pressionless work gang docilely placed down their tools a⋯
formed an inspection line before their Druid masters.

"A press gang!" wheezed the haj.

Thorhall nodded glumly. A press gang it was for ce⋯
tain—a hundred chained men, half-starved and drugged u⋯
der the influence of the evil Seeds, toiling in the pits f⋯
sixteen hours a day and more, suffering within that bru⋯
hole where the temperatures were intolerable and many pe⋯
ished for lack of a single swallow of water. A Druid pre⋯
gang, where hunger and depravity were the rule, and only t⋯
strongest of the strongest could hope to survive more than⋯
few seasons.

It took some time for the last of the slaves to reach t⋯
surface. Transfixed and dazed, they waited like children wh⋯
the taskmaster took them all to account for their day's lab⋯
One of the soldiers worked his way slowly through the sile⋯
lines of sweaty, exhausted men and seemingly on a wh⋯
chose one from here and one from there. Those selected f⋯
lowed him meekly and knelt while another Druid, a fat be⋯
of a man, flexed a gruesome bullwhip. Then with a cr⋯
grin, he beat them mercilessly.

Sickened and incensed, the haj slipped out his dagger. ⋯
gyle quickly grabbed the swineherd by the arm. "Don't be⋯
fool!" he reprimanded. "What good do you think that w⋯
do? They'll be all over us like flies."

Burlu nodded; he sheathed his weapon, too stunned by⋯
all to have words for reply.

"But we can't just stand here and watch," object⋯
Ramagar, feeling for the prisoners' plight. "Isn't there a⋯
thing to be done?"

A sudden scream turned every head back to the gri⋯
scene. One of the whipped slaves had been forcibly picked⋯
by a handful of soldiers and sadistically heaved into one⋯
the uncovered vats. The prisoner splashed in the molten l⋯
uid, his flesh sizzling to cinder.

"Mercy of heaven!" cried the haj in despair. No one e⋯
uttered a sound; they all looked on in disbelief, recalling ⋯

320

grim tales they had been told of such terrible doings, but never once dreaming they would come face to face with such a thing themselves. It was ghastly, a shameless act, without reason and without sanity.

"The prisoners must have caused a bit of trouble today," Thorhall explained knowingly. "The Druids enjoy making examples of those who disobey their orders. But at least this poor fellow went quickly. I've witnessed others who were racked and tortured for days on end until they died . . ."

The press gang taskmaster continued to exhort his charges for a few minutes more, carrying on as if nothing had happened. When he was finished, his men marched the prisoners off toward a grouping of ill-constructed shacks where they were fed their daily allotment of slop. Then their legs were unshackled and they were permitted to sleep.

Ramagar shuddered; the wretched existence of these slaves had made its mark upon him, and for the first time he truly understood the fanatical drive of the Prince—a drive that would never cease until his people and the world were rid of such terrible barbarity.

"We'd best get away from here," said Thorhall after a time. "Who knows what guards may be about on patrol—"

The haj tapped the Aranian lightly on the shoulder; Thorhall slowly turned his head and glanced beyond the deadened stumps leading back down the hill. Hands on hips, a black-bearded Druid stood watching them with a grim smile. And although there were five men and he was alone, he didn't seem the least bit perturbed.

Argyle grasped his fearsome ax and made ready to rush at him. The Druid held out a hand and snapped his fingers.

A rainfall of short, snubbed arrows came sailing over their heads; the adventurers leaped to their feet as the darts smacked into the ground all around them. Then from behind boulders and stumps a cohort of Druids raised themselves, reloading crossbows similar to those used on the Dragon Ships, and waiting for the next signal to be given by their captain.

"Throw down your weapons," came the terse command from the grinning Druid, speaking in the language of the North.

The band hesitated. Ramagar glanced to Argyle, both men having made a quick assessment of the situation. By now the archers had finished loading and were taking dead aim. There was no chance against such firepower; before they reached the bottom of the hill the next volley would cut them down.

321

"Better do as he says," advised the thief, slipping his dagger from its sheath and tossing it toward the impatient soldier.

With a grunt and a growl, Argyle threw down his ax. The haj sighed and let his own knife fall; Homer did the same. Thorhall overcame his own reluctance, scowling as his blade dropped from his hand.

All at once the Druids moved in, swarming over them like a plague of locusts.

"Are they going to kill us?" said the haj, turning to Thorhall as their hands were bound behind their backs.

"To what purpose?" replied the fugitive Aranian bitterly. "Laboring in the mines will do it for them. You see, we're as good as dead already, my good friends. After a few days of such misery, we'll regret ever being taken alive."

"Az'il!" grumbled Mariana, wincing with the sting as she bathed her blistered foot in the shallow water of the murky stream. She rubbed at the instep and then leaned back along the coarse bank. Overhead, the white mist still swirled, only thinner than before. Marching all night had taken them virtually to the end of the dreaded canyon, and the road to the citadel lay directly before them.

The Prince sat in deep contemplation of the dangerous task ahead. Through the haze, he could almost make out the fuzzy outline of the tower itself. It was a huge structure, built of gray stone, rising so high that its upper limits were completely shrouded by the clouds. And from the Black Forest which itself tapered and ended at the limits of the tower chalk cliffs rose up and up, moss- and lichen-covered, to merge gradually with the more massive stones of the edifice.

Mariana focused her attention on the distant structure and marveled at the architectural feat. She wondered just how human hands could have ever constructed such a thing, and how she, feeling so small and pitiful, could ever be expected to reach the top, those lofty heights unmatched anywhere in the world.

Specian dawn crept slowly across the sky, an eerie soft yellow pall glowing at the edges of the black clouds. Mariana did not turn her gaze from the awesome sight; rather, she continued to watch in deep fascination, thinking that she had come to the very edge of the world. From here there could be no return—only the strange silence that foretold her demise. For coming face to face with the enemy had left her convinced that her task was as hopeless as the fulfillment of her dreams.

"Are you ready?" said the Prince suddenly, snapping her from her thoughts.

Mariana stood warily and nodded. Oro picked himself up slowly and grimaced. Drying his moist palms on his worn tunic, the hunchback shivered at the landscape before them. "We'll never make it to the tower without being seen," he grumbled.

"Ah, but that's where you're wrong," said the Prince with the hint of a smile. "There are hidden catacombs leading to the tower, with secret entrances as far as a league away."

"And how will we find these secret passages?" huffed Oro in his sourest voice.

The Prince had a ready answer for that as well. "Each entrance is marked with ancient runes," he told them. "Specian runes from my forefathers' time. Remember, the tower had been begun long before Druid domination. And all we have to do is be able to recognize them."

Then without waiting for the hunchback to argue the point, Mariana and the Prince started the long walk. By midday, they were well away from the Valley of Morose, and Mariana paused to look back at the craggy heights where Ramagar would still be searching for her. Now and again she heard the shrill cry of a Death-Stalker plying the valley's skies, and she shuddered. The carrion would be carefully watching. She could only hope that the Prince would find one of these hidden passages before the birds of prey spotted them.

Across a barren plain of empty fields they walked, stepping cautiously across the pebbly trail. The air felt thicker, clammier; it became difficult to breathe. The magic of the Seeds of Destruction was already encumbering them, it seemed, slowing them down and beginning to bring a haze of lethargy to play around the edges of their minds. Only the greatest will and effort on all their parts would keep the deadly poison at bay for at least a while.

Oro was the first to show signs of his sapping strength; the hunchback's breathing became labored, and his moans steadily increased the closer to the source they came. Mariana and the Prince fixed all their thoughts on a single goal: reaching the Devil's Tower—and with deep concentration they fended off the poison's potency almost completely. But even they knew the dangerous game they played, for sooner or later

323

they, too, would succumb, as all trespassers onto this bleak and sad land must.

The mountain wind was blowing strong again; frightful wails and cries whistled through the deadened trees and over the plain. And the hope of finding the tunnel was all that kept them going.

23

Ramagar stared through a slit in the stone wall of the bleak barrack. He could see a handful of dark Druid stallions thundering along the Black Forest road and scattering clouds of dust as they reached the wired perimeter of the sulphur mine.

From the corner of his eye he could see the grim shacks of the slaves and hear the sound of picks against rock as the night crew labored in the pit. Although confined to this cell, he had learned much of this place in the past hours. The frequency of patrols told him that a Druid garrison or fortress was close; the sickening powder smell in the air told him that sulphur was the product being mined. And the telltale pale yellow traces to be seen everywhere only solidified his belief.

Undaunted by the threatening gestures of his guard, the same taskmaster who had so cruelly beaten the slaves, he sat in silence and returned his gaze to the bare plank floor to await the interrogation.

At his side sat the haj, also with the same stiffened resolve not to tell their captors a word. The two men exchanged nary a glance as they contemplated their fate, even when, for reasons unknown, their companions were dragged out and taken to cells of their own.

The gruesome Druid before them grew restless; bullwhip behind his back, he paced before them, slitted eyes darting from one prisoner to the other.

The stallions' hoofbeats became louder; Ramagar listened carefully as the horses came to an abrupt halt outside. There was the sound of heavy boots drawing near, and the taskmaster smiled a thin and disturbing smile. Suddenly the door was flung open wide and two dark figures entered. One, by the look and color of his uniform, was a soldier of some rank. But from his gait and his subservience to his companion, Ramagar dismissed him as no one of great importance, certainly no more than a garrison commander at best, here to escort the other visitor. But looking at this second man, Ramagar began to feel ripples of goose bumps crawl up along his neck.

He seemed a strange sort, this new arrival: a gaunt man, hooded, wearing a deep violet toga and a cloak of purple that swept behind.

At length, the man pushed back his hood, exposing a creased face almost yellow in color. He was clean-shaven, with a pointed chin and a long hawk-shaped beak of a nose that reminded the thief all too much of a carrion. His eyes were set wide apart beneath thin, joining brows, deeply recessed so that they caused shadows to form above his cheekbones. The visitor studied both prisoners briefly, and Ramagar saw that the pupils of his eyes were mere diluted pinpricks within a sea of white, crimson pupils like those he had seen on the Dragon Ships. There was high intelligence in those orbs, and cunning. But more than that, there was unmistakable evil—and the thief hid a shudder.

Bejeweled with onyx and ivory rings on every finger, the visitor played with a small silver pendant around his neck; then he imperiously flung his cloak over his shoulder and put his hands to his hips. Everything about him connoted authority and power. And from the uneasy looks on the soldiers' faces, Ramagar knew this authority to be no empty boast. This man commanded respect, demanded respect, the kind that could only be afforded a king or a wizard.

Without looking at the taskmaster, the wizard said, "Where were they found?"

"Beyond the wire, my lord. They were spying. We thought perhaps they were the ones you were seeking—"

The wizard cut him off curtly, a thin smile of satisfaction parting his cruel lips. Looking at Ramagar, he said, "Who are you? Where have you come from?" He twirled a small emerald ring on his index finger while waiting for a reply. There was none.

"Better for you if you answer," said the taskmaster, flexing the bullwhip before their eyes.

"We have nothing to say," whispered the haj.

"Tell me your name!" demanded the wizard. He tapped the toe of his fine leather boot and hunched his shoulders with tightly balled fists at his hips.

When there was still no answer, the taskmaster lashed the whip, stinging Burlu's feet. The haj moved not a muscle.

325

"Give these two to me, my lord," the taskmaster growled. "I know how to deal with them. I'll make them squirm . . ."

The wizard narrowed his eyes and glared at the thief. "That won't be necessary," he said with confidence. "This matter will be handled by me—personally."

The taskmaster's eyes widened and Ramagar could see fear behind them. "As you say, my lord," he stammered.

The wizard snapped his fingers, and both the taskmaster and the accompanying soldier withdrew from the hot cell, leaving the visitor alone to carry on the interrogation. After the door had shut behind them, the wizard smiled again. "We know you came here in a ship," he said. "A ship that sailed from Aran . . ."

He knows! thought Ramagar. This devil knows about the *Vulture!*

As if reading the thief's thoughts, the wizard smiled broadly and pressed his face close to Ramagar's. "Yes," he hissed. "We know many things about you, and about your companions as well."

"I don't know what you're talking about," replied Ramagar.

The wizard curled his lip. "We know a ship reached our shores—and we know why you have come. Our carrion spied you and your pitiful companions days ago."

The thief sneered. "If you know all this, what need have you to ask us questions? Surely your magic has ways of learning everything."

The insidious smile vanished; the wizard stepped back as if appraising the prisoner anew. For him such disregard for his authority was unprecedented; the prisoner showed both courage and character in his reply and the wizard's curiosity was fueled.

"Do you know who I am?" said the wizard.

Ramagar shook his head. "A sorcerer, no doubt," came the reply.

A set of large white teeth glinted in the dim light. "I have been called that, yes. I am the Grand Vizier. And word of your capture hastened me from the citadel to greet you."

Ramagar shuddered with the realization that he was in the presence of the very man who ruled this vast realm of perpetual darkness. That he had journeyed all the way from the Druid city assured the thief that his capture was considered important.

326

"Do you still refuse to answer my questions?" the wizard said.

Ramagar looked at him blankly, then lowered his gaze to the floor.

The Vizier shrugged. "A small matter, my friend. There are ways to make you speak."

The haj shot him an angry glance. "Torture us if you like! We'll not say anything!"

The wizard slanted his dark brows; he nodded slowly, gravely. "There are many kinds of pain," he said. "Some far worse than others. I could have you both racked, have your bones broken one by one, have your fingernails torn out bit by bit. But such methods," here he smiled again, "lack finesse. My own methods are far subtler—as you shall learn." And with that, he reached inside his toga and withdrew a small vial. The vial fit easily into the palm of his hand, and the wizard pulled off the cap. A thin green vapor slowly spread into the air, twisting and dancing above their heads.

Suddenly Ramagar was dizzy; he knew he was losing consciousness and he struggled with all his might to regain it. The face of the wizard grinned malevolently through the misty haze, and Ramagar fought to loose the bonds around his hands.

The haj slumped over and passed out. Ramagar was only vaguely aware now of what was happening. The wizard was leaning over him, forcing open his eyes. Ramagar tried to speak, but only low gurgles emerged from his throat. He knew he was powerless to move or to say anything; he could no longer think straight, his mind had been fogged by the vapor, and he realized he was completely at the wizard's mercy.

The wizard deftly recapped his vial and knelt beside the unconscious prisoners. He asked his questions quickly, in a soft and lulling voice. Then he smiled with satisfaction as, against their will, the prisoners replied. When he had done, and the air had all but cleared, he stood and clapped his hands, calling the soldiers back inside.

"They will no longer be a problem," he told the taskmaster.

The sadist grinned. "Shall I have them tortured?"

The Vizier shook his head. "They are both strong. Send them down into the mine when they awake. We have need of such men to labor for us." And then he strode from the room, lifting his hood and crossing the shadows to reach his horse. None who saw him were aware of the knitted brow of

worry; none had read the deep concern within his strange
eyes. The sorcerer had learned much about these foreigners,
all that there was to know. And it was with fear that he
heard the thief speak of Blue Fire—the one magic that could
threaten the Druid empire, the one magic that he and his
king had feared above all else.

Those in possession of the blade must be found, must be
caught and stopped at once—before they exerted the power
within their grasp.

24

Ducking from view behind a twisted stump, Mariana peered
up breathlessly at the sky and bit her lip as a grim Death
Stalker came gliding downward, sweeping in low above their
heads before it zoomed back toward the clouds. The huge
bird danced in a figure-eight pattern, made another pass over
the rocky plain, and then was gone.

The Prince stood and dusted off his tunic, watching the
diminishing speck until it disappeared.

"Do you think we were seen?" panted Mariana. It had
been the fourth time this morning they had been forced to
run for cover; carrion had been making constant forays and
the intervals between appearances were becoming ever shor-
ter.

"I think we saw him first," the Prince replied. "The bird
wouldn't have been so quick to run off if we'd been spotted."

Mariana shivered. "I don't like it. Something must be
wrong. It's almost as if these carrions know just who we
are—and where to look." She clasped her arms and warily
looked back to the sky. "And why that second pass? They've
never come over twice before . . ."

"Of course they're looking for us, you fools!" wheezed
highly agitated Oro. "Don't you think the Druids know all
about us by now?"

Mariana ignored the remark and forced herself up from
her hiding place. As the hunchback continued to rant she
contemplated the gloomy trail ahead. By this time, the Devil
Tower had become more than a distant haze on the horizon.
Its bulk had taken sharper form, and Mariana realized now
that its size was so massive, so awesome, that it literally
328

ocked out the tall mountains stretching behind it, dwarfing oth peaks and cliffs. And beyond the tower, she could also e the first walls of the citadel itself—the very heart of ruid power and authority—looming in the melancholy eakness.

Mariana shook her head. With so much distance yet to avel, and so little time in which to do it, their task seemed ore impossible than ever. "How much time do we have ft?" she asked the Prince.

"Less than a day and a half. We'll have to reach the tunls soon—if we're to reach them at all."

Oro laughed a malevolent little laugh. "Still dreaming, eh? ill thinking you can take on the might of an empire—and ush it by yourself."

They pretended not to hear and fending off fatigue, aveled onward, even deeper across the plain. Where the nstantly winding trail was leading they did not know, not en if it would finally take them to the hidden underground ssages that Specian engineers had designed so many cenries ago.

All at once the flatness of the plain gave way to thickening pses of trees, which the travelers followed in an eerie lf-light of day under an almost closed roof of branches. d finally these trees themselves gave way, bringing them ain into the open, only this time beside a poorly paved ad, whose loose gravel near the center gave testimony to e frequent passage of Druid stallions. Now and again eath-Stalkers were clearly seen roaming the faraway skies in arch of intruders, although they seemed to stay well away om the road and the three lonely travelers upon it.

With the wind picking up and a light drizzle descending, e Prince looked around miserably, sensing the closeness of eir destination, yet feeling the conclusion of their mission as stant as ever. Mind swirling with the effects of the Seeds, he shed aside all thoughts of failure and forced them all on, ssing by vast fields once abundant with produce and now rren and wasted.

Rain was still falling and a storm growled and cackled ove the dark mountains when they came upon the marking. was Oro who had seen it first; quite by accident, the nchback had noticed a peculiar formation of rocks set side a dark patch at the end of a field. Hurrying to exam- e it, the Prince stared in wonder. At his feet, partially ried by an accumulation of weed and gravel, was a stone

329

slab. Bending to his knees, he cleared away as much of t
debris as possible and stared at the runes embedded into t
stone.

Mariana stood at his side while the Prince translat
aloud: *"Let no man cross this gate unwarned. Within the
bowels the ravishes of hell shall be found."*

Mariana kneeled and ran her fingers lightly across the a
cient letters. "Who might have written then?" she asked.

The Prince shook his head gloomily. "Perhaps some run
way slave, or maybe a lost soul who never—"

Mariana's hand on the Prince's shoulder stopped him mi
sentence. Scattered amid the nearby weeds and moss lay :
assortment of bones, human bones, devoid of marrow ar
brittle to the touch. The Prince leaned over and picked o
up in his hand; the bone crumbled.

"Poor, poor fellow," mumbled the Prince sadly. "The c;
rion must have found him and done this . . ."

Pushing down her sickness, Mariana returned her attentic
to the message. "What does it mean, 'let no man cross th
gate'?" she said.

"This must be an entrance," replied the Prince. He look
about uneasily. "But where it leads, I don't know."

"Seems more like a grave," grunted Oro with a shiver. A
a grim smile crossed the Prince's face.

"For once, you're probably right. Mariana, lend a hand
And he dug his own hands under the stone, straining to mo
it.

With the dancing girl adding her own weight, and eve
Oro helping to push, the slab of dark rock began to slide
the side, exposing a narrow set of crumbling steps leadir
down into a black abyss. A putrid smell of death filled the
nostrils as fresh air entered the hidden cavern for the fir
time in centuries. Mariana put her hand to cover her mou
and nose and peered inside.

Can you see anything?" asked the Prince.

She shook her head. Then, without waiting, she swung h
lithe body over the side and gingerly stepped onto the fir
landing of steps. Then the second, then the third.

"Be careful, Mariana!" cried the Prince.

Nodding, she descended farther until she was almost go;
from their sight. Soon she stopped, and her voice echoed c
the walls as she called for the others to follow.

When the Prince reached her he stared in shock. "
graveyard, indeed," he whispered to the stunned Oro. Bo
330

en gasped at the gaping cavern before them. As wide as a
ver, the soft dirt floor was littered with skeletons, thousands
f them, scattered from wall to wall and piled high atop one
nother. Skulls peered up at the strangers from their resting
aces, and greeted the intruders with sardonic smiles.

Mariana swallowed hard and shut her eyes. "It's
uesome," she panted.

The Prince stepped down from the last of the steps, his
et crunching over bone as he sat himself firmly on the soft
rt. Spiders drew back from overhanging webs, and a small
dent dashed for safety under another pile of rotting bone.

"Are . . . are these Druid remains?" said Oro, his eyes
xed on the watching spiders.

"Slaves, no doubt," replied the Prince with a shake of his
ead. "Their Druid masters must have a hundred graveyards
ke this."

"Let's get away from here," said Oro, ill at the stench rush-
g up his nostrils.

The Prince was about to concur when Mariana hushed
em both. They stood immobile, listening to the dim sound
nich came to their ears. All three exchanged puzzled
ances.

"It sounds like . . . like chanting," said the girl, perplexed.

The voices were distant and low, but a song it surely was.
choir of deep voices, chanting verse in an unknown
ngue.

The Prince worked his way between mounds of rubble and
ossed the cavern slowly, coming to a small arch set deep in
e shadows. He beckoned to Mariana, and both she and the
nchback hastily made their way to his side.

"This doorway must lead to the tunnels!" gasped the
ince in sudden realization of their discovery. Then he
pped just over the threshold, letting his hand slip to his
gger, and carefully scrutinized the ill-lighted passage. It
s very dim, but the walls of rock themselves eminated a
ll glow, which would provide enough light for them to
ss. He could also hear the chanting, louder than before,
ming from some far off point. The very sound of it sent
ills racing down his spine.

"This passage looks like it goes on forever," said Mariana,
ching her way beside him.

"And we'll have to follow it until we're sure where it
ads," added the Prince. The name of the Devil's Tower re-
ained unspoken, but was fully understood.

331

Stumbling, they moved on, away from the graveyard. [It] seemed as if they had been pressing onward for hours by th[e] time they reached the first downward turn. Clinging to eac[h] other, unsure of their footing, they followed the sounds of th[e] chant, growing ever closer and louder.

Unaccountably, the passageway grew lighter. The narro[w] tunnel widened, its ceiling rose. A grim reddish pall reflecte[d] off the walls; here and there runes had been etched in[to] stone, Druid markings, a language far removed from those [of] the North or any the Prince was familiar with.

As they came to a wide opening, they realized that the tun[-] nel turned off, and they were now at a crossroads, confront[ed] by three new passages, each dark and long, each leadin[g] down far below the earth.

The grim song of the chanters suddenly diminished [in] tempo, if not in fervor. Holding breath, the travelers stopp[ed] in their tracks and listened while a solo voice rose above th[e] others, a falsetto ringing in their ears an unholy wail.

Mariana shuddered, finding a mocking similarity to th[e] calls to prayer chanted from minarets by the holy men [of] Kalimar. But these dark calls were not prayers to heave[n.] They could only be a plea to the powers of Evil, wiza[rd] priests conjuring some grim sorcery, asking for godle[ss] blessing in their profane rites.

"I'll examine the tunnel on the right, you take the left[,"] said the Prince. "Meet me back here in five minutes to rep[ort] what you see."

Mariana nodded.

"What am I supposed to do?" cried Oro, shaken at th[e] thought of being left by himself under such dire circu[m-] stances.

"You wait here." The Prince smiled at the dancing gi[rl.] "Ready?"

"Ready." And she moved on alone, cautiously slinki[ng] along the downward spiral into the darkness. After lo[ng] minutes she became aware of the passage's end. And the[re] they were, perhaps a hundred of them, dark-robed a[nd] hooded men, all gathered in a great torchlit cavern beyo[nd] the edge of the tunnel.

She moved very slowly now, keeping her back as close [to] the wall as possible, strangely attracted by the subdued colo[r] glowing from the chamber. And it was cold, curiously co[ld.] Clenching her chattering teeth, she boldly moved from h[er] place to a slight recess in the wall at the very edge of the pa[ssage]

...ge. There, she knelt and stared out into the unusual pro-
...edings, her eyes wide in disbelief.

...The ornate cavern was humming with the low song of the
...zards. Holding their arms high into the air, rustling the fab-
...c of their richly embroidered robes, they sang in unison
...ile another priest stood at an altar and lifted a small bas-
...t above his head.

...The simply woven basket was filled with what Mariana
...ok at first to be eggs; quickly she realized that they were
...nes, multicolored rocks that cast an eerie glow of dark, op-
...essing color across the walls and ceiling. And the wild
...umping of her heart assured her that these Stones were
...mples of the Seeds. Seeds of Destruction were here being
...epared for scattering into Speca's black skies.

...A sudden gong sent thrumming waves through the in-
...nse-laden air. The chant ceased, and the hundred wor-
...ipers fell to their knees as another wizard entered
...ajestically from the secret door behind the altar. This man
...od taller than the others, his air one of arrogance and au-
...ority.

..."Hail the Vizier!" cried the priest with the basket, lowering
...s gaze in the man's presence. "Hail the Grand Vizier!"

...And the cry was picked up by every other robed man in
...e chamber.

...The Grand Vizier swept his glance across the hall. He
...umbled an incantation that left Mariana trembling, then
...ok hold of an ornamental incense brazier and placed it
...ntly inside the basket of Seeds. Immediately the glow of the
...nes increased, and a wine-tinted hue was cast over the
...vern, changing slowly into a fiery red.

...Mariana held her breath; the scene was frighteningly famil-
...r. She recalled the glow of Blue Fire and the way it also
...d shrouded the world around it in color. Only the dagger
...d given her a sense of tranquillity and peace; these Stones
...ade her cringe with fear. And then she understood. The
...gger had brought forth the forces of Good; the red glow of
...e Seeds was Evil.

...A slight, wicked smile cracked the Vizier's thin lips; he
...pped to one side and bowed his head. The incense-filled
...amber was becoming foggy; Mariana had to strain her eyes
... see what was happening. She heard great creaks and
...ans, and looked on in wonder while the far wall slowly
...d open and a procession of instrument-carrying priests
...arched somberly into the chamber. Grim pipes played an

unhappy tune, followed by the shrill cry of ebony trumpe[t]
heralding the arrival of someone of importance. But who?

The girl gasped; she put a hand to her mouth and tried [to]
control her shaking.

It was a little man who entered, slightly deformed, rotun[d]
with round squat features; he reminded her of Oro. But th[e]
man walked with haughty airs of self-importance, and h[is]
jeweled silk garments attested to the incredible wealth wi[th]
which he adorned his person. Behind him, carrying a golde[n]
pillow, came a servant; and upon the pillow sat a crown, [a]
jewel-studded crown so magnificent that the blaze of the pr[e-]
cious stones almost hurt her eyes.

Mariana felt a wave of apprehension overtake her; s[he]
leaned back into the shadows, ready to run as fast as s[he]
could. But the sight of the little man left her intrigued, and [it]
was not long until she realized that she looked upon t[he]
Dwarf-king himself, the Druid man/god whose satanic pow[er]
was rivaled only by that of the Grand Vizier himself. He w[as]
the scion of a line of dwarfs whose ancestral vendettas, assa[s-]
sinations, and regicides had assured their line its power [to]
rule forever.

The Dwarf-king stood in silence while the Vizier plac[ed]
the crown upon his liege's head. There was fire in the kin[g's]
crimson eyes. As one demented he peered from priest [to]
priest, smilingly witlessly and glowing with satisfaction. Th[en]
he clapped his hands—once.

To Mariana's horror, a young girl was brought for[th.]
Specian, if her blond hair and blue eyes were any indicatio[n.]
Clad only in a simple, loose tunic, she stood as though tra[nce]
fixed before the Vizier, her eyes drugged and glassy.

The Dwarf-king grinned maniacally; fondling her, [he]
slipped the dress from her shapely form, and taking her [by]
the hand led her to lie upon the altar. The girl complied wi[th-]
out a murmur.

The chamber returned to silence. The Vizier stretched o[ut]
his hand and sprinkled her naked body with a blue powd[er.]
The drugged girl began to writhe and shiver, as if the powd[er]
were as cold as ice.

Then the Vizier handed the king a dagger, a black dagg[er]
encrusted with rubies at the hilt. The Dwarf-king smiled; [he]
played with the blade for a moment as though it were [a]
special toy. Then he lifted it high and brought it down with [a]
furious thrust, tearing it through the girl's flesh. Blood spla[t-]
tered across the grinning liege's finery and crazed face. S[he]

334

oaned, arms clutching into the air, and fell back dead. Thin
nes of blood trickled down her arms and onto the floor.

The Dwarf-king was shaking; he bent over the corpse and
issed the dead girl's lips. At this the host of priests began to
eer, boldly shouting of their liege's skill and prowess.

Mariana looked away in terrified awe. Her heart was bro-
en for the poor victim of this horrible murder. How many
mes had this terrible ritual taken place in the past? How
any other victims had fallen prey to the abhorrent rites of
e evil Druids? Mariana clutched her arms around herself to
op her trembling.

The wizards began their chant again; the Dwarf-king
aited while his crown was removed, and then he strode
om the chamber in the same fashion in which he had come.
ariana watched in revulsion while the dead girl was lifted
d carried behind him, followed first by the Grand Vizier,
d then by the priest with the basket of Seeds. Soon all the
hers began to leave, filing out in grim procession while the
ft unholy music of the pipes continued to play.

Mariana turned to run back. She had stayed far too long,
d the Prince would be worried. She must get back as
uickly as possible and tell him what she had witnessed. But
ould he believe her? Although she had seen it herself, she
ll wasn't sure it had all really happened. The haze, the in-
nse, the Seeds, had they all somehow combined to warp her
ind? Could this have been nothing more than a nightmarish
llucination?

Running as fast as she could, stumbling up the tunnel pas-
ge, she knew all too well that it was real. And she prayed
at somehow she could make certain it never happened
ain.

25

Ramagar lay sprawled on the foul straw mat and allowed h
half-opened eyes to close again. They stung with the resid
of sulphur, burned and teared every bit as much as they h
in the mine. To save his sight he had found a rag and car
fully wrapped it around his head, making sure his eyes we
well covered. In the depths of the shaft there was little ne
to see; one needed only his pick or shovel and a strong ba
to carry the fruits of the day's labor up to the top in hea
sacks.

The sadistic taskmaster had laughed as the new arriv
were shunted below for their first shift; he had held his
belly with both hands and chortled while young Hon
falling from the weight of his tools, was flogged nea
unconscious by a dim-witted overseer intent on punishing t
lad for his inability. And then down they were broug
forced to march a thousand meters beneath the earth wher
breath of fresh air was considered a luxury and a swallow
water a prize over which a man might kill another.

It was here that they toiled, side by side with the dozens
silent, drugged Specian slaves, while other overseers watch
from their posts, eager to whip or beat any laborer who
much as turned his head.

It was grueling work they faced; Ramagar wondered h
the slaves managed to last through even a week of such ha
ship. Sixteen hours with only the briefest period of rest
lowed, during which time a group of kitchen slaves brou
down a bucket of slimy water and doled out a tiny allotm
to each of the workers. The haj had tasted his swill and s
it out, so offending the guards that ten lashes of the bullw
assured he would never show such impertinence again.

As for Argyle and Thorhall, they had subdued their d
ance, completing their tasks without question and biding th
time while Thorhall plotted escape. It was a most unlik
possibility, Ramagar knew, but still a chance to cling
Without it, despair would be total.

At long last the shift was done. Cloth sacks loaded, t
carried them over their backs step by painful step until
overseer put the burdens on the scales to see if each man h

done his apportioned day's work. Everyone had, or so it seemed, for the new arrivals were at last allowed to come back out into the light and enjoy the single meal.

Unshackled for the night, each was handed a metal bowl of cold mealie stew and a single slice of hard bread. The haj had taken his fare thankfully and put the crust to his mouth, but when he saw the host of maggots working their way from the center he put the bread down in revulsion. As for the mealie, it was hardly any better. The foul lumps that passed for meat had turned green with mold; the thin soup in which they sat crawled with insects both large and small. Meanwhile, as the slaves were forced to exist on this sustenance, the Druid guards taunted them with slabs of fresh beef and hot mutton cooked especially for the camp's warders.

Disgusted, Ramagar had given his own supper to another, an unspeaking Specian whose months of malnutrition had withered his body until his frame looked as though it would snap like a twig.

While the hideous vats boiled outside and permeated the air with a terrible heat, the prisoners were at last allowed to go to their hovels for sleep. A loud whistle signaled the time for all talk to cease, although in truth there was hardly a word passed between any of the camp's prisoners.

And so in the dank darkness Ramagar lay alone with these thoughts, his heart filled with worry and sorrow for his lost Mariana. He rued the bleak day they had all landed upon these sorry shores, and now could think of only one thing—somehow finding a way to break loose and find the dancing girl.

"Are you asleep, Ramagar?"

The whispered voice was raspy and tense; Ramagar twisted his frame slowly around, careful not to arouse the curiosity of the watching sentries. The thief opened his eyes and looked into Thorhall's agitated visage.

"I'm awake," he whispered back. "What is it? What's the matter?"

"Do you know what the morrow is?" said the Aranian.

Ramagar nodded slowly. "The first day of Moon Time . . ."

Thorhall sighed, bobbing his head sourly. Like the rest of the band, he had remained acutely aware of the hours left until the Druid Dark Rites were to be held. Shifting closer to Ramagar, he said, "The day of commemoration will be celebrated in full—even here in the camp."

"So?"

"So, this time is revered by them as no other. I can recall the occasions well, during my former imprisonment . . ."

Ramagar looked at him impatiently. "What are you getting at?"

A dark frown crossed Thorhall's thin mouth. "There will be a celebration once the sky has been seeded. All labors shall cease, a priest will likely come from the citadel, and our masters shall revere him while the period of Ritual is sung throughout the land."

"I still don't know why you're telling me all this," said the thief. "What has any of this to do with us?"

Here Thorhall smiled; he sucked in a deep breath and peered at his companion with twinkling eyes. "Escape, Ramagar! That's what I'm talking about! Tomorrow will provide us with an opportunity that may never come again."

"But won't we still be shackled and sent down into the mine?"

"Shackled, yes, but not to toil below. All prisoners will be drugged during Holy Time, chained to our places while the Rites are celebrated. Often I have seen priestesses— whores—brought from the temples to offer their pleasures to the taskmasters. And the Druids will partake of every known sin that—"

The harsh patter of boots on the hard floor broke off the conversation. Ramagar quickly turned back to his sleeping position and feigned deep slumber while a lone guard passed among the rows of prisoners. The guard lingered a moment beside the thief and peered down with intent, watchful eyes. Then, convinced that the thief was actually asleep, he glanced at Thorhall and moved on.

It was some time until the sentry was out of sight, and when they were certain he was out of earshot, Thorhall pushed at Ramagar's shoulder, saying, "What do you say? Are you with me? The religious rituals will take hours, and the overseers will be too involved to miss a handful of laborers until the count is taken before mealtime."

Ramagar grunted warily. "And what about these shackles they put on us? How far do you think we can run with chains around our legs?"

The wily Thorhall grinned; reaching inside his dirty shirt he pulled out a long jagged rock—a rock whose edges had been honed into razorsharp fineness.

"How did you get that?" marveled the thief.

"I found it yesterday while we were below. I worked it fo

hours, testing its edge, even trying to loosen the links of my chains. Then just before they brought us up for weighing the sulphur I tried it out. It cuts, Ramagar! Not as well as a hacksaw, perhaps, but well enough! I'm positive that once the festivities begin I can free us both."

"What about the others?"

"Don't worry. Once you and I are unchained we can steal better tools from our praying masters. Weapons as well. I've been keeping my eyes open, Ramagar; I know exactly where the overseers store their blades . . ."

The thief of Kalimar laughed soundlessly; he also had made careful note of such matters. All they would need were a few simple tools: a pick, a chisel, and a few good steel swords. With such as these in his hands a whole cohort of Druid soldiers couldn't keep him pinned down in this godless place.

Thorhall's cold eyes glinted in the dark. "What do you say, then? Are you with me?"

The cunning smile etched into Ramagar's rugged features left no need for words. Come tomorrow, one way or another, he would pay a few debts that could no longer wait.

26

The Prince stood silently at the edge of the shadows, looking about him in the dark, cavernous hall that Mariana had found. It was as grim and barbaric a temple of human sacrifice as he had even imagined—a painful reminder of the bitter tyranny which his land was forced to endure.

Because of the dim light he had to strain his eyes as he peered from icon to icon, noting the devilish statues and artifacts, then letting his glance wander back toward the altar itself, where tiny pools of unwashed blood still lay upon the floor.

Torches had been fixed in metal brackets, and several were aflame, streaking shadows across the high ceiling. In the poisonous air the yellow flames lolled this way and that, with a spurt of resin now and then flaring off or a knot in a torch's wood exploding with a crack.

The ruby eyes of the icons stared at the visitors, their carved, twisted mouths mocking and scornful. On the wall behind the altar hung a serpent's head, and at its side images of great carrion, Death-Stalkers, with wings fully spread and talons projected. This room was the Druid world in miniature: evil surrounded by evil.

"Do you believe me now?" said Mariana, shivering as the memory of the death rite she had witnessed came flooding back at her.

The Prince nodded; he took her hand and squeezed it firmly. "I never doubted you," he replied. Then he crossed behind the altar and examined the slab wall for the hidden passage from which the Dwarf-king had made his splendorous entrance.

Oro meekly came beside the girl, his teeth clattering loudly. "What . . . what do you suppose we'll find on the other side?" he said, imagining a host of devils ready to fly at them the moment the door was opened.

"I expect we'll find the passage to the tower," replied Mariana.

The hunchback shuddered. "Maybe we should go back and look for another tunnel—"

Something gave way at the touch of the Prince's fingertips. The wall began to creak and groan, and as the Prince stood back in awe, the thick slab of rock began to slide off to the side, exposing a winding corridor filled with glowing red light and leading off into a rabbit warren of passages.

Mariana gulped. A strong residue of incense came rushing at her and she felt sickened again.

"Come on," said the Prince, yanking her by the arm and pulling her across the threshold. "We don't know how long the door will remain open."

Mariana turned back toward Oro, whose knees were quivering so badly that he couldn't walk. "Are you coming?" she said sharply. "Or do you want to stay behind?"

The hunchback wiped his sweaty brow and took a single step forward. Then reluctantly he halted, hesitating over whether to venture forth and face this new hell, or remain behind in the hell he already knew. The rumble of the wall beginning to slide back into place made up his mind for him. He took a single leap and passed into the corridor, just as the slab door was about to slam shut. A hollow clang echoed down the passage and the three intruders stood glued to their tracks, holding breath, listening and watching for the presence of priests or Druid sentries patrolling the labyrinth.

The passage remained empty and silent. The Prince drew

340

his magic scimitar, the blade slipping from its scabbard and glimmering in the red light. Without a word he moved forward and signaled the others to follow.

It was a smooth marble floor they raced across, with walls so fine and polished that they almost reflected the images of the three strangers.

"Which way now?" asked Mariana as they came to a series of smaller passages.

The Prince chose the one whose incline became steadily sharper as it worked its way to ground level. There was a bright glowing light at the end, and the low chanting of priests.

"We must be near the Holy Temple," said the Prince, pointing to where the tunnel ended and opened into a vestibule. As the song of the wizards grew louder, the Prince inched his way to the entrance, looking on while three hooded priests kneeled with clasped hands in prayer as they mumbled their incantations. A smoking brazier sent thin clouds of incense streaming toward the low ceiling. Behind a small altar stood a huge arched doorway with a wide row of stone steps leading on an upward spiral. And from far away they could all hear more chanting, a chorus of voices in unison.

"It's begun," mumbled the Prince. "The hour is at hand. The priests must be carrying the Seeds up to the tower."

Mariana swallowed and nodded; she wiped perspiring hands onto the folds of her tunic and narrowed her eyes at the three priests blocking the way to the arched door. Within the folds of their dark robes she could see the outlines of swords.

"They're armed!" she gasped.

The Prince gloomily fondled Blue Fire. "As I suspected. They must be guarding the vestibule . . ."

"We'll never get past them," ruminated Oro.

Passing the dagger from hand to hand, the Prince smiled coldly. "Get down, both of you. Stay put until I signal." Then he fell to his knees and crawled from the tunnel into the chamber.

The wizards were lost in their song; the first hardly groaned as the Prince silently sneaked behind him, swept up his head, and slit his throat.

Like cats his two companions were up, faces ashen, crimson eyes ablaze. The Prince knocked the first one down with balled fist. The second drew his long curved sword and

341

thrust it in a broad sweep. Deftly the Prince dodged to the side; the edge of the weapon cut into the side of the wooden altar. Blue Fire swung up as the priest made to charge. The dagger cut through the robe; the wizard staggered, his hands to his belly as his sword clattered onto the floor. The last of the wizards jumped to his feet and slammed at the Prince with all his weight. The Prince rolled to the floor, and both men grappled for the sword.

Mariana raced into the chamber; she grabbed hold of a small emerald-encrusted stone icon, and while the priest pinned the Prince to the ground she heaved it over his head. A low gurgling sound rose from the wizard's throat. Slowly he loosened his grip, eyes rolling in their sockets, and fell prostrate, the side of his head caved in like a crushed grape.

The Prince briefly examined the corpses and then quickly stripped the first priest of his robe. "Here, put this on," he called to the surprised girl.

Mariana donned the dark garment, carefully fitting it over the hem of her tunic. The Prince meanwhile had stolen the robes from the other corpses. He threw one over his own body and handed the second to Oro.

"Why are we doing this?" asked Mariana, as she secured the belt and placed her own dagger inside the folds of the long sleeve.

The Prince eyed her coolly. "We're going to slip past the procession—dressed as wizards. Be sure to keep your hoods tightly around your faces. And don't look at anyone! Our eyes aren't crimson like theirs; they'll give us away the moment we're spotted. Now, is everyone ready?"

After hurried nods they scrambled through the arched door and up the long flight of winding steps until they could see the gathering of wizard priests as they filed solemnly into the Shrine Chamber of the Holy Temple, at the base of the Thirty Thousand Steps.

In grim array the wizards came, literally hundreds of them, with heads bowed low, arms at their sides, and a ghoulish song upon their lips. Behind them came the Carriers—wizards also, but muted, sorcerers whose tongues had been wrenched from their mouths so they could never speak of the secrets they knew. It was these Carriers, heads shaven and bodies hairless, who brought forth the baskets from which the Seeds of Destruction would be thrown. And it was they whom the Prince knew they must foil, for in their hands a

342

this very moment lay the Seeds, prepared and tested, waiting only for the time to arrive.

Hiding in a recess at the foot of the Shrine Chamber, Mariana watched and then gasped. In the forefront of the gruesome procession came none other than the feared Grand Vizier himself. Adorned in black silken finery, wearing jewelry of ebony and flaming crimson, he walked slowly toward the icon-infested altar, sprinkling a dark powder this way and that, mysteriously creating a thin haze all around him.

The walls of the chamber were slanted, the high ceiling a pyramid. Grisly paintings covered the walls: demons, dragons, and devils, which in the haze seemed to come to life while the singers completed their chant.

And again the hideous Dwarf-king appeared, and Mariana trembled at the sight. The Grand Vizier greeted his liege with a deep bow, and the grim song of the priests ceased. Pipes blared and a drum beat slowly; the demented king grinned as he peered above the heads of his multitude. The Carriers knelt before him; they placed down their Seed-filled baskets and lay prostrate at his feet. It was then that the Vizier invoked a new incantation. From a vial he poured a thick red liquid into the baskets, a liquid Mariana knew to be blood. The Dwarf-king cupped his hands and held them out, letting blood pour over his palms and between his fingers and drip down his golden-seamed black robes.

The Grand Vizier cried out to the black powers of hell. Mutes silently brought another basket and held it before him. This one, though, held no Seeds. Mariana retched at the sight of the organs—human organs that could only have belonged to the sacrificed girl. The Vizier held up the blood-soaked heart and quietly let the liquid pour over the Seeds. His incantation grew louder; his chant was picked up by the masses in attendance until the din became frightening and terrible.

Joined by the sacred instruments, the swelling music had a strange, pungent sweetness about it that lulled both mind and soul. It sounded like no song that Mariana had ever heard before, so ethereal, so powerful was the pull of the unholy symphony.

Suddenly there was a hissing noise and swirling bands of color lowering from the ceiling. The prince saw it and watched in horror. "Poison!" he gasped. "They're spewing poisons into the air!"

And the noxious gas slowly descended upon the gathered

343

crowd. But the priests did not run from it, nor even turn their faces. They seemed to welcome the fumes, inhaling deeply, smiling as they continued to sing, opening their arms in acceptance while the gas filled their lungs.

"Fall to the floor quickly!" cried the Prince. "Cover your mouths and noses—and hold your breath for as long as you can!"

The spreading mist permeated the air in radiant color, swirling and twisting as it was piped in from hidden vents near the ceiling. And all the while the Druid chant continued to rise in pitch. The drums, the pipes, all were swelling to a life-shattering fervor. Glassy-eyed, the host of priest-wizards hailed the foul gods of the Dark, calling many by name and shuddering in reverence as the Vizier hailed their Dwarf-king as the savior of the world.

With her lungs bursting and her head swimming, Mariana watched the scintillating forms of color and substance dance before her eyes. She could feel a sickening lack of orientation; it was as if time, distance, depth, and sound were all now somehow meaningless. Reality had ceased to exist. There was the music, oh yes, above all there was the music. Soft and loud, harsh yet gentle, subtle yet poignant, lifting her from this plane onto one higher, one which she dreaded yet welcomed.

Drifting. The world was drifting. The Prince had also felt the effects. Gasping for fresh air, he fought for control of his mind. The pull of the magic was strong—stronger than he had realized, and he damned the Vizier for this insidious attack.

And then a gusty wind was upon them all. Sweeping down from above, it cleared the air of the gases and sent the colors shattering, fading into oblivion. The priests fell to their knees, still chanting, still glorifying their liege as a god.

Mariana rested with her back against the wall, struggling to regain her senses. Her forehead was beaded with sweat and she put her head in her hands. Besides the entrance to the chamber Oro lay in a stupor; as always the effects of Speca seemed to have a firmer grip on him than the others.

"Are . . . are you all right?" wheezed the Prince, crawling close to the dazed girl.

Mariana nodded. "I . . . I will be . . . soon . . ."

The soft voices of the choir again drew her attention. She saw the throng of priests standing, now in salutation to the Carriers before them. The mutes had picked up their charges

344

ke mothers fondling their infants, and began to march in a
ngle file from the hall. The Vizier's incantation was done;
oth he and the Dwarf-king marched behind. And slowly the
ows of followers did likewise.

"They're preparing to climb the steps!" cried the Prince,
olted out of his light-headedness.

Mariana pulled herself up and cleared her thoughts.
We've got to hurry! They mustn't reach the top before we
o—it's our only hope!"

Oro stirred; he drew back in revulsion at the very mention
f the dreaded Devil's Tower and its Thirty Thousand Steps.
acing an army of hallucinating ghouls was more than he
as prepared for.

"Dressed as we are, we can probably slip past the sentries
t the landing," said the Prince. "But from then on it's going
o be a race—and the Vizier will know we're coming . . ."

"Then we'd best be quick," replied Mariana. She swung
round and entered the emptying hall, easily mingling with
ne last group of drugged wizards.

At the side of the exit guards had been posted. The Prince
overed his eyes with his hands and walked grimly past, the
roning song of the Druids upon his lips. Stoic and silent, the
entries paid scant heed to the last three priests leaving the
all.

The procession of pipes led the way; the sorcerers had en-
red a wide, open plaza outside the Holy Temple's labyrinth
f chambers. It was a dismal morning even for Speca. The
ind was blowing with ferocity; the sky was as lifeless and
hreatening as Mariana had ever seen it. From the narrow
alkway leading past the Holy Temple's grounds, the three
sguised adventurers made all haste away from the looming
uttressed walls where horn-helmeted Druids kept careful
atch on the sweeping plain below. Beyond the sacred
ounds lay the road to the citadel and the Dwarf-king's
eep. Mariana let her gaze carry beyond the walls, along the
arp slope of hills to the dark roofs of the lower city—once
ajestic and beautiful, a city whose renown crossed every
order and danced on every tongue.

Speca—the fabled land of myth and history whose glories
panned millennia, whose deeds filled volumes during times
hen the rest of the world dwelled in its darkest ages. Speca
f a thousand tales lay before Mariana now: a crumbling
ty, wasted and forlorn, its paved streets cracked and bro-
en, its alleys and byways haunted by ghosts of ages past, its

345

splendor turned to ashes heaped upon the rubble of its falle
might.

Mariana gazed in wonder, her inner self trembling at th
sunless panorama of neglect; a city lying dormant, its peopl
ravished and broken, while Evil forced itself upon the onc
proud nation, and prevailed. For league upon league th
great walls still stood, but they were decayed and broken fo
as far as she could see. The harbor, where once the world'
finest ships sailed with banners aflutter, now lay grim an
barren, empty wharves decaying, rotting into the tepid blac
waters. It was an awesome sight, not to be believed except b
the beholder. And the reality of it made her cringe.

A bell began its morbid toll; the wizards gathered at th
foot of the tower to recite once more their vile incantatio
before the trek to the sky began. Mariana stood close besid
the Prince; she could feel the bite of the wind through he
black sorcerer's robes. The Prince stood with head bowed, hi
eyes closed to stop the tears. The sight of his ravished hom
had been a crueler blow than expected; it was all he could d
to hold back his anger and not use Blue Fire right now t
slay the wicked Dwarf and his Vizier.

The Vizier extolled his followers with promises of glorie
yet to come. He spoke of the North, of the fair islands th
lay ripe for the taking. He spoke of war and of war machin
that would run rampant in the name of the Darkness; of th
powerful armies that would sweep the land and crush i
peoples; of new spells yet to be cast, and of heinous Dragc
Ships that even now prepared to sail.

Mariana listened with growing horror as the monoto
voice condemned half a world to its demise. Aran would t
first, she knew. Then Cenulam and all the other seafarir
lands. How much time was left before the Druid hord
descended upon the East itself?

The mutes stood in a single line and proudly held hig
their baskets, offering the Seeds to the heavens as a gift fro
the gods below. Mariana looked at the granite tower, th
terrible tower whose pinnacle reached so far into the clou
that no man on the ground had ever seen it. And the be
rang again. It was almost time. Moon Time.

The crowd had been worked into a frenzy. The Prince sa
that the priests, who stood with blazing eyes, had given the
very souls for their god/king and his Vizier. Drugged and f
natical, they hailed the Forces of Darkness in a cry so lou
346

at its echo vibrated across the fortified citadel and through
ut the dead city.

"Death to all infidels!" cried the Vizier, his arms out-
retched.

"Death to those who would alter our destiny!" chimed in
e sadistic Dwarf, his face twisting into a hideous mask.

The priests picked up the cry, over and over, shouting at
e top of their lungs as veins bulged from their throats.

The Vizier smiled cruelly; he put out his arm and pointed
ward the far edge of the crowd, right to where Mariana
d the Prince were standing.

Mariana felt her heart leap into her throat as the Vizier
ied, "Death to those who would betray us! The infidels are
mong us *now!*"

"He knows who we are!" rasped the girl. And a tremen-
us roar of anger rose from the gathering, intent on murder
r the three strangers in their midst.

With the speed of a lizard the Prince grabbed Mariana by
e arm and jerked her away as three frenzied priests drew
ng daggers from the folds of their robes and attacked. Bolt-
g for the entrance to the steps, the Prince slashed wildly
th Blue Fire, fighting off a host of screaming wizards who
d charged across the stone floor of the plaza. The scimitar
t high into the air; a priest caught the edge of the blade
uarely across his face. Pulsing dark blood spouted like a
untain; as he staggered, the Prince pushed him back, top-
ing him into a group of raging oncomers.

"To the steps!" shouted the Prince, working his way from
e side of the mob to the other.

Witless and wild, the drugged priests began to press the be-
ged strangers. Oro deftly flung off his robe, swinging it
adly and momentarily blocking the thrust of a brutish mute
o had jumped down from the line of Seed-Bearers.

"Catch them!" thundered the Grand Vizier, his crimson
es smoldering with rage.

The Prince fended off blow after blow. Mariana, too, her
n knife in her hand, cut a frenzied path to the bottom of
steps. And up the first flight they raced. A burly sentry
me leaping down, sword singing from his hand. The Prince
estepped and brought the dagger up. Midflight the soldier
aned as Blue Fire tore through his belly.

Mariana scrambled past, Oro right behind. A demented
st of priests yapped at their heels like dogs. The Prince
ged his companions on, then turned and, flinging his cloak

347

in their faces, pushed the first assailant backward with all h
might. Sprawling, the wizard slammed into his companior
and halted their advance.

"Run, Mariana!" shouted the Prince. "And don't stop!"

The race had begun. The dancing girl was scrambling u
the twisting spiral, never once glancing over her shoulder
scc the foaming multitudes in pursuit. The stairway narrowe
then broadened. Straining and panting she glanced upwar
only to feel her heart sink with the realization of how fa
there was to go. The steps seemingly had no end. Up and u
they climbed, a coarse defile of stone surrounded by the cor
cave walls of granite that pressed in on all sides.

From recessed windows the wind blew, tossing her ha
wildly before her face. Exhausted, she had to fight for eve
breath.

Suddenly a side door sprang open; Mariana spun in shoc
as another soldier darted at her from the hidden stairwe
With an evil grin the Druid lunged, his steel sword slashir
savagely through the air. Mariana ducked; sparks flew as t
weapon scraped against granite. The girl rolled on the step
the Prince was close behind, Oro just a few paces farth
back. But both were still too far to come to her aid.

The Druid laughed sadistically at the girl's plight. Drawi
the curved blade with both hands, he made to plunge
through her breast. Mariana lunged forward, yanking the sc
dier's leg and pulling him slightly off balance. In that sp
second before he could right himself, her knife was up—a
into the Druid's groin. His scream echoed up and down t
lower flights, a scream so awful she put her hands to her ea
to block it out. And then he fell, tumbling, tumbling dov
the steps.

Mariana stood up gasping. Her head was reeling and s
fought to fight off the waves of nausea sweeping over he
"Take the side stairway!" she heard the Prince shout, a
without time to think she did as he asked. Seconds later
was a terrible commotion at the door. Oro had slipp
through without any trouble, but the Prince had to fend
the first rank of the mob who were desperately trying to wo
their way inside.

Crazed priests hacked and slashed with all manner
weaponry. And from far out across the citadel came the de
tones of the great brass bells, the Druid signal that infid
were on the loose. It was a sound so chilling that it fill
Mariana's heart with new dread. The whole of the Druid e

348

ire was now in pursuit, and no force on earth was powerful
nough to stop them.

The Prince whirled about, Blue Fire dancing in his hands.
he bitter fight had barely begun; body after body choked
he small threshold to the side stairwell, and the Prince knew
e could not hold out much longer.

"We must shut the door!" he cried to the petrified girl.
Mariana, close it behind me!"

But doing so would leave the Prince at their mercy, and
ather than escape alone Mariana decided to share the
rince's fate. Forgetting her fear, she grabbed the sword of a
allen priest and played a wheel of flying death all around.
irisly screams rollicked through the air, the brittle crunch of
one against rock drowning out the whistles of furious
lades.

The charge slowed and then almost died. The Prince slid
etween the half-shut door and the stairs. "We held them!"
e laughted jubilantly. But his merriment was short-lived. A
ying wizard leaped to his knees, crimson eyes burning with
ate, and with his last effort, he plunged his dagger, catching
he Prince in the small of his back.

The Prince groaned; he forced his way inside, and
ammed the iron door shut behind. Fists began to pound;
ere was the furtive patter of a hundred footsteps racing to
ach the landing.

"I'm all right," wheezed the Prince to the startled girl.

Mariana gasped at the sight of his wound. It was deep—
o deep for the Prince to go on.

"We've got to take care of you," she cried.

The Prince shook his head. He grimaced to subdue the ris-
g pain. "I can make it . . . I promise you. I didn't come all
is way just to die here. Not now . . ." And then he half
llapsed in her arms.

Mariana gazed up the endless flight. She could almost see
e clouds scudding before her at a place where the stairway
oke out into the open onto a terrace.

The Prince hobbled to his feet, refusing any aid the danc-
g girl tried to give. Oro looked on in desperation at the
oming terrace in the clouds. "We can't go on!" he wailed.

"And we can't go back!" snapped the girl. "Listen! Can
u hear? They're breaking down the door! It's either up or
thing!"

Sweating like a caged animal, Oro pondered his choices—

and clearly Mariana was right. No matter how bad the wa
up might seem, down was worse.

They climbed and climbed, hearing the awful din of th
hammers growing increasingly louder. The Prince was breath
ing haltingly; Mariana's eyes flooded with tears at the though
of his wound. Why must it have been him? It should hav
been me! He, of us all, is the only one who can call on th
dagger's powers!

The wind was blowing down the passage with incredible i
tensity. The closer they came to the terrace, the more difficu
the climb became. It was as though the forces of hell itse
were pushing them back, making it impossible for them t
reach the top.

Suddenly the Prince staggered; his hands went to h
wound and he fell on the steps. Sobbing, Mariana kne
beside him. "Get up," she cried. "We need you! *I* need yo
Speca needs you!"

The Prince looked deeply into her wet, luminous eyes an
shook his head slowly. "No, Mariana. I can't . . . I can
make it . . ."

"You can! You *can!*" she sniffed. "I'll help you! Oro w
help you, too!"

The hunchback bent over the Prince and nodded. "I'll
anything I can . . ."

The Prince coughed as he smiled. "You mean well, both
you," he whispered faintly. "But I could never make it. V
haven't yet climbed a third of the steps . . ."

The banging still echoed from below; Mariana looked ba
down the flight to see the door beginning to bend on i
hinges. It was only a matter of minutes until the wizar
broke through.

Tears streaming down her face, Mariana said, "What a
we to do without you? What use are we if you're gone?"

The Prince too had tears in his eyes. His strength was sa
ping, and there was so little time for him to explain. He la
a steady hand over Mariana's, clasping it with all the streng
he could draw. "You must do what has to be done," he to
her. "You don't need me any longer; you can complete o
task yourself . . ."

The frightened girl recoiled. "What are you saying?" S
wept, feeling the weakening pulse of her constant friend. "\
need you! Only you possess the ability to control Blue Fire

"Trust in me, Mariana. You're wrong; the blade can
used by others as easily as I have learned . . ."

Mariana firmly shook her head. "It . . . it can't be," she replied, almost pleading. "No one else in the world knows the dagger's secrets and magic. You told me so yourself."

"Then let me teach you, Mariana. Let me show you what must be done . . ."

The distraught girl shut her eyes and drew a breath. "Please, don't ask me," she said with a shudder. "Only *you* can save Speca. Blue Fire is yours; it is your inherited right."

The pain was growing; the Prince moved his head agonizingly and tightened his grip on her trembling hand. At the bottom of the landing, meanwhile, the heavy door had all but blown off its massive hinges and they could easily hear the Vizier's frantic voice above the din shouting for his lackeys to hurry.

"I am going to die, gentle Mariana . . ."

She suppressed a gasp. "No . . . no, you're not . . ."

His expression was stern now, like an older brother taking her to task. "It is true. Perhaps I have always known this is how it would be. Perhaps the Fates had never intended for me to regain this land . . ."

A pulse leaped in the hollow of her throat; she pulled her gaze away even as he forced her to look at him.

"There is no time for grief now, girl," he reprimanded. "A man's destiny cannot be altered—not even that of a prince. I know now that it was indeed my fate to come home, but only to show you the way. Yes, Mariana. You are the one. Only you can redeem Speca . . ."

"I won't listen!" she cried, beside herself with sorrow. "You'll not die! You'll not!"

The aged door moaned as it withstood the Druid heavings. Oro stared at the girl in terror. "Mariana! They've almost broken in! Hurry, we have to get away!"

"I'll not leave him here!" she wailed.

The Prince smiled through his pain; his fevered eyes shone with pride in her fierce loyalty. Yes, he had been fortunate to find the companions he did that dark night in Kalimar's alleys. Blue Fire could know no better or stronger hands—even if Mariana did not yet realize it.

"There is no more time," he said flatly. "Oro is right; you have to flee, both of you. Take the dagger—take it now."

Although her sobs threatened to burst forth she held them back and did as he asked. The scabbard was cold, as cold as death itself, and she shivered at the touch.

"This . . . this is wrong," she whispered painfully.

351

"No, Mariana. This is right, the way it was meant to b from the beginning. My people are waiting to be freed. Yo must not let them down. You cannot fail. Do you understan that?"

She inclined her head slightly.

"Then take the power, and use it well."

"What . . . what must I do?" she sniffed.

"Only as little as I myself would have done. Carry th blade to the zenith, to the pinnacle of the Thirty Thousan Steps. And from the Darkness itself you must hurl th blade—as high and as far as you can. Then, and only the can the world be set free . . ."

"But how?" she blurted. What good are these things whe I cannot call upon the Fire? Only you can touch the scimit: while it glows—you told us that a dozen times"

His smile was faint. "Then we must share the secret . . ."

Mariana was still shivering as she tightened her hold on th magical blade. And to her amazement she felt it quive within her grasp with a life force of its own. She stared at th Prince with wide, reddened eyes, and she knew then that I was right. He'd been right all along. Whether he was to liv or die, there was no way he could accomplish the task alon It was up to her to carry the burden of the blade's awesom power, and the responsibility for the world's safety.

"How do I call the Fire?" she said at last, resolved to con plete what had begun so long before.

With a mighty thud the door rocked against the landin the clatter of boots and swords resounded against the stor steps.

"Quickly," said the Prince, drawing her closer. "Hold t scimitar tightly with both hands. Shut your eyes—and s that you believe . . ."

"That I *believe*?"

"That is the only secret. Trust me, Mariana. Please. Dra all your concentration and repeat it again and again. But s it not falsely, or the cold fires will burn you as readily as th will another. Faith is the secret, Mariana. Have such fai and the blade will do your bidding. Think otherwise, and y shall fail. And the Druids shall win; Evil will triumph ov Good . . ."

Nodding, she clutched the scimitar and pushed away t world around her. Wizards were leaping up the steps, bour ing over three at a time, swearing terrible oaths and despe ately trying to reach the beleaguered trio.

I believe, she panted. I believe. *I believe!*

Nothing. Nothing happened.

"Hurry, Mariana!" whined Oro.

"Concentrate!" hissed the Prince.

Tears fell; her arm was shaking and her head swimming. *I believe! I believe! If there are heavens above as surely as there be hell below, then know that I believe!*

Frantic, ready to give up, she hung her head and sobbed. But then it happened. Merely another quiver at first, so faint that she was hardly aware of it. The blade was no longer cold, hints of heat were rising along the edges of the scabbard. Then hotter and hotter the blade became until she felt that her hand itself was on fire. Her eyes opened wide and she stared in amazement at the blue aura which shone above her hand.

"Faith, Mariana!" cried the dying Prince. "You almost have it! Don't give up now!"

A desire to throw the blade away came over her, an urging that she almost could not suppress. But she knew this to be the Evil of the Druids playing at the corners of her mind; she knew this was their desperate attempt to wrest from her the strongest force of good the world possessed.

"I believe!" she shouted raising the scimitar high in the air and shaking it at the charging priests. *"I do believe!"*

And the dagger burst into flame, glorious flame that rose and swelled, and bathed the unholy stairwell in its brilliant light.

The first ranks were upon her; the front wizards drew back in horror while the flame intensified and rose with the blowing wind. Screams of agony swept the steps as a finger of fire touched the lead priest. All at once his dark garments were ablaze, his hair a torch, his flesh blackening into ash. He fell back, back, back, his soul doomed to everlasting torment, and the fires fanning from his corpse spread over the faces and garments of his companions, drowning them in an ocean of searing blue tongues.

"Run!" cried the Prince with his last breath. "Run while you can!"

"Must I still leave you?" she wept, staring down at the man who had touched her life and changed it forever.

There were tears in the Prince's eyes as he said, "Yes, Mariana. Leave me. Leave me now, to be consumed together with those I came to destroy . . ."

The dancing girl nodded with understanding; she knelt

353

beside her fallen friend and kissed him softly with a kiss th
would bridge the realms of heaven and earth. Then she stoc
her eyes no longer wet, but dark and fiery. While the dyi
wizards twisted and cavorted, she could see other sorcere
break into the entrance below. And among the mutes and
sassins came the Grand Vizier himself, spreading magic
tions into the air to counteract the roaring blue flames.

"Goodbye, my friend," she whispered. And without looki
back she and Oro left the Prince behind, running as fast
their feet would carry them toward the pinnacle of the tower

The wind was blowing harder as they reached the terra
Mariana held on for dear life at the banister, fearfully loc
ing out at the whirling clouds above and the miniature wall
city spread below. Ten thousand steps they had climbe
there were twenty thousand to go. And she knew that
Vizier and his liege would do everything in their power
stop her before the heights of the tower could be reached.

Oro's feet pattered across the stone of the terrace;
glanced down and gulped. Gathering in the plaza were c
horts of fierce Druid soldiers, some taking up firing positio
along the turrets of the high walls, others dashing inside t
tower itself, helping the king to give chase to the intruders.

The force of the wind nearly pushed Mariana off as s
groped across the narrow balcony and reached the twisti
steps that curled up along the outer wall.

"We'll never make it!" cried Oro, shading his eyes a
gauging the terrible heights into which they must ascend.

"We've got to try!" rejoined Mariana. And with h
wizard's robes blowing wildly behind, she began the treach
ous climb.

Scant moments later she heard a flurry below. The Viz
and his liege, accompanied by a handful of brutish mut
had reached the open landing. Still sprinkling his potions, t
Vizier bounded like a demon possessed from one end of t
terrace to the other, urging his henchmen to hurry th
climb.

The glow of Blue Fire sent great dancing shadows over t
grim walls as Mariana carried the bright scimitar upwa
step after step, turn after turn, never glancing back.

From the walls over the citadel, a hundred meters below
symphony of arrows whistled. Ducking and scrambling, Ma
ana and Oro dashed this way and that, hugging the w
while shafts bounced off the metal steps at their feet.

And still the Vizier followed.

To her dismay, Mariana saw that the incline of the stairs head became even steeper, as they continued their revolving scent. Black shadows loomed ahead; there was another landing somewhere above—but the route to reach it was even more hazardous than the one they were on now.

Lashing gusts swept all around; the shadows grew closer. They had almost reached the second terrace, almost gained twenty thousand steps. A horrid shriek filled the air; both the dancing girl and the hunchback stared up in fear. Coming from the dense mists of Darkness raced a pair of carrion, vicious and wild, Death-Stalkers as heinous and foul as any they had yet encountered.

Trying to fend them off while still on the steps would be almost impossible. With a sudden burst of energy Mariana yanked at Oro and half dived to reach the landing's precarious safety.

Oro screamed as he hit the smooth floor. The first bird swept its huge, pointed talons above Oro's head and nearly tore it from his neck.

Mariana slashed with the dagger; flames of Blue Fire danced, but the grisly bird showed little fear. Flapping its enormous wings, it soared high above the searing fingers, zooming back into the dark. And then the second carrion was upon them. Shrieking like some ghoul from the dimmest recesses of a nightmare, the Death-Stalker dived for the dancing girl. Mariana whirled, dagger in hand, swinging the blade high above her head. The carrion flapped its wings, red eyes blazing, its beak open wide and spitting fire. These were no ordinary carrions, Mariana realized—but guardians of the sacred tower itself, cursed demons who would fight to the last to protect their Druid masters.

Again the bird roared fire; Mariana swayed and nearly fell from the hot, putrid blast. Then she lunged again with her blade, a crackle of sparks in the air as the blue flames battled with the red.

The bird pressed; she rolled on the ground, feeling a sharp sting as the carrion's talons grazed the side of her head. A gruesome cackle spit from the parted beak. The bird was laughing at the frightened girl, daring her to come at him again.

As she parried and struck, keeping the fiend at bay, the second carrion had reappeared, zooming back down from the sky at the top of its speed, circling above.

Blue Fire throbbed in Mariana's hand; she cut and slashed

355

as she crawled closer to the center of the terrace where there was more room to maneuver. Then up went the scimitar again, its fires burning with greater intensity. The carrion wavered for just an instant, providing Mariana with time to regain her feet. Then she leaped up, diving at the repulsive bird with no thought for her own safety. The blade touched flesh, the carrion reared back as if in unspeakable torment. Crazed, it charged forward, and Mariana felt herself momentarily dazed by the weight of its body. She staggered and fell, eyes open wide; the bird wailed, shaking all over. And then its whole body changed color. Flames of blue singed its innards, burning the beast from within. Vainly it tried to fly backward, its beady eyes bulging and rolling in their sockets.

The second bird screeched horribly as its companion gasped and wailed. Losing no time, Mariana held Blue Fire with both her slim hands and ripped at the oncoming carrion with all her strength. The bird's wings tried to lift it from harm's way—but to no avail. Black feathers roared into lusty blaze; red eyes screamed soundlessly while the searing flames incinerated it alive. While the first carrion exploded from within, the second pirouetted in the air, its beak open wide, trying to spew its devilish fire, a horrid moan rising from somewhere deep in its throat.

Then down, down it plummeted, twisting in circles as it fell toward the plaza below. Oro crawled to the edge of the ledge and peered down. He could see the frantic running of soldiers, panic-stricken and witless as the bird crashed with tremendous thud and sent billows of blue-tinted smoke rising high into the sky. Blue sparks jumped among the Druids. A ball of blue flame ignited, and soldiers scrambled in every direction, throwing down their cumbersome weapons and running like madmen at sight of the fanning fires. Many reached the safety of the citadel's walls, but many did not. Crying and moaning, they fell victim to Blue Fire's wrath. Within moments after the carrion had plunged to its death, the whole of the plaza had become a fiery inferno.

Wiping her eyes, Mariana caught her breath and searched for the continuation of the steps.

"There she is!" came a loud cry. She spun to find a handful of the dreaded mutes reaching the landing. Swords flashing, sardonic smiles exposing teeth like fangs, the mutes clambered onto the terrace in a frenzied attempt to stop the girl before she could go any farther.

356

"Mariana, look out!" cried the hunchback.

The dancing girl whirled, cloak flowing behind. A massive [fi]st came smashing at her, but she sidestepped the blow just [in] time, grabbed the mute by the arm, spun him around, and [p]ushed.

His arms flailed, his sword dropped. Over the side he went, [c]avorting as he fell into the roaring fires below.

Another mute swung his broadsword. The edge of the [b]lade clanged loudly against the wall. Mariana arched back [a]nd thrust the scimitar. Blue flame touched his garment, and [h]e ignited into a ball of human flame.

Others were coming, making their way onto the landing. [M]ariana dashed to the far end of the terrace and found the [r]ow of steps leading higher. Two at a time she scrambled, [O]ro right behind, and the Vizier himself close on her heels.

It was a race that could not be lost. Her lungs were burst[i]ng, her heart pounding so fast that it made her dizzy. All [a]round the clouds and mists were thickening and the wind [w]as howling like never before. Harsh rain began to fall, so [h]eavily that she could not see. Her feet clattered on the metal [st]eps, leading her on and upward into the sky itself. And be[h]ind, like a plague of locusts, came the wizards and mutes, [th]e Dwarf-king, and the Vizier.

"They're gaining on us, Mariana!" wailed Oro fretfully, [gl]ancing over his shoulder and seeing yet another awesome [m]ute leading the charge. The mute hurled a javelin; the spear [sa]iled inches past Mariana's head, and she hunched her [sh]oulders as she fought her way forward against the wind.

The Vizier called upon every devilish god he knew; upon [th]e demons of hell, upon the black spirits that walk the earth [in] the shroud of Darkness, upon the flying demons whose [so]uls had been damned since the world's creation.

Pain shot like arrows through Mariana's mind: the pain of [th]e tormented, the pain of affliction brought upon her by the [m]agic of the Seeds of Destruction. Desperately she clung to [h]er sanity even while these demon spirits called on her to [su]bmit her will to their own, to hurl the blade back down, to [th]row herself into the abyss and greet her peaceful death in [th]e arms of the black gods below.

Reeling, feeling the weight of the magic bear down as [n]ever before, she felt every step as a new agony. And she [co]uld plainly hear the Vizier's dark voice calling to her, ex[ho]lling her to give up now, to join him in the service of Evil.

She shook her head violently, fighting off wave after wave

of willingness to turn back. *I believe!* she cried again an
again in her thoughts. She thought of Ramagar; she thoug
of the Prince whom she had loved more than a brother; o
her grandfather, the haj; and of all her friends whose ver
lives depended on her now. But more than all this, sh
thought of the fate of the world, and the knowledge of wh
would happen to it should she weaken and give in to th
wizard's calling.

And Blue Fire raged in her hand. She stared at the blad
drawing both strength and courage from its power. And u
up she fled, blocking from her mind the thousand laughir
devils intent on destroying her soul.

The steps seemed never-ending, twisting and winding aloi
the sides of the tower, taking her where no man or woman o
Good had ever gone before. The clouds were so dense no
that even the scimitar itself gave hardly enough brightness fo
her to see. It was growing steadily colder, colder even tha
those long nights on the *Vulture* when the ship first saile
into the far North. And a lashing, driving wind screamed lih
the devils themselves.

"Look ahead! Look ahead, Mariana!" Oro was calling.

She drew herself from her thoughts, and clinging to th
banister she dared to lift her head and gaze up.

The steps ended at a broad platform with low, crenellate
walls, a circular terrace that hugged the very pinnacle of th
tower. She gasped and shut her eyes, crying with the realiz
tion that they had almost reached the top. If only she cou
make it just that much farther . . .

The *whish* of a sword brought her back to reality. Behir
her, Oro was bravely grappling with another surging mut
The wizard had all but pinned the hunchback against th
wall, and was trying to throw the little man over the side.

Mariana jumped back down three steps. Blue Fire dance
the mute staggered back, his weapon clattering down, and p
his hands to his eyes, screaming soundlessly. Oro pushed wi
all his waning strength, and the mute dropped clumsily in
the clouds, where the raging wind began to toss his boc
about.

Pulling up the shaking Oro by his tunic, Mariana took h
hand and led him to the edge of the terrace. The rain ha
mysteriously stopped, the wind ceased to howl. It was a gri
world; she could see nothing below, nothing above, save f
the clouds themselves and the cold mists swirling around her.

Turning her attention to Oro, she saw that a strange loc
358

of calm had overtaken the hunchback. The figures still racing up the steps were distant, and Oro seemed to pay no heed to the coming Dwarf-king and his Grand Vizier.

"Guard the steps," she snapped, turning to hurl the scimitar.

Oro shook his head. "No, Mariana. This is the end of the road for both of us."

Her dark eyes narrowed suspiciously. "What are you talking about?"

He held out his hand. "The blade, Mariana. Give it to me."

"Are you mad?"

A cruel smile parted his lips and she recoiled. "I've planned for this moment ever since I first saw the scimitar. It's mine. It belongs to me—and no one can stop me, not even you!"

"You *are* insane!" she cried.

"Do you think I've traveled half a world to see you throw away such a priceless jewel? To see it lost forever here, in such a forsaken land?" He chuckled. "No, Mariana. I will take the scimitar from you—"

"And do what, you fool? What good is it to you now? The Druids will only kill you for it!"

"Will they?" he barked cunningly. "I think not, Mariana. The scimitar will make me a king. Yes, even here, should I choose. You forget that the Vizier covets it, too. What price would these wizards not pay me to possess it themselves, eh? I could return home the richest man in the world. A king, with all the finest wealth in my hands. Gold, jewels . . ." He smiled a wicked smile, and Mariana knew that his treachery had at last surfaced. She had been a fool to let him come; she should have let Ramagar have his way long before they reached these shores.

"And what about Speca?" she flared. "What about Aran and the bondage that awaits the North?"

Oro sneered. "What care I about such trivial matters? I did not make them slaves. If they are unhappy, let them rise up themselves. I did not come to save the world, Mariana. Only enrich myself. And now, I give you a choice: come with me, as my bride, or stay here and die . . ."

"You pig!" she hissed. "Death is a far better choice!"

A dark scowl crossed the hunchback's features. Snapping his fingers, he said, "Very well, if that's the way you want it.

But I have no more time for games. Give me the scimitar—
now!"

The dancing girl gulped and stepped slowly backward
wielding the dagger in front of her. "If you take just one
step, I'll kill you," she vowed. "I don't want to do it, but I
will if you force me."

Oro laughed. "Ah, but have you forgotten? I, too, know
how to call upon the blade's powers. When the Prince told
the secret, I was there as well. Listening, practicing. So you
see, the scimitar cannot harm me—any more than it can
harm you. Now hand it over!"

Mariana flashed a dark smile of her own. "Never! Come
and take it!"

The fire was blazing at its height as the hunchback lunged
for her. As they grappled, his hands firmly around her wrists
the Vizier and the Dwarf-king reached the foot of the steps
and stared frozen.

Oro screamed when the girl bit his hand; he wrenched her
away, and she stumbled against the crenellated wall. Oro
slapped her arm, and the scimitar fell to the ground. As
Mariana reached to sweep it up, Oro's fist slammed against
her face and she went sprawling backward in a daze.

"It's mine!" chortled the hunchback. "Mine, at last!" And
his stubby fingers grabbed at the hilt.

"Do not touch it!" commanded the Vizier, quickly slipping
onto the terrace.

The hunchback paid no heed; repeating the secret words
he scooped up the dazzling dagger and laughed aloud at the
realization that indeed he knew the secret; and now that it
was in his hands there was no need for him ever to give it
up. Why should he? He could have this spindly Vizier and his
ugly, demented liege at their knees right this moment if he
chose.

"Get back!" he shouted to the Vizier. "Get back or I'll
throw it!"

Slyly, recognizing the look of greed, the Vizier pretended
to do as asked. "Put your prize down," he said in a low, commanding voice. "Place it on the floor and I shall give you
anything you ask. Rubies, diamonds, gold. Women . . . beautiful, exotic priestesses for your everlasting pleasure. Prolong-
ed life among us as a deity. Yes, we shall make of you a
deity. Every wish shall be a command . . ."

Oro smiled thinly. "That's not enough. I want an army.

et of ships to conquer my own lands . . . And I want
owledge of all the Dark Arts . . ."

The Vizier nodded; signaling for the Dwarf-king to hold
: place, he took a single step. "All that and more shall be
urs. By the powers of Darkness, by the Shrine of the Spir-
, I swear this to you. Now put down the scimitar . . ."

Lulled by the soft, compelling voice and the allure of
:hes, Oro wavered. Mariana listened while the Vizier con-
ued to make promises, and with her mind still reeling she
awled in the shadows of the wall, inching her way forward
til, unnoticed, she was almost at Oro's back.

The hunchback, meanwhile, held a nervous hand on the
ide. "Then we have a bargain, you and I?" he said.

The Vizier nodded solemnly, even as from the corner of
: eye he saw his liege carefully slip closer to the excited
nchback. "Everything you want is yours for the taking,"
sured the Vizier. Everything you want . . ."

"And I can have the girl? She won't be harmed?"

"The girl, too. I promise . . ."

Oro gleamed in the darkness. "Then here. Take the—
of!"

Mariana's strong push caught him off balance. Oro heaved
ainst the wall and the girl sank her teeth deeply into his
ist. The scimitar fell.

"Stop her!" shouted the Vizier. And the demented Dwarf-
ig, bejeweled in his finery, leaped past the shaken hunch-
ck to grab the quick-stepping woman. Mariana thrust the
ide forward; it caught the fringes of the king's garments,
d all at once his whole body exploded into flame. Scream-
; in pain, flailing his arms madly in the air, the Dwarf
shed to close his hands around Mariana's throat—but Oro
od between them. As Mariana ducked and the Vizier
oked on aghast, the Dwarf-king hurled himself mistakenly
ainst Oro and the two of them entwined into a single ball
searing blue fire. Struggling to break free, Oro pressed
ck at the depression in the low wall. The king, out of his
nd and in agony, tore at his burning hair and pushed them
th forward until they slipped from the precipice.

"Mariana, help me!" cried Oro, his hand groping to find
rs as the king dragged him down. Frozen to her place, the
ncing girl watched stunned as both men fell, a burning
ap together, down, down into the clouds, a flaming torch of
sh, to smash upon the marble plaza below.

Mariana spun to avoid the grabbing hands of the Vizier.

361

She ran to another part of the wall, holding the dagger h
and drawing back her arm.

"Don't!" thundered the Vizier. "You can't! You can't!"

"I can and I will!" rejoined the shaken girl. And she ai
the scimitar high, just as the Prince had instructed, a
hurled Blue Fire with all her ebbing strength and courage.

"You fool!" cried the Vizier, his hands to his face. "Y
don't know what you've done! It's the end, the end of us all!

Mariana was crying, and she laughed through her te
Now she was prepared for anything, even death. The bur
had been lifted from her shoulders forever.

The air became suddenly still; there was no longer eve
breeze. Mariana stared out into the pervasive void. Abo
the clouds still hung in the black sky as though nothing
happened. The glow of the dagger had vanished, become
in the oblivion of the Eternal Darkness, and for a mom
she wondered if its powers had been too pitiful to battle
poisoned air of Evil.

But then it happened; slowly at first, but frightening a
awesome. Thunder rumbled in the distance; lightni
cracked. The mists began to swirl. And from somewh
above there came a glow, dim at first but steadily brighteni
a blue glow that worked its way along the edges of the s
and slipped thin fingers among the clouds. Then there w
crackles of electricity and red sparks snapped through the
mosphere.

White-knuckled, Mariana clutched the wall, holding
breath as the wind roared once more, only this time with
force of a hurricane. The Vizier held out his arms and fell
his knees in sobs. The tower itself began to shake, and wh
the thunder boomed it seemed the whole world swayed w
it.

Across the sky dark colors were ripping; blue fire lash
among shadows. Roar after terrible roar filled her ears u
Mariana could no longer stand it. Stones loosened in
walls and tumbled down. The bedrock tower had begun
crack, huge fissures forming among the stones and rippli
downward back to the earth.

Crying, Mariana shielded herself and waited for the gra
to crumble around her. The Vizier was writhing on the flo
calling out to his gods of the Darkness, his lips dark a
trembling. It was as if the earth itself were exploding. Migl
lightning bolts struck again and again, crossed swords in t

362

ky, weapons of anger, furiously charged and pelting the land
with terrible retribution.

Rock crumbled everywhere. Mariana threw back her head
and stared out into the multicolored sky. The battle was hotly
contested. Good against Evil. Faith against damnation. The
foul and disgusting civilization of the Druids would surely
come to an end. And even should fair Speca herself be tossed
beneath the sea, Mariana was sure she had done the right
thing.

With a shattering crash of lightning one side of the terrace
split before Mariana's startled eyes and caved in completely.
Still lost in his anguish, the Vizier was hardly aware when the
ledge gave way and loose stones came crashing over his head.
Then the balcony buckled and Mariana saw him tossed into
the air, his crimson eyes wide and fearful, his shrieks piercing
the night as he was thrown into the raging vortex. Singed by
the ravishes of blue fire and the devilish scarlet flame he himself had spawned, he tumbled ever downward to a fiendish
grave.

As the tumult of a sky gone mad surrounded her with its
fury, Mariana folded her shivering arms and stood waiting.
Her own demise would be swift in coming, and with neither
fears nor sorrow she held her pitiful meter of ground while
the Devil's Tower crumbled to dust about her.

27

The celebration of the Seeding had long since been under
way throughout Speca. Set apart from the merrymaking taskmasters, Ramagar and the other shackled slaves sat miserable
and cold in their smelly hovels. Thorhall had successfully cut
through his own bonds and had nearly succeeded in freeing
the thief.

Ramagar winced with pain, his bruised ankle throbbing
and swelling, as the wily Aranian finally sawed through the
iron links. The metal snapped suddenly and the thief hur-
riedly pulled the chain off. He rubbed at his ankle and drew
a long sigh of relief. In the darkness of the shack and amid
the loud carryings-on of the taskmasters and their priestess
whores, no one was yet aware of the strange bursts of light
brightening the sky.

"Shh . . ." said Thorhall, a finger to his lips.

Ramagar's eyes slitted like a panther's. "What is it? Ar there guards about?"

The Aranian shook his head; he slinked to the boarde wall and peered through a crack. There were distant rolls thunder, he noted, a not uncommon occurrence in the climes, yet there was also a strange accompanying glow fro the direction of the citadel itself.

"What do you make of that?" said Thorhall, moving asid and beckoning for the thief to have a look. Ramagar peeke through the opening and shook his head in wonder. "The sk is sparking . . . Look at that! It's . . . It's . . . crackling lik timber!"

They exchanged long, fretful glances. "Could this be pa of the celebration?" asked the thief.

"I've never seen this sort of thing before," Thorhall admi ted, as puzzled as the thief.

Suddenly they heard a bugle blast, a loud shrill wail horns blaring in the Darkness. "It's the Call to Arms!" crie the startled Aranian. "Coming from the garrison, no doub and signaling all soldiers back to duty!"

The thunder grew closer, the lightning more terrible. Ou side, several of the overseers were clanging bells and hoc ing through whistles. "Quick! We won't have much tin now," said Ramagar. And he pulled the sharpened ston away from Thorhall and began to free the haj. The old ma grunted, then smiled with satisfaction as his bonds broke.

A burly sentry stepped inside, weapon in hand. Ramag sprang from the shadows and knocked him down. With on move he broke the soldier's neck, scooped up his sword, ar tossed it into the waiting hands of the haj. While Bur slipped to the entrance to watch the ensuing commotio Ramagar worked feverishly to free Argyle and young Hom

The haj inched outside, crawling on his belly. Across tl open field in front, frightened whores, half naked, can scampering from the Druid barracks. And behind the shirtless and sweaty, came the taskmasters and other noncon missioned officers, caught literally with their pants down the moment of their empire's most dire emergency.

Black stallions came galloping out of the Darkness, crin son-eyed messengers restraining their steeds from bolti while they gave the news. But by this time there was little tell that could not be seen. The sky was raging in hues

364

e, and the ground itself rumbled and shook. A shattering
rricane wind raged over the grim and barren landscape.

Ramagar reached the unlocked door and flung it wide. He
elded his eyes from flying dust and stared at the incredible
ht. In the sky, thick black clouds were bursting, tingling
h ripples of strange colorful brightness, and spinning about
zily while the glow of deep blue spread rapidly from one
l of the horizon to the other. It was a blue that could not
mistaken.

"Blue Fire!" Ramagar cried in jubilation. He spun and
ked to his equally stunned companions. "The Prince . . .
riana . . . They're alive! They've reached the Devil's
wer and thrown the dagger!"

"There is no other explanation," stammered Argyle in
eement.

Bursting with the new realization that his beloved was not
t, the thief of Kalimar subdued a racing heart and watched
e Druid soldiers scrambling through the camp to answer the
ll to Arms amid the raging havoc.

"Now it's our turn to play a role," he grunted. "Druid
gic may well be at an end, but this fiendish army still reins intact."

"Aye," said Thorhall grimly. "Every one of these devils
l be mustered and rampaging over the land within hours.
ey'll be bent on destruction, you can be sure. A slaughter
inst the helpless Specians such as the world has never
n . . ."

"And their Dragon Ships will ply the coasts in vengeance,"
led Argyle knowingly. "They must be stopped."

Ramagar gritted his teeth. "Then what are we waiting for,
friends? We came here to fight, didn't we? Let's put an
l to their plans before they begin!"

And with that, the thief bolted from the hovel daringly
le the wind roared against him.

A single soldier came running in his direction, weapon
wn. Ramagar drew back his arm and slammed his fist into
Druid's face before the soldier could duck. Snatching up
fallen sword, he raced into the fray.

War cries upon their lips, both Thorhall and Argyle dashed
oss the compound. Those few unfortunate enough to get
heir way were quickly dispatched, and the Aranians made
haste to reach the carefully protected mine—a mine
ose bowels of sulphur would create a fire that would dev-
ate the Black Forest itself.

Druids rushed to block the charge. Mighty Argyle swive[ ]
in his place, a curved broadsword held tightly with b[ ]
hands. The blade whizzed above his head, coming down w[ ]
terrible speed and power and smashing heads at every si[ ]
Druids staggered at his feet, tumbling atop one another. T[ ]
came at him from the left and from the right; Thorhall c[ ]
ered at his back, and young Homer slashed a dagger wil[ ]
to keep other pressing soldiers at bay.

The haj, meanwhile, had made his way to the shed wh[ ]
weapons were stored. On his heels Ramagar arrived a[ ]
made short shrift of the single soldier on guard. The [ ]
sought out their own weapons, making special note to f[ ]
Argyle's ax. Then, arms burdened with weapons, the two m[ ]
rushed back outside to aid their besieged friends.

"Here, catch this!" cried the haj, tossing the huge ax in [ ]
gyle's direction. The Aranian's eyes glinted in the dark [ ]
glad smile spreading over his shadowed face. And with his [ ]
firmly in hand, he marked out a new and more feroci[ ]
circle of death, sending limbs and appendages flying a[ ]
dozen Druids fell in bloodied heaps.

Horsemen were thundering into the camp, fresh tro[ ]
from the Black Forest garrison. Riding insanely into [ ]
wind, they crouched low, swinging their steel swords, tear[ ]
into the ranks of helpless, dazed Specians.

Ramagar leaped from Thorhall's side and brought do[ ]
the first of the line with a tremendous blow of his sword. [ ]
black stallion reared in panic as its rider crumpled from [ ]
saddle. And all at once the thief mounted. Spurring the [ ]
mal on, he rode directly among the cavalry, hacking [ ]
slashing, creating a bold diversion so that the shackled Sp[ ]
ans could run.

"The vats!" he cried aloud. "Spill the vats!"

The haj spun and stared at the huge pots of boiling mi[ ]
als set against the sides of the mine's entrance. Bracing [ ]
shoulder, he strained to overturn the first, veins popping fr[ ]
his throat in the effort. Argyle and Thorhall were soon at [ ]
side. "Heave!" shouted the seafaring Aranian. "Heave!"

The thick, hot vessel gave; the adventurers scurried to [ ]
side. As the vat fell over, great billows of molten liq[ ]
spilled with the roar of the tide, splashing over the flat terr[ ]
and burning the earth with white-hot heat.

Horses were screaming in pain from the liquid, stagger[ ]
and falling, rendering their riders helpless to go on with t[ ]
charge. Ramagar leaped from his own agonized steed o[ ]

e sloped roof of a hovel. Arrows and spears came flying at
im, a host of archers having taken aim from their strong
ositions beside the barracks. From roof to roof the coura-
eous thief clambered, dodging and spinning while feathered
hafts whistled inches from his head.

Argyle and Thorhall were making for cover behind the
igh piles of sulphur sacks while brave Homer and the haj
esperately tried to clear a path for the anguished slaves who
ere running helter-skelter in an effort to get away. Soaring
rrows cut a third of them down, and forced the rest to cower
mong the white-hot flames of the burning liquid.

Ramagar spun at the sound of a hoarse, cruel voice.
rouching, he peered beyond the flames; then, inching to the
dge of the sloped roof he found himself staring at the task-
aster himself, bullwhip in his hand. He was barking orders
 frantic soldiers while lashing at a handful of frightened,
ornered slaves. Taking great pleasure in his sadistic game, he
ughed with bounding glee as the slaves begged and moaned
nd the whip pushed them back directly into the fires.

The bellicose fat man had not yet caught sight of the fleet-
g silhouette above. Shrouded by billows of thick, fuming
noke that danced in the wind, Ramagar grasped his small
agger firmly and slid down.

"Taskmaster!" he called, landing evenly on his feet.

The overseer turned in trepidation; he faced the daring for-
gner before him dumbly, shaken by this new turn of events.
ut slowly his fear vanished and a broad grin crossed his
ce. His potbelly quivered with his mirth and he lashed the
ullwhip at Ramagar's feet. Hours of pleasure could be found
 torturing this particular prisoner.

The Vizier himself had of course commanded that none of
ese strangers be molested in mind or body—yet the wizard
as not here now, and the taskmaster could only chortle at
e prospect of at last having his own way. He would rip the
sh from the arrogant thief, layer by layer, watching him
uirm, until his screams begged for death.

Thunder rumbled and the ground shook. Ramagar paced
hile the sweaty overseer drew back the whip. Lightning
ared and struck nearby; the cries of panicked horses rose
ove the din. The overseer lunged, Ramagar ducked. Then
th the awful winds at his back, the thief threw his body
to the air, striking feet first and bowling the fat man over.
gether they struggled in hand-to-hand combat, the thief

367

rolling on the ground while the sadist's hand tried to clo
around his throat.

The sky was in a tumult, crackling and thundering. A d
luge of rain now was turning the caked soil into mu
Ramagar slammed an elbow into the taskmaster's jaw. T
man was stunned. Ramagar raised his dagger and plunged
into soft flesh. The taskmaster groaned, hand to his belly.
thin trickle of blood stained his muddied tunic; he stagger
to his feet and staggered backward and wobbled, finge
crimson with his blood.

"The keys!" cried one of the slaves. "He has the keys
our shackles!"

Without a thought for the white-hot flame already seari
the overseer's bloated body, Ramagar scrambled to the ed
of the pool of liquid, straining to pull the flaming taskmas
free. While driving rain kept the flames subdued, the fe
some wind sent tongues of flame licking at the thief's g
ments.

The taskmaster was still alive, screaming and writhing
Ramagar's nimble fingers tried to pry the key chain from
belt. Finally the thief used his dagger to cut off the belt. Th
he tossed it to the waiting prisoners.

"Here, free yourselves!" he shouted. And while the amaz
Specians struggled to unlock their shackles, Ramagar made
hasty retreat, his hands sheltering his face, just as the f
spread and consumed the moaning sadist.

Argyle and the others were badly under siege; though t
piled bags of sulphur offered good protection, they were co
pletely surrounded and pinned down by squads of Drui
Constant barrages of whistling arrows sailed amid the r
and wind, forcing the bold adventurers to keep down low
their positions.

The sky itself seemed afire when Ramagar finally work
his way to their side. The haj bellowed in warning, a
Ramagar whirled, greeting head-on a fearsome soldier thro
from his steed and now trying to bolt free from the mayhe
Ramagar deftly upended the man and sent him flying i
Argyle's waiting arms. The glittering ax came down, and w
a single thrust severed the soldier's head from his shoulde
sending it tumbling to the ground.

"We'll never be able to hold!" cried Thorhall in desp
"They're coming at us from every side—and more are on
way. Look!" He pointed down the dark, muddy road
where Druid cavalry were racing from the shadows.

The Druids were pressing steadily closer; they plunged from the road and over the fences of the camp, sweeping running slaves before them and trampling them down like chattel, with crashes and thuds lifting men off their feet and snapping their necks and backs.

Howls of dismay rose from the prisoners as they realized their situation. Freed at last from their chains, they were now given a choice of being cut down by the oncoming cavalry or retreating to face a fiery death from the burning minerals.

"They're done for," commented the haj, his heart broken at the sight.

"And so will we be," added Argyle in somber response.

"Unless we can reach the mine," said Ramagar. "If we can blow it, we can stop their entire advance."

But the situation seemed hopeless. The moment they broke from their cover, a host of Druid arrows would assail them.

Anguished, the brave band looked on. But suddenly their ears caught the faint blast from afar—a sound that made them all expect the worst.

"What is it?" said Ramagar.

Thorhall shook his head. "I . . . I don't know . . . I'm not sure . . ." But then it came again: the sound of a horn, five short blasts in rapid succession. Thorhall strained to peer over the sides of the sacks, heedless of the snub-nosed arrows smacking clumsily into the dirt.

"It is!" he cried. "It's them!"

And while his companions stared in confusion, a large group of shadowy figures came leaping and bounding over the fences, broad-shouldered, swarthy men, with hate in their eyes and minds intent on battle.

Thorhall's wildmen had joined the contest.

The fearless barbarians scaled the wired perimeters, shouting war cries of old, attacking with the full force of their numbers into the lines of Druid archers and cavalry and rendering savage blows.

With the new element added to the fight the melee raged at a more furious pitch than ever. Wildmen slashed and hacked their way from one fortified line to the next, causing total havoc and forcing the hard-pressed Druids to make one hasty retreat after another. And while all this was happening, the freed Specian slaves began to come out of their drugged stupors and, sweeping up the enemy's fallen weapons, added further fuel to the din of battle.

Argyle and Thorhall looked at each other and laughed.

369

Then bolting from their places, they full-heartedly joined the fray.

"Now's our chance," exhorted Ramagar. With the haj and Homer beside him, the thief dashed into the open and across the bloodied field. The ground was carpeted with bodies; slaves, wildmen, dozens upon dozens of fallen Druids. Arrow shafts poked up from the earth like grisly blades of grass; there were helmets and spears, knives and swords, limbs and torsos stuck in mud and pools of dark blood. Boiling minerals sizzled as the Specians turned over the last of the vats, spilling the liquid at the oncoming Druid horsemen. Rain was pouring down, the ground shook with thunder, and lightning flashed while searing color raced across the heavens.

Ramagar stooped and picked up a thick stick. While the haj watched with puzzlement, the thief tore strips of linen from his shirt, wrapped them carefully around the head of the stick, and ignited his torch by poking it into a pool of fiery mineral. The torch sprang magnificently into flame, sending streaks of fire spinning in the wind. Then on toward the entrance to the mine they ran, mindless of the danger to themselves.

Three mail-clad Druids charged from the side. Distant cavalry pressed to reach the thief and stop him. Eyes wild with desperation, the mail-clad soldiers lunged for the haj. Burlu met the first with an overhand blow that crushed both helmet and skull, then quickly wove a web of flying steel at the others while Ramagar slipped closer to the dark, descending shaft.

"Hurry, Ramagar!" called the worried haj, fending off blows and keeping a wary eye to the approaching cavalry.

The thief grunted, and replied, "Run like the devil when I throw!" Onto his belly he dived as spears came flying. The sordid smell of sulphur burst upon his nostrils; gathering a handful of loose sulphur he quickly spread it thinly in snaking line down to the shaft, a short fuse giving perhaps ten or fifteen seconds' time to make his getaway.

The haj thrust, countered, parried, and thrust again. His blade caught the second soldier unaware and the Druid reeled back, hands to his throat where his jugular had been cut. The last of the enemy abandoned all defensive tactics; wildly he threw himself at the aging swineherd. Burlu lost touch with his opponent's blade; holding breath, he leaned aside, dodging the thrust, then came back up with one of his own. He could

370

feel the bite of steel as it grazed his arm, feel his own weapon pulse up through the Druid's gut and tear into his heart. The soldier fell with the blade; the haj turned to seek out the coming horses. "Now, Ramagar! Now!"

The thief backstepped outside; he lifted the torch and threw it down at the edge of the fuse. Sulphur sizzled and the flames danced. And back toward the piles of sacks they ran with reckless abandon. The charging cavalrymen pulled sharply on the reins and tried to turn their steeds about. At sight of the lighted fuse the horses bolted in terror, screaming and bucking.

The fuse wisped its way lower and lower into the shaft, out of sight now, save for the crimson shadows reflected by the dull earthen walls.

Ramagar and the haj leaped for shelter. The first explosion rocked the camp like nothing they had ever seen; horses and riders were sent flying into the air like dolls, scream upon scream, limbs being wrenched from their bodies as a flood of dragon-like fire spewed from the shaft.

Ramagar scrambled to his knees, feeling as though his head had been beaten by a sledgehammer. Druids were trying to run in every direction before him, but the second explosion sent them slamming to the ground again, unable even to move while a new fire tore across the length of the camp. The wooden edifices were turning into raging timber, flames rising higher and higher until the entire camp had become an oven.

Through the scorching terrain Ramagar and the haj broke, reaching the edge of the open road. There, the wildmen, under the direction of Thorhall and the wounded Argyle, were routing the last of the cavalry and preparing to attack the Black Forest garrison itself.

"The citadel," gasped Ramagar, panting for air, "we have to get down to the city at once to free the slaves and give our signal to the *Vulture* . . ."

"The fires are spreading everywhere," said Thorhall. And he glanced back at the devastated camp. "You'll have to cross the flames to reach the road."

"No matter," replied the thief, thinking now only of finding Mariana amid the raging of battle and rescuing her before marauding Druids combed the land.

From behind came the whinnying of frightened horses; Ramagar turned with blade in hand. Standing tense and poised he stared as Homer appeared from within the dense

371

clouds of smoke, riding a fine black stallion. His face wa
black with ash and smoke, his clothing smeared, but the grir
he wore stretched from ear to ear.

"The compound is freed!" he cried merrily. "We can rejoi
the Prince!"

"He's right," said the haj. "Best we hasten to the citadel a
fast as we can."

"That's why I rounded up these," replied Homer, and h
gestured to the two horses on short rein standing docilely be
hind his own. "With luck we can be there in a few hours."

"The sooner the better," said Ramagar. He took the bridl
of one in hand and soothed the mare's flanks. "Captain Osar
must be close to port by now, and we can't keep him wait
ing." And losing no time, he expertly mounted and prepare
to ride.

"Farewell until the battle is done," called Thorhall as th
haj mounted his own steed. Then as he and Argyle began th
march to overtake the garrison and free the countryside, th
three companions from Kalimar waved briefly and gallope
off in the opposite direction.

Through thundering flame they spurred the horses on, rid
ing a course right through the burning camp where onl
hours before a thousand slaves had languished. Across th
shattered and smoking terrain, mindless of the stench o
death and the pitiful sobs of dying men resounding in thei
ears, they clattered over debris, beyond the splintered fence:
and onto open land.

Back toward the Valley of Morose they raced, where eve:
at this distance they could make out the lines of the forebod
ing Devil's Tower as it swayed amid the terrible winds an
began to crumble.

The sky blazed now in whirling color as the riders reache
the flatland. It glowed as black as coal, then white almost a
the day; flashes of scarlet and amber dizzily danced above
changing to silver and gray and returning at length to bur
feverishly with blue fire. The poisoned clouds churned demor
ically in a vortex; it was hail that suddenly pelted the eartl
spewing harmless venom to the ground while the thunde
clapped in deafening roars and the winds continued to howl.

Over field and bogs they hurried, winding along th
tremor-filled road, while from faraway points they could hea
the low droning of bells, hundreds of bells, deep an
resonant. They clanged like the wails of demons, and th
riders shuddered with every chime.

Drawing close to the citadel, they paused upon a rise and peered out for the first time at the city itself and the port beyond. Ramagar stared in wonder. The sea had begun to roll, with wave after mountainous wave lashing furiously against the ancient wharves and low reefs at the harbor's mouth, breaking over both, smashing them like kindling. Into the stoic walls of the capital they crashed; like a flood the torrent of ocean came, crushing seawalls asunder, pouring like a tempest over deadened scapes and withered lands.

Then atop the heights near the jagged chalk cliffs the riders took pause again. Peering down at the city, they watched a sight unlike anything they had ever seen. Even as the bite of the sea tore at the Druid fortress from without, a great tumult had begun to rage from within. Great fires were spreading everywhere, and beneath the explosions of the sky above, it seemed as though the entire land of Speca was crumbling before their eyes. From shore to shore the land was shaking; the din of rampant mobs broken free attested to the thousands of slaves rid of their shackles and now ripping apart every vestige of Druid domination.

Mighty statues came smashing to the ground; grim temples and marble plazas were devastated as the earth quaked underneath. As once-fierce Druid cavalry and archers vainly tried to stem the raging tide, scores of half-crazed mobs burnt everything in sight. Dragon Ships were rocking and tossing upon the angry sea, rendered virtually helpless with the maelstrom. Slowly, though, the dark vessels plowed closer to the port, weapons of destruction aimed at the heart of the city itself.

"They're going to destroy the capital!" cried Ramagar, watching as the sail-less ships fought their way toward the shore.

"Aye," agreed the somber haj. "They hope to raze the city and ravish the land. The lords of Darkness demand as much. Druid culture must perish, then so shall all others . . ."

Ramagar looked on helplessly; already the first balls of steel had been flung from the catapults, smashing over the walls and killing all who stood in the way. The crowds were fleeing helter-skelter, scrambling over the corpses of fallen comrades and slain Druids. And onward the Dragon Ships pressed, in unholy vengeance against the pitiful city.

The Dragon Ship prows struck westward, past the broken seawalls; the sea was black with the shadows of crimson ships dancing upon the tossing waves. But then, even as they drew

373

closer to target, other vessels began to appear beneath th
twisting clouds to the east. Tiny dots at first, shapeless an
unrecognizable, but drawing steadily closer to Speca's barre
shores. The horizon became dotted with them from edge t
edge, until it showed itself to be a mighty armada strainin
forward to join the fight.

The Dragon Ships stopped in their places; some began t
turn, others held fast. Orders bellowed from vessel to vesse
as the awesome Dragon Ships massed into battle formation

"They're turning from the city!" gasped the haj, astounde
The thief of Kalimar laughed. "Look! Can't you see? Loo
to the sails!"

The first of the approaching ships came into full view, an
both Homer and the haj stared in disbelief. It was the *Vu*
ture, sails full and swelled, leading what seemed to be half
thousand sleek *knaars* into battle.

True to its word, Aran had come.

The *knaars* of Aran covered the horizon, their long, sli
shapes built for sturdiness in battle as well as speed. Hug
sails billowed in the winds, and across their decks the rugge
warriors prepared for battle, proudly defying both the ragin
weather and the dreaded Druid forces.

It was not long before the first of the *knaars* reached th
shattered barriers. War cries resounded through the air; th
Druids pelted the bold fighting ships with every weapon the
had, but still the *knaars* came, slashing through the waves.

Catapults twanged lustily; decks smashed, masts brok
prows dipped below the waves. But the veterans of Ara
knew only courage. Under direction of their battle-seasone
captains, they surrounded the Dragon Ships and hurled bla
ing balls of fire from stem to stern.

For almost an hour the battle raged; casualties mounted o
both sides, the sea became littered with drowned combatant
Skillfully, the *knaars* tightened their web around the flounde
ing larger ships, forcing them to stall upon the reefs whil
grappling ropes were flung over the sides and thousands o
fierce sea warriors clambered to reach the enemy.

Ramagar and his friends mounted their steeds and rode t
the citadel. Hooves trampled over smashed statues of dar
lords and fiendish devils. Through the heat of smoldering fir
they reached the plaza with weapons drawn. Fallen pries
and Druid troops lay in disarray; bells were still chimin
from the city, but fewer and fewer with the passing of tim
Scorched and blackened walls greeted them silently, glaze
374

eyed soldiers dead in the streets blocked their path at every turn. Hug clouds of smoke fanned out everywhere, and Ramagar, his face sooty and grim, stared about at the total destruction.

The Devil's Tower stood straight before him, a crushed shell of its former self, a lifeless hulk still swaying at its zenith. Mangled and charred corpses told something of the fight to reach the top; the haj covered his face with his hands to block out the stench of death, and sat bewildered in his saddle while the roar of the mobs in the city heightened. All around was a shambles; untold thousands had died this day, and still the battle was far from over.

The sea battles still raged furiously and the fires in the city swelled as Ramagar and the others came to the entrance of the tower. Dismounting from his saddle, the thief made ready to fight his way through the rubble in search of Mariana. But suddenly he stopped. A strange quiet had overtaken the sky, a shattering silence that left him startled.

The haj stared up questioningly. The sky had turned black again; the rain and hail had ceased and the winds strangely calmed. There was no more thunder or lightning, and in that very moment it seemed the world itself had stopped spinning, as if nature held her breath until the lull subsided.

Perplexed, Ramagar and his companions exchanged long, worried glances. The din of the mobs had ended as well, and the freed slaves lifted their own gazes toward the sky. Something different was happening, something no one could explain.

The stallions stirred uneasily, sensing the eerie dispassion. Holding firmly on the reins, the haj swept his glance past the unseen top of the shattered tower. A thin, dark haze was spreading across the heavens, like a fog, shrouding the land from shore to shore. But as the haze descended it began to dissipate.

Homer rubbed at his eyes, turning away from the falling vapor. And when at last he peered up again he gasped. "The clouds!" he stammered. "The clouds are breaking up!"

Distant screams came from the city accompanied by frantic calls from woeful priests yet in their temples. Ramagar blinked and shut his eyes. Something was hurting, hurting his eyes so that he could not see. And it was the same for the shaken haj Burlu, who found himself unable to look up. "Fire!" he gasped. "The sky is on fire!"

Homer bravely defied his own pain and struggled to peer

375

toward the clouds. Tears streamed down his diluted pupils from the brightness, but he had begun to laugh, loudly and deeply. "There is no fire!" he cried. "Look again! Look again my friends! It's the sun! *The sun has broken through!*"

And so it was; needle shafts of brilliant sunlight had begun to stream down over the city, slowly at first, but then faster and faster. Crimson-eyed Druids fell to their knees and wailed, unable to stand the light. Blinded, they moaned and cried while a jubilant roar of happiness resounded down every street.

On the sea, the Dragon Ships had ceased to attack. Blinded helmsmen staggered and stumbled while hordes of Aran's warriors greeted the blazing ball of fire in the sky with cheers. The sun was shining fully now, spreading its glowing warmth over the barren hills and wasted rivers, through forests and fields, into crevices and recesses that had never known its light, from the peaks of the mountains down to the valleys below. Everywhere. Everywhere there was light golden brightness bursting majestically for the first time in more than ten centuries.

Ramagar shaded his eyes for a time, letting them readjust to the brightness he had not seen in weeks. The dark haze that descended was now all but gone, burning through the last vestiges of poison and wiping it away forever. Some high clouds still scattered above, but they were soft clouds of white, gently rolling in from the sea, tinted at the edges with a flaming crimson as the sun set in the west at the end of day.

And what a glorious day it had been! Against a sudden sky of deep, rich blue the battle was won. The Druid empire had crumbled to nothing within a single day's time. And the sun had returned, a sight to gladden any heart, to give comfort to every soul.

The lost land of Speca was free at last.

28

Dressed in a soft yellow brocaded gown of silk and lace Mariana walked alone from her quarters toward the open veranda of the Specian palace where long ago great and heroic kings had guided the land from triumph to triumph.

376

The ordeals of past days were still fresh in her mind; she could still feel the sting of bitter tears welling in her eyes. Yet these many events, as fresh and recent as they were, also seemed lost in some distant past, as if the memories were more of vivid dreams than of reality. Yet real they were, she knew, and no matter how much time might pass, she could never forget. Nor would she want to. During her most frightening hours, when she had been forced to fight her way back down the Thirty Thousand Steps, battling for her very existence while the Devil's Tower cracked around her, she had wanted nothing more than to blot these days from her mind, erase them completely. Now, though, even that wish was past. She was prepared to face the future without fear or doubt.

It was early morning. The rising sun glittered on the clear, chilly Northern waters, and cast soft shadows across the stone structures of the city.

Mariana paused in her walk to the veranda, and standing at the low balcony wall she gazed out at the calm sea, as restful as she had ever seen it. Birds were in the air, seagulls, squawking and diving towards the reefs. She hardly took notice of the shattered hulks of Dragon Ships, many still smoldering, smashed upon those same reefs and slowly breaking up, to be carried far out by the tides and lost forever. Mariana smiled and sighed; she knew she would be content with her memories, even the most painful.

There was a small flight of steps at the end of the balcony leading down to the veranda. The haj stood patiently waiting, dressed in a fine Eastern robe, his bronzed face aglitter with smiles. Mariana gave him her hand, and side by side they came to join the gathered crowd.

All her friends were there, waiting for her arrival, chatting quietly among themselves. Captain Osari and Argyle shared some small mirth, while Thorhall, accompanied by his lovely daughters and father-in-law, spoke briefly with the aged Sage of the Sklar. Homer beamed when he saw Mariana; he nudged Ramagar in the ribs, and the thief excused himself from the others to greet her with a kiss.

"Ah, Mariana," said the Sage, turning toward her, and bowing politely. "You look beautiful." His eyes sparkled and the dancing girl blushed.

Argyle took her hand and kissed it, saying, "I hope you passed the night well."

The girl nodded and smiled, not mentioning to him the

377

tears she had quietly shed after the funeral bier was s
adrift. Her eyes wandered back to the sea, back to where tl
blazing craft carrying the body of the Prince had bee
launched. The fires of the boat had lighted up the sky,
lonely and forlorn flame drifting endlessly along the shores
Speca until the sea itself consumed it and brought his so
into its bosom.

Mariana heaved a deep sigh, thinking on how briefly sl
had really known the mysterious Prince whose life ha
changed her own. Like Blue Fire itself he had come an
gone, both living for the same purpose, dying for the sam
cause. Mariana knew she had loved the Prince, and her onl
regret was that she could not tell him so now. He had bee
more than a brother, but his memory would remain strong i
her thoughts forever, and she knew that Ramagar felt th
same.

The haj put his hands on his hips and swelled his lung
with fresh salty air. With a single quick glance he looke
across the harbor at the hundreds of anchored *knaars*, sai
furled, waiting to return to Aran. Then he turned his atte
tion toward the quay and to the berthed *Vulture*. All hanc
of the merchant vessel were busily readying the ship for sai
preparing happily for the long voyage back to Cenulam.
the city itself the newly freed citizens were thronging th
streets, still cheering the armada before beginning the task
rebuilding their civilization.

"It's a good sight to see, isn't it?" observed Captain Osa
to the haj.

Burlu nodded. "It is. But I fear it shall take many lifetime
before the memory of the scourge is wiped away."

"Not so," interrupted Old Man, sightlessly lifting his gaz
toward the sun. Children were playing in the courtyards b
low, laughing and dancing in the sunlight as children alway
do. "*They* are our future," the philosopher went on. "The
and their own children after them. We must make certai
that they grow strong and wise, for from them shall con
Speca's new leaders."

"And the new Provisional Council will see to it," said tl
aged Sage of Aran in agreement. He looked down at the chi
dren and smiled. "It shall take time, but not as long as yc
think."

"The Prince would be pleased," said Captain Osari with
sigh. "All his goals have been achieved. And I for one a
glad to have been able to help."

378

Mariana looked to the contented mariner. "When are you scheduled to sail?" she asked.

Osari grinned merrily, his thoughts now on home. "With the evening tide, Mariana," he replied. "I've found everything I came here for and more. This new trade route shall make Cenulam a wealthy nation again—and I shall certainly share in those profits."

Thorhall laughed heartily. "Aye, I'm sure you will. A free Speca shall surely add to the world's wealth and knowledge. But tell me, have you decided not to stay here, to help in rebuilding the land? There is need of you . . ."

The rugged sailor shook his head. "The sea is still my calling; that can never change for me. But I'll be back, again and again, to carry home the first cargoes and to watch the land grow."

Thorhall nodded. He clasped the mariner's hand and shook firmly.

"But what about you?" Mariana asked of the wily Aranian. "Aren't you going back to Aran? It's more than twenty years since you've seen your home."

Thorhall took the hands of both his pretty daughters and squeezed them tightly. "My home is here," he answered, smiling and looking from one blushing girl to the other. "We have talked it over and decided. We want to help rebuild the land, do everything for her that we can. We want to see the land grow fertile, see the grasses return to the hills. Give us that much, and we shall be more than content."

"And I feel the same," said Homer with a beam in his eye and a smile directed at Thorhall's eldest daughter. "The Provisional Council has asked me to take charge in city matters—a task that I hope to live up to in every way. I, too, have found my destiny here." And the hint of a tear came to his eyes. "It was the Prince who altered the course of my life," he continued. "Without him, I would yet be a worthless urchin in the back alleys of the Jandari. Aiding my new friends in Speca is but a small part of repaying that debt of gratitude."

The wise Sage of Aran clasped Homer's shoulder. "And I know that the Prince would be proud of this moment," he told the youth. "It is both good and right that you are among us today. There is much we can all learn from you." Then turning from the tearful lad, he looked to the haj. "And what of you, my friend? Shall you remain to become a part of the new Speca as well?"

Burlu smiled wistfully and hesitated in his reply. "Would that it were possible!" he told them all. "Alas, I cannot. have too many duties that must be attended to at home. M' family awaits my return, and I must hasten back to Kalima' as soon as possible. I leave today on board Captain Osari' ship. My sons-in-law by now have me ruined, no doubt, an' my grandchildren will have missed me sorely. But know this these past months have given an old man such adventures a I never dreamed of. I am more than gratified to have live them and done my own small part in freeing this fair lanc Now I must take my leave."

Old Man nodded his head slowly. "You shall be missec good haj. Speca shall never forget your courage . . ."

The haj turned away to hide his tears, thinking that stayin would have been a pleasure for him; he could have spent h' last years in true peace, close to Mariana and Ramagar, per haps living long enough to see his granddaughter's childre raise families of their own. But those at home could not b denied, either, and back to his herds he must go, as surely a the moon follows the sun.

At length both Old Man and the Sage looked to Ramaga' "And what shall be your future?" Old Man wanted to know "You have journeyed half a world to be upon these shores. don't have to tell you that you and Mariana hold special an' honored places among us. You may ask anything of what w have and it shall be granted . . ."

Ramagar thanked him; sighing, he folded his arms an' gazed up at the cloudless blue sky, exulting in the mild breez blowing in from the sea. Events and adventures had hap pened so fast these past days, that in truth he and Mariar had not spent a single moment discussing what they woul do. The storms were at last over, though, and now the tim for choice was at hand. Their home could be almost an' where they decided, with a golden rainbow waiting shoul that choice be Speca.

"What do you say, my love?" he asked, looking sharply : the dark-haired girl whose eyes still glowed with tiny fires.

"Stay here with us, Mariana," said Thorhall in hopeful o fering. "You'll never regret it, I promise. We are all yo friends. We want you and we need you. It was you mo' than any of us who saved this land from its doom, and think you'll find Speca more than grateful."

"Yes, Mariana," chimed in Homer. "Do stay with us. T' Prince would ask as much were he here today."

380

A single tear rolled down her soft cheek and Mariana
~sed her dark lashes over her eyes. Speca was a wonderful
~d. A marvelous land with new wonders waiting to be
~nd every day. Yet it wasn't home. "I . . . I *do* want to
y," she said truthfully, trying not to cry. "Truly, I do . . ."
~t her thoughts carried her back to her dreams; her dreams
~ golden sands and deserts, of palm trees swaying in an
~stern sun, of darkly tanned children playing along green,
~wered hills. She reached out and took Ramagar by the
~nd, her bright eyes smiling. "What is your wish, dearest?"
~ asked. "Do you want to stay?"

Ramagar kissed her gently. "My happiness is where yours
~ be found. You choose, Mariana. Choose and I'll follow."

The dancing girl sniffed and smiled. "I think," she said to
~eryone, "that the rainbow awaiting both of us can only be
~nd at home . . ."

"Home?" sputtered Captain Osari, startled. "But you can't!
~u can never return to Kalimar! Have you forgotten that
~magar is still a fugitive from justice? The moment you
~me back he'll be charged as a murderer and sent to the gal-
~vs!"

Ramagar sighed deeply. "He's right, you know," he said to
~ariana. "As much as I also would like to see the East
~ain, it cannot be. The thief of Kalimar can never
~urn . . ."

"But the thief of Kalimar is dead!" interrupted the haj.

Ramagar looked at Burlu curiously. "What are you talking
~ut, man? I'm as alive as you are!"

The haj smiled slyly and then laughed. "Ah, but that is not
~ I assure you." He looked at Mariana and winked. "The
~ef was killed—months ago aboard the *Vulture* while lead-
~; an abortive mutiny. I, Burlu the Swineherd, haj of the
~untain Lands, shall swear as much to the authorities upon
~ return . . ."

"And so shall I!" chimed in the grinning captain in dawn-
~; comprehension of the ploy before him. "The ship's diary
~ give added weight. Ramagar the thief is dead. The man
~o returns to Kalimar is the husband of haj Burlu's
~nddaughter."

"Come back with me, my children," pleaded the haj, tak-
~; them both by the hand. "All that is mine shall be yours.
~turn with me this day, to our true home, and there you
~ll find the rainbow of happiness you've been seeking for so
~g."

381

Ramagar lowered his gaze and nodded with emotion. Mar
ana clung to him tightly and smiled.

"Then you have decided," Old Man said regretfully.

"It's what was meant to be," whispered the girl.

"We are sorry to see you go," Thorhall said truthful
"But if this is what you want, then do it with all c
blessings. But never forget that a home among us is alwa
waiting for you. You both have secured a special place in c
hearts."

Homer swallowed to push down his own emotion. "A
we'll be expecting you to come and visit, with your ch
dren . . ."

"Thank you," replied Mariana, bursting into tears; s
threw her arms around the youth, hugging him with all h
strength. "Take good care of yourself," she wept, "all of y
dear friends. Ramagar and I shall never forget . . ."

"And we *will* come back," promised the thief. "To s
Speca as she prospers . . ."

"The *Vulture* is at your command," said Osari, himself
most in tears at the parting. "Any time, any day. You alwa
know where to find me."

Mariana kissed each and every one in turn, smiling as st
Argyle tried not to cry. Then, her brief goodbyes comple
she returned to Ramagar's side. "Well?" she sniffed. "Had
we better gather our belongings? The *Vulture* wc
wait . . ."

"And look for our rainbow within the tents of the ha
asked the thief. "Where, perhaps, it has always been wa
ing?"

Mariana grinned. "You have doubts?"

Ramagar laughed and looked deeply into her wet, lu
nous eyes. "You really believe it, don't you? You really
lieve it's waiting?"

Tall and proud, Mariana threw back her hair and smil
"My dear, dear husband," she chided, "haven't you lear
by now? Anything in life is possible. Anything at all—if y
believe."

About the Author

raham Diamond has been inventing incredible tales and
riting them down since he was ten years old. He is the
uthor of the highly acclaimed HAVEN series, and in
s spare time he works as an editorial artist with the
ew *York Times*. He lives in Queens, N.Y. His young
aughters, Rochelle and Leslie, were an inspiration for this
ok.

FREE
Fawcett Books Listing

There is Romance, Mystery, Suspense, and Adventure waiting for you inside the Fawcett Books Order Form. And it's yours to browse through and use to get all the books you've been wanting . . . but possibly couldn't find in your bookstore.

This easy-to-use order form is divided into categories and contains over 1500 titles by your favorite authors.

So don't delay—take advantage of this special opportunity to increase your reading pleasure.

Just send us your name and address and 35¢ (to help defray postage and handling costs).

FAWCETT BOOKS GROUP
P.O. Box C730, 524 Myrtle Ave., Pratt Station, Brooklyn, N.Y. 11205

Name_____
(please print)

Address_____
City_____ State_____ Zip_____

Do you know someone who enjoys books? Just give us their names and addresses and we'll send them an order form too!

Name_____
Address_____
City_____ State_____ Zip_____

Name_____
Address_____
City_____ State_____ Zip_____